CRAF

1 4 APR 2012

- 8 SEP 2012

4/12/18

- Please return items before closing time
  on the last date stamped to avoid charges.
- Renew books by phoning 01305 224311 or
  online www.dorsetforyou.com/libraries
- Items may be returned to any Dorset library.
- Please note that children's books issued on
  an adult card will incur overdue charges.

Dorset County Council
Library Service

DL/2372 dd05450

PENGUIN BOOKS

Sweet Little Lies

Alison Bond worked as an agent for writers and directors in film and television for ten years before stepping to the other side. She has been published in a handful of national newspapers and magazines and when not busy working on her next novel she has been known to dabble in hopeful screenplays. She lives in a country cottage with her young family.

Sweet Little Lies

ALISON BOND

PENGUIN BOOKS

Published by the Penguin Group
Penguin Books Ltd, 80 Strand, London WC2R ORL, England
Penguin Group (USA) Inc., 375 Hudson Street, New York, New York 10014, USA
Penguin Group (Canada), 90 Eglinton Avenue East, Suite 700, Toronto, Ontario, Canada M4P 2Y3
(a division of Pearson Penguin Canada Inc.)
Penguin Ireland, 25 St Stephen's Green, Dublin 2, Ireland (a division of Penguin Books Ltd)
Penguin Group (Australia), 250 Camberwell Road,
Camberwell, Victoria 3124, Australia (a division of Pearson Australia Group Pty Ltd)
Penguin Books India Pvt Ltd, 11 Community Centre,
Panchsheel Park, New Delhi – 110 017, India
Penguin Group (NZ), 67 Apollo Drive, Rosedale, Auckland 0632, New Zealand
(a division of Pearson New Zealand Ltd)
Penguin Books (South Africa) (Pty) Ltd, 24 Sturdee Avenue,
Rosebank, Johannesburg 2196, South Africa

Penguin Books Ltd, Registered Offices: 80 Strand, London WC2R ORL, England

www.penguin.com

First published 2011
1

Copyright © Alison Bond, 2011
All rights reserved

The moral right of the author has been asserted

Set in 12.5/14.75pt Garamond MT
Typeset by Jouve (UK), Milton Keynes
Printed in England by Clays Ltd, St Ives plc

ISBN: 978-0-141-02682-4

www.greenpenguin.co.uk

The door opens and Anna Page looks up once again in case it is her best friend. But it isn't. She shifts in her seat and orders another cup of coffee to give her something to do while she waits. Outside the summer is starting to fade to gold and soon the evenings will draw in. Ten years have passed since they first met. How many times in her life has she waited for Chrissie? Too many. Chrissie: the popular one, the pretty one, the impossible one. After everything that has happened Anna supposes that she should hate Chrissie now, though the truth is she can't help but be excited to see her again.

She wonders if Chrissie is married. If she is happy. Or if she is still the same.

Anna used to think that people did not change; not really.

She wants Chrissie to see how she is now, how treading the difficult path to success has given her the poise and confidence she always lacked, how the love of a constant man has rid her of her self-doubt, how the satisfaction of achievement has calmed her nervous disposition. How her trials have blown away that feeling – that sickly, caustic feeling – of never having enough of whatever it is that matters.

Her coffee comes and she blows across the surface to cool it down.

She thinks about everything that Chrissie did to her, everything she ruined, everything she destroyed. Because Chrissie Morton has a nasty habit of taking things that Anna holds dear and tearing them down.

And now it is Anna's turn.

Except the prospect of revenge is not the thrill that she thought it would be.

Finally, Anna Page has everything she ever wanted. And she realizes that perhaps she has had it all along.

The door opens. It is Chrissie. And she hasn't changed at all.

One

When Anna met Chrissie it was not love at first sight. Anna had other things on her mind. Important things like survival. Apparently it was perfectly natural to be scared on your first day at a brand-new school. Her father said if she didn't have butterflies then she wouldn't be normal. Anna had long considered herself to be far from normal, and not in a good way, so his reassurances were lukewarm comfort. Still, it was nice of him to try.

'You'll love it,' he said, over breakfast. He blinked twice, which meant he was lying.

'Will I?'

'Of course you will. A school like this, it's a dream come true.'

She put on her fighting face and smiled. She didn't want him to feel bad. 'You're right,' she said. 'A few nerves are perfectly acceptable. Only natural.'

'Are you being sarcastic?' he said.

'No,' she said. 'I was trying to be positive.'

'Then you can see why I might be suspicious.'

'Everyone, please pay attention. This is Anna Page. Her father is taking over as Head of Maths this year and so Clareville House has offered Anna a place in Year 10.'

Anna groaned inwardly. Now everyone would know that it was neither excellence nor affluence that brought her here. And that anything they said in front of her might get back to her dad. Being the teacher's daughter was going to be a challenge.

A class of around twenty girls, each one a flourishing combination of inexperience and hormones. At fourteen and fifteen they were the kind of girls that men who should know better would soon be lusting over, if they weren't already. The girls sat in rows of identical blue V-neck jumpers, grey blazers on the back of every chair, and collectively blanked her. The faces, dazzlingly similar in their disinterest, swam before her eyes; perhaps she was about to faint. How embarrassing. To be forever known as the girl who fainted on her first day. No, worse: the *fat* girl who fainted on her first day. The very thought of it was enough to pull her vision sharply back into focus and she realized she was now expected to take a seat.

She looked at her feet as she walked to a spare place near the back of the class. The shiny black toes of her Doc Marten boots were oddly reassuring. She could remember seeing them in the safety of her bedroom. She took a deep breath. It was time for her nerves to go now. They weren't helping.

She sat down and slumped low in the chair, wondering why she was bothering to make herself invisible when they had barely noticed her anyway. Nobody was looking at her. Was it possible to feel paranoid and ignored at the same time? Nobody would appreciate that she had spent an extra hour this morning blow-drying her hair so that it would perhaps be described as sophisticated dark auburn, rather than that loathsome word 'ginger'. She hadn't worn her regulation black eyeliner because her dad had told her she'd be going back to her old school if she so much as dared. She was happy to obey him. At least for the first day.

Anna tucked her feet under the desk and delved into her bag, not for anything in particular, merely for something to do now that she could no longer see her reassuring boots. She didn't want to be the only person in the room paying attention. First impressions last, so she concentrated on trying not to make any impression at all. It was an art she had mastered at her old school, where eventually she sank so far into the background that she almost disappeared altogether.

'At the beginning of every day we make sure that all the day girls are accounted for and none of the boarders have absconded in the night,' said Miss Webb. Her laugh at her own joke then disintegrated like candyfloss in the rain. She proceeded to call the register in a meek voice that diminished still further as the girls took delight in answering her with excessive force, shouting their replies for sport. This seemed unnecessarily vicious and Anna felt sorry for the teacher. A shiver of apprehension tickled the back of Anna's neck.

Halfway through the register Miss Webb was quaking in her thoroughly sensible shoes.

'Chrissie Morton?' she said, her voice breaking on the M.

'HERE!' yelled Chrissie, loudest yet by far, and four or five girls began to laugh. Chrissie flicked her shiny brown bob like a show pony and tittered behind her hand.

'Everyone, please,' said Miss Webb. 'What must Anna be thinking?'

Anna's head flicked up at the mention of her name. She was thinking: please don't drag me into this; I'm trying hard to be invisible.

'Wasn't Chrissie hilarious?' someone said as they walked out an undisciplined half-hour later.

'Ohmigod, hilarious!'

Anna smirked a little, a tiny bit, an involuntary twitch at the corner of her mouth, a hint of Anna the Cynic. Her dad once said that cynicism was all the young had in place of wisdom. It took her a couple of days to realize this had not been a compliment.

'Do we have a problem, new girl?' dripped a honeyed voice in her ear.

Anna flinched. That was all it ever took. The wrong kind of glance, a mistimed giggle, a word where silence would be better, silence where a word was needed. Teenagers didn't need much to pick each other out and slap on labels. At her old school she had gone through 'teacher's pet', to 'weirdo', and eventually 'grass', the latter because she had seen a classmate pull a knife on his girlfriend and voiced her concerns at the staffroom door.

Even though they were more or less the same height Chrissie Morton gave the impression she was looking down on Anna from somewhere higher. Chrissie was a flashy beauty, all glossy pink lips and radiant teeth, a smile that had probably parried her out of all sorts of trouble. 'What is it?' she asked. 'Don't you think I'm hilarious?'

'It's my first day,' said Anna. 'I don't think anything.' Chrissie narrowed her eyes. Anna hadn't meant to sound lippy, but maybe that's how it came out. Getting things wrong was something that Anna seemed to excel at.

Chrissie looked the way that Anna had always wanted to look. Effortless and relevant, getting everything right without appearing to try. Quickly Anna surmised that if she wanted to fit in she would have to start blow-drying her hair straight every day. She would have to get a paper round and save every penny so that she could buy a tan leather school bag and a good pair of grey suede ankle boots, which seemed to be standard issue for Clareville this term. Actually the boots weren't too bad. But if she wanted to belong she would have to start wearing sheer tights, not 70 denier opaques, and pluck her eyebrows and French manicure her nails instead of painting them dark petrol blue and get her crooked teeth fixed. It could get expensive. She would take on two paper rounds. Between the paper rounds and all the blow-drying she would have to start getting up before the sun.

'So you're this year's charity case,' said Chrissie.

Anna wondered what would happen if she turned around and ran away down the corridor. If she was six years old she might have got away with it, but sadly she wasn't so she just had to stand there like a punch bag and take Chrissie's sly little jabs. Things were so much easier when you were six.

'I always love the waifs and strays,' Chrissie continued. 'Scholarships, daughters of staff, special circumstances.' She made special circumstances sound on a par with special needs. 'Thick but pretty, clever but ugly, you know what I mean?'

Chrissie Morton's father was a well-known media mogul based in the Orient, from where he oversaw the Asian media market, specifically the enormous chunk of it that he controlled. Chrissie liked fashion, no surprises there, and was a girl who wore *outfits* as opposed to just clothes. Anna had learnt this much about her in the space of one half-hour registration class. Chrissie smiled without warmth and patted Anna's shoulder. 'Is it *terribly* exciting to be going to a school you can't afford?' she said.

'It's an honour,' said Anna and she meant it. She believed

7

that it was always best to tell the truth and hard to make enemies that way.

Around them there was a murmur of confusion. Was the new girl trying to be sarcastic? Clever? What? Once more Anna wished she had kept her mouth shut.

For a long moment they stared at each other until, sweeping her pert little nose into the air, Chrissie tucked both her arms through those of her waiting minions. 'Come on,' she said. 'I wonder if the new maths teacher is as freaky as his fat ginger daughter.'

Anna watched her go and let out all the breath that she hadn't realized she was holding. The class bitch was, of course, also the most popular girl in school. Perhaps the leap from comprehensive to Clareville House wouldn't turn out to be so wide after all.

By the end of her first week Anna had managed to speak to two people, both times she'd been asking directions. By now her classmates would have labelled her as shy or pathetic or pathetically shy. The Brain. So what? She wasn't here to make friends, she was here to get ten A stars at GCSE and four As at A level so that she would get into Oxbridge and never feel inferior again.

All her life her parents had told her that she was clever. She had always assumed they were trying to make her feel better about not being pretty but maybe, just maybe, they were right. She could thrive here. She tried to keep it under her hat but the truth was that Anna liked school, she always had, and now her father had arranged their lives so that she could go to this one she was infinitely grateful and determined to make the most of the opportunity.

During Friday assembly the teachers all sat on the stage in the big hall. She saw her father was chatting amiably to a grey-haired man sitting on his left as the girls filed in. See? He was managing to make friends. It wasn't impossible. Maybe making friends was one of those things that got easier as you got older, like staying awake after midnight or golf.

Their headmistress looked like a retired model, too elegant to be a stuffy old headmistress. Her name was Catriona Mackenzie, which was a fantastic name.

Mrs Mackenzie clearly wanted to impress upon the girls at the beginning of this new term the importance of making the most of their time.

'Sixteen short weeks from now,' she said, 'this term will be over and what will you be able to say you have achieved? I would like all of you to be able to say that you have achieved everything you wanted to and more besides.'

Right now all Anna wanted to achieve was making it through the next week. She couldn't possibly be expected to think any further ahead than that.

'As most of you know it is customary at the first assembly of the school year for our new head girl to address the students over at St Anthony's. Jane Heggarty is there as I speak and I'm sure she's having a marvellous time.'

A few titters for Jane, who would no doubt be struggling with making a speech and scoping the boys at the same time. Then the whispers started and a young man seated at the very edge of the stage stood up.

She saw the flash of a navy-blue blazer, the movement of his hand raking through his artfully messed-up hair. A murmur grew from the girls, rising up from them like steam. As one, they squirmed pleasurably on their hard wooden seats.

'And now I am happy to introduce to you her counterpart, the new head boy at St Anthony's, Ben Latimer, everybody. Ben?'

Anna never forgot that first moment when she saw him. For years to come she could close her eyes and see him there again, striding across the stage as if to collect an award. He was the best-looking boy she'd ever seen in real life. Also, underneath the hem of his trousers he was sporting some pretty cool Adidas.

The applause was muted as Ben turned to face his audience, three hundred girls all trying to play it cool. There was a collective inaudible sigh at the sight of him, like a puff of warm Colgate-scented air.

He wore his school uniform like a bespoke tuxedo, the body which had won numerous tennis and swimming trophies filling it out beautifully.

Nice.

Ben paused for a very long time, casting his gaze slowly into the crowd so that each girl felt as if she had a moment, a perfect moment, when Ben Latimer was looking directly at her. For Anna this moment coincided with a short flare of heat in her knickers.

The communal sexual tension was excruciating.

'Hello,' he said.

The hall giggled.

Catriona Mackenzie resisted the temptation to roll her eyes. She didn't know whether it was reassuring or tragic that these girls of hers were so terribly predictable.

'I rode my bike over here,' said Ben, instantly conjuring a disarming mental image of those powerful calves of his thrusting on the pedals and a thin line of sweat sliding down his back underneath his clothes. 'And halfway here I started thinking about what I was going to say.'

Nobody else but Ben would have the balls to admit that they gave this speech less than ten minutes' thought, at least not while there were teachers present, but such insouciance only made him seem more intelligent: a quick thinker, daring and bold.

'I decided,' he said, 'to talk about love.'

This time Catriona Mackenzie *did* roll her eyes, she couldn't stop herself and she thought that she caught one or two of the other teachers doing the same thing, the happily married teachers, the ones who knew that what a sixteen-year-old boy could tell them about love was not worth knowing.

'Hands up here who wants to fall in love?'

They all did. Especially the older girls who were already falling in love with some of the St Anthony's boys in the car park behind the village shop every Saturday afternoon.

Anna wanted to fall in love too, preferably with someone who loved her back, so she waved her hand with the rest of them and wondered if the other boys at St Anthony's were quite so good-looking. She'd have to be willing to fall in love with one of them as Ben was so clearly, stratospherically, out of her league.

'Me too,' said Ben. 'I want to fall in love very much. And I think that in love as in life forewarned is forearmed. I think preparation is the key to everything. So let's all practise love. Shall we?'

Okay.

God, she hoped she hadn't said that out loud.

She looked down the line of girls and saw Chrissie

giggling with one of her cronies, her hands spaced several inches apart as if she was saying, 'This big.' Maybe Chrissie was Ben's girlfriend. The sharp pang of jealousy made Anna wince and narrow her eyes as if she had sucked on a wedge of lemon. She turned back to the stage.

'Do I sound ridiculous?' Ben tugged at the lock of hair that fell forward so charmingly on his unblemished forehead, the self-effacing gesture adding modesty to his many admirable qualities. He didn't sound ridiculous at all, he sounded as if he was about to tell his captive audience the secret of life.

'I went to Nepal with my dad last Christmas,' he said. 'And at Everest Base Camp I told my dad that I loved him. And then when we got home I told my mum that I loved her too.'

The hairs were standing up on her arms and she felt as if she was going to start steaming *down there* if she didn't stop looking at him but she couldn't drag her eyes away. The sound of three hundred girls thinking that was at once so brave and yet so sweet hummed through the air like a swarm of biting insects looking for blood.

Ben dived into the heart of his speech, confident of the effect he was having on these women, on all these beautiful women. He had worked his arse off to become head boy and if this was the highlight then it was worth all the effort. He'd studied Jung last year and thought he remembered something about collective consciousness; this must have been the kind of thing he meant. 'I thought about love,' he continued, 'and how, sure, maybe romantic love, the once-in-a-lifetime love we are striving towards, is impossible to practise, hard to prepare for. It happens without warning. But perhaps if we love each other a bit more, love our families, our friends, our classmates, our teachers . . .' a laugh from the hall at the thought '. . . if we surround ourselves with love, then true love, when it comes along, will be easy.'

Catriona Mackenzie was surprised to find that she actually quite liked the sentiment. If Ben could bring a little more harmony to the hotbed of teenage rivalry and bitchiness over which she usually presided then bless him, he was a sweetie.

And so, just like that, Ben won over the last resister.

The whole hall was his.

'We just have to love each other,' he concluded. 'That's all I wanted to say.'

In her head Anna was cheering, in her imagination her palms stung with the force of her applause, but in reality she just watched dumbstruck as he sat back down and for that moment she wished she was his chair.

Ben was nothing, *nothing*, like the boys at her old school.

They were all little boys pretending to be men, she could see that now, more concerned with fighting among themselves than paying attention to the girls. And if they did, miraculously, find themselves with a girlfriend they proved their masculinity by mistreating her, and scored points by racing through as many as they could in as short a time as possible. Ben would never do that. When Ben Latimer fell in love, it would be forever, she could tell.

The opening chords of the day's hymn were bashed out on the piano and three hundred girls lifted their voices in song, singing in praise of him. Not Him as in God, him as in Ben. Ben, mmm.

Anna, like a host of others, felt first-love's rose bloom inside her. She sucked in her stomach and stuck out her chest. Boys liked boobs and she had good ones. There was nothing she could do about being ginger.

Ben sang 'All Things Bright and Beautiful' with gusto, aware of all the eyes on him, enjoying the attention. It was a heaven-sent opportunity to have the entire school in front of him to survey. He flicked his gaze over the delicious crop of Year 11s and wondered which ones he'd defile. His attention was drawn to a busty little redhead he hadn't seen before. She was nearer the front, with the Year 10s, staring at him, hazy-eyed with longing.

Cute. He'd never normally consider anything under sixteen, frankly it wasn't worth the hassle and they never knew what to do anyway, but this new girl looked like she'd know plenty, like she might want to have some fun instead of doling out kisses like rewards, as was the habit of most of these little teases. Three out of ten for face – unmissable nose, pasty skin – but her breasts were a ten. And the look in her eyes was an eleven. He grinned at her.

Bloody hell. Is he looking at me?

Anna looked behind her but when she turned back he was still looking, still grinning, with something resembling a question in the lift of his eyebrows. She could smile back, but the moment seemed to demand more than that. She had next to no time to think about it – this was her chance to make an impression he might not forget. She winked.

And that was how it started.

'I'm going to ask Ben to be my mixed-doubles partner,' said Chrissie to everyone within earshot in the changing rooms after tennis. Anna's ears pricked up at the sound of his name.

'Chrissie, you can't,' said one of her friends. 'He's been teamed up with Jayne Borham since forever.'

'Jayne Borham has no net game,' said Chrissie. 'She didn't even make the first team last season so there's no way Ben will stay with her. He'll be looking and I want to make sure I'm the one he sees.'

'But he's sixteen.'

'So?'

'You're fourteen.'

'Almost fifteen. And I have twice as many trophies as Jayne bloody Borham.'

Chrissie and Ben would make a tennis pair that would look as if they were two models on a break from a Ralph Lauren shoot.

'Ben will go to one of the older girls.'

'Don't be a dickhead,' said Chrissie. 'No decent player in Year 11 is going to want a new partner, not if they're winning. What's the point?'

'The chance to hang out with Ben,' said one girl dreamily.

'Tough,' said Chrissie, 'because he'll be hanging out with me.'

But it was not to be. The following week Ben Latimer did what very few had ever dared to do. He said no to Chrissie Morton. The news spread around Clareville like wildfire.

'Watch out, Chrissie will be a total bitch today,' said Jemima.

Jemima sat next to Anna in registration and was now the nearest thing Anna had to a friend. Sometimes a clumsy silence stretched between them, but nevertheless it was a relief to have someone to eat lunch with once in a while. She liked Jemima but she couldn't imagine trusting her with secrets. Wasn't that what real friendship was? A willingness to share what you thought, who you really were? To offer more of yourself than you gave to the world in general. She wouldn't tell Jemima, for example, that she was nurturing something of an obsession with Ben Latimer. Nor that she liked to watch Chrissie Morton from a safe distance, convinced that she could learn something from her, even though she was not yet sure exactly what that would be.

'She even asked her father to ask his father,' said Jemima, 'they know each other from some NGO board, but Ben's answer was a still a firm no.'

'Do we know why?'

'Apparently he's not even playing tennis this year. Teri Spencer in Year 11 said that's been on the cards for ages. He needs good exam results.'

'What for?' What would someone as privileged and good-looking as Ben need with exam results?

'Dunno,' said Jemima, obviously thinking the same.

'Poor Chrissie.' Chrissie had been boasting all week about how she and Ben were going to storm the national championships. How humiliating. 'She must be devastated.' It was surprisingly straightforward to feel sympathy for someone quite so beautiful, fashionable and rich.

Jemima snorted. 'She was so convinced and now she's made a total tit of herself. I'm not sure if anyone's said no to her before. Ever.'

'Don't you think she must find it hard to live up to herself sometimes?' High standards could be a bitch to maintain. Often she wished that people would stop referring to her as academically gifted so that she might be congratulated for her achievements rather than terrified of getting a B. Normal people were able to feel scared about failing, but she constantly had to excel otherwise she'd draw attention to her limitations. Probably Chrissie felt the same way about popularity.

Jemima looked at her as if she was out of her mind. 'What I wouldn't give for her problems. Apparently she's been crying in the toilets all morning.'

Anna had five spare minutes before French and so she ducked into the girls' toilets on the third floor. Most likely Chrissie would be surrounded by girls offering commiserations and she could nip in and out unnoticed. She just couldn't bear to think of anyone crying in the toilets all alone. Even if it was Chrissie Morton in a bad mood.

At first the third-floor toilets appeared to be empty, but then she heard a thick unctuous sniff. She bent down and peered under the doors of the stalls, looking carefully so that eventually she saw Chrissie tucking up her grey Chanel boots in a half-hearted attempt to hide her feet.

She knocked gently on the toilet door, her fingers tracing the gouged graffiti that had been painted over more than once but would never disappear. I ♥ ROB, it said, and she wondered how it felt to like someone so much that you needed to tell the world.

'Chrissie?' she ventured. 'Are you all right?'

'Piss off and leave me alone.'

'Teri Spencer said he was going to retire this year anyway.'

The door was flung open and there stood the most popular girl in school with watery eyes and a red nose. Her immaculate complexion was blotchy with distress. 'Bloody hell,' she said. 'It's you. What are you doing here?' Chrissie looked past her, as if checking that there wasn't something better over her shoulder.

'Somebody told me you were crying. I wanted to see if you were all right.' When you stared directly into Chrissie's eyes, especially now when they were red-rimmed, she looked younger and more real. The warm brown of them was probably the softest thing about her. Anna turned away.

'You haven't the faintest idea,' snapped Chrissie. 'I have plenty of friends, why would I talk to you?'

'I just thought . . .'

'. . . that I'd be all, like, *oh how sweet of you*? We'd chat and then we'd be the best of friends? Please. Half the time I forget you're at this school and the other half I think your name is Hannah. Now bugger off and leave me with my misery.'

'Is there anything you need?' People were touchy when they were upset. Chrissie didn't mean it.

'Have you got a cigarette?' said Chrissie.

'I could ask around?'

'For a cigarette? Don't bother. Forget I asked. Forget you ever saw me. Forget I'm alive.' She dissolved into fetching sobs.

Anna rolled her eyes and dug deep into her canvas knapsack, unearthing a crumpled packet of Lucky Strike. 'It's my last one,' she said. 'We'll have to share it.'

Chrissie stopped crying immediately and looked over in shock. She took the lone cigarette from the pack, lit it with her silver Zippo, took a deep drag and then passed it back. 'I didn't know you smoked,' she said.

Anna didn't, not really. A bit, that's all. It was something she'd tried a few times. The pack had been in her bag for weeks, mainly so that her parents wouldn't find it and give her a hard time about it. 'You think my name is

Hannah,' said Anna. 'I think that tells us how many things you know about me.'

Chrissie pushed open a window. 'Sorry, but sometimes it's a pain in arse being popular,' she said. 'People care about what you do.' She poached the cigarette back for a second pull. 'You wouldn't understand.'

'No, probably not,' said Anna.

Chrissie blew out her cigarette smoke in a practised plume that went straight outside. 'You've got very cool eyes. But you should wear less eyeliner.'

'You sound like my dad.'

Chrissie laughed and when she did Anna wondered why that single peal of laughter made her feel more proud than a week of straight As.

'I'm sorry about Ben,' she said.

Chrissie kicked the toilet pedestal with her foot. 'Wanker.'

'Twat,' offered Anna.

'Yeah,' said Chrissie. 'That too.'

Sixteen weeks raced by and at the end of term it felt as if she had achieved loads. She said as much to Mrs Mackenzie when they had a little chat.

'I'm asking all the new girls to see me,' she said. 'Just to be sure that you've settled in. Are you making friends?'

What was she supposed to say? She was still as unsettled as on her very first day. She was a wallflower, clinging to the edges of every situation and eclipsed by brighter blooms. But she got away with it by permanently pretending to be in a bad mood, hoping to build a reputation as something of an enigma. Her father wanted her to make the most of this opportunity and had warned against isolating herself, as she had done at her last school. But it was hard to fit in when you were unsure of your place.

If friendship was a genuine interest in others then she would have to say that her only friend was Chrissie. She had a confidence that was compelling. Chrissie seemed to know who she was and where she was going. Yet Chrissie barely acknowledged her existence.

'Everybody's being very friendly, thank you,' she said, appropriately bland and inoffensive.

Catriona Mackenzie was thinking that Anna was one of the most self-contained young ladies she had come across in a while. 'Are you happy?' she said.

'What fifteen-year-old girl ever is?' said Anna mournfully. 'I'm kidding,' she added, when she saw alarm cloud Mrs Mackenzie's face. 'I'm perfectly happy.'

'I'm hearing good things about you.'

'It's an honour just to be here,' she said. 'Seriously, I mean that.'

'And have you given any thought to what kind of career you might want to pursue?'

Of course she had. When she was five years old she had wanted to be a mermaid; at nine, a teacher like her dad; now she was currently consumed by the idea of being a world-renowned journalist, reporting back from disaster zones in fatigues and a flak jacket. But Mrs Mackenzie probably meant her question to apply to the real world.

When she'd talked to her dad about it he said there were two kinds of people in the world. Those who watched the world and those who shaped it.

'A good journalist, a really good one, can be either,' he'd said, tapping his index finger on a story he was reading in the newspaper about an unknown struggle in a forgotten corner of Africa. 'You could shape the world, Anna, imagine that.'

'Maybe a writer?' she said now to Mrs Mackenzie, knowing that she didn't sound very convincing. 'Right now I'm focused on getting to a good university; I have my heart set on Oxford or Cambridge,' she said. 'There're bound to be more opportunities to decide the greater future there.' An Oxbridge education was the country's great leveller. She knew that. Graduate from one or the other and it didn't matter where you came from, everybody watched where you were going instead.

Her sensible answer left Mrs Mackenzie reassured.

'I'm very happy,' she said again and Mrs Mackenzie let her go.

The truth was that she felt more pressure than ever pushing her forward to a brilliant future now that this magnificent Clareville education had been bestowed upon her. Her father had been well into his forties by the time she was born; now in his late fifties it was a risky time for a career move. He had done it for her. He had given up everything to work at this school, swallowing left-wing principles entrenched since his own student days, and entering the rarefied world of private education. It was his way of saying, 'I love you'.

The problem with everyone telling you that you're destined for great things is feeling like you're letting them down when you do something stupid.

And Anna felt as if she did stupid things all the time.

On the penultimate day of term there was to be a ball. It sounded suspiciously like some streamers in the assembly hall and a busload of St Anthony's boys to be exasperated by, so it was a struggle to get excited. Anna said as much to Jemima.

'But what will you do instead?' asked Jemima.

'Start my English literature essay,' she said and watched her gasp, actually gasp, with unconcealed pity. 'I'm *joking*.'

'You could wear that dress you bought in the sale last weekend. It's a great dress, it makes you look all sort of voluptuous,' said Jemima.

The dress she hadn't dared show to her parents. She'd bought new underwear too.

'Ben will be there,' added Jemima with a little giggle.

A lesser girl would have blushed, and though she did feel the heat rising to her face she controlled it, an odd talent her father said she had inherited from his side of the family.

She knew that she wasn't the prettiest girl at the party, and she wasn't the nicest either, but from the way the boys kept looking at her, and the way she felt inside, she sensed that perhaps she was sort of sexy? Anna felt a buzz of confidence, which instinctively made her suck in her stomach and walk a little taller.

Am I?

She felt the familiar pull to blend into the background, to sit out all the dances in the shadows with a detached cynical air. She had never had a boyfriend, hardly even been kissed unless you counted the off-target lunge by a spotty youth outside Streatham KFC last year (which she most definitely did not), and though the St Anthony's boys all looked very handsome in their smart shirts and trousers she didn't have a clue what she would say to any of them.

Voluptuous, Jemima had said.

Wasn't that just a posh word for chubby?

Luckily it was a typically segregated school dance and only the established couples and the downright whorish started snogging before the slow dances. Meanwhile the boys snaffled smuggled alcohol on the sidelines while the girls danced in circles of four or five and pretended their shoes didn't hurt, so she had plenty of time to sit around and look moody.

It was hours before the two schools began to mix properly. Only when the pace of the disco began to slow, and the boys saw their chances of a smooch and snog narrow, did they start to make belated forays across the gender divide.

Anna saw a St Anthony's boy she didn't know making his way straight towards her.

Her heart sank and she tried to think of something, anything, to talk about. Would he ask her to dance? She didn't even know if she could. Would she be expected to put her arms around a virtual stranger and hold him as close as she'd ever held anyone?

And what then? What when the music ended?

All these worries blurred together into a bellyful of anxiety and she could only pray that she wasn't getting a rash on her neck the way she sometimes did when she was terrified. She was in desperate need of a glass of water.

The unknown boy was getting closer and closer. But then she saw him stop short and veer away. She turned that way to see what had dissuaded him and found herself face to perfect face with her crush. It was clear that the other boy had spotted Ben moving in and decided that he didn't stand a chance.

'I'm Ben Latimer.' Ben smiled and artfully manoeuvred himself so that he was closer to her than any boy had ever been, including the one who had kissed her.

'Anna,' she said. 'Anna Page.'

'Lovely.'

Ben was so popular he was practically famous. He was beautiful. All she could do was stare up at him hopelessly, clenching her hands into fists to stop herself from reaching out like a total loser and pushing back the lock of hair that fell onto his forehead. He was asking her about her plans for the weekend and she managed to bumble something crap about 'family' and 'telly'.

'How come I don't know you?' he said.

'I have no idea,' she blurted, and felt like an idiot.

'Do you want to go for a bit of a walk out back? Or something?'

He had a handful of tiny freckles on his upper lip that she wanted to lick. She was breathing so heavily she was convinced that he would be able to hear her. She must stink of desire. 'Sure,' she murmured.

She did not see the death stares that were coming at her from the other side of the room.

He placed his hand around her waist and guided her through the crowd with his palm on the small of her back.

People were looking at them.

He kept his mouth close to her ear and she could feel the warmth of his breath with every word so it felt as if they were inside a bubble, oblivious. He could have taken her anywhere. If he'd led her up to the edge of a cliff and told her to fly off she would have thought that she could. He was so tall that he had to stoop to be close to her. He wanted to be close to her. She hoped that someone some-where was taking their picture so that later, when she was able to convince herself that it didn't really happen, she would have proof.

'St Anthony's has loads of dark corners,' he said. 'I think that's why they always have these things here at Clareville. They pretend we come to you in the spirit of chivalry, but really they need to keep an eye on us. Luckily . . .'

He banged his backside against a fire door and it opened, letting in a flood of cool air.

'. . . they don't alarm the building when there's a func-tion going on.'

They emerged into the cold damp night a few metres away from the hall, the muted music thumping a dead-ened bass into the dark playing fields. Ben immediately wrapped his arm tighter around her, so that leaning into his chest seemed the most natural thing to do.

'Or else you'll freeze,' he said.

She silently thanked her parents for choosing Clare-ville, for moving the family home, for choosing each other, for giving birth to her. Without them she wouldn't be here. Here. With Ben. All sorts of crazy tickles were racing through her body, before settling between her bare thighs and making her hypersensitive to every inch of him so close to her. The part of her beneath the weight of his arm felt in danger of melting. When he looked down into her eyes and grinned she thought she might be having a heart attack.

Is this normal?

They walked away from the hall, further into the darkness until they were shielded by the back wall of a maintenance shed. She was getting mud on her best shoes. She didn't care. She licked her lips, they felt warm. Out in the dark with Ben.

'Do you want to smoke?' he said.

She spoke without really thinking. 'Maybe after,' she said. And Ben knew he was going to like this girl.

She wasn't sure who smiled first but slowly they both did, the smile growing with anticipation and understanding, until they were grinning at each other and the tickles between her legs had turned to fireworks. She wanted him to touch her.

'After?' he said, tipping his head to one side and wondering if she was real. He had a bulge in his trousers. The inky pupils at the centre of his eyes pulsed and grew bigger as she watched them. She was suffused with a heady feeling, as if she was floating. It was so cold, but she felt as if she was burning.

He lowered his mouth onto hers.

Oh my God.

His lips were warm and wet, and he pressed her mouth so that it opened slightly. As he did so his roaming hand traced the seam of her dress under her arm and trailed lightly along the swell of her breast.

Her pelvis flip-flopped. *I'm kissing Ben.*

Her thoughts faded until she was left with only sensation under the skilled touch of his hands. He caressed every inch of her available skin, and gradually slipped his fingertips in and out of her neckline, grazing the top of her breasts with his palms until her body was urging him to press harder, to kiss more savagely. She kissed him like she wanted to be kissed and he pulled her closer to him, pressing their lower bodies together in a coarse movement that made her legs give way. He hooked one hand under the curve of her bum to hold her upright and rammed his tongue into her while she recovered. Then finally he grabbed a handful of the spectacular boobs that he had wanted all along. He took great satisfaction from her groan of pleasure. Thanks to his steady pace his wandering fingers had figured out exactly how to unfasten her dress. He deftly did so and peeled the top half away from her, never losing the lip-to-lip contact she seemed so hungry for.

How on earth had he managed to unhook and unzip her dress? But she didn't have time to mind as the hot sensations continued to curl her spine on its end.

Panting, he stepped back and took in the sight of those tits in a fancy bra. She was so pale that she lit herself. Then he set about familiarizing himself with the fastenings of her bra by touch alone.

'You are gorgeous,' he whispered, 'so sexy, so horny. I just want to kiss you.'

Never in her wildest fantasies would she have imagined that her first real kiss would be with someone like Ben. Until tonight she had wondered if she would ever be kissed properly at all. So going from nothing to this was making her head spin. Was this too far? Should she tell him to stop? But why? Why would she tell him to stop when she wanted him to go on and on and on?

When her bra fell open, she knew that now she really should say something but she didn't; instead she caught her breath while he stepped back to look at her. She stood in the dark wet grass, her new dress pushed down around her waist, and felt utterly desirable, a feeling which sent shockwaves of pleasure rippling through her until she thought she might pass out from the sheer thrill of it.

She placed her own hands on her shoulders and ran them across her curves. They locked eyes and she moaned softly without thinking, licking her lips and feeling more excited than she had when they were kissing.

This is heaven.

Ben's hands, when he lay them on her bare skin, were tentative and icy cold, kick-starting more tremors that escalated when, after a couple of minutes of ecstatic groping, he bent his mouth to her stiffened nipples and kissed her.

'You,' he said between mouthfuls, 'are disgracefully sexy, and you know it.'

She felt in control, more in control than she ever had before, acutely aware that she was driving him wild, that she had something he wanted, badly, but then the voice of caution came from deep down in her staunchly sensible gut, and she knew that she had to say no.

'Enough,' she said.

He broke off, panting slightly, and was very slow to smile. She reached down for the straps of her bra, then her dress, and struggled briefly with the fastenings while he watched her. His mouth was set in a neutral line and she hoped that he wasn't pissed off with her for stopping him. He flipped two cigarettes out of his packet and lit one for her. When his breathing returned to normal so did his easy grin, his perfect teeth gleaming. She was relieved. The bleak, soggy school playing fields were fine for a first kiss, but there was no way she was losing her virginity against the wall of a maintenance shed. At fifteen. Though after tonight she could hardly wait to lose it.

If this was kissing then sex would be *awesome*.

*

They entered the school the way they had come, slipping back into the crowded hall.

'You probably want to see your friends,' he said. 'But later we could, you know, maybe . . .'

'Maybe,' she said. He squeezed her hand and then let it go. She watched him walk away. She was shaking slightly and she no longer knew whether it was from the cold, or from him.

She slipped into the girls' toilets and found an empty cubicle, flipped the seat shut and sat down.

Oh. My. GOD. She closed her eyes to recall the sensation of standing half-naked in front of him, how grateful he had been, how for a brief moment when he had seemed nervous and unsure she had been the one in command. She had felt unbelievably powerful. Her breasts were still tingling with lust. She sat for a while and collected her thoughts. For a moment she wondered if they might have been observed, if someone might have seen her standing bare-breasted in a field. How had she found the nerve? Ben, that was how. He made her feel confident in herself.

She was a brain, a bore, a mouse. He could have anyone, *anyone*, and he had chosen her. She felt invincible all of sudden, like the world was hers, offering her every opportunity she could think of. A silly grin crept over her face and she hugged her knees to her chest with suppressed glee.

Back in the assembly hall Jemima ran towards her, stumbling in her kitten heels in an effort to hear all the gossip first, and as soon as humanly possible. With Jemima were a handful of girls Anna hardly knew.

'Ohmigod, did you kiss him?'

'What happened?'

'What was it like?'

'What did he say?'

'What did you say?'

'How do you *feel?*'

Before she could summon an answer, Chrissie Morton cut through the crowd like a queen at court. When the girls parted to let her through they even dipped their heads in a half bow, perhaps in deference to Chrissie's superior popularity.

Chrissie laced an arm through Anna's in a sisterly fashion, neatly ignoring the fact that they had barely spoken all term. 'Tell me everything,' she said, leaning in so close to Anna that their foreheads were practically touching.

Jemima and the others backed off, jaws slack. Anna caught and savoured a glimpse of their faces as she, the new girl, was drawn into the confidence of the ultimate alpha-teen. Where should she begin?

'Ben has never paid that kind of attention to a girl in our year before,' said Chrissie. 'Never. You must be special. Watch out for Bethany Ewart, though, she's snogged Ben a few times, probably thinks she's his bloody girlfriend. She might start on you.'

'Start?'

'Stick with me,' said Chrissie. 'They'll all leave you alone when they see that we're friends.'

The stamp of approval from the most gorgeous, most popular, most desired boy in town still felt fresh on her lips. 'We're not friends, Chrissie,' she said. 'Are we?'

'Of course we are!'

Two

Chrissie Morton knew what counted in this world. Looks and money. When she was five years old, on her very first day at school, Chrissie selected her first best friend. She chose a blonde girl with blue eyes to perfectly offset her own persuasive Bambi browns. The girl was almost as pretty as she was.

Almost.

But nowhere near as rich.

Though she had changed her best friend several times over the years she had consistently given the impression of immense popularity, though she knew deep down that nobody came close to understanding her and this some-times made her feel lonely and sad. Nevertheless, Chrissie Morton was the princess of Year 10. Looks and money were hers; she had everything that mattered.

And anyone who dared to disagree was quite obviously jealous.

When school started again after the holidays, Chrissie and Anna started walking the halls of Clareville together and many over-plucked eyebrows were raised at this new and unlikely friendship, but Chrissie would have let her natural roots grow back in before she admitted the full story. Anna was clever. That was obvious to all. And Chrissie was not. She needed a friend like Anna.

Her intellectual failings were something she had man-aged to conceal quite artfully up to this point, but now that school was getting, like, hard, she needed to make a little extra effort. She got a C minus once. She pretended that she'd had a hangover but the flare of shame – a brand-new and deeply unwelcome sensation – made Chrissie apply herself wholeheartedly to improving her academic standards. Clearly, she needed a clever friend.

Et voilà, Anna Page. (See? Her French was improving already.)

Plus, and this was something she still didn't fully understand, it was as though being pretty simply didn't count for everything any more. You had to be sexy too.

Chrissie assumed she was sexy in the same way that she assumed she was popular, but when she thought about those St Anthony's boys at the ball all lusting over Anna it was plain that Chrissie lacked a little something. She'd almost jumped out of her gold prom dress with shock when she saw Ben L leave the hall with her soon-to-be new best friend. If the top-tier boys were going to be paying attention to Anna then Chrissie damn well wanted to be in the vicinity at all times. And if it meant that she could also cadge essays and the like, then so much the better.

It was multitasking. Sort of.

Anna wasn't into it at first, she could tell. There was a wariness about Anna and you never really knew what she was thinking. Chrissie, who was used to being able to get what she wanted from anyone, found this frustrating. But Chrissie knew she'd be able to crack her eventually. There was nothing more cool than being popular, no matter what the geeks might tell themselves. Plus, Chrissie knew the way to Anna's heart. She'd seen the raw desire on her face at the ball when she'd haltingly recounted their little assignation out on the playing field. She knew that Anna wasn't too cool for a crush.

'Don't get carried away,' she cautioned. 'You'd only be embarrassing yourself. It's not as if you can ask him to go for a drink or something. You're fifteen and the pubs round here are draconian.'

'I know.'

'So don't spoil things by putting unrealistic expectations on the relationship,' said Chrissie. 'Don't do anything stupid.'

Usually, when it came to boys, everything Anna did was stupid and so she allowed Chrissie to be her guide in this new and slightly terrifying world.

'I want to see him again,' said Anna. 'What do I do?'

'There're parties,' said Chrissie. 'And weekend passes, events and stuff. We'll hang out at this little café in Tunbridge Wells. Everybody does. Your paths will cross again, and when they do I'll make sure you're prepared. I've known Ben Latimer since I was six years old. But timing is everything, so be patient.'

She gave Anna tips on her hair, her make-up and her clothes and soon she was perfectly presentable. Chrissie was smart enough to know that recreating this new best friend in her own image was never going to work and so she encouraged her towards a style all of her own. A fifties look that suited her figure and was, by virtue of its retro vibe, timeless.

'Women used to be way fatter,' explained Chrissie kindly.

She told her to wash her school jumper on hot a couple of times so that it was as tight as the skin on a pear. She taught her how to tease the end of the liquid eyeliner just so, then painstakingly plucked her eyebrows so that her green eyes were more startling than ever.

'The goth look was doing you no favours at all,' she said. 'You could be quite pretty. Have you ever considered surgery?'

'What?' said Anna, looking down at her cumbersome boobs. 'On these?'

'No,' said Chrissie, flicking Anna's nose with her thumb, 'on this.'

'You say that to me with that chin of yours?'

Chrissie opened her mouth to argue back but there was nothing there. Much to her surprise she found The Brain (as they had all previously known Anna) to be excellent company. She was the only girl who stood up to her, quick as a poison arrow; the others were generally bent double, licking her arse.

There were rich girls at Clareville but Chrissie's family fortune made paupers of them all.

'I'm new money,' she'd explained. 'My father made his first million by the age of seventeen but before that he had nothing. Lower middle class at best, which is the worst really because you can't even be a working-class hero with a background like his. His father ran a chain of shoe shops and his mother helped out. But he is addicted to money, totally addicted. Lucky me – not so much to the manor born as buying it for cash when that lot can no longer afford to heat the place. Those posh girls hate that, they just hate it.'

'Doesn't it bother you?' asked Anna.

'No, of course not, that would be ridiculous. Don't worry, I'm not one of those rich and pretty girls who's secretly *dying* on the inside, hoping that misery gives her depth.'

'And I'm not this year's charity case,' said Anna, with a

saccharine smile. 'Don't you just hate it when people make assumptions?'

'Fair point,' said Chrissie. 'You're so wise.' Then she mimicked Anna's sickly smile until they both started laughing. As always it was impossible to tell who started laughing first. And, as always, nobody else on earth would think their back and forth was that funny. But they did. And that was all that mattered.

They became inseparable, spending most of their free time together. Chrissie's former best friend, a snide little piece inappropriately named Honor, could only watch miserably as Chrissie paraded Anna round the halls like they owned the place, the weaknesses of one balancing the strengths of the other, a team, bezzies.

They had their favourite table at Otto's in town, a sweet little coffee place with gooey cakes which Chrissie didn't like to order but was happy to share. Whatever she stole from Anna's plate was merely helping her friend with her figure. If their favourite table was taken by other Clareville girls those other girls were quick to move. It was immensely comforting to live in a world where everybody knew their place.

'Do you see those Year 8s staring at you?' asked Chrissie. 'Over there?'

Anna turned around and saw three little heads quickly flick away and pretend to be studying the back of their hands. 'Do I have chocolate on my nose or something?'

'No, there's nothing wrong with you. They want to *be* you,' said Chrissie. 'Isn't that nice?'

'Why would anybody want to be me?'

'Get used to it,' said Chrissie. 'I have.'

*

The half-term holidays came and went and spring took hold. By now Chrissie was a regular visitor at Anna's house, helping herself from the fridge and learning the whereabouts of the spare key. The camp bed in Anna's bedroom was eventually left permanently out as Chrissie would rather spend weekends with Anna, gossiping for forty-eight hours straight, than with her own mother or in her four-bed dorm at Clareville.

'You're always going on about how much you hate boarding,' said Anna. 'Why board if you don't have to?'

'But I do have to,' said Chrissie.

'Why?'

'It was the only way my mother would agree to have custody of me after the divorce.'

'Are you serious?'

Chrissie shrugged. 'It wasn't exactly *Kramer vs Kramer*.'

'I never thought –' Anna stopped mid-sentence.

'What?'

'Nothing. It's just . . . I would never have expected to feel sorry for a girl like you.'

'Then don't. Remember, when they die I get everything.' Her voice cracked on the final word of her dark joke. Usually Chrissie avoided hugs as a general rule but Anna's hugs were fierce and encouraging, a lot like Anna, and rare, like the friendship they both knew they had found.

What is love? Finding happiness in your own skin. Being real. Feeling free. Closing the boundless gaps between what you think and what you say and who you are in a single breathless leap of faith.

This was not a romance, this was friendship. But it was love.

Anna opened her mouth to share all this with Chrissie but then remembered it was very, very late and they were both supposed to be asleep.

'Chrissie? Are you awake?' she whispered.

'Yes. Um, are you?'

Anna exploded with laughter and smothered the sound with a pillow. Her mum had threatened to ground her if she had to come in one more time to tell them to be quiet.

'Will we always be friends?' asked Anna.

In the darkness she heard Chrissie shift on the old camp bed. The springs creaked, metal ground on metal as the legs took the strain of each movement, even though her skinny friend weighed nothing. 'I hope so,' said Chrissie. 'I hope that we'll be friends forever. No matter what.'

The love in Anna's heart bubbled up like fizzing coke in a shaken bottle, drenching her with sweetness. She turned on her bed so that she and Chrissie were face to face. The faint light of an approaching dawn revealed the flicker of an eye, the flash of a perfect smile in the shadows.

'No matter what?' echoed Anna.

'No matter what.'

At last, just when Anna thought it was never going to happen, the perfect opportunity arose to casually bump into Ben again.

'House party,' hissed Chrissie. They were sitting at the back of the class at the beginning of a double history lesson. Anna used to sit at the front but Chrissie persuaded her to move to the back by promising to pay attention, most of the time. As a result of this concession Chrissie's grades were steadily improving while Anna's were managing to hold steady. 'Small party, but not too small,' she said. 'Posh, but not so posh that you'll feel like a total out-sider. Maybe try speaking less.'

'I'm sorry,' said Anna. 'Is my accent not snotty enough for your crowd?'

'Not just the accent, babe, the words too,' said Chrissie.

Anna grinned. 'Where?' she said.

'Hampstead. His cousin's, which is good because he'll know all the nooks and crannies. Spare bedrooms, that sort of thing.'

Anna paled.

'Oh relax, fridg-o,' said Chrissie. 'I'm kidding. You'll have a couple of drinks, maybe a snog, whatever . . . either way it'll get you back on his radar.'

'And we're invited?'

The history teacher was walking around the class hand-ing back homework while everybody prepared to learn by checking mobile phones surreptitiously and turning to the relevant page of the textbook, or staring out of the window and dreaming of the day when they could spend an afternoon like this one outside in the sun.

'Sort of,' said Chrissie. 'I am, and they'd expect me to bring an extra girl or two. It's fine.'

'When?'

'Saturday night,' said Chrissie. 'But your dad teaching here makes it so complicated. I can't tell school I'm stay-ing at yours, and you can't say you're staying here in the dorm, so we'll have to stay with my mother.'

'In Dulwich? But isn't that miles away from Hamp-stead?'

'We won't actually stay there, idiot, we'll crash at the party, but you can tell your parents and I can tell school and then we can do what we like.'

'What about your mum?' said Anna. 'What will you tell her?'

'Doesn't matter what I tell her,' said Chrissie. 'She won't care.' Staying with her mum was like staying with some cool aunt who'd occasionally forget she was only fifteen. Too many drugs, first recreational, then prescriptive, had relaxed her will. 'We're to bring rum, apparently.'

The teacher shushed the pair of them as she reached the back row with last week's essays. As she dropped Chrissie's in front of her the teacher nodded her head and almost smiled. Chrissie looked down. A. She checked that it wasn't a mistake, that the name on the top was hers and that she hadn't been given Anna's essay by mistake. Yes, they had done their homework together, and okay maybe Anna had helped her to understand the finer points of the subject, but the A was hers, all hers. It felt good.

As she waited for Anna at the train station on Saturday night Chrissie tried calling her father. She got through to his assistant Fuji, even though it would be early on a Sunday morning where he was. 'Can I help at all?' said Fuji warmly. 'Did you need something?'

'No,' said Chrissie. 'I wanted to tell him . . . I just wanted to talk to him. Is he there?'

'He's on a call,' said Fuji. 'He could be a while.'

'Maybe he could call me back?'

'Is it important?'

'I'm his daughter, is that important enough?' She wanted to tell him about the A she received in history. She was excited at the prospect of telling him but her enthusiasm was slowly dripping to the ground. She glanced up at the departures board and saw that there were fifteen minutes until the next London train. Anna should be here by now. Where was she? It wasn't like Anna to be late.

'Maybe I can hold?' she said.

'You're sure I can't take a message?'

'Fuji, I would like to speak to my father. Do you think between us we could facilitate that?' she snapped, using the kind of language a good personal assistant should be able to understand.

'As you wish,' said Fuji and the line cut through to a hissing tone punctuated by an annoying beep every now and again, which she supposed was to reassure the caller that they hadn't been cut off. No muzak for Kendall Morton. Nothing as tacky as that.

She was on hold.

Holding for her own father.

A few minutes later Fuji came back on the line. 'I'm so sorry to keep you waiting,' she said, sounding not very sorry at all.

'Does he know I'm on the line, that it's me? Have you told him?'

'I have, yes,' said Fuji, which made Chrissie feel even worse than she already did.

Five more minutes passed. Quietly, entirely without her usual histrionics, Chrissie began to cry. She walked up and down the station platform and with every step she willed her father to take her bloody call.

When Fuji came back on the line for the final time she had the good grace to sound faintly embarrassed. 'Chrissie, he has asked me to take a message.'

'Is that what he said? That you should take a message?' Chrissie made every effort to keep her distress out of her voice; she didn't want anyone to know how hurtful this was, not even Fuji, who knew better than most how Kendall treated his daughter. 'My own father keeps me on hold forever and then gets you to take a message?'

'He's extremely busy today. It's a very complicated time.'

'I *know* he's busy. He's always busy. Tell him . . . just tell him . . . Forget it. Forget I even called.'

'No message?'

'No message.'

Chrissie slumped down onto a bench and put her head in her hands. She rubbed the soft pad of her thumbs across her closed eyes and then calmly pulled her compact mirror from her bag to check the damage to her make-up. She saw Anna approaching and quickly tidied her face. By the time her friend sat down next to her she was repaired.

'Excited?' said Chrissie.

Anna paused. 'Is everything okay?' And Chrissie realized that Anna had been watching her for a while. It wasn't like Anna to be late.

'Why wouldn't it be okay?'

'You're sure?'

The London train roared into the station and Chrissie jumped up brightly. 'Of course I'm sure,' she said, pulling Anna onto the train. 'Now come on, let's see if we can't rid you of that pesky virginity.'

A middle-aged woman boarding with them overheard this comment and frowned, shooting them a disapproving stare. Her expression was sour and the deep furrows on her forehead didn't help. She moved further down the carriage away from the two spirited girls.

Chrissie and Anna looked at each other and sniggered. 'Don't ever let me turn out like that,' said Anna.

'You never could,' said Chrissie. So her father was too busy to talk to her? So what? At least she had Anna.

Ben's cousin's parents were obviously out of town. The party was already getting messy and it wasn't even ten o'clock by the time they arrived.

Outside the front door Anna pulled on Chrissie's arm to stop her before they went in. 'I just want to say thank you,' she said.

'For what?' said Chrissie.

Anna gestured expansively at her hair, her make-up, her clothes, her confidence. All of it thanks to her friend. 'This,' she said. 'Me. Here at a cool party. With you.'

'Are you making a pass at me? Calm down,' said Chrissie. 'Besides, we don't know if this party is cool yet.'

'You know what I mean,' said Anna.

'You're not as hopeless as you like to think, you know,' said Chrissie, generously. 'You're the cleverest girl I ever met, you're fun, funny, you get on well with your parents, and one day I might get boobs like yours but I'd have to pay big money for them. So drop the act, and let's get in there and find your boyfriend.'

'He's not my boyfriend.'

'Not yet,' said Chrissie. 'And then you really will have everything.'

She pushed Anna through the door and into the party.

'Everyone's drinking Dark and Stormies,' said the boy in the kitchen who relieved them of their Navy rum and threw it casually into one of two plastic dustbins full of bottles and ice. 'It's a cocktail.'

'Lovely! Two, please,' said Chrissie, winking at Anna.

'Do I look like a barman?'

'Yes,' they said in unison, which made them both laugh so much that he gave them a funny look and assumed they were already a bit drunk.

They quickly found the wow-factor roof garden where the party was focused. Chrissie sipped her drink and noticed that Anna had nearly finished hers. 'Pace yourself,' she said. 'I don't think he's here yet.'

'This house is beautiful,' said Anna.

'I wouldn't go that far.' The views of the London skyline were impressive enough but the fixtures were dated and as a family home it was on the small side. Still, one could see how a girl like Anna would be impressed.

Chrissie passed her gaze across the people who had gathered. There were a couple of pretty girls, but nobody she had to fear. In fact the only girl who was clearly 'sexy' was the ginger-haired teacher's daughter standing next to her, ample bosom squeezed into one of Chrissie's Vivienne Westwood corsets. For the first time she wondered if it might be too much, making friends with someone who looked the way that Anna did. Then she dismissed the thought immediately. Chrissie had always been able to handle competition. She positively thrived on it.

'More drinks?' said Anna brightly.

Over an hour passed before Chrissie spotted Ben arriving in the heart of a large post-pub contingent. He knew everyone, of course, and his arrival was greeted like that of a star on the red carpet. You really did have to admire how the boy managed to stay cool without letting the attention turn him into a complete dickhead. She turned to look for Anna but she was out of sight, which surprised her; at a party like this she might have expected

Anna to be clinging to her skirt. It irked her that Anna could possibly be somewhere else having a better time.

Where was she?

She tried the kitchen first. Anna would be talking to someone next to the fridge or helping to wash a few glasses. But the kitchen was empty, except for the ice-filled dustbins dripping condensation onto the trendy rubber floor. She poked her head outside and peered into the gloomy back garden. 'Anna?'

Nothing.

Was it possible that she might have left? Where would she have gone? They were miles away from anywhere or anyone that Anna knew. Surely she wouldn't wander out onto the London streets alone? Silly girl. It might be Hampstead but that didn't make it nutter-proof.

She started checking the bathrooms, this house had a lot of bathrooms, and was just surveying the Japanese-style master en-suite when she heard a strangled sob from the walk-in closet.

She pushed open the door and there she was, crouched behind it, her body curled up into a tight knot. She was crying so hard she had a disgusting trail of snot seeping from her left nostril. 'Anna? What's wrong? Has something happened?'

Then Chrissie noticed the tumbler laced with the dregs of a Dark and Stormy clenched determinedly in Anna's hand. 'You're drunk,' she said.

Her friend stared up with bleary, forlorn eyes. 'A bit.'

'A bit? How many of these have you had?'

Anna paused, exhaled with a deep sigh and screwed up her brow in concentration. 'Four,' she said eventually. 'I don't know. Don't worry about me. Go back to your friends.' She spat out the last word and then slugged back what was left of her drink.

Chrissie groaned. 'Oh no, not the self-pitying drunk,' she said. 'That's the second most humiliating kind of drunk there is.'

Anna tilted her face sideways and scrunched her left eye as if trying to focus. 'What's the first?'

'The slutty drunk,' she said. 'Speaking of which . . .'

Anna buried her head back in her knees. 'Ben?' she wailed. 'I can't. He won't . . .'

'And why not?'

Anna moaned slightly then slurred into the bottom of her empty glass. 'Look at you all,' she said. 'I've never been to a party like this. Nobody is mucking about, there're no games, you're all just drinking cocktails and talking about things I don't understand. I feel like the Disney character who has wandered into the independent film set. I don't know any of the people you're talking about, I don't even know any of the *music* . . .'

Chrissie rolled her eyes and sighed. Given enough alcohol this happened to the best of people, this paranoid attack of the horrors, but it was never pretty. In her experience the best way to snap out of it was quick and painful.

She pulled back her hand and slapped Anna crisply round the face.

Anna stopped crying immediately, looked at Chrissie aghast for a fraction of a second, and then slapped her back, just as hard if not harder.

'Listen to me,' said Chrissie, glad to have her attention at last. 'You're not really unhappy. It's the rum. You are way better than this party. You hear me? This party is actually a bit crap. You, on the other hand, look sensational and need to shake off this booze-induced misery and start enjoying yourself, okay? Now take a deep breath.'

She did.

'And another, please, just like that. You feel better?'

Anna nodded, took a third breath voluntarily, and soon her shoulders no longer trembled. Only then did she look up with something approaching awe on her tear-ravaged face. 'You slapped me,' said Anna faintly.

'You slapped me too, girl. Call it even?'

'Ben's here?'

'I say we spend a few minutes re-doing your face and then I'll go up and tell him I've lost you and send him in here to look for you. That way you get to say hello privately but you can come straight back to the party after a couple of minutes. Not long enough to get nervous. Good plan?'

Anna saw herself in the mirror and flinched. Luckily none of the dripping mascara had gone as far as the Vivienne Westwood corset. Chrissie had promised to totally kill her if she didn't take exceptional care of it. 'I like this plan,' she said. 'Anyone ever tell you you're good in a crisis?'

'I'm good at most things,' said Chrissie with a smile that made it look as if she was joking, then she dived into her Fendi clutch and got out the repair kit.

The house was empty yet the roof terrace was crammed. Nevertheless it was relatively straightforward to locate Ben and throw a damsel-in-distress number. 'You know my little friend Anna?' she said, all fretful and feminine, 'the redhead from the ball? I can't find her! She doesn't know anyone here and I'm worried that she'll get lost if she tries to make it home on her own.'

Ben looked concerned and immediately offered to help look, as she had known he would. Deep down Ben was a good boy – so not really her type; her friend was welcome to him. She subtly steered him off in the direction of the freshly primped Anna feeling like a proud aunt. She back-tracked to the terrace and refreshed her drink, happily engaging with two of the dreary girls knowing that she wouldn't have long to wait and soon she would get a line-by-line account from Anna of her first one-to-one with Ben since the ball.

Except that after fifteen minutes she was still pretending to be interested in a conversation about which she had long since stopped caring.

This wasn't what was supposed to happen. Anna had been coached to give an enigmatic taster of herself to Ben and then come straight back here and tell Chrissie about it. What on earth could she be doing? She had a terrible feeling that Anna's courage may have deserted her and she had hidden herself in the walk-in wardrobe again instead of sitting at the dressing table as they had discussed. Ben might not have found her. He might have gone out into the night on a wild goose chase leaving Anna bereft in the dark.

'Bugger.'

'Excuse me?'

'Sorry,' said Chrissie to the dreary girls. 'I have to . . .' She got up and left the sentence hanging in thin air.

She fully expected to have to coax Anna out of the closet but as she turned into the hallway she ran straight into her, followed closely by Ben.

They both looked guilty.

'I found her,' said Ben.

'So I see.'

'Catch you later.' Ben raced back upstairs as if he couldn't get away fast enough.

Chrissie turned to her friend, her imagination running riot. '*Well?*'

'Can we just go home?'

'Ohmigod, what happened? Where've your lips gone? All the gloss? Did he snog it all off you? He did, didn't he? You two!' And she felt an unexpected stab of jealousy. Not because she wanted her lips kissed off by Ben – she didn't – but because she wanted her lips kissed off by somebody. She wanted that blush in her cheeks that Anna had, that breathlessness. And despite all her schoolgirl kisses she knew that none of them had been as exciting as all that.

'I'm not telling you,' said Anna. 'Please? I just want to get out of here.' She walked downstairs and Chrissie followed.

'We're supposed to be staying here,' said Chrissie.

'Well, I won't,' said Anna. 'So either take me back to your mother's or I'll have to sleep on the streets, won't I?'

'Oh relax, drama queen. We'll go.' It was then that she noticed Anna's corset was done up unevenly, as if in haste.

Dirty bitch! What the hell had gone on in the master bedroom? This was huge. Huge!

They couldn't find a taxi willing to take them all the way to Dulwich, so they caught the last Northern Line tube southbound. Anna took the only remaining seat in the carriage while Chrissie remained standing near the doors so conversation was impossible.

At Kennington they emerged onto the street to try their luck again at finding a taxi and Chrissie renewed her efforts to be taken into Anna's confidence.

'Did you shag him?' she ventured.

'No.'

'You were gone an awfully long time. Something must have happened. Blow job?'

'It's none of your business.'

'I beg your pardon?' Chrissie stared at her friend but Anna was too busy scanning the roads for an available cab, or at least pretending to be.

'I said it's none of your business. Okay? I don't want to talk about it.'

'Fine,' huffed Chrissie. 'I'll ask Ben.'

Anna rolled her eyes. 'No you won't,' she said. 'Don't be ridiculous.'

'You're the one who's being ridiculous. What's the big deal? I'd never keep a secret from you.'

'You really can't deal with this, can you?' said Anna. 'You can't cope with there being a bit of my evening – a bit of my life – that I want to keep private.'

'Get over yourself. Like I care. Whatever.'

'Passive aggressive won't work either.'

'You wouldn't even have been at the party if it wasn't for me.'

'Neither will trying to guilt me. Give it up, Chrissie, I'll never tell.'

This was getting beyond funny. How dare the little teacher's daughter keep stupid secrets after she, Chrissie, had plucked Anna from her dull life and elevated her into the kind of social scene most ordinary girls would trade their best shoes for?

'What's so special about Ben anyway? Talk about predictable. I mean, half the school fancies him.'

She thought she saw Anna flinch a little and knew that

she was getting to her. Good. 'It's not like you're the first girl he's ever been with,' she said. 'He's a bit of a knob, really.'

'Shut up, Chrissie. I like him, so shut up.'

Tonight was supposed to be a laugh, a night for the girls. Ben was supposed to have a walk-on part, not be the star of the whole show. What if he became her *boyfriend*? Who would she hang out with then? If Anna rejected her, if a socially defunct, ginger-haired, middle-class weirdo rejected her then what would everyone think? It was okay for Anna. She had things to fall back on, places in which to dig deep and find self-esteem that didn't rely on looks and money. Chrissie, on the other hand, had nothing. She couldn't remember the last time either of her parents had told her that they loved her. Her dad was all business and her mum acted like someone who had woken up one day to find that she had accidentally had a child. Chrissie had grown up always feeling inconvenient and quite lonely.

'You *like* him?' said Chrissie. 'Oh Anna, I thought you just wanted to shag him.'

'What is your problem?' snapped Anna. 'Why do you have to ruin everything? Are you jealous?'

'Sweetheart, been there, done that.'

'What?' Anna stopped looking down the street for a taxi.

'You heard.' Chrissie flicked back her hair. Anna had absolutely no way of knowing whether or not she was telling the truth. But it wasn't like it was way beyond the realms of possibility. Everybody knew that Ben and Chrissie had known each other since they were children. Surely half the school would assume that they had done it at some point.

'I don't believe you.'

'Believe what you like.'

'If you and Ben had so much as held hands you would have told me about it, you would have told everyone about it. You don't know how to keep a secret. You're just making it up to hurt me.' Anna didn't look as if she was about to cry any more. Instead she looked angry. Her eyes burnt bright, two spots of colour appeared on her pale cheeks and suddenly it was easy to see why the boys liked her, why Ben liked her.

'I can be discreet,' said Chrissie, holding fast to her lie and hoping that she wasn't blushing. Now she'd said it she couldn't go back without looking like a fool.

'Please,' said Anna disparagingly, 'the only thing you like more than talking about other people is talking about yourself.'

'You say that like it's a bad thing,' said Chrissie. 'You, with all those questions, constantly on at me: what would *you* do, Chrissie? What would you say? What would you wear? Who should I be? I tried to help you, I *did* help you. You think you'd have had your ten minutes of passion with lover boy if I hadn't thrown the pair of you together? Ben likes the damsel-in-distress number; he finds it a real turn-on.' She smiled. 'Among other things.'

'This is stupid,' said Anna. 'You're lying.'

'Says you.'

'Fine,' said Anna. 'Let's call Ben and ask him, shall we?'

'You don't have his number.'

'He gave it to me about half an hour ago. Hang on, let me find it. He told me to call any time.' She started scrolling through the contacts in her mobile phone.

Chrissie panicked. Anna was bluffing, she had to be

bluffing. A few hours ago she was terrified of being in the same room as Ben so she was hardly likely to phone him now, was she? Or was she?

Two black cabs sailed by with their orange lights blazing but neither girl noticed.

'Here we go – Ben. This is him. Ready?' Her eyes flashed with the thrill of a challenge.

'He'll deny it,' said Chrissie frantically.

'And why, pray, would he want to do that?'

Chrissie hated the sing-song voice that Anna was using. It made her want to clamp her hands over her ears and scream. Ben would deny it, of course, as it wasn't true, and she would end up looking like an idiot. A liar or, worse still (if she maintained the lie she already bitterly regretted), somebody he was ashamed of sleeping with. It was lose/lose. She was mortified. 'Wait,' she said. 'Stop.'

Anna stopped. The red brake lights of passing traffic crossed her face like a strobe and made her look devilishly triumphant. The other side of lose/lose was win/win. Anna knew she had Chrissie beaten. But almost as soon as the look of triumph appeared it dissolved into concern and her gaze probed Chrissie so deeply that it was uncomfortable. God, Anna was such a loser. She couldn't even argue properly. Any minute now she would want her to talk about her feelings and envelop her in one of those hugs that made Chrissie feel exposed and vulnerable, like an open wound. If Anna knew her, really knew her, she would never want to be her. Nobody would. To her horror Chrissie felt a sob surge up from absolutely nowhere and threaten to blow her cool.

'You think you're so bloody clever,' said Chrissie. 'You'd be nothing without me, *nothing*.'

'What's the matter, Chrissie?' said Anna softly. 'Is this about your dad?'

'*What?* What has my father got to do with anything?'

'I saw you on the station platform. I heard. That couldn't have been very nice.'

She *knew* Anna had been there. Eavesdropping little bitch. Oh God, she would have seen Chrissie crying over him and everything. Hot shame rushed through her body like the warmth from a shot of rum but without the buzz. She tried to drag the conversation back to more comfortable territory.

'Take my advice,' said Chrissie, 'and stay well away from Ben Latimer. He would never go for a girl like you. You'll only end up with a broken heart.'

'I'm right, aren't I?' said Anna.

'Shut up,' said Chrissie. 'Just shut up, okay? You know nothing about my father and me.'

'I know enough,' said Anna. 'You go on and on about how fabulous he is but I know he's difficult. I know how upset you get when he doesn't show up for any school stuff. I know how much he hurt you this evening. Is that what gets you down sometimes?'

'I don't get down,' said Chrissie.

'Of course you do, everyone does. How am I supposed to be your friend when you tell so many lies?'

'Then don't be,' said Chrissie. 'Don't be my friend. I don't give a shit about you, not really. I was just using you anyway. As if I'd be friends with a girl like you. It was your brain, Anna. I didn't want to fail maths. Or French, or history for that matter. Ha! You really thought we were friends. That's pathetic.'

'No,' said Anna. 'You're pathetic.'

'You think? Fine.' She wanted to get as far away from Anna as she could. She spotted a taxi and used her fingers to whistle loudly the way that she had been able to do since she was nine years old. She might not be the smartest girl in the classroom but she could still hail a cab across three lanes of traffic. Let's see The Brain try to do that.

'I know why you don't let people get close to you,' yelled Anna. 'They'd see what a total fake you are. People should know the truth about you, Chrissie. Let's see if you're still the princess of Clareville then.'

Chrissie climbed into the taxi without looking back. Maybe it was mean to leave Anna alone in the city in the middle of the night but she'd be fine, wouldn't she? She'd call her precious father and he'd drive and pick her up no matter how late it was, no matter how far. Chrissie's face burnt with humiliation. How dare she? How *dare* she? First thing tomorrow Chrissie was going to come up with a plan to make sure that she never had to set eyes on Anna Page again.

Three

Chrissie slipped through the door to the maths classroom. Mr Page was marking exercise books at his desk and didn't look up until he heard her soft little cough. She assumed her most innocent expression, taking two steps into the room and noticing that he had the same bad posture as his daughter. A ripple of apprehension tickled her conscience. For that brief moment she considered an alternative plan, telling him that his little girl had screwed the head boy of St Anthony's in the master bedroom of a Hampstead townhouse. That should be enough to get Anna into the shit with her beloved Daddy, especially if she told him that she'd probably smoked a cigarette afterwards.

But that wouldn't get rid of her.

They had never recovered from the fight they had that night on the street. She had dropped Anna immediately, and started a whispering campaign that quickly turned most of the others against her too, but it wasn't enough.

Anna had to go.

Chrissie hated the way she felt now that someone had burrowed beneath her artfully constructed persona and was able to see what a mess she was under there. She felt permanently itchy and paranoid. She kept thinking people were laughing at her because Anna had told them how she had made up a stupid lie about Ben because she was jealous, or smirking behind her back because Anna had told them that she wasn't daddy's little girl, she was his after-thought. The shame of being pitied was unimaginable. She couldn't live like this. She never should have befriended Anna. You couldn't trust anyone in this world. Chrissie had remembered that just in time.

She closed the door of the maths classroom behind her and it clicked shut.

'Hello, sir.'

He looked up and perhaps he could have said some-thing then. As part of an unofficial open-door policy that Clareville House believed would encourage pupils to ask for help more often it was rare for a classroom door to be closed after lessons had ended. But he didn't say a word. It was an error of judgement that allowed her to proceed.

So she did.

'I need you,' she said, reaching down into her lower register to deliver the line in a sultry yet entirely girlish way.

'Chrissie?'

'I wanted to ask you about this week's homework, Mr Page. I think you might have made a mistake.'

She knew Mr Page didn't really like her. He had toler-ated her as his daughter's best friend, but as that was obviously no longer the case his true feelings were becom-ing apparent. He didn't like the way that she assumed superiority over everybody she came in contact with, he didn't like the way she sometimes came to class wearing more make-up than anybody else so that the first few minutes of each lesson were disrupted as she was asked to go and remove it. Big deal.

'What is it, Chrissie? I'm expecting someone any minute.'

She knew. He was expecting Mrs Mackenzie. The reason she knew was that she had sneaked into the secretary's office and made a note of his appointment with the headmistress and then precisely timed this play accordingly. You don't pull off something like this without a lot of preparation. And people had the audacity to suggest that she was stupid.

Slowly and deliberately she set her honeyed trap.

She took her maths book out of her bag and laid it on the desk in front of him. 'Here,' she said, 'which angle am I supposed to use for the equation?'

He sighed. 'We went over this weeks ago, Chrissie.'

'I know, but I forgot.'

Patiently, for even if he couldn't stand her he still had a duty as her teacher, he explained the different angles in a triangle.

Chrissie edged closer. 'One more time?' she said.

And one more time he explained.

When the door opened a minute later she was practically in his lap though he was too intent on his explanation to notice.

Chrissie looked up at the doorway and jumped away from him with a gasp that had disarmed a dozen St Anthony's boys, loaded as it was with sexuality, the gasp of a girl about to come. He looked up at the sudden movement and was flustered by the sound. The combination appeared damning.

Catriona Mackenzie wasn't sure what she'd just seen but she sensed an uneasy atmosphere in the room. Chrissie looked scared. He just looked embarrassed.

'Mr Page?'

'Come in,' he said, 'please.'

Chrissie gathered her things, studiously avoiding the headmistress's eyes. 'I . . . er . . . okay, Mr Page, I think I understand that now, thanks.'

She sounded as if she was lying.

She scurried out past Mrs Mackenzie looking down at the floor, adjusting the neckline of her blue V-neck jumper, knowing that the headmistress would remember this. Around the corner she slowed down and allowed herself the satisfied smile of a job well done. Nobody tangled with Chrissie Morton. And she was sick of people underestimating how clever she was. She was, frankly, brilliant.

Now Chrissie had one tearful phone call to make to her father and then she could easily imagine what would happen next.

A few days later Mr Page was called into the headmistress's office. Even as Mrs Mackenzie told him that there had been a serious complaint, he continued to smile, eager to fix whatever problem had arisen, keen to prove that he was still one of the best maths teachers that Clareville had ever had, determined to learn how to be better still.

'A complaint?'

'Yes.'

'About me?'

'Yes.'

'Oh dear.'

'Chrissie Morton has made a number of allegations, very grave allegations, against you.'

He looked back at her with the same professional dedication and amiable disposition that he had shown throughout his tenure. She watched his face cloud first with confusion and then with horror as she outlined the charges against him. Chrissie told of a series of sexual advances towards her, said that at first she had been surprised, then flattered, then charmed to the point of reciprocation.

'She's lying.' These things were hard to defend or prove. It was his word against hers. 'She's lying,' he repeated. 'She's making it up.'

Chrissie alleged that they had embarked on a clandestine affair but the guilt had grown overwhelming; now not only did she realize that the relationship was deeply wrong, but she also felt that she had been manipulated, that Mr Page had used his superior position and maturity to gain her trust for his own perverted gain.

'I have to ask about Wednesday,' said Mrs Mackenzie, 'when I came across the pair of you. What was going on?'

He couldn't immediately focus on her question, more concerned with relocating the bottom that appeared to be dropping out of his world.

'Because Mr Morton asked me if I had noticed any suspicious behaviour and . . .'

'Mr Morton?'

'His lawyer.'

And then he realized the enormity of the situation. It was unsalvageable.

'And you told him that you had? You think I'm . . . suspicious?'

He had a sudden urge to put his head between his knees and force the blood back to his brain.

'I didn't tell him anything. I said I would speak to you. I must warn you, though, that Chrissie was incredibly upset. She left school after our conference and has refused to come back until this situation is resolved.'

'Resolved?'

'Yes.'

Mrs Mackenzie seemed painfully conflicted. On the one hand she had a teenage girl, and one she had a responsibility to protect, making accusations so serious that it was hard to believe anyone was capable of such malicious spite, and on the other she had a fine teacher protesting his innocence. Without a shred of evidence to back up her claim how could Chrissie have such a damning effect?

'She's setting me up. She had the most insubstantial reason for speaking with me on Wednesday. She must have known you were coming to see me and was trying to make it look suspicious. Please, I have a daughter, I would never . . .'

'I know, and I'm sorry, but I'm going to have to ask you to take a leave of absence until we can sort this out. It's the end of term next week. We can make it look perfectly proper. News like this travels so fast . . .'

'It's not news, it's gossip, unfounded and cruel gossip.'

'Still, I wouldn't want any of the other parents to learn that we had allowed you to stay on the staff, given the situation.'

'What situation? She's having some sort of spat with my daughter. Let me speak to Chrissie, get her to drop whatever ridiculous game she's playing.'

'That's quite out of the question.'

'But you believe me?'

Mrs Mackenzie looked into his honest and open eyes and he realized that she did. But it was out of her hands.

'Please try to understand my position. I have asked Mr Morton to consider allowing the police to question you in your own home. Yesterday he wanted to have you dragged out in front of the entire school.'

'The police?'

'Chrissie is only fifteen years old, Alan,' said Mrs Mackenzie. She was trying to be gentle.

'The police?' A faint echo of his earlier disbelief.

These kinds of accusations followed a man wherever he went. Even if proven innocent he would certainly never teach again.

'It's not right,' he said, 'that a girl like Chrissie can wield this much power. The system needs to change. I can't let this happen.'

'I'm afraid you don't have much of a choice.'

'But I must. Don't you see? I have a family to support.'

'I'm sorry.'

'Mrs Mackenzie, Catriona, please. You have to help me. She can't get away with this. She's making it up.'

'That's as may be, but . . .'

'*That's as may be*? This is my *career*, this is my *life*. Please. I wouldn't just be taking on Chrissie, I'd be taking on her father. Kendall Morton. The man probably has a hundred lawyers. Please.'

There was nothing that she could do except wait for him to regain his composure, then calmly ask him to leave.

He stood in the doorway of her office and implored her to keep this away from his family. 'Anna,' he said. 'She must never know. Never. I'll tell her something else . . . that I'm unhappy . . . I'll think of something.'

Catriona nodded. 'Of course. And I really do sincerely hope this all blows over and we will be able to welcome you back soon.'

But right now neither of them saw how that would be possible.

That night Chrissie received a phone call from one of her father's lawyers.

'Is it taken care of?' she said.

'Yeah,' said the young lawyer. It was the first direct order he had received from Kendall Morton, and though he had followed it to the letter he had misgivings. If these accusations were true then the police should surely be involved. If they were not . . . well, then he'd just dumped a pile of shit on an innocent man. This was not why he went to law school.

'I'll be sure to tell my father how helpful you've been,' said Chrissie. It was a struggle to keep the satisfied delight out of her voice. Her father employed thousands of people across the world and it was reassuring to know that all of them would bend over backwards for her if called upon to do so. She was Chrissie Morton and that meant something. It meant everything.

Anna who?

Four

Anna knew that meeting up with Ben was a bad idea. Immature. Unrealistic. Desperate. At least that's what Chrissie would say. But seeing as how Chrissie was no longer speaking to her it really didn't matter what she said, did it? Ever since that night in Kennington Chrissie had been a total superbitch.

She went over and over their argument in her head, trying to work out what it was that she had said that was so awful and would justify being summarily dumped, but she couldn't put her finger on it. It was as if Chrissie was afraid of being seen for what she really was: a normal girl with all the usual insecurities and doubts that came with finding your place in the world. Glimpses of what was lost danced in front of her eyes. It should have been Anna and Chrissie forever. Why had she said what she had said to Chrissie and made her so angry? Everyone was entitled to their secrets so why had she tried to force Chrissie to reveal more of herself than she was willing to show? Now they were parting on really dreadful terms. Anna had dared to see past Chrissie's hard-as-nails front, and she had looked forward to seeing more the longer they were friends, the closer they became. Now all she saw of Chrissie was the stupid little sneer she gave her if their eyes should happen to meet. Getting involved with Chrissie Morton had been a bad decision.

Then last week Anna's father had announced that they were moving back to London and that her short and socially disastrous foray into private education was at an end.

It felt like the end of so much more.

They told her together, her mum and her dad, sitting next to each other on the sofa wearing their most serious faces. Her first thought was that they were getting a divorce, which was ridiculous because they were quite obviously still very happy together after twenty years of marriage, but she was so appalled by the thought of going back to her old school that she thought divorce might be preferable. It didn't make any sense. All her life the importance of getting a good education had been drummed into her, and now that she was finally settled in a school with a glowing academic record they wanted her to go back to the inner-city school where the teaching was not so much about educating as crowd control and bright young things like Anna went largely ignored.

She begged them to reconsider, but her father said his mind was made up, he would not be returning to Clareville and so neither would she. It would be as if none of this had ever happened.

Her dream of an Oxbridge education, which seemed so close, started to drift away and she thought she might as well let it. What was the point?

'Is it my fault?' she asked. 'Did I do something wrong?'

'It was a bad fit,' said her father, but he wouldn't be drawn any further.

So soon it was time to say goodbye. And, confused and frustrated as she was, there was still one person she wanted to say goodbye to.

Everybody else hated her anyway. Chrissie had seen to that.

Standing a short distance from St Anthony's gates she felt as conspicuous as a bad case of acne on school photo day and she took solace once again in staring at the toes of her shoes. Only her shoes were no longer shiny black Doc Martens but grey suede ankle boots that marked her out as one of the cool kids. Temporarily cool, only to be thrust back where she belonged.

And what chance would there be now with Ben? The first boy to kiss her. Could any kisses still to come in her life measure up? It seemed impossible that out there somewhere might be someone whose kisses would make her feel as sexy, as blissful and as complete as his did. She hated her father for taking her away from the possibility of more of the same.

She lifted her eyes to watch the boys drift past in packs, deflecting the occasional smirking glance with the death stare she had been obliged to perfect since her popularity took a nosedive.

Then she saw Ben and she held her breath for no other reason than she seemed to have forgotten how to breathe. She drank in his perfect face, fixing it in her mind to be recalled later in the privacy of her own bed and whenever she chose. The image of the two of them kissing in the dark leapt into her mind's eye and brought with it those delicious sensations, desire that zigzagged through her body like boiling blood in her veins. She remembered the touch of his fingertips on her skin, the smell of his neck when she rested her head there, the way his mouth felt against her eager, happy lips.

'*Ben.*' Her voice came out like the hoarse whisper of a cackling witch. She cleared her throat and tried again. 'Ben?'

He saw her and he raised his hand and said something to the two lesser boys that he was with. They didn't dissolve into laughter, which she took as a good sign. She watched him lope over to her with his easy stride, a curious smile on his beautiful face. She sucked in her stomach and stuck out her chest. 'Hi.'

'Hello.' He wasn't angry that she was there or embarrassed. If anything he looked pleased. Sadly the power of speech temporarily deserted her but probably he was used to girls staring dumbstruck into his yummy eyes. 'How've you been?' he asked.

'I'm leaving,' she said.

'Was it something I said?'

'Clareville, I mean. I'm leaving, we're leaving. My dad was offered a better job.' She had pre-planned this white lie in the absence of an actual reason she could believe.

'Oh,' he said. 'Well, that's a shame.'

'I wanted to see you and, you know, say goodbye.' She fought back a blush. Did that sound like a come-on? The sexual tension flitted between them like a hummingbird. Could he feel it too?

'It's Hannah, right?'

She felt a slow sinking sensation in her chest. 'Anna,' she said softly.

'Right. I did know that, honestly. That's pretty shit of me. Sorry. Anna.' He looked back towards his friends and jammed his hands in his pockets. 'Well, bye then, Anna. Take care. See you around, okay?'

'You won't actually.'

'Sorry?'

'You won't see me around.' Something that felt an awful lot like fury was brewing in her guts. 'I can't picture you walking down Streatham High Street any weekend and I doubt very much I'll be invited to one of your cousin's parties again, so you see, you won't see me around, you won't see me at all.'

She waited for him to say something but he just stood there looking at her like she was a mental case, and probably she was. He didn't even know her *name* and she was here making speeches like he'd give a damn. She never should have come here. What kind of a masochist was she? She should just prostrate herself on the pavement before him and her humiliation would be complete.

Then Ben gestured to his friends to go on without him and they did.

'Have I done something wrong?' he asked gently.

'No,' she said. 'It's just . . .'

'What?'

'It doesn't matter.' So one more person had let her down. So what? The sooner she could parcel up this whole experience and shove it to the very back of her mind for good the better she would be. They were all spoilt, pretentious disappointments, every last one of them.

'I heard about you and Chrissie,' said Ben.

'Yeah? What did you hear?' She forced the nails of her right hand into the yielding flesh of her palm to distract her from the tears she could feel welling up somewhere behind the bridge of her nose. This was not going to plan.

'You had a big fight.'

Anna nodded and focused on the stabbing pain in her palm and not the one in her heart.

'If it makes you feel better,' he said, 'I've known Chrissie for years, forever, we went to same primary school, and I know she never sticks with anything, especially not friends.'

'Well,' she said, 'that kind of makes me feel worse.'

'Oh. Sorry.'

He scuffed his feet on the pavement and looked as if he was about to leave.

Her mind start to race with excuses to make him stay just a little bit longer but then a slow smile twitched the corners of his mouth and spread into a mischievous grin.

'Want to get back at her a little bit?' he said.

'What makes you so sure it was her fault?'

'Like I said, I've known her forever.'

The pavement tables outside Otto's were packed as boys and girls made the most of their after-school freedom by sipping one cup of coffee for two hours. When Anna realized that this was where they were heading her feet stopped moving one in front of the other and Ben had to gently coax her down the high street towards the café where she was absolutely certain Chrissie would be holding court.

'Come on,' said Ben.

'We'll never get a table.'

'We don't need a table.'

They could see Chrissie well before they got there, sitting in the prime people-watching spot, sunglasses on like she was a movie star, Honor on her right-hand side, two more girls to her left. Anna couldn't help thinking of all the hours they had spent there together.

Then Ben took her hand, and though she couldn't be certain she thought she saw Chrissie's gaze behind those silly sunglasses resting on the pair of them as they walked on the opposite side of the street, hand in hand.

Nerves prickled at her skin and she felt cold all over,

except for her hand, which was red hot as Ben laced his fingers through hers just as if they had held hands a hundred times before.

Now it was unmistakable. Chrissie's entire table was blatantly staring.

Ben leant down close to her ear and nudged her with his elbow. 'Say something.'

'Like what?'

'Anything. Whisper in my ear.'

She stretched up on tiptoes, cupped her hand around her mouth and said the first thing that came into her head. 'You're very sweet for doing this.'

Ben laughed loudly as if she'd just said something clever and hilarious, then he wrapped his arm around her shoulders, pulling her close. His other arm went low around her waist and his hand hovered at the top of her bum as he looked directly at Chrissie and laughed some more.

Chrissie was all smiles, but Anna knew her well enough to know that she was seething. Her unpopularity plan decreed that Anna should be hiding in a corner licking her wounds, not parading around town with the biggest boy catch that there was.

On impulse she stretched up on her toes again and kissed Ben on the mouth.

She looped her arms up around him and tasted the salty tang of his lips, caressed the warm spot at the base of his neck where the little hairs were as soft as feathers, felt his strong safe hands on her hips and pressed her body against his, wanting to remember this always. They kissed and kissed until a wolf-whistle from one of the St Anthony's boys at Otto's made them break apart.

Ben grinned, Anna grinned back.

'Well,' he said, as flustered as she had ever seen him. 'That should do it. Come on, let's go.'

Hand in hand they sauntered past Otto's, ignoring the expressions of awestruck disbelief on the faces there. And though she knew she shouldn't, Anna couldn't help one last glance back at Chrissie. If happiness is counted out in giggles and grins then the time spent with Chrissie were the happiest hours of Anna's life. She would miss her so much.

The truth was that she already did.

To her surprise Chrissie was smiling.

It wasn't a vindictive smirk or a badly disguised grimace, but the genuine smile that Anna had grown to love. As the conversation at Otto's picked up again Chrissie ignored it and kept her shaded eyes fixed on Anna and Ben.

Anna waved, just barely.

Chrissie waved back, a small quick movement that went unnoticed by her chattering friends.

Then Anna felt the squeeze of Ben's hand and they walked away together.

Fifteen minutes later and he was still holding her hand. They walked right on to the other side of town until the traffic thinned and the road climbed up towards the woods on the hill. The sunlight fell through the trees in ripples, patches of shade and brightness playing with her vision until finally she closed her eyes, trusting Ben to lead the way for a minute or two. As the world around her fell away she listened to the birds singing and the crunch of small twigs and dried leaves beneath her feet, she felt the downy hairs on the back of his hand under her trembling fingertips and she savoured this walk in the woods. Her mind settled. She thought how liberating it felt to allow someone to take control, to place your life in somebody else's hands and have a break, however brief, from making decisions and worrying constantly that you were making all the wrong ones. It felt like being a small child again, with all the freedom to be whoever you chose to be and none of the anxiety about the future, about popularity and friendship, about how to be a good daughter and a good friend, the uncertainty that had kept her in a constant state of confusion for so long. All that she needed to do was breathe and have faith that the hand that held hers would keep her safe. To say, take me I'm yours.

This must be what love feels like.

A short moment later he noticed that she wasn't looking and started to laugh.

'Why have you got your eyes closed?'

'I thought it would be interesting.'

'You're a very strange girl, Anna.'

'Don't say that,' she said, ducking her head and looking down at the muddy trail beneath their feet, her grey suede suffering, his black leather scuffed and sexy.

'Why not?' he said. 'It's not a bad thing to be a bit different.'

'Only someone as popular as you would think that was true.'

He kissed her then but she pulled away. 'You don't have to,' she said.

'I want to.'

'Do you mind if we don't?' She knew that it would be goodbye and she might never see him again. What was the point? What was the point of having one more perfect kiss? And if things escalated in this beautiful woodland setting until they tumbled to the ground and she was overwhelmed by the heat of his kisses and the surging desire in her belly, what then? The more they did the more she would have to remember him by and she was ready to start forgetting. But her body trembled at the memory of his touch and she had to draw on all her reserves of self-control. However, when Anna lost her virginity aged eighteen to a dull musician, who she stopped seeing three months later, she wished that she had lain with Ben that day in the dappled sunlight among the ferns and the wild flowers and asked him to make love to her.

She thought that pulling away from his kiss would make it easier to stop thinking about him. But in the end she found him impossible to forget.

Five

Anna's remaining schooldays did not present her with a new best friend. She looked but she did not find one. Then she worked steadily through four years at university without forging the kind of enduring camaraderie that seemed to come so easily to people around her. She remembered what it was like to have a best friend and started to wonder if she would ever feel that way again. She would watch enviously from the sidelines as double-acts laughed raucously from the corner of a bar, or twosomes leant so far into intense conversation that their foreheads almost touched. She saw how close friends could finish each other's sentences and share a joke with little more than a glance or a nod. She watched pretty girls mop up the heartbroken tears of the pretty girl next to them and wondered how long they had known each other, how well they knew each other and if there was anything they couldn't say to one another. She had acquaintances, people to share a few drinks with after lectures, house-mates to laugh with and fall out with over chores and the contents of the fridge, but she didn't feel that strange kind of bliss that comes from being entirely unguarded in the presence of another. She didn't know how to take a friendship higher. It was almost as if Chrissie had broken her heart and she was afraid to love again. Which was silly, because they were friends, they were not in love. And so when she found her thoughts drifting to those times she forced herself to think of Ben instead as it made a lot more sense to romanticize your first kiss rather than your first friendship. And Anna liked it most when things made sense.

She felt the same way about relationships as she did about friendship. With every failed attempt came the sense that something was missing, that there should be more to a love affair than this, and so after a few months, maybe a year, she would finish it and feel very little. As the years passed the memory of Ben took on a magnitude that it didn't deserve. He went from being her first kiss to her first love and if she awoke in the middle of the night and felt lonely she would latch on gratefully to a recollection of him and dream of maybe seeing him again one day.

People who knew Anna would describe her as a loner. A hard worker. Close to her family. Friendly, but reserved. And nobody knew why.

By the time Anna was twenty-two years old and halfway through a master's degree in international journalism she had resigned herself to a life spent somewhere on the edges. Seven years had passed since she last saw Chrissie.

Anna sat towards the back of the crowded lecture hall and pushed her hand up into the air to answer a provocative question. Way down on the stage the man speaking didn't call on her. Why would he? He never did. John Mackintosh, award-winning journalist with the sort of career that Anna liked to fantasize about when she was feeling blue, was the Writer-in-Residence at City University and he spoke to the entire department once a month. She thought carefully about what dazzling points to make, and then panicked every time she dared to put her hand in the air. Twenty-two years old and still scared of being noticed.

Anna had found a place in the world where she felt comfortable and it was usually somewhere near the back.

Seven years ago she had been poised to lift off and soar into the sky. Friends with the most popular girl in a brilliant school and nurturing a fledgling romance with someone who made her heart hammer in her chest, it seemed there was nothing between her and the stars except her own fears. Since then her life had been unspectacularly grounded. It was depressing to think that those few short months all that time ago might have been the best of her days. The past sparkled like a moment of sunlight in an otherwise dreary afternoon.

All those dreams she'd had that never came true. Was it any wonder she had stopped dreaming, except for those that came at night?

Last night she dreamt about John Mackintosh. Remembering the dream now made her blush even though she couldn't recall the exact nature of it. She refused to have a crush on him like half the students around her, the female half. She admired his talent. Though she was fairly certain that wasn't what her dream had been about.

His mellow voice captured his audience with its slow insistence, effortlessly filling the echoing space with thoughts and theories and making the cold hall come alive with the awakening of ideas. This wasn't like ordinary lectures, which were sometimes a bit uninspiring; you could miss them and miss nothing (not that she ever did). But this was quite possibly the highlight of her month. Also pretty depressing when you thought about it.

Facts and comment, that's what he was talking about.

The twin components of news delivery. Could they ever be separated? And should they? What use were cold hard facts without context? How constructive was comment without facts to back it up?

'Nobody ever got fired for sticking to the facts,' he concluded. 'But nobody ever got promoted either.'

Anna liked the truth. She liked things that could be proven and demonstrated. For Anna facts were like the stepping stones across a dangerous river of hypothesis and speculation. Only by treading circumspectly on these stones could she get to the other side. That, some would say, made her boring. Stepping stones would only take her so far in life. And she wasn't sure that would ever be enough.

Rumour, on the other hand, could take you anywhere. Rumour had it that John Mackintosh had been offered a number of editorships over the course of his peripatetic career but had turned them all down, which would seem financially irresponsible had he not been offered a rumoured high six-figure sum from a US publisher for the diaries of his time in Western Africa.

Rumour also had it that he had a thing for his students.

She could see that some women would find him attractive. If you liked that sort of thing: the well-travelled journalist. He looked ageless, anywhere between thirty-ish and forty-something, she supposed, and had the kind of face that you instinctively trusted, eyes that crinkled in the corners as if he'd spent too much time on a sun-baked road, hair looking desperately in need of a trim, a strong jaw which permanently suggested that he just hadn't had the time to shave when he clambered out of bed that day. His smile seemed a little melancholic to her, wistful, like that of a man who knew that joy and pain are two sides of the same coin because of something that happened once a long time ago.

Looks and money. All that and brains too.

Around her people began to gather their things as the lecture came to an end. She sat where she was for a moment, glancing at her notes, reviewing them at speed while they were still fresh in her mind, writing a few words in the margins to remind her of something later, crossing out irrelevancies so they didn't distract her many months from now when she was trying to revise for her exams and wondering why she had made a particular note. It was a habit now, thinking about exams, thinking about the future. The future, Anna had decided, was where she would shine.

She stood up and walked down the steps to the door. As she passed the stage he called out to her. 'Miss Page, a word, if you don't mind.'

Anna panicked although she had no idea what she had done. After all this time she should be pleased that he even knew her name, but she had the sense that she was in trouble; it was the same sort of anxious feeling she used to get when she and Chrissie were shouted at for whispering at the back of the classroom when they should have been working out the boiling point of ethanol.

She lingered at the front near the stage while the rest of the students filed out, ignoring every glance that was thrown her way until it was just the two of them left alone in the vast empty space. She watched as he finished making a note on some paperwork in front of him. When he looked up he seemed surprised that she was there.

'Yes?' he said.

'You asked me to stay.' She didn't trust the way his eyebrows worked independently of one another. Up close you could tell that Oxford blue shirt he was wearing needed an iron, possibly a wash.

'Miss Page. Right. Of course.' He reached into his bag for a stack of essays and then paused. 'You smoke?'

'Not at the moment.'

'That's a shame. I could do with my fix. I'm afraid that without it I might hurt your feelings.'

'Go ahead,' she said. 'I can take it.'

He rifled through the essays until he found hers. 'I'd like you to revisit this,' he said.

'What's wrong with it?' she replied.

'Nothing really. It's a pass, a fairly decent pass, and you raise some interesting points.'

'Then what's the problem?' She thought of all the hours she had put into that essay and her heart plummeted at the thought of starting all over again.

'Balance,' he said, 'is best left to the tightrope walker.'

'Sorry?'

'You know, like in a circus?' He smiled, just barely, and reached for the pocket of his battered brown jacket, taking out a packet of cigarettes, removing one and tapping its end on the lectern in front of him.

'I know what a tightrope walker is,' said Anna. 'I don't understand your point. You didn't like the balance of my essay?'

He tucked the cigarette into his shirt pocket then lifted the pages of her essay and placed them on the upturned tip of his index finger so that they tottered there, balancing between him and Anna. 'It's perfectly proportioned,' he said, 'much like yourself. But without your voice, without your unique insight, it's as shallow as an entire evening spent flirting without sex at the end of the night. Which is not why I came to the party.'

The salacious tone in his voice irked her. He was such a wonderful writer, how could his conversational ability be reduced to badly veiled references to sex?

'I disagree,' she said. 'Flirting with a stranger doesn't always have to lead somewhere in order to be enjoyable.'

'I'm not a stranger, Miss Page, I'm your editor, your readership, I'm a working man with a twenty-minute window to read my newspaper and I don't have time to consider all the angles. I read you because I rely on you, and I need you to tell me what to think. Rewrite the ending, Anna, tell me how you feel.'

His eyes locked on to hers and she noticed that they were the same shade of dirty blue as his shirt. She started to worry that he would see into her limited imagination and realize that she held on to her opinions because she was scared. When you tell people how you feel sometimes it gets thrown back in your face.

'Fine,' she said, and snatched the essay from its precarious perch.

'You sure you don't smoke?' he said, with a suggestive tilt of one eyebrow.

She shook her head and had to stop herself from telling him that he was being inappropriate. He was one wink away from coming on to her and she didn't like it.

'Was there anything else?'

'That's all.'

A small group of her friends, people she knew from various overlapping classes, were standing outside smoking their little rolled-up cigarettes and discussing whether or not to go to a new club where a new band that were rumoured to be quite good were rumoured to be playing.

'I can't,' she said. 'I have to work.' She worked three nights a week, teaching French to recalcitrant teenagers above a fast-food place in Oxford Street.

Her rebuff passed without comment because this group, the nearest thing she had to friends, were used to Anna declining invitations, and the chatter quickly moved on to where to go for a cheap drink beforehand.

When she slipped away a few minutes later nobody noticed.

Why was she so quick to turn down any invitation? She could have gone out tonight; there were always people eager and willing to pick up extra classes. It wasn't just that, was it? It was the almost certain knowledge that an hour or two into the evening she would have wanted to go home. Was she old before her time, or what? Standing in a packed venue that smelt of sweat and beer, and shouting to make herself heard over the amateur rock and roll thumping out from a small and badly lit stage. It wasn't her idea of a good time.

Anna liked the walk home from work. She talked to people. There were hordes of tourists in this part of central London and the ones that needed help were always easy to spot. Young Europeans, still wearing their backpacks, hunched over a bad street map looking for their hostel, older Americans peering cautiously at the menu in the window of a restaurant that would overcharge them for plates of underdone chips, solitary travellers clutching a second-hand paperback and counting out their change a

penny at a time. Anna liked all of them. She would interrupt confused visitors to this, her city, and guide the
backpackers to the hostel on Gower Street, politely suggest to the Americans that they tried Browns on St
Martin's Lane instead, and strike up a conversation with
the lone traveller, who would be grateful for someone
briefly breaking the monotony that came with being alone.

When it came to being lost, confused or lonely Anna
was something of an expert.

It was late by the time she got home. Her textbooks
were out of her bag before she'd even closed the door and
she picked up one of John Mackintosh's books to read
while she cooked herself some dinner. Work had been
bearable, she'd recycled a lesson plan she had used a dozen
times before to teach the kids how to order food in a restaurant and the right way to pronounce knife, fork, spoon,
plate and twenty other pieces of a food-related vocabu-
lary, but it had made her exceptionally hungry. She piled a
huge handful of spinach into a wok and shook sesame oil
and a dash of water over the dark leaves before clamping
on the lid. Then she added boiling water from the kettle
and a handful of thread noodles to a smear of oily miso
paste in a pan and tipped in some fresh prawns that had
been waiting in her fridge since this morning. She watched
them turn pink in the time it took to slice some chilli and
spring onions and then she poured the whole lot over the
wilted spinach, which she'd tipped into a deep bowl. It
was in her mouth five minutes after walking through the
door.

She turned on her computer, opened her essay and
worked hard for almost an hour without a pause, then she
stopped and stared hopelessly at what she had written.

Suddenly it seemed like every word was lifted from John Mackintosh's own work; it was nothing more than a weak imitation, practically plagiarism. Success at this, at becoming a journalist, a writer of the calibre she wanted to be had never before seemed so unattainable. Her protracted education would soon come to its natural conclusion and then what would she do? She wanted to hurl the laptop against the wall, curl up into a ball and cry.

She had been so angry with her parents for taking her away from the chance of a good education. Farewell Oxford, so long Cambridge. It was only a last-minute panic that saw her emerge with good grades at all. Good, but not excellent. That was now the story of her life. Good but not good enough.

'You don't seem *engaged* any more,' her father had said when she scraped through her GCSEs. She stormed out and came home with a tattoo. She self-sabotaged her mock A level exams to prove her point and failed to get an offer from Oxford or Cambridge. She said she didn't care. 'It's what you always wanted,' he said. She stormed out again and came home with a boyfriend. A feckless youth, the type she knew her dad hated. It didn't last longer than a couple of months. They had nothing to talk about once she had paraded him around the house a few times to enjoy the expression on her father's face.

The stupid thing was that deep down Anna was still the kind of daughter he could be proud of. She shared his values, she liked all the things that he liked – reading, thinking, a big sky, a simple life – she just pretended to be a difficult teenager. It was stupid, but it was her way of letting him know that she still hadn't forgiven him for ruining her life.

But then life has a way of taking the stupid things you do and throwing them back in your face somewhere down the line.

He was sick, her dad was sick and all the cruel words that had passed between them seemed like such a waste. She wished she could take back every single one of them and replace all that spite with something more meaningful. He would die, maybe soon, and the thought of him still thinking that she hated him as he was dying kept Anna awake at night.

The only way she could make it up to him was to try to claw her way back to the top of the pile. To make something of her life, something he could be proud of, even if he could never really know it. She would know and that would be enough. She didn't want to let him down again.

Perhaps the few short months she spent at Clareville had ruined her forever. They had certainly shaped her. If not, then why did her thoughts drift to those days more than she would have liked them to?

She thought about them all the time. Chrissie, Jemima, Ben. But mostly, it had to be said, Chrissie. How could it be possible to love someone and hate them at the same time? And as so often happened when Anna felt nostalgic and slightly sad, thinking of what she did not have, she wondered where Chrissie Morton was right now and what she was doing.

Six

Kendall Morton was locked in a battle of wills. He always held his ground, no matter how devious his opponent. But he could sense his notorious iron grip on the situation beginning to slacken.

When she wanted to get her own way Chrissie Morton knew how to make her father's palms sweat.

'Daddy, listen to me,' she said, twisting the band of diamonds set in platinum he had bought from Tiffany's in New York for her twenty-first birthday. 'I can't help thinking that you don't quite understand the concept of a gap year.' Her big brown eyes were deliberately perplexed. She had yet to add tears to the mix but from the whining tone at the edge of her voice it could surely be only a matter of time.

For the last forty years Kendall had ruthlessly tackled some of the world's most influential figures without hesitation. He had ridden the Asian tiger all the way to immense money and power because anyone who stood between him and that which he thought was right could expect to be challenged. He angled one single longing glance at the bank of screens in front of him, the columns of scrolling figures representing his millions, and then he turned to face his only daughter. The cleft between his eyebrows was dark and deep. 'I'm an educated man, princess, so let's assume that I do.'

She presented her argument as if it was an absolute

right. 'I didn't have a gap year before university, so I deserve to have one now. When I get back you can sign me up for as many MBAs or post-graduate doo-dahs as you like, but I don't understand why you're being so mean.' She stuck out her lower lip in the exact same way that she had done just a few hours after she was born, cracking him open to the possibility of love.

'You need to get some new tricks,' he said, 'because the old pout isn't working, baby. You didn't have a gap year because you were retaking the exams you failed the first time around.'

'Don't be mean.'

'You'll get over it.'

'I don't understand you sometimes,' said Chrissie, toying with the solid silver paperweight on his desk with her pale pink fingernails, fidgeting, like she didn't really care, jealous of his fascination with a ticker of figures and the constant bleeps that reminded her of life-support systems around a hospital bed. 'I thought you'd love the idea of me changing the world.'

'And how did you plan to do that?'

'I don't know,' she said. 'Build an orphanage in India or something?'

Kendall's glance flicked back to his screens. He had less than an hour before Shanghai closed and every minute that this conversation continued was likely to be costing him upwards of twenty thousand dollars as his TSE securities company waited for confirmation from him before trading. He needed to conclude things with Chrissie within the next three minutes, preferably less than two.

He looked out of his full-length windows and focused on the gaudy Tokyo Tower, which he pretended to hate but privately loved. In Japan you had to move relentlessly upwards to stay at the top. The tower was an outdated symbol of modern Japanese progress, rapidly eclipsed by bigger and better structures; had it not been obediently painted a vile air-safety orange it may even have been beautiful once. It made him smile in a world where very little did. His reflection hovered there, as insubstantial as a ghost, merciful to his silvering hair and the lines that gathered on his face with a speed that alarmed him. Looking at his shadowy reflection he could still convince himself he was young. Almost as young as his daughter, and with all her passionate indignation too. After all, this was all for her one day, wasn't it? Every hour worked, every dollar earned, or pound or yen. She knew it, he knew it. Which is why stressing the importance of a good education sounded as hollow as a drum. 'Listen to me,' he said. 'You managed to scrape up a halfway decent degree in the end, despite everything, better than mine. So unless you intend to get a job, you can damn well take up a postgraduate *doo-dah* and be grateful that I'm willing to pay for it. Now where's it to be?'

'This is so unfair, what about what *I* want?'

Kendall tried to find that place in his heart that she had opened, his compassion, his softness, the part that had stayed up all night long when they got home from the hospital with the new baby just to watch her first sleep. But after the depressing, expensive divorce from her mother, that place had been locked and he'd had access only to a steely determination for Chrissie to become a daughter he could be proud of.

And so far, so far, they both knew he could not.

'Baby, you and I both know that if you took a gap year,

the closest you'd get to Indian orphans would be wearing some shoes from a sweatshop full of them.'

'Oh please,' said Chrissie. 'Like I'd wear anything mass-produced.'

They both grinned. Smiles that matched exactly, the same teeth, the same lips, the same lift in the apple of their cheeks. He wished that she could be more like him; she wished that he liked her more.

'I could get a job, I suppose,' she said. 'Can I come and work with you, Daddy?'

'Really work? Or drift from a late start, through lunch, to an early finish? No, I thought not. You need to find something to be passionate about apart from money.'

'Oh, like you, you mean?'

'Don't piss me off today, Chrissie,' he said. 'Did it ever occur to you that I might want you to learn from my mistakes? Maybe I want your life to turn out a little differently from mine.'

Their lives had been so different already. He left school at sixteen, no money, no connections, and from nothing he had built an empire. She was born pretty and privileged, and the closest she was likely to get to building an empire was commissioning an empire waist from one of the absurdly expensive young designers she favoured in New York and London. Why this incessant need to get her to *do* something with her life? Wasn't being beautiful and charming enough to earn his respect? It worked on everyone else but him. The only person that mattered.

'If you were married and pregnant maybe I could understand,' he said. 'But I worry that you'll be lonely,' he said.

I'm already lonely.

*

Chrissie stalked out as best she could when the object of her frustration had already turned his back. Thirty-seven floors down she stepped through the marble lobby onto Omotesando Street, flicking away the offer of a taxi from the genuflecting doorman. Instead she joined the surge of pedestrian traffic heading south, ducking and weaving a fast path through tightly packed Tokyo crowds, like in Harrods on Christmas Eve, working out her frustrations with her father on the spotless pavement. Clearly she had mistimed her approach; she should have waited until he was more distracted. Damn it. But she wasn't giving up that easily.

She stayed on Omotesando, finally escaping the crush as the people trickled down side passages in the direction of Takeshita-dori like a mighty river washing into a delta. On another day she might have followed one of those twisting side streets away from the hordes, getting lost on purpose then looking for a bar she'd never been to before, in the hope that it might change her life. But she couldn't handle all the Harajuku girls today, their fashion so edgy it pained the eye, expressing their beloved *kawaii* in the most cutely cartoonish outfits. Because somehow those girls were uniform even in their non-conformity: obedient little rebels. Typical Japanese.

No, she needed to be with people she trusted – Prada, Cartier, Chloé – the holy trinity of Omotesando Street, conveniently grouped together in one florid architectural adventure after another. There was a bench opposite them and sometimes she liked to sit there with a cup of darkly sensuous miso and just look at them, simply because the buildings were so beautiful, ignoring the looks she got from rich Japanese women who didn't think anyone should be seen eating in public.

But today she needed her shopping hard and fast.

She glided into Prada and bought a pair of red patent T-bar shoes within fifteen minutes, relaxing as soon as she handed over her credit card, enjoying the exemplary Japanese service. As far as she was concerned a Japanese salesman combined American sincerity with British reserve, which was as close to perfect as she could imagine. The very second the transaction was complete she felt the familiar soothing warmth that came with having spent money well.

'*Arigato*,' she said, and enjoyed the way her thanks were accepted with much bowing and scraping and offers to carry her bag to the door.

The credit card she used to buy these adorable red shoes rightfully belonged to her mother, but she'd been using it for almost five years now and neither of her parents had yet to notice. Clearly her father thought this particular card was one of many her mother retained privileges to during the oh-so-amicable divorce, while her mother was under the mistaken belief that it was one of those that had been cancelled. Just knowing that she was getting something past both her parents in one swipe gave Chrissie an enormous amount of satisfaction.

And lately satisfaction had been in short supply.

This talk of her future was becoming tiresome. Now he had vetoed the gap year she would be back to the classroom for yet another mind-numbing stint from which she was bound to emerge with a bad diploma and more memories of feeling intellectually out of her depth.

She had *tried* at school, my God, she'd had to. After the humiliation of failing her A levels, her father had immediately employed no fewer than seven private tutors, each of them patently on incentive bonuses. They had spoon-fed her information that she could regurgitate under exam conditions, so after the retakes she was able to call her father and tell him her results without being scared. Then university had been harder than she expected and twice she had transferred between schools and continents because she knew she was in danger of failing. She swapped Bristol for Berkeley and back again until at last she knuckled down to American Studies at the University of Tokyo, where life was so *dull* you couldn't help but study.

Please, no more. She might not be very clever but she was clever enough to know that if you were bad at something you should do it as little as possible.

She could get a job.

Yeah, right.

So now what? If she didn't want to get a job what was she supposed to do? Get pregnant? Kendall had clear ideas about the sort of man his daughter would one day marry, and since it coincided neatly with her own – rich, good-looking, malleable – she had no arguments there. But there was a distinct shortage of same in downtown Tokyo. Chrissie got the level of male attention that would make most women buckle under pressure but she could always find room for more. She would quite happily get married to Mr Right, even Mr Right Now, to avoid being responsible for herself, but she had nobody in mind.

Was marriage the answer?

She looked at the diamond solitaires in the tiny display cases set into the plasma windows of Cartier.

It would be fun to get married. Then after the wedding

and a Seychelles honeymoon they would move into the small terrace on Dovehouse Street that she suspected had always been earmarked for her wedding gift.

Her eye was caught by a five-carat solitaire that would look awesome if her nails were French-manicured or painted with that cute Sahara shade from Chanel.

After the honeymoon period the visions became hazy. But to be a young bride . . . there was something very rock and roll about that. If you waited until after twenty-five to get married then a unique opportunity for dewy radiance was lost forever. Those forty-year-old brides might look happy and sophisticated but truly they were fooling nobody. Everybody could tell that they were just extraordinarily relieved.

She slipped open her new Nokia and hit speed dial one. 'Rev? It's me. I was thinking of an early supper?'

He had a real name but she called him Rev because it was easier. He was vice-president of one of her father's companies but that didn't really mean anything; Kendall had hundreds of vice-presidents and probably just as many companies. Rev wasn't like most of the Japanese men she had met, probably because he was Korean, something he had taken great pains to hide from everyone, herself included. But she went through his things one morning when he was in the shower and saw his passport.

They met regularly in various hotels. Usually at the company's expense, which gave her a thrill. They'd had more sex than they'd had conversations. Rev helped to make Tokyo bearable. He had a good body for an Oriental and the most perfect skin she had ever tasted, pale gold and sweet like cinder toffee. He liked her to wash her hands thoroughly after sex and he wouldn't kiss her at all if she swallowed. God, this impossible country.

Forty-five minutes later she was stretched out in a killer suite at the Hyatt feeling like she was having what she knew would only be a mediocre orgasm bullied out of her by his insistent, but probably spotless, hand.

'Will you marry me?' she said.

His slim, warm fingers stopped what they were doing and she felt his weight shift until he was level with her. 'I'm sorry?' His face quivered like that of a deer staring down the barrel of a shotgun.

'I was asking you to marry me.' She placed his hand back between her legs and twisted her ankles together, pushing up at him with her hips. Rev would look fabulous in a morning suit. And her dad would be furious at her for marrying a local yet totally unable to say anything for fear of appearing racist.

'For real?'

Rev used the heel of his hand to rub down hard, which she didn't like and so she stopped him. 'Yes,' she said. 'For real.'

'Chrissie, I don't know what to say.'

She couldn't help but notice his erection shrivel up and die so she knew exactly where this was heading. Pig. He should be so lucky. He had always given the impression that he was nuts about her and now he looked at her like that? With raw fear in brown eyes as deeply liquid as her own? She felt the power in their relationship abandon her with such a momentous shift that she understood why men were nervous when they proposed. And Rev was significantly silent.

'I'm joking!' she said. 'Of course I'm joking. Sorry, it was a stupid joke.'

'Good. Because I like you very much, but you know I can't marry you, don't you?'

'You can't?'

'You're not Japanese,' he said.

'So? Neither are you.'

'I would not disrespect my family like that.'

'Excuse me?' To think that a few minutes ago she'd had him in a morning suit and sharing a terrace house on Dovehouse Street.

'Chris,' he said, a contraction of her name she hated, 'you always said this was just sex.'

'And I always got the impression you were wild about me,' she said. Proposing to him had been a ridiculous whim but the rejection still burnt like acid.

'Because you always said this was just sex,' he said, exasperated.

And he was right, she had, and sex was all it was. Rev was an absurd choice. Why complicate things when she could marry a decent English boy who would understand who she was and everything she had to offer? She needed somebody who was similar to her, who would understand the problems that came with privilege, who would know how it feels to have enormous expectations placed on blatantly inadequate (though aesthetically perfect) shoulders. Not Rev, not a guy who hero-worshipped her father and thought that orgasms should be shared out evenly like dividends.

'Get out,' she said.

'Angel,' he said, 'don't spoil everything.'

'There's nothing left to spoil.'

*

A few hours later she stormed back into her father's office.

'I'm leaving,' she said. 'I hate Japan. You know I do.'

'And where exactly will you be going?'

'I'll go back to London, to Mother's.'

'Have you asked her?'

Chrissie squealed with frustration and Kendall merely looked amused. 'I shouldn't have to *ask*,' she said. 'You're my parents.'

'I suppose you want me to pay for your flight?'

God, why was he being so difficult? It wasn't as if she had asked for the jet. A first-class ticket to London cost the kind of money he would drop on a set of shirts without even thinking about it. What was she supposed to do? Pay for her own flight out of her allowance?

'Find something to do with your life, Chrissie. Or you and I are going to have a major falling-out.'

'I'll go back to school,' she said, thinking quickly that that sounded like the easiest option, at least until she found herself a marriage. 'I'm sorry, Daddy. I think I'm just nervous.'

She left Tokyo within the week. She was looking for a short, sweet, childless marriage and then a discreet divorce. Her father would hardly snatch Dovehouse Street from a grieving divorcee. With a bit of luck she'd bounce back before she was twenty-six or twenty-seven, when the question of university would no longer apply. And there was always an outside chance she might fall in love for real.

Either way she'd get to keep the ring.

A little over a month later Chrissie held her breath and tiptoed through the master bedroom of the Dulwich house, keeping her eyes trained on the prostrate form of her mother, who was sleeping off far too much gin at lunchtime. It was a big bedroom and a long walk, and by the time Chrissie reached the safety of the en-suite and locked the door, her chest burnt with the effort. She barely glanced at herself in the mirrored doors of the medicine cabinet before throwing them open with a satisfied smile.

Excellent. Her mother was hoarding enough drugs to supply a coachload of clubbers with a nice safe pharmaceutical buzz.

She pushed past the Prozac, idly flicking a stray diazepam into her mouth to while away the afternoon, and texted the labels of a few things she didn't recognize to the small-time dealer who had told her he'd be willing to swap some prescription drugs (what he had called Housewife's Candy) for a couple of grams of naughty salt (or what she preferred to call cocaine).

Three texts later and they had a deal.

She was glad she had chosen to stay with her mother in Dulwich while she pretended to study. Yes, it was over an hour in a taxi from Dulwich to the London School of Economics in Bloomsbury, so it was no great surprise that she'd missed one or two lectures. Or perhaps a few more. Whatever. But at least in Dulwich the bathroom cabinet was stacked.

'How was school, darling?' her mother would unfailingly ask, like she was six years old and about to pull a finger painting out of her Mulberry tote.

'Fine,' said Chrissie, wondering why her mother's constantly addled state didn't bother her.

Yesterday she called on an old Clareville friend, Honor, who was in her final year at Kings, and invited her to go out. 'Come on,' said Chrissie. 'It'll be fun. Crush is the best Friday night there is, apparently.'

'Can you get hold of some charlie?' Honor had asked.

'Probably,' said Chrissie, who wasn't averse to a line or two, hence the swaperoo.

Lord knows she would need something to make it through the night. Crush sounded like a grotesque meat market, but every girl in want of a good husband has to start somewhere.

There was a big line outside the venue filled with the sort of student bodies she usually went out of her way to avoid. Loud Americans midway through their Big British Adventure, all mouth and Tommy Hilfiger trousers, acting like they owned the city in which they were little more than tourists. And terribly earnest English boys from the provinces who wouldn't dare speak to girls until five pints later, when they were too sweaty and stupid to make any sense. Chrissie looked at the pickings with despair. What if she failed to meet someone she could marry and ended up twelve months down the line failing her exams and having to go through the ordeal all over again?

This was a mistake. She should have gone straight to 192. She considered ditching Honor even as she was waiting for her, wishing that she was looking forward to seeing her more, longing for a friend. When Honor turned up she was wearing sky-high heels and a purple handkerchief, fitting in with the dress sense of the female half of the crowd perfectly but leaving Chrissie disappointed and even more certain that coming here tonight was a colossal misstep. She looked down at her own outfit, a knee-length Chloé skirt in soft silver suede, which she'd teamed with a white vest from Gap. She realized it made her look older, and more boring, than anybody there. She didn't care.

'If you like,' said Honor, 'we could find some scissors and I could kind of customize that skirt. It'd look fine with a few inches off it.'

Too late Chrissie remembered that she hadn't really liked Honor that much at school.

Once inside, their wrists branded with purple ink, Honor wasted no time in hoovering up more than her fair share of the coke. Chrissie was just barely in the mood.

'Don't fancy it?' said Honor hungrily.

'Don't need it,' said Chrissie.

They wandered into the body of the club and the opportunity for further discussion was lost in the resonant bass of the summer's chunkiest house track. Honor's feet were already gently bouncing in time to the music and she wasted no time at all in getting the drinks in.

Around midnight vile-smelling foam fell from the ceiling of the rammed nightclub and Chrissie's skirt was promptly ruined. She looked for Honor to suggest that they left and found her with her tongue rammed down the throat of a young man with four earrings in his left ear and a stud through his eyebrow.

She walked out and knew she wouldn't be bothering to keep in touch.

She wasn't fifteen any more and so she didn't intend to act like it.

She did however quite take to the old Shaw Library. A warm and vaguely stylish nook on campus, if you liked the Gentlemen's Club look, which she did, the Shaw was an oasis of calm in the maddening melée. Overstuffed velvet armchairs were tucked behind the sprawling stacks and a row of desks was well lit with single spots, but the rest of the library oozed with promising shadows. Maybe she would meet somebody there, the studious type who'd read her Keats after dinner and take her to see the sights of Ancient Egypt. That could work.

On one rainy Tuesday afternoon she was supposed to attend an emergency tutorial with her anthropology professor to explain why she had so far failed to submit a single piece of written work. The truthful answer was that she had yet to make it in for a lecture, the anthropology module taking place at the ungodly hour of nine a.m. Surely she couldn't be the only one who had struggled with that kind of unreasonable timetable? She was hoping to find inspiration for a better answer before they met, and where better to be inspired for storytelling than a library? She generally felt quite academic and purposeful once she found herself a quiet corner of Shaw and began reading *Elle* magazine.

The cute librarian smiled at her when she walked in, that's how regular she was here, at a library no less. Her father would be so proud.

Annoyingly, someone was already sitting in her favourite chair, the one near a window at the back that overlooked the hubbub of Clare Market below, buffered between Modern Philosophy and Military History.

It was a girl. Her pale hand hung motionless above a dropped book, and the tilt of her head suggested that she was asleep. Perhaps if she accidentally woke her then this girl with the unpainted fingernails would be disorientated enough to grab her eco-shopper and her tatty leather jacket and vacate Chrissie's favourite chair.

With a sense of purpose she selected the heaviest tome to hand, something hardback on the Napoleonic wars, and let it fall to the floor with a bang.

But the hand did not so much as twitch.

Chrissie edged closer. She was sleeping so peacefully, her right arm outstretched while her left was curled up under her head like a pillow. Suddenly she could see the girl's face.

Anna.

The guilt slammed into her stomach like a punch.

Anna Page.

I'm so sorry.

The taste of shame in Chrissie's mouth made her feel sick and she wanted to run screaming from the Shaw Library, to get back to the state she had existed in mere moments ago, where Anna and the dreadful thing that Chrissie had done to her had been softened by the passage of time. But even as she closed her eyes, partly to stem the tears and partly to block out the familiar face, she could still feel the sting of reprehension behind her eyelids, and in the very centre of her soul it felt as if all of her good qualities were bleeding away leaving only the nasty little bitch who had gone way too far.

Also, she couldn't help noticing, Anna hadn't lost the puppy fat.

There was no doubt about it, what she'd done to Anna's father had been bad.

Very bad.

So, so sorry.

She had wanted rid of her classmate and friend because it was embarrassing having to look at her every day. And the panic of embarrassment felt so very much like anger. She had acted in haste. She had been wrong.

She thought a hundred times about walking into the headmistress's office and confessing, begging for Mr Page to be reinstated, prepared to face the consequences – expulsion, surely, maybe even a civil suit. She imagined her confession repeatedly, varying what she wore and whether or not she had her hair up or down, what Mrs Mackenzie was wearing, what the weather was like, but in these imaginings she could never quite think what to say beyond 'I have something to say . . .'

And then she would think of how disappointed her father would be in her; she pictured his face and she was scared, too scared to walk into the headmistress's office after all.

So not only was she a nasty little bitch but she was a coward too.

This was what she would think late at night in the dark when she awoke unexpectedly panicked as if the weight of guilt itself had roused her.

A coward.

A bitch.

A liar.

But, *but*, she had been a child. She wouldn't do something like that now, obviously, of course not; she had grown up, morally as well as physically. That was the very pinnacle of her misdoings and it had been all change, change, change since then.

Wasn't that change, in a way, a sort of repentance? Didn't that make it right? It must do, because the guilt was lighter to bear with every passing year, and if she woke up at night these days it was usually only because she wanted to pee. Besides, perhaps things didn't turn out badly; maybe what she did was a blessing in disguise?

But seeing Anna again, a flesh and blood reminder of her personal low, felt like standing on the edge of a high cliff, swaying as the warm air from the ravine below unsettled your feet and you lost the ability to balance. What she did to Anna and her father was the one thing in her life she knew that she could never make into a funny story because there was no way to spin it. It had a taken only a few short weeks to realize this, when the thrill of victory had worn off and left a humiliating sense of self-loathing and a dirty secret to keep forever.

Anna stirred in her sleep and Chrissie felt her heart lurch into a gallop, but then she merely shifted her (still considerable) weight and settled back again. Chrissie could see the book now, something terribly dreary-looking by a John Mackintosh, and she smiled even as her eyes swam with tears. Still clever, then.

Chrissie cursed her misfortune. And just as she was getting over the guilt thing too.

She should just go, now, leave the library, leave the university even, if she could think of a good enough excuse to give her father. Quick, before Anna woke up. Apply herself diligently to burying the memory once more. Before that familiar panic got its claws back into her life. Now! Quick! That way she could . . .

'Chrissie Morton?'

The fake smile came to her mouth instinctively. The false look of delight she had mastered over the years to react to disappointing presents or party invitations. Bright eyes, bright grin, bright voice. 'Ohmigod, Anna? Is that you?'

'Chrissie. Well, if it isn't my worst best friend.'

'Your what?'

Anna bent to pick up her book, her red hair tumbling artlessly over her shoulders as she did so but she threw it all back with a single flick of her head. She muttered something under her breath, and whatever it was it didn't sound complimentary. 'Excuse me,' she said, 'I have to be somewhere . . . else.'

'Are you kidding me?'

Anna shrugged.

Chrissie liked what she was wearing. Anna looked all grown up, wearing a smart party dress and heels but throwing on the battered leather jacket to complete the look. She could use some make-up but it was nice to see that Chrissie had left her old friend with something useful, something meaningful. Style.

Perhaps there was more she could do. Perhaps she was supposed to make amends.

Perhaps this was fate.

If she could make things better, for Anna, maybe for her family too, then the guilt that dogged her charmed little life might abate. She could – what was the word? – grow. It was about facing your past, confronting your fears, admitting your mistakes. Well, perhaps not *admitting* them exactly, not out loud anyway. What would be the good in that?

Besides, it was always nice to have a project.

'Give me your number,' said Chrissie. 'We have to have a drink or something and catch up. What course are you on?'

'You're a student here? Seriously?'

'What do you mean, *seriously*?'

'I thought maybe you were just browsing.' Anna pulled her crappy bag higher onto her shoulder and looked at a non-existent watch on her wrist. 'Well, this has been lovely. Good luck with everything.'

'Anna!' Chrissie was bewildered. 'Stop, will you?' She didn't like to get the brush-off from anyone, not even her worst enemies. Yes, they'd had their run-ins but that was eons ago and Anna didn't even know the worst of it.

Or maybe she did. What if she knew the dark secret but was hoarding it for her own use? Like a named bullet that hadn't yet met its mark.

'What is it?' said Chrissie. 'Why so bitchy?'

'Why? Do you have an exclusive on that?'

She couldn't know. Nobody did. If they did, surely Chrissie would have been taken to task, no matter who her father was. But what if she did? 'You don't still hold a grudge?' said Chrissie tentatively. 'I couldn't have been more than fourteen when I saw you last.'

'Fifteen,' said Anna. 'A grudge for what? Dumping me? Being a bully? Making sure that everybody hated me? No, I don't hold a grudge. Maybe I should, but I don't.'

'Then what is it?' Even as she pushed the point there was a little voice inside her saying, 'Stop! Go now. It's not too late to disappear.' But she kept picking away at the scab though she knew that she might scar. 'Come on, Anna, we used to be such good friends.'

'No we didn't,' said Anna, 'not really. And I'm fairly confident that I shouldn't want to be friends with a girl like you. So I'm not going to give you my number. And I doubt I'll ever come to this library again, even though it was always pretty much my favourite place in London. You spoil the place. I think I'd rather read in the cold at home.'

Harsh. Chrissie had forgotten the smart mouth Anna

had on her. It had been one of the few things they had in common and one of the best things about their friendship.

'Maybe I've changed,' said Chrissie.

'People don't change that much.'

'I think you're wrong. I mean, look at you – a few years back you would have pushed people out of the way to have a drink with me.'

'A few years ago I was an idiot,' said Anna coldly.

'Hello? And so what does that make you now? Hmm?'

'You're still a bitch.'

'You say that like it's a bad thing.'

There was something. An amused twitch at the corner of Anna's mouth, a twinkle in her eye. Chrissie leapt on it. She was going to make amends whether Anna wanted her to or not.

'Come on, babe,' she said. 'Let's catch up. I can't believe you're a student here too.'

'I'm not,' said Anna. 'I mean, I was, as an undergrad, but I'm at City now. Round the corner.'

'So running into me is even more serendipitous.'

'That's a big word, Chrissie. Don't tell me you've been reading?'

'Now who's being bitchy?'

The sigh which came out of Anna's mouth was perfectly pitched between weariness and disdain and yet Chrissie could still glimpse the vulnerable side of Anna behind the smart mouth, the side of her that found it hard to say no, and she knew that eventually Anna would do the polite thing and accept her invitation. So she waited, hopeful.

'One drink,' said Anna eventually. 'I can tell you won't leave me alone until I say yes.'

Chrissie squealed, jumped up and down and clapped her hands, earning a stern glance from the cute librarian and an elaborate eye-roll from Anna. She loved it when she got her own way.

They ended up at One Aldwych because it was the first place Chrissie could think of nearby. Almost as soon as they walked in she knew she should have chosen a more down-at-heel venue, something a little more, well, studenty. The only problem was that she didn't know anywhere like that. Still, they were here now, she would push on, push past, power through. It was time to make friends.

'We should get a bottle, I think,' she said, as she perched on the edge of a modernist blue daybed and curled her feet up underneath her while she looked at the wine list.

Anna had refused to check her coat and so it sat by the side of them making the place look crumpled and scruffy. 'Just one glass for me. I told you, I have stuff I have to do.'

'Everyone has stuff to do,' said Chrissie, waving away the very idea that there could be something more important pressing for time. 'Take a couple of hours off from it and share a bottle of champagne with me.'

'In other words, do as I'm told?'

'Exactly. I'm going to need a minimum of two glasses to put the past behind me so a bottle will probably work out cheaper than buying by the glass. Isn't that the kind of thing they teach you at the London School of Economics?'

'Since when did you start worrying about money?' said Anna.

'Who says I'm worried? I just want you to loosen up and by the looks of it one glass won't do it.'

'Then I'll have to stay the way I am. Poor me.'

'I always buy a bottle even if I leave half of it,' said Chrissie. 'Buying by the glass is sort of tacky.'

Anna finally submitted to the smile that had been in her eyes for thirty minutes or more and let it make its way to her mouth. When Chrissie ordered a bottle of Billecart-Salmon from a passing waiter, Anna didn't protest. Instead she remarked on the copy of *The Times* that Chrissie had with her and then forced herself not to smile when Chrissie flashed her the *Elle* magazine tucked in its pages.

'Tell me everything about your life,' said Chrissie expansively after her first sip of perfectly chilled dusty pink bubbles. With every passing moment she was becoming more convinced that her secret was safe and this made her warm to her old friend even more. Anna might try to deny it but the old energy was straining to be back between them, the cut and thrust of banter that made outsiders wonder if they were missing the joke.

Anna painted an amusing picture of her days and nights. Living in converted halls on Tottenham Court Road, small, she said, with privacy issues, but great to be in the centre of town. Work in the evenings, teaching French to teenagers. It was obvious that money, or a lack of it, played a significant role in her lifestyle, if it could be called that. Anna was a girl on a budget. Everything she did – galleries and exhibitions, festivals, concerts – was either free or cheap. Everywhere she ate sounded dreadful.

Chrissie poured them both another glass and asked the Big Question, trying to sound as casual as she possibly could. 'How's your dad? Still teaching?'

'Why do you ask?'

Chrissie's hand trembled and the almost empty champagne bottle slipped and clattered back into the ice bucket with a tremendous echoing crash, then the bucket toppled and unbalanced, ice cascading all over the floor, and the bottle tottered to a noisy, lazy circle on the glass tabletop.

The peaceful ambience of the sophisticated bar was decisively shattered. Several curious stares turned on them and Chrissie felt as if she had an audience as her past was closing in, stealing her breath like the damp warm air of a Tokyo summer, oppressive and inescapable. Ice cubes skittered around her feet.

Waiters busied themselves clearing the mess and the Right Thing loomed huge in Chrissie's mind.

She could tell the truth. Throw herself at Anna's mercy and see what happened. That was the right thing to do. Perhaps the only thing to do. That must be why their paths had crossed once more. It was meant to be. She had to confess. The cool surety of knowing that you were right washed away her fear.

'Is he still teaching?'

'No, he's not.' Anna smiled fondly. 'Clareville was his last job, as it happens. He was writing a book for a while, non-fiction, about early childhood education, but, well, he isn't any more.'

'What's he doing?'

'Not much of anything.' She looked around her, as if for an exit, then grimly sipped some more champagne. 'He's not very well.' She started playing with the hair at the nape of her neck, twisting it and untwisting it, her eyes losing their clarity and turning gloomy. Chrissie felt like a brick had lodged itself in the pit of her stomach and dreaded what was to come.

'He was diagnosed with early onset Alzheimer's at the beginning of last year, it's . . . I mean, he's . . . It's difficult.'

'But that's awful.'

'Yeah. So you can see why I don't really care who did what to whom at school. I can hardly bring to mind anything about Clareville, except that's the last time I remember him completely . . . intact. He struggled to get another job, I think, and at first we put it, you know, his slips of the mind, down to boredom, but then after a few months it was obviously something more.'

'Is that why you didn't do the Oxbridge thing?'

'I kind of messed up my exams.'

'The stress.'

'No, it wasn't diagnosed until later. We fell out, Dad and me. I chose precisely the wrong time to go through my rebellious phase and now . . .'

Chrissie's mouth dried up suddenly and the bubbles in the champagne only seemed to scour it painfully when she took a sip.

'Doctors, people, keep telling my mum that at least he's not in pain, like that's supposed to help when he forgets who she is, his wife, the love of his life, and he's terrified of her, accuses her of breaking into his house. It's like one minute he was fifty-eight and now he's ninety.'

'I'm so sorry,' whispered Chrissie. She looked back on her actions with more shame than ever, shame that felt hot, liquid, permanent. So, today, regret tasted like pink champagne.

'Maybe if I'd stayed at Clareville, who knows? At least this way I got to stay close to them.'

'But hang on,' said Chrissie. 'You went to LSE, and now City. You're not exactly a failure.'

'It's not what I wanted,' said Anna. 'It's not what he wanted either. And the worst thing is, I don't think he knows how hard I'm trying now, how hard I'm trying to put things right. I think . . . honestly, I think he thinks I hate him.'

'Is he –' said Chrissie, scrambling for the right word and gripping onto the only one she could find – 'bad?'

Anna nodded.

Chrissie fell back into her seat as if a few inches could put some real distance between her and the dark realization that she was a truly awful person. The tears sparkling in her friend's eyes made her feel physically sick. The impulse to confess scuttled back into the shadowy recesses of her mind. She must learn to live with the dirty secret, because she couldn't come clean, she just couldn't. Instead she thought back to their schooldays before any of this happened.

'I was jealous of you at school, you know,' said Chrissie. 'I think a lot of us were. It was obvious you two were crazy about each other, you and your dad, I mean. The way he looked at you when he thought nobody was looking. So proud. I wasn't the only one there whose dad was half a world away. And you had him so close.'

'Too close,' said Anna lightly.

'We all want what we haven't got,' said Chrissie. She lifted her glass. 'A toast,' she said. 'To Mr Page.'

'To Dad.'

They both drained their glasses.

Anna was embarrassed. 'I never usually talk about this,' she said. 'Maybe I was wrong. Maybe we are friends.'

'Do you need one?' Chrissie decided that she would be the best friend that ever there was. Perhaps she was impaling herself on the stake of her shameful secret, but keeping her distance hadn't worked one bit. She could no sooner forget what she had done than forget who she was. Anna was about to see, again, that having Chrissie Morton on your side made everything a little bit easier.

'Do you?' said Anna.

Chrissie shrugged. 'I have to find a husband otherwise my dad will make me get a job.'

Anna chuckled and shook her head. Chrissie reached across to squeeze her hand and with that single touch they were friends again.

Some secrets are meant to be kept forever.

Seven

Anna stood in front of her parents' house, the only place she had ever called home, and it occurred to her that she could walk away. She pulled her coat around her a little tighter, slouching down into it as if she might make herself disappear. She could turn around, catch the bus back to halls and spend her Saturday shopping in the West End for things she didn't need, have a normal twenty-something's Saturday, the sort of Saturday she hadn't had for ages.

She still had a key but she never used it. She rang the bell to give her mum a few vital seconds to pull it together if it had fallen apart. From experience she knew that coping was about the illusion of normality as much as anything else. 'I can cope,' her mum always said, and she did. But the cost of her sacrifice could be measured by the speed with which she left the house every Saturday when Anna arrived.

She really had no idea exactly what her mum did with her Saturdays, sometimes she told her, sometimes she didn't, and it didn't matter. Anna was here to give her a break. What she did with that break was entirely up to her.

'Hello, love.' Her mum's smile was warm and light, so it must have been a good morning. 'You look nice; did you get your hair cut?'

She hadn't had a haircut for three months, and that wasn't even a good cut, just a walk-in somewhere in Soho that she wouldn't be going back to. 'Not for a while,' she said, but her mum wasn't really listening, she was getting her things together and looking for her keys. 'Where is he?'

'He's taking a nap in his chair,' she said. 'It's been about twenty minutes, so you should probably wake him up in a bit. The shopping arrived but I haven't unpacked it, is that okay?'

'That's fine, don't worry.'

'There's a newspaper on the kitchen table.'

'Just like every other Saturday?'

'Don't be cheeky.' Her mum tucked a silk scarf down under the collar of her coat and glanced in the mirror. 'I wish you could come with me today,' she said. 'There's a new exhibition at the Horniman. Do you remember, I used to take you there when you were little?'

'I love the Horniman,' said Anna. 'Is that café still nearby? The one that did the hot chocolate ice cream?'

'I don't know,' said her mum. 'I'll look. If it is, we'll go back together another time.'

They couldn't hold each other's gaze. They both knew that there would be no mother/daughter outings, not any more, because if they both went out at the same time then who would be there to mind Dad?

When he was sleeping there was nothing to distinguish him from the father that he was once was. He took naps in his chair back then too, the chair that had sat in the small conservatory off the kitchen for as long as she could remember. Her mum sometimes told the story of how he bought it at an antiques auction a few weeks after they were married, persuading her to part with seven of their precious pounds by telling her how beautiful it would be once he had sanded it down and re-covered it. For six months it was the only chair the newly-weds had. 'And I always let you sit on it, didn't I, love?' he'd say.

'Until we got another chair,' she'd say, 'and I haven't been allowed to sit in it since.'

He had never refurbished it. The rich red upholstery was worn so thin at the arms that you could see the weave beneath. The wooden frame was chipped and peeling.

But the chair would outlast him.

'Dad,' she said softly. 'Come on, Dad, time to wake up.'

It was better to wake him than to let him wake up naturally. He was always quite frightened when he woke up, so it was best to gently coax him into the real world – such as it was for him – and be there with a reassuring word.

He stirred. In those few short moments before he opened his eyes she wondered if he would know her. She knew in her heart that it was unlikely. It had been weeks since she saw the light of recognition spark something in him, months since he had said her name. But she had been unable to stop hoping that he might.

He opened his eyes and turned to face her, panic creeping into his eyes.

'Hello,' she said. 'It's me, Anna. It's okay, you were sleeping, that's all.'

Then the fear left him and in its place – nothing.

There was a supermarket delivery piled up on the kitchen table. Anna put most of it away in the cupboards and the fridge, leaving out the onions and the potatoes and a few other things that she would need first. She was in the habit of cooking a few dishes for later in the week and leaving them in the freezer. She ordered the ingredients online and spent the day pottering in the kitchen. Her dad kept very close to her as she moved around, and though she kept up a constant stream of chatter, he didn't say anything. She told him how well she was doing at City, knowing how much he once wanted for her. Her mum used to say that he gave up on dreams of his own the day that she was born, and even though she knew that he probably didn't comprehend what she was saying she wanted to tell him that she was making it happen, everything they had talked about before he got sick.

Okay, so perhaps it wasn't Oxbridge any more, her road to success had taken a slightly different path, but she could still be a journalist, she could still shape the world just like he always insisted that she could.

Every now and again she squeezed his hand or asked him a question, trying not to let it get to her when both actions went unanswered. She gave him an easy task to do, putting the potatoes in the water after she had peeled them, but he just looked at the cold peeled potato in his hand with no idea what it was doing there until she took it back from him.

Was he worse than last week or was he still the same?

The speed of his deterioration had surprised everyone. It took three years to diagnose him, which was two years too many for anti-dementia drugs to do any good. But perhaps there would be a new drug one day soon. Hope refused to be quashed, no matter how slight.

He leant into her and put his head on her shoulder, as trusting as a child, as helpless as a baby, and she gave him a cuddle. She chopped the onions for the Bolognese sauce savagely, blaming them for the tears that pricked her eyes.

His face was familiar, his arms were the same shape, the smell of him was the same as it had always been. He was still there, but she missed her father with all her heart. The man who taught her to throw a ball, to read a book, to swim in the sea. She just wanted to chat to him, to ask his advice, to make him happy, to make him angry. She wanted her dad back. She wanted him back but she knew she would probably never get the chance to speak to him again.

She threw the onions into a pan and they sizzled when they hit the hot oil, which made him laugh, a thin, wavering laugh that she had grown to hate. It was a million miles from the hearty chuckles that she used to say made him sound like Santa Claus.

At first the doctors gave him a life-expectancy of twelve to fifteen years, but then last year his descent had been sharp and terrifying and the medical estimate dropped to ten to twelve years, then five to seven, and then the doctors just stopped counting and it felt like they were all on borrowed time. Her mum was exhausted. They were permanently skint, the house was on the market once but refused to budge and they took it off again. Perhaps the pervasive air of melancholy was palpable to everyone who walked through the front door. Anna was glad to cook every Saturday because the alternative would be to go into the front room with the harmless, shuffling old man who was no longer her daddy and they would have nothing to do there but sit. She would gladly tear off her left hand for a chance to chat to her dad just one more time.

She must have had thousands, tens of thousands, of conversations with him.

But one more, that's the one she wanted.

A memory haunted her. Her dad, lucid and enthusiastic, clutching onto a brief moment of friendliness amid all the angst she unjustly subjected him to. They were discussing the possibility of taking a short trip to New York as a family. He had been there several times but not for years and she was interested enough to give him a few minutes without storming off to her room and slamming the door. 'You'll love it,' he said. But then she remembered that she didn't like him any more so she had rebuffed him, told him that she didn't think she'd have the time, not that summer anyway. Now time was all she had and he had none of it. In no time at all.

That evening Anna stayed for supper and a glass of wine with her mum. The café *was* still there in Forest Hill, said her mum, and the hot chocolate ice cream tasted exactly the same.

'How was he?' she asked.

'The usual, more or less,' said Anna. 'No dramas.'

'I've put another lock on the back door; that should stop him wandering off again.'

Last week she was caught on the phone and took her eye off him for a minute or two. He had been found taking a piss over a neighbour's Californian lilac.

'Have you heard from Carol? Or Brenda?' Anna said, naming the first of her mum's friends that came to mind.

'Not for a while.'

Immediately she was angry at them. Her mum and dad used to be off every weekend, crossing the country to have a night with some or other of their dizzying number of scattered old friends. And now, when she needed them most, they had drifted away.

'People don't know what to say,' said her mum. 'They get upset and I just end up trying to make them feel better.'

Anna struggled to make close friends because she never wanted to tell strangers about her dad, and yet the thought of him was so omnipresent that to others she always appeared to be hiding something. Chrissie was the first person she had told about her father in years. It had felt natural too, as easy as discussing the weather.

'How's . . . Peter?' asked her mum, reaching for the name of the boy her daughter had mentioned once and then never again.

'History,' said Anna.

'Well, it was only a matter of time.'

She watched her mum playing with the neck of her wine glass. She was drinking faster than Anna, and seemed tense. They turned the television on but her mum flicked through the channels to such an extent that eventually Anna turned it off again and they sat in soft silence, both exhausted from a long day.

When her mum spoke again her tone was serious and vulnerable. 'Can I ask you something?' she said.

'Of course you can.' This was it. Her mum was going to start looking for a full-time care home for him. It was something they had never discussed but it hung in the air like a stick they could beat themselves with when things were bad.

But that wasn't the question.

'If it's like this for me,' said her mum, 'if I get sick like your dad, I mean, and I can't . . . take care of myself any more, if I'm not me, then I want you to finish it.'

The request ricocheted into stunned silence then Anna found her voice. 'What? No! Don't talk like that. I don't want to hear it. Why? Are you sick? Do you feel okay?'

'I feel fine, love, I'm fine. I've years left. Sorry, I didn't mean to scare you.'

Anna fought off the tight grip of panic. She had already lost one parent and she couldn't contemplate losing them both. She wanted to reach out for her mother but she didn't dare. She was afraid that if one of them started to cry then the thin illusion of normality that they clung to like a life raft would drift away in a torrent of tears and they would both be drowned.

Saturday nights with Chrissie became a welcome addition to Anna's weekend routine. This time they were in Hoxton, where Chrissie'd told Anna she had a big surprise for her. They met in a café at ten and almost two hours later Anna was jangling from caffeine and irritated by the fact that there were trendy drinking dens nearby but Chrissie wouldn't take her to any of them yet because they would be 'utterly dead' before midnight.

'Hey, I don't make the rules,' said Chrissie.

'But you do so love to follow them.'

'What's the alternative? Being a *rebel*? Isn't that just another word for loser?'

'You'd know.'

'As if.' Chrissie balled up an empty sugar wrapper and flicked it into Anna's face, perfectly aimed. It bounced off her nose and into the empty coffee cup in front of her.

'If you can do that again I'll give you a fiver,' said Anna.

'Keep your money for the nose job, babe.'

'Still about looks and money, huh?'

'Always.'

Anna glanced out of the window and smirked. Despite

the caffeine and another Saturday she had just endured with Dad, she was happy. Over the last couple of months, being friends again was like finding a missing link. It was also proof positive that neither of them had changed as much as they thought, perhaps hoped, they had. While running around London trying to find Chrissie a prospective spouse they had to take care not to scare off any candidates with their shameless displays of immature mischief.

'You bring out the absolute worst in me,' Anna said once.

'You're welcome,' said Chrissie.

At last Chrissie decreed that they could move on. The place was just a few minutes away, and they walked past several wine bars and gastropubs spilling clientele out onto the pavements. Everyone was young and happy, mostly they were beautiful. London was the friendliest place on earth when you were on your ups; when you were miserable it was hell. Anna had had it with being miserable. Her eyes met with the flirtatious smile of a stranger and she ducked them instinctively but then raised her head to smile back. Chrissie had taken an interest in her love life and had made some ominous hints about fixing her up with an old friend of hers. Anna's knee-jerk reaction was to say that she was too busy with her studies but she knew how pathetic that sounded and couldn't face the ribbing.

Besides, maybe she could be with someone. Maybe she could fall in love.

'We're here,' said Chrissie, as they approached a roped doorway where a small queue had gathered. She gave the queue one, almost pitying, glance before walking directly to the doorman and fluttering her eyelashes. Anna was impressed. It worked. It always worked.

Once it would have been a grand townhouse, a family home perhaps, but now it was a pleasure palace, the original features ripped out to make room for fire exits and bathrooms and a solid marble champagne bar. A girl on the door to take your money, another in a cloakroom to take your coat, overbearing dance music and the clatter of glasses and conversation, the reflection on the mirrored bar area making kaleidoscopes out of every bottle, fractured disco lights bouncing across every footstep. The mirrors reflected the pair of them in multiples, as if they were walking two by two into infinity.

'Original flooring,' said Chrissie, pointing down at the burnished oak parquet beneath their feet. Anna was blinded by the razzamatazz and surprised that Chrissie cared enough to point it out.

They were shown to a table and it was only when Chrissie tipped the hostess ten pounds to find them a table closer to the stage that Anna noticed there was a stage at all, a stage that was halfway to being a catwalk, spiked with three silver poles around which near-naked women twirled and arched in lazy patterns, bending their perfect bodies and obscuring their faces by flinging around lots of long hair. Nearby a man was enjoying a private dance while two of his friends looked on and made badly timed jokes. At the neighbouring table two white girls in threads of sparkly clothing were sitting with a group of Chinese men, drinking champagne and flirting. As soon as you'd spotted one working girl you quickly saw more. It was like seeing fish in the surf.

'A lap-dancing club?' said Anna.

'The best place to meet men,' said Chrissie.

'Lonely, desperate men, maybe.'

'My favourite kind.'

The table next to theirs groaned under the weight of happy, horny, thirty-something men sipping at their overpriced drinks without taking their eyes away from the women, conversing spasmodically without making eye contact. One man was sitting in the middle of a lap dance, rigid with the effort of keeping his hands to himself.

'Look,' said Anna. 'You can practically see him making a deposit in the wank-bank with every move she makes.'

'Hush,' said Chrissie. 'Whatever happens you mustn't voice your opinion on lap-dancing clubs, or the men who go to them. If you absolutely have to you can go on at me tomorrow, so try to contain all your pseudo-feminist objections until then.'

'What makes you think I'd have pseudo-feminist objections?'

'I dunno. The way you look in that dress? Couldn't you at least have worn some more make-up? We look like a couple of dykes.'

'I like this dress,' said Anna. And she did. It was vintage Givenchy, a real find in a dusty provincial shop, round-necked and full-skirted, nipped in at the waist, classic. 'It's the most expensive piece of clothing I own.'

Chrissie gave the dress a second look but that didn't change her opinion. 'You look Amish,' she said.

Anna poked out her tongue. 'Piss off. You must have some lipgloss or something. Give it to me and I'll go to the Ladies and tart myself up a bit. I thought we were going to a café, didn't I? Not the Moulin bloody Rouge.'

'I don't know how you think you're going to meet someone without making an effort. Here,' she said, digging into her Burberry bag and pulling out a tube of lipgloss. 'Keep it.'

'You keep giving me things, Chrissie, it feels weird.'

'Oh get over it, I have loads.'

'Okay, well, thanks,' said Anna. 'If you're sure.'

'I'm sure.' Chrissie added a Laura Mercier highlighter and Maybelline mascara to the cache of cosmetics then waved Anna off to the bathroom.

It was true that the face that she looked at in the mirror could take some enhancement. But she knew that no matter how much make-up she applied she could never look as stunning as Chrissie. She just didn't have that grace and self-assurance, and no amount of lipgloss would change that. She applied the highlighter sparingly around her eyes before two coats of the mascara and just enough gloss to stop Chrissie making her turn back and put more on. She pressed her lips together, trying to enjoy the unfamiliar stickiness but instead feeling as if she had yet to wipe her mouth after a slice of bread and jam. How did one drink without smearing the rim of the glass, she wondered. Then realized that would be why God invented straws.

When she came back to the table she looked distinctly less drab. 'That's better,' said Chrissie, and then she patted the wave of Anna's hair like an anxious aunt. She suggested drinks as her eyes kept casting around the room.

'Seen any husband candidates?' said Anna.

'Nope.' They were all too old. That was the problem. When she pictured her rock-and-roll wedding it wasn't to a paunch and a prostate problem, it was to a guy who would make all the other girls jealous. 'I'm looking for something younger and hotter.'

'But why would a young sex machine want to get married?' asked Anna. 'No offence.'

'You're right. It's a stupid idea,' said Chrissie. 'I should just give up the husband hunt and resign myself to a life of hard labour. Do you think I'd be a good journalist?'

'I think,' said Anna cautiously, 'that journalism is going to be pretty competitive.'

'I'm competitive.'

Anna sucked down hard on her straw to avoid comment. Chrissie liked to be the best at everything, that was true, but perhaps she felt as if she was running out of things to be the best at.

Chrissie checked her watch and then suggested they take a look upstairs.

'For what?' asked Anna.

'You never know,' chirped Chrissie. Anna began to suspect there was a reason they were here tonight and it wasn't just to find Chrissie a starter marriage. She followed her friend nervously up the narrow stairs at the back of the converted townhouse. Her suspicions were confirmed as Chrissie tried to casually check out every single table on the second floor. She was looking for something, or someone, and several minutes later she found him. She stopped short, pointing.

A table of men, indistinct from all the others, the host of the party clearly the slim silver-haired man to whom all other faces were turned. Most of his companions were around his age but there was one achingly familiar young face sipping from a vodka rocks and grinning just as he had in a thousand of her dreams.

'Hey,' said Chrissie, in a pathetic attempt to sound surprised. 'Isn't that . . .'

'Ben,' said Anna. 'Yes, it is.'

Was it possible that he looked exactly the same? It couldn't be, otherwise he would look out of place, a sixteen-year-old schoolboy in a lap-dancing club. But his hair was the same, the way he pushed it out of his eyes was identical. His body was throbbing with youth and vitality and his smile, his charming smile, was precisely the same smile that used to make all the girls melt. Her hand went to her mouth and she felt a slightly sick sensation, like vertigo, but it passed.

She instantly recalled the last time she had seen him, his lips on hers, his conspiratorial whisper warm on the soft downy skin of her earlobe. *Ben*.

'Surprise!' said Chrissie, with glee.

Anna's voice was shrill and breathless. 'You knew he was going to be here? Why? Why did you think this was a good idea?' She looked towards the door, her instincts urging her to flee.

'We keep in touch. We're friends, you know? I saw this on his Facebook and I thought it'd be a laugh to bump into him,' said Chrissie.

'We're not invited?'

'It's his dad's stag do. So no, of course not. This is a coincidence. Sort of.'

'What were you thinking?'

'Honestly?' said Chrissie. 'I thought you'd be pleased. I'm sorry.'

Anna paused, pressed her lips together and closed her eyes tightly for a second. The shock of seeing him subsided with each calming breath. When she looked up again she was smiling and looking for all the world like she wasn't so nervous that she could barely stand upright. It seemed crucially important not to let Chrissie know just how affected she was by the sight of him. 'I am,' she said. 'Apology accepted. Forget it.'

'Chrissie?' said a voice close to her shoulder. 'I'm right – it is you, isn't it?'

'Ben!' They said his name in high-pitched unison, which set them both off laughing. Anna felt more of the tension seep out of her. She could handle this; it wasn't that big a deal. She wasn't a virgin schoolgirl any longer, just as he was no longer the most popular boy in the world.

Ben clapped his hands and rubbed them together. He seemed genuinely delighted, which helped with the awkwardness. Or lack of it. It was quite possible, even likely, that neither Ben nor Chrissie felt awkward at all.

'This is great,' he said. 'Come on over and I'll introduce you to my dad. God, he'll love you two.'

'I remember your dad,' said Chrissie, looking over at Ben's table. 'He's getting married?'

'Again,' said Ben. 'Third time's the charm, right? Come on, grab a chair. Do you have drinks?'

'We can't,' said Anna abruptly.

Ben and Chrissie looked at her in confusion. 'Is something wrong?'

'It's just that it's so late,' she protested.

'What's your point?' said Chrissie. 'Come on, I never crashed a stag night before.'

'Girls aren't allowed on stag nights.'

'I'm sure we can make an exception. Chrissie, you look fabulous, as always. And you . . .'

She tensed, waiting for him to get her name wrong.

But he didn't.

'Anna,' he said. 'The one who ran away.' He reached out his hand and when she took it she imagined their skin fusing together and never being able to let go. She would follow him anywhere.

Ben had limped out of University College London with a degree that bore the scars of too much partying. 'Dad persuaded his brother to find me a junior analyst position at Casenove but with the markets the way they are nobody feels secure, not even the boss's nephew. Especially not the boss's nephew. I'm not good enough at the job to make it my own.'

'I'm sure you are,' said Anna.

'Anna, I don't even fully understand what it is that I do,' he said solemnly. 'It's to do with numbers and confidence and I'm only strong in one of those areas.'

At the table his dad was enjoying a private dance from a scantily clad lovely, with his friends looking on and Chrissie being a good-humoured cheerleader for them all. Yet Ben seemed content to sit at the bar with Anna and catch up on the intervening years.

'But you'll improve,' she said, trying to be positive. 'As you learn.'

'I've been there for a year,' he said. 'And the only thing I'm good at is pretending that I know what I'm doing. Honestly, I sometimes wonder if there aren't dozens like me in the company, in the industry.'

'In the world, I imagine,' said Anna. 'I seem to spend most of my *life* pretending that I know what I'm doing.'

'Really? You seem so, I don't know, sorted. Like one of those people who has it all, who has it all together.'

She shrugged.

He looked at her for a long moment, as if trying to catch her out. 'Well, if you're faking it then you're very good at it. Want another drink?'

She did. And another and another. If she could she would drink enough to make this night last forever. Ben hadn't changed at all.

There was a lot of hooting and hollering from their table and they both turned round to see Chrissie staging a mock lap dance for Ben's father, to the obvious displeasure of the on-looking professionals. 'On second thoughts,' he said, 'maybe it's time to move on somewhere else,' he said.

She prepared herself to say goodbye. Would he ask if they could see each other again or was it not that kind of conversation? Was he being nice to her because he liked her or just because he was, you know, nice?

He stood up and walked back to the table where Chrissie was pretending to take her top off and he pretended to stop her to the good-natured pretend boos of his father and his father's friends. Ben and Chrissie both laughed as she pretended to fight him off with girly slaps.

Everyone was faking it in one way or another. So she shouldn't feel like a liar for not correcting him and telling him that most of the time she felt like a mess.

'You ladies will join us, of course?' he said, aiming his question towards Anna. She nodded dumbly. She couldn't stop staring at his arm, which had somehow wrapped itself around Chrissie's shoulders.

By the end of the chaotic night Anna decided that they were just friends, all three of them. Though the qualifying 'just' seemed as insufficient as it ever had. Ben was the perfect third wheel, the butt of their jokes, the jam in their sandwich.

It was almost four when they emerged blinking and dry-mouthed onto the ghostly streets of London.

'Will you come to the wedding?' he asked.

'We'd love to,' said Anna politely, propping up Chrissie, a drunken deadweight on her arm.

'I love you too,' slurred Chrissie.

Eight

The next morning Chrissie woke up feeling like she had been punched in the head. All she wanted to do was go back to sleep, moaning softly, but as it was also immediately apparent that she had not woken up in her own bed this was not a realistic option.

She was in a sleeping bag (a first for her and if she didn't feel quite so wretched she might have enjoyed the novelty), on a scratchy red sofa in a room she didn't recognize.

Oh the shame.

She had no idea where she was. Opposite her there was a single bed with a human-shaped lump under the duvet. She must have allowed herself to be picked up by some guy.

She looked around without moving her head, hoping to see something that might jog her memory. One of life's most depressing rooms, with white walls, a grey tiled ceiling and a carpet the colour of Blu-Tack. The furniture was so cheap it looked like cardboard. A tiny cracked sink oozed damply in the far corner. There was a makeshift kitchen, consisting of a kettle and a hotplate on top of a cheap pine table shoved against the wall. There was a humming fridge underneath it.

It occurred to Chrissie that she was in what they called a 'bedsit'. This was turning out to be a day of firsts.

She looked at the figure in the single bed.

Please be gorgeous. It was the only excuse she could accept for going home with someone who lived in a dump like this.

Chrissie's coat and bag were strewn across the floor and her dress was hanging from the back of the door. She was still wearing her underwear, so it wasn't as bad as all that. She closed her eyes.

Think, think.

They had gone off with Ben and his lot – hadn't they? – to a club, in a basement somewhere near Holborn, and there had been more drinks, some dancing. The night had taken on a surreal quality and there was lots of laughter, almost too much; she remembered feeling breathless and giddy with it. Then where? Soho maybe? Somewhere with strippers, not as sophisticated as the first place, and the boys hadn't wanted the girls to tag along but she had made such a fuss and everyone was having a good time and his dad, the stag, had the final say so they had gone to the strip club and there was a crazy strobe light on the stairs and many mojitos and then . . .

And then . . .

She opened her eyes again and shuddered.

She remembered a guy. He wasn't someone with their party, not a chance. He had been foreign – Macedonian, or Moldavian, or (possibly) Moroccan – and he had that way that some non-English men have of being very physical very quickly. Or maybe that was the vibe she'd been giving off. She'd been . . . dancing? Could that be right? And he had put his hands on her like he adored her and she'd let him. He had been smiling, smiling, smiling and then . . .

Kisses, hot kisses tasting of sour breath, rum and

excitement. Where? A dark corridor somewhere, the music from the club muffled by the walls around them. A cupboard? Surely not. Another shudder as she remembered his hands, those dark hands with dirty nails, roaming over her body as he kept kissing her, sloppy and overeager. She hadn't been scared, not for a moment. He had been far too *grateful* to feel like a threat. And then . . . What had possessed her to go home with a stranger? Silly little kisses she could forgive, but no more. She felt itchy, like she needed a shower. A fresh wave of pain drilled into her head.

Gently, so gently, she eased herself off the sofa, being as careful as she could, but the lump made a noise and, though she froze immediately, it moved.

'You,' the lump said chirpily, 'were certainly on form last night.'

'Anna?' She felt so relieved to see that ginger frizz emerge from beneath the duvet that even her headache subsided.

'How do you feel?' said Anna, one degree of chirpiness below irritating.

'This is where you *live*?' said Chrissie, the realization saddening her. 'Oh you poor, poor girl.' She slumped back onto the sofa, the memory of the Macedonian (or something) retreating back into the box marked 'Drunken Misbehaviour'. Ha! She knew she wasn't a slag, she just knew it.

'We tried to get you a cab to Dulwich,' said Anna, 'but nobody would take you, except this one very persistent minicab driver that Ben had to ask to back off.'

'Ben?'

'You don't remember?'

'Not much after the strip club.'

'But you remember the strip club?' pressed Anna.

'Not much there either, to be honest.' What must she have looked like, drunk and messy? Had anyone seen her with her dodgy paramour? Had they been laughing at her? 'Those mojitos were evil.'

Then another, far more frightening thought occurred to her and a needle of anxiety pierced her thumping head. Rationally, she knew everything was sound. Anna was smiling, clearly they were still okay, but what if she'd lost control and launched into a self-pitying confession and told Anna about her dreadful lie? She must be more careful.

She propped herself up on her elbow and tied back her hair. The smell of it was making her feel sick. 'Was I hideous?'

'You weren't too bad,' said Anna. 'Funny, mostly. You kept apologizing to everyone.'

'For what?' Somehow she kept her expression neutral. 'Who knows?'

Anna swung her legs out of bed and walked over to the fridge, taking out two cans of drink. 'Lemon Fanta?' She pushed a can into Chrissie's hand. 'Trust me. It's good for what ails you.' She popped open the tab and got back into bed.

Chrissie sipped the liquid gingerly and found the ice-cold combination of sweet and sour went down well. 'Did we have a good time?'

'We had an *excellent* time.'

'What is it? You're lying. You're never this enthusiastic.'

'We did,' said Anna, 'honestly. Ben and his dad's mates were lovely. I think at least one of them plans to ask you out. Or at least he did until you announced to everyone that you wanted to get married as soon as humanly possible.'

'I didn't.'

'I'm afraid you did. And he'd already been married. Didn't fancy it again.'

Well, there were worse things she could have said, she supposed. It was a little humiliating though. Quickly she turned it into a joke before the mortification could take hold. 'But do they realize I come with a terraced house in Chelsea and a commitment to divorce in a few years after some childless good times?'

'Yep,' grinned Anna. 'You made that very clear. A number of times. Do you remember falling asleep with your head on the table?'

'I fell asleep?'

'Passed out, whatever.'

Anna didn't mention the seedy little two-minute romance so perhaps she was fortunate, perhaps it had gone unnoticed. There had been many nights exactly like this in Japan, too many. It was how things started with Rev, a few drinks, a few more and then a desperate hunger for some physical contact, to link up, to coalesce. She wasn't hurting anyone. The embarrassment would quickly fade.

'And what about you and Ben?'

'What?'

'Did anything happen?'

'Why would anything happen?'

'I thought you liked him,' said Chrissie. 'That's all.'

'A thousand years ago, maybe.'

Then what a total waste of time it had been trying to set them up.

Chrissie slumped back down on the scratchy sofa and

looked straight up at the ceiling until the ominous brown spots up there started to bother her. She was trying so hard to give Anna what she wanted, but it was impossible to guess what that was. Being this nice made one weary. 'And this is where you live,' she said. 'No wonder you've never had me back before.'

'What's wrong with it?'

'The furniture, the curtains, the carpet, the . . . scent. I don't know where to start.' There was really no excuse for bad taste.

'The location is perfect. It's cheap and the furniture came with it.' Anna was snippy and defensive. Why, Chrissie had no idea. This place was a non-negotiable dump.

'You should burn it. Nobody over the age of twelve should ever sleep in a single bed.'

Anna was pulling on her clothes. 'I don't care,' she said.

'Of course you do.'

'So, what? I should spend all the money I don't have tarting up the place where I live, which nobody ever sees?'

'Yes. Your surroundings are a reflection of who you are. You'll feel better, trust me. And then who knows who'll visit?'

She saw a flicker of interest cross Anna's face and jumped on it.

'You still like him,' said Chrissie.

'Ben? Oh Chrissie, maybe a bit. Will you shut up about it now?'

'You should absolutely go for it.'

'You're being ridiculous. Ben is rich and charming and good-looking and funny and I'm . . . Anna.'

'And?'

'What do I have to interest a guy like Ben?'

'You're Anna,' said Chrissie.

'That's not enough.'

'It's a good start.'

Anna had finished dressing in no time at all. Yet again Chrissie had to admire how pulled together she looked on next to no sleep and no doubt a fair number of mojitos of her own. She wore black skinny jeans and a white shirt fresh from the hanger. She was pushing her feet into well-worn brown leather boots and then she would be ready to go. Chrissie could never look so chic so quickly and she was the one with a walk-in wardrobe and a limitless amount to spend on clothes. A quick glance in her compact mirror confirmed what she had strongly suspected: she had fallen asleep with her make-up on yet again, whereas Anna's clear skin glowed with the testament of a lifetime's good habits.

'Come on,' said Anna, as she scragged her hair back into a lazy topknot. 'Get a move on.'

'Where are we going?'

'Breakfast. A fry-up. Don't pull that face, you need one.'

The truth was it sounded ideal, with lots of toast to soak up the hangover, both physical and emotional. 'Okay,' she said. 'But you have to give me a few minutes to shower. Where's the bathroom?'

'Out of the door, turn left, down the stairs to the half-landing, the door on the right.'

'You share a bathroom?' This really was too much. She grabbed her dress off the floor and pulled it over her head. 'Forget it.'

There were many things that she was willing to do for Anna, but taking a shower in a place that was likely to make her feel grubbier than she did to begin with was not one of them.

Out on the street Chrissie recoiled from the bright sunlight and wished she had her shades.

'We're invited to the wedding next month,' said Anna. 'Remember? Think of the possibilities. There could be someone for you there.'

'Or you,' said Chrissie.

'I don't want to get married.'

'Ever?'

'Not next month,' she said.

On the way back to Dulwich that afternoon Chrissie had her next fabulous idea. It was because she could hardly bear thinking about that unloved scrap of Bloomsbury that Anna called a home, the forlorn single bed, the cracked sink and the grimy carpet. Wouldn't giving her flat a makeover be another nice thing to do for her new best friend?

Not enough, said a dark little voice at the back of her mind, not nearly enough to make up for what you did.

People change.

Still, she ordered her black cab to stop as they passed a newsagent and ran in to scoop up *Elle Decoration*, already picturing drifting muslin curtains and sanded wooden boards.

The following day she was alarmed to see that she had a tutorial scheduled for mid-morning that she had forgotten to rearrange. She didn't have a diary clash or anything like that, she had just realized pretty early on that these things could be rescheduled repeatedly, hence avoided for ever. But rather stupidly she had allowed this one to remain in her diary and now she had three unattractive choices. She could cancel at the last minute or just not show up at all. Or, of course, she could keep the appointment and see what it entailed. The third option was likely to be the one that got her into the least amount of trouble. It wouldn't do to draw attention to the fact that she had so far managed to avoid doing any serious work at all.

'I don't know why you bother,' Anna had said, when she learnt of Chrissie's loose interpretation of higher education.

'What else would I do?' said Chrissie reasonably.

'You should really go to the tutorial,' said Anna earnestly. 'It might be important.'

'As if.'

'Aren't you afraid that they might throw you out of school?'

'Could they do that?' said Chrissie. That would be awful. What would she tell her father?

It took her a while to find the appropriate tutorial office, a grim room at the end of a bland institutional corridor. The heels on her sky-high Manolos flitted over the nylon carpet in disgust. She decided that afterwards she would treat herself to lunch at the Wolseley to make up for this unfortunate waste of a morning. She rapped on the door and wondered how long this would take.

'Miss Morton?'

She smiled her most charming smile. 'That's right.'

'I'm Rosie, your sociology tutor, which you'd know if you'd managed to keep any of our previous five appointments.'

'Gosh, is it as many as that?' She hadn't been expecting

a woman. Probably that had been written down some-where but if it had she'd missed it. If she'd known she would have worn different shoes and less make-up. She sat down and tried to look demure.

'We had a meeting about you last week,' said Rosie.

'We?'

'Myself, two of your professors, your personal tutor. You were supposed to be there but as you couldn't make it we pressed on without you.'

This did not appear to be going well. If she didn't make lunch she would settle for afternoon tea.

'Had you failed to show up today,' continued Rosie, who was fast becoming one of Chrissie's least favourite people, 'there was a strong possibility that we would have had to fail you for this module and the associated con-tent.'

'But I'm here,' said Chrissie.

'Yes,' said Rosie, palpably disappointed. 'Yes, you are. And would you happen to have any of your overdue assignments with you?'

Chrissie looked down at her slim little clutch bag and laughed lightly. 'I'm afraid I don't,' she said. Oh well, it was bound to happen sooner or later, she had just hoped it would be later, that's all, preferably when she had found herself a prospective husband. With the practised skill of a true artist she started to cry. 'I'm so sorry,' she said. 'I've had some, well, some problems, some personal problems.'

Rosie's frost thawed slightly. 'I see.'

'I can't . . .' Chrissie sobbed delicately and then com-posed herself with a show of considerable effort. 'I can't seem to get out of bed in the mornings, not since . . . since . . .'

The end of the broken-off sentence pushed into the cold space between them and waited for someone to pick it up again. Chrissie could feel the doubts coming her way in big waves of suspicion, but in this day and age she knew that all she had to do was hold her ground and then she would get away with it. The university would be in a legal disaster area if she went home and topped herself the same day she had asked for help and been refused.

Rosie looked in her desk drawer and passed her a piece of paper from it. 'Here,' she said, 'if you need to talk to someone. The university has some excellent counsellors.'

Chrissie took the page and looked at it in what she hoped was a suitably dazed and mortified manner. 'I . . . do you think so? I mean, maybe. I don't know.'

'Miss Morton, if I may say so, you are one doctor's note away from failing this diploma. I suggest you either see someone about these problems of yours or rise above them and apply yourself to making up for lost time.'

'Thank you,' whispered Chrissie, and she scurried from the smelly little office before she could be asked to stay longer.

Once outside she called Ben to see if he fancied meeting her for lunch.

The best thing about the Wolseley was that they had the kind of menu that allowed you to drift from lunch to tea with only a couple of glasses of champagne in between. Ben needed very little persuasion to ditch work for the afternoon and they sat there beneath the chandeliers and talked about this and that until they were both pleasantly relaxed.

Ben suggested that they call Anna and they did. She didn't pick up. Chrissie was somewhat relieved.

'Do you like her?' said Chrissie.

'She's great,' he said.

She could have pushed for more but she didn't feel like sharing Ben's attention when she had him all to herself. And she really didn't want Anna asking how her tutorial had gone either and reminding her of the academic trouble she was managing to ignore.

'Are you seeing anyone special?' she said.

'By special you mean . . .?'

'Serious.'

'Why would I want to see anyone serious?'

'Are you dodging the question?'

'Are you asking me out?'

She laughed. 'I'm paying for lunch, aren't I?'

'Oh dear,' he said, checking the time, 'if this is a date I should be trying to get you into bed by now.'

'If this was a date,' she said, 'I'd probably let you.'

Over the second glass of champagne, prompted by an anecdote of his involving a married woman and a midnight flit, Chrissie started talking about confessions. 'If you did something wrong to someone,' she said, 'years ago, and you had the opportunity to confess, would you?'

'That depends,' he said.

'On what?'

'Would my confession change anything? Or would I just be confessing to make myself feel better?'

She toyed with the cupcake he had ordered and nibbled at the corner even though she had insisted that she was stuffed after lunch. 'Isn't feeling better change enough?'

'I meant change things for them. If the only reason you have for confessing is that you feel bad then I think feeling bad is just the price you pay for doing wrong. Why? What have you done?'

'Me?' said Chrissie, wide-eyed and innocent. 'I haven't done anything.'

'Somehow,' he said, 'I find that very unlikely.'

Nine

Within minutes of seeing him again Anna's old familiar feelings for Ben had resurfaced, the twisting heat in her knickers, the dry mouth, the insatiable hunger to know him better, to breathe in his presence, to be in his world. Crush: a violent word meaning to defeat or subdue completely. Still, seven years on, she didn't dare do anything about it. Who was she? Plain old Anna Page. Whereas he would always be the best-looking boy in school. People didn't change, no matter what Chrissie said.

It was thoroughly depressing.

'What about Ben?' she said to Chrissie shortly after their night out.

'What about him?'

'You could marry Ben.' The thought that her best friend might do exactly that had been haunting her night and day. After all, who wouldn't want to marry Ben? Ben, with his perfect smile and his gentle manner, the way he subtly ensured that everyone was happy, nobody was left wanting for an engaging sentence. If a smile dropped for more than a minute there he was, drawing the attention to a new topic of conversation. Ben had an innate skill for looking after people. And Anna was sorely in need of somebody to look after her. But standing beside Chrissie and all that she could offer – looks, money, the whole package – what hope was there for anyone else?

'He'd never go for it,' said Chrissie. 'And he knows me far too well to be fooled.'

A spark of jealousy flared and faded. Anna wanted to be the one who knew him well.

'Besides,' said Chrissie, 'I think he still likes you.'

'He never *liked* me,' said Anna, though her heart can-canned bawdily at the prospect. 'We were kids.' She could confess how she felt but doing so might open her up to ridicule. What she felt for Ben seemed too fragile to share, as insubstantial as a cobweb.

By the time Ben's father's wedding came around Anna had almost convinced herself that nothing was going to happen. Until she saw him.

She'd never been to a Jewish wedding before. 'I didn't even know Ben was Jewish,' she said, wondering fleetingly whether if they had children she would be expected to raise them in the Jewish faith.

'He isn't,' said Chrissie. 'It's the new wife.'

'Good. I mean, not good, I mean good as in okay.' She cringed. Chrissie must have noticed how she stumbled over every sentence close to his name and how many times she had changed her mind about what to wear today and how briskly she was walking towards the synagogue on Hallam Street knowing that she would see him again.

Chrissie checked the invitation. 'Ben said we're on his table.'

'You spoke to Ben?' Although they had exchanged a handful of texts she hadn't actually spoken to him on the phone.

'Email,' she said, and Anna couldn't decide which was

worse. Would it have been one of those short, choppy emails with terse information and nothing else? Or perhaps it was one of those emails with paragraphs and little jokes and open-ended questions so that a reply might be forthcoming. And was it one email? Or several?

The conversation moved on so she tried to stop worrying that Ben liked Chrissie more. Can there really ever be a battle if only one of the people knows they are competing?

She looked good. She had dressed up the Givenchy with a rose corsage from Portobello the same colour as her lipstick and borrowed a pair of red Prada heels from Chrissie (which she said she could keep), that also matched her lipstick. This morning she had been wearing a hat, but had taken it off at the last minute because she decided it looked stupid. Today, when she found the courage, she would move things with Ben onto another level. Immediately her mind danced towards the possibility, imagining a stolen moment of mutual desire.

Where better than a wedding for a romantic confession? There would be a moment; it was a wedding, there was bound to be a moment.

'We're here,' said Chrissie. 'My feet are killing me. I told you we should have got a cab.'

The temple in Hallam Street was beautiful. Ornate without being imposing, grand without being grandiose. When she stepped inside she felt the warmth of a community and the depth of history and briefly wished for a faith of her own. They found a couple of seats at the back and Anna studied the beautiful art on the walls while Chrissie looked for available men.

And then, in a skipped heartbeat, there was Ben,

looking handsome and at ease (did he ever look anything but?), walking his dad down the aisle with an elderly woman she assumed must be his gran. When the bride saw them approaching her face broke into a delighted smile that brought a tear to many of the watching eyes.

It was a friendly, inclusive sort of ceremony. The rabbi warmly welcomed the hotchpotch of family members squeezing under the chuppah, as if he knew them all personally, Ben from the groom's first marriage, two young daughters from the bride's. Although the groom was a decade or two older than his wife they were both ablaze with happiness, yet by the time they smashed a glass beneath their feet to ward off evil spirits Anna found herself wishing them the best but thinking the worst.

Weddings made her sad.

She used to think she was so lucky, having parents who were still together. Every week it seemed that another divorce was being wept for in the classrooms of her youth. But forced to watch her mother keep her vows of sickness and health, she found herself wishing that her parents had gone their separate ways years before. Anything to save her mother from his slow, excruciating slide towards his oblivion, dragging her down with him like a drowning man clinging on. That was marriage: a journey that started with laughter and a smashed glass and ended with tears and smashed dreams, one way or another. Did it matter if it was divorce or death? Which would be more painful?

Everybody cheered, but what she really wanted to do was shake them apart and tell them to reconsider.

The wedding reception was held beneath the soaring palm trees of the atrium at the Landmark Hotel.

'Like the Holy Land,' said Chrissie, and Anna shushed her.

They didn't know anyone so they stuck to each other and giggled about the spinster at the cloakroom, who probably hated every Saturday of her job and the weddings that it brought.

'I think I'd be a good Jew,' said Chrissie. 'Don't you?'

'What is it, Chrissie? Seen someone you like the look of?'

'Over there,' said Chrissie, 'the one with the lavender necktie. Doesn't he look cute in his yarmulke? I'm going over to say hi.'

Anna took a caviar blini from a passing tray and watched Chrissie for a little while, the introduction, the flirtation. Chrissie laughed at something that he said and placed a hand on his arm, and as she did so she caught Anna's eye and tipped her the wink.

'That girl,' said a voice behind her, 'is shameless.'

Her heart bounced and she hoped that he couldn't smell fish eggs on her breath when she kissed his cheek. 'Ben! Congratulations.'

'Thanks,' he said. 'Dad's a lucky sod, but then he always was.'

He looked lovely in his dark suit, pale blue shirt and no tie, and she blushed as she told him so.

'You look nice too,' he said.

Did he mean it? Or was he just saying it in a 'nice to meet you too' kind of way? A standard response to her compliment.

Get a grip. What was it about him that turned her into a poor excuse for herself?

'I wonder if he knows what's hitting on him?' said Ben, nodding towards Chrissie and her no-holds-barred flirtation with the lavender tie, all hair flicks and giggles and any excuse to touch him.

'I thought men liked a girl with no inhibitions,' she said.

'And what sorely mistaken woman's magazine told you that? We like our girls to be hidden, so we can discover them, unearth them. Come on too strong with what you're all about and maybe we'll sleep with you, but afterwards we'll run like little boys back to mama.'

'Unearth them? Who are you? Indiana Jones?'

'A particular hero of mine, as it happens.'

'I like his whip.'

Ben's eyes widened. 'Steady,' he said.

A silence stretched until he cleared his throat and changed the subject. She hoped it might be sexual tension but more likely it was awkwardness that had made the words dry up. 'I've gotta chat to some family, maiden aunts, duty, you know?'

She traced a circle on the floor with the toe of her shoe. She had embarrassed him and now it would be all uncomfortable between them.

'Sure,' she said. 'Don't let me keep you. I wouldn't want to stand in the way of duty.'

He took a couple of steps away from her and then hesitated. 'You want to come with me?'

Of course she did. She wanted to be with him everywhere. 'Okay.'

'I'm warning you, they might think you're my girlfriend.'

Even better.

The third time around for the groom, the second for the bride. It was as if those had been trial runs and taken away

147

all the pressure, which meant it was a fantastic wedding. The food was delicious, the drink plentiful, the speeches were hilarious and, best of all, Ben was right by her side for the entire thing. Chrissie had switched tables to keep talking to the lavender tie and so she had him all to herself.

'Hey,' said Ben, in the middle of a conversation about family. 'How's your dad? He used to teach at Clareville, didn't he?'

'Yeah, that's right,' said Anna, tucking her hair behind her ear and wishing that he hadn't asked. 'He's fine.' She sipped her wine. 'What are your new stepsisters like?'

'Young and pretty,' said Ben. 'Trouble.'

'Well, they have you to look after them now.'

'You should meet them,' he said. 'They could do with a positive female influence. All their friends appear totally spoilt to me, and their mother, my stepmum ... well, heaven help them really. She's making my dad very happy in ways I don't want to contemplate, but she's not exactly a role model.'

'She seems lovely,' said Anna.

'That's because she's drunk,' he said.

She didn't want this day to end. She felt alive, she felt beautiful and every moment that passed without pushing beyond the boundaries of friendship felt like a moment wasted. Outside the sun was setting.

Discover me. I want you to discover me.

'Do you remember the first time we kissed?' she said, her voice husky with longing and nervousness. She wanted him to desire her, she wanted to see hunger on his face, she wanted the space between them to jump with sparks of attraction, and the space between his legs to burn with longing.

'You and me?' he said, raising a quizzical eyebrow. 'We did?'

As her heart plummeted into her red Prada shoes he laughed and punched her shoulder. 'Of course I do,' he said. 'You were wearing a green dress, as I recall, and you wouldn't let me put my hand up your skirt.'

'I was a teenager,' she said. 'It was cold and we were in the middle of a field.'

'And now?'

'It isn't cold.'

'And we're not teenagers.'

She held his gaze. The loaded moment hung between them and her eyes fluttered closed.

Then with a surge of exuberance Chrissie, stupid bloody Chrissie, was suddenly upon them, squealing and killing the moment as surely as a belch. 'I swear,' she screeched, 'I am totally head-over-heels in bloody love with your cousin.'

Anna screamed inside, furious at Chrissie for ruining the moment but unable to say anything about it.

Chrissie, oblivious, checked her reflection in the blade of a cheese knife.

'He's not my cousin,' said Ben. 'He was married to one once.'

'Married?' said Chrissie, pursing her lips. 'He never told me that.'

Go away.

'Fancy,' said Anna. 'And after you two had all those long getting-to-know-you dinner dates and everything.'

'Don't be sarcastic.'

'Has he asked you out yet?' said Anna, thinking of the

nearly, the almost, the closed eyes and the feel of Ben's lips that close to hers.

'Not exactly,' said Chrissie. 'But I'm working on it.'

Every moment that she was there wittering on about her new flame Anna felt tense until, to her despair, Ben stood up and excused himself. 'I have to check the bar tab,' he said. 'My dad asked me to keep it under five K.'

'How are you supposed to do that, exactly?'

'I don't know,' said Ben. 'Push the cava?'

Then he left and after a while Anna convinced herself that she had imagined that moment and her wonderful mood drained away with the sunlight. Chrissie was soon off again in dogged pursuit of the lavender tie and Anna was left alone.

Again.

When the happy couple took to the dance floor for their first dance her head started to ache, and no matter how much fizzy water she tried to dull it with the niggling pain remained. She thought about going home but she was still clinging to the pathetic notion that she might get another chance with Ben.

It was then that she saw a familiar face propping up the bar. John Mackintosh was sharing a bottle of red wine with a girl who might have been his daughter. But as she watched he snaked his hand up the girl's thigh, higher than was decent, and she realized that wasn't the case.

It felt strange seeing him here outside the lecture theatre, as if that part of her life which she had under absolute control was intruding on this one where she couldn't get the words out. John Mackintosh represented a future that she could work towards with careful, premeditated steps. A future where hard work and application would eventually be rewarded. But each step she took towards Ben was like the backward heel of some unfamiliar tango.

She couldn't drag her eyes away from John and the girl he was with. The attraction between them was so obvious, as was the understanding they shared that tonight they would be having sex. What did people see when they looked at her and Ben? They would read into the awkward body language and the lack of intimacy that they were two friends having a conversation, not two lovers enjoying a confident preamble to bed. And they wouldn't be wrong.

He started laughing loudly at something the girl had said, using his amusement as an excuse to move his hand from her thigh to the base of her back, which was left bare by the daring cut of her dress. The girl didn't seem to mind. Perhaps after a certain age all you needed to appeal to young intelligent women was your own hair and a Pulitzer prize. The girl got up and left him alone, after placing the palm of her hand on the side of his face to assure him she would be back.

He sat at the bar in comfortable solitude looking so pleased with himself that it annoyed her. Yes, the girl was beautiful and very sexy, but did he have to look so *smug* about it? It just made people feel bad.

Then he caught her staring and after a moment of amused hesitation he lifted his glass to her. She lowered her head and pretended to be fascinated by the floral arrangement on her table. When she glanced up again he was still looking at her.

John Mackintosh's date came back to the bar and his momentary fascination with her was instantly over. She swallowed down a burst of irrational disappointment. It was just a look, that was all. They hadn't even spoken.

Still, it took her a long moment to recover her thoughts. What exactly was it about him that was so compelling?

One more darting look confirmed that she was no longer of interest to him, so she forced herself to move on.

Where was Chrissie?

She saw lavender tie in the corner of the dance floor smooching up to a blonde who definitely wasn't Chrissie and wondered if she was watching. Perhaps they had had an argument that ended the shortest relationship in history, a record even for a butterfly like her friend.

She saw the bride and groom, their dancing duties over, at the centre of the loudest, happiest circle of people – exactly where they should be – and it made her think of her own parents and their tiny wedding in the town where they were both born and raised. It had rained, they told her, it had poured down all day long but it didn't matter, nobody cared. Besides, rain on your wedding day was supposed to bring good luck.

The dance floor was filling up. The band played the reliable crowd pleasers that dragged people to their feet no matter how many helpings of cake they had consumed. High heels tapped alongside polished toes, shuffling through the glitter-strewn dance floor, the sound of conversation and laughter lifting above the music and making Anna feel more light-hearted, hopeful and happy.

She wandered off towards the bathrooms thinking that perhaps she would find her friend in there, touching up her make-up in preparation for a second offensive, but then she heard Chrissie's familiar throaty chuckle from a dark corner near the kitchen and stopped, confused. If not lavender tie, then who?

She followed the sound, curious.

Chrissie and Ben sprang apart when they saw her. They both had that excitable flush that comes with drunken kissing; her lips were swollen and glistening. 'We were just talking,' said Chrissie immediately and giggled. 'Where did you get to?'

'Nowhere,' said Anna. 'I was right there. Right where you left me.'

She could hardly bear to look at Ben and when she did he smiled helplessly at her and tugged at his collar. She noticed the tiny shimmer of lipgloss at the corner of his mouth and fought the urge to wipe it away with the back of her hand.

Ben rocked back on his heels. 'Who wants another drink?' he said.

'I'm going home,' said Anna, fighting to keep the emotion out of her voice. Ben and *Chrissie*?

'Why?' wailed Chrissie. 'It's still so early.'

'I'll get a bottle of champagne,' said Ben, manoeuvring himself past Anna without touching her, exchanging a private little look with Chrissie that both angered and devastated Anna.

'I thought you were supposed to be pushing the cava?' she said.

She knew she sounded petulant but she couldn't help it. A nasty idea took the fight out of her. What if this wasn't the first time? After all, hadn't they both always been more street-smart and sophisticated than her?

Ben went off to the bar, sheepishly dragging his heels and not bothering to look back.

Chrissie grabbed hold of her hand. 'Are you pissed off with me?' she said. 'It's just a stupid wedding thing. We're just messing around.'

'Why would I be pissed off?'

'I don't know, you seem mad.' Chrissie's brow was furrowed and her smile was unsure and fading.

'I've got a headache.' The thought of Chrissie and Ben messing around. The thought of his lips, the very lips that she ached for, being on those of her friend was like a squeal inside her skull. 'I'm going to get a cab.'

'Are you *sulking*?' said Chrissie, incredulous. 'You're acting like a child. A kiss doesn't have to mean anything. And so what if it did? You don't like him like that, remember?'

'And so now you do?'

'Not really. I was bored, Anna, if that's okay with you. I don't need your permission to amuse myself.'

Why had she ever thought that this time their friendship could be different? Chrissie was wrong. People don't change. '*Slut*.' It came out like a hiss.

Chrissie merely laughed. 'You know what I think?' she said, and Anna realized she was drunk. 'I think you *do* like him, you just can't bear the thought of rejection so you'd rather linger around your feelings and pick up crumbs than actually say anything.'

She kept her face impassive so that Chrissie wouldn't see how shrewdly she had aimed her jibe. 'Whatever happens with Ben, just remember this,' said Anna, 'I kissed him first.'

She watched Chrissie's face contort with frustration and hoped that she had ruined her night. Just like Chrissie had ruined hers.

She kept her head up, even though it was an effort not to put her chin on her chest and weep. Chrissie didn't need to see the hot flush on her neck from shame and disappointment.

Ben and *Chrissie*?

Shortly she was outside where it was dark and she was hopeful that she would be able to find a taxi and maybe even get all the way home before she lost it completely. Didn't Chrissie have enough without taking the one thing that Anna wanted most of all?

'Everything okay?'

John Mackintosh emerged from the shadows, his face creased in genuine concern, and she realized that she didn't look as together as she might have hoped. He was holding a lit cigarette; she could see the orange tip of it and smell the familiar scent.

'I'm fine.'

'Do I know you? I think I do.'

'Not really,' she said, for that was true enough. He hardly knew her at all. Not even enough to put a name to her face. Was she so very forgettable? She couldn't imagine Chrissie was forgotten very often, not perfect Chrissie, not with that face, not with that figure, not with that attitude, and – lest we forget – the Morton name to tow her through life in its silvered slipstream. Was she now to have Ben too?

'I'm Mac,' he said. 'Friend of the bride.' But Anna ignored him. 'You want a cigarette?' He held out a packet of Lucky Strike and she shook her head.

'I want a taxi,' she said, scanning up and down the busy street. The hotel was set back from the main road to soften the roar of passing traffic.

'Let me get one of the doormen,' said Mac, flicking his cigarette to the ground.

'It's okay,' she said. Marylebone Road was four busy lanes and she could see the orange lights of many taxis, any of which would be glad to take her the short distance back to Bloomsbury. All she needed to do was step away from the hotel forecourt. 'There's no need, I'll be fine.'

'Allow me,' he said, tucking her hand through the crook of his arm.

She shook him off. 'Please don't touch me.'

He held up his hands. 'Just trying to show some common courtesy.'

'Ha!'

'I beg your pardon?'

'It seems to me, *Mac*, that's not really your thing. Public displays of affection, if affection isn't too soft a word, with a girl half your age might be what passes for courtesy in your opinion but as you keep reminding us that it's all about facts as well as opinion, let me tell you a fact or two. Men your age chase younger women because they are trying to recapture their youth, and you know what?'

'Please,' he said, irritatingly amused, 'do tell me.'

'Your youth has gone, and you won't find it up her skirt.'

'I didn't hear her complaining.'

'That's true,' said Anna. 'So I presume that she's either drunk, or acting out some repressed issues she has with her father.'

He smiled. 'Maybe she'd rather be an old man's sweetheart than a young man's fool.'

She had nothing to say to that. For a little while they just stared at each other, he amused, she frustrated.

Then he grinned. 'It's Anna, right?' he said, clicking his fingers and looking pleased with himself. 'Anna Page, the book-smart one at the back, right? Great Hall, City University. International Journalism. Put your hand up whenever I ask something objective, but couldn't come up with an opinion if her entire vintage wardrobe depended on it.'

She nodded sorrowfully. She wanted good grades from him, not sympathy for what he must clearly see was displaced anger, anger which he had probably already deduced was over a boy. Why else would he have made that comment about her being a fool?

'Want to grab a coffee somewhere?' he said.

'What about your . . . that girl, the woman inside?'

'Oh yeah,' he said. 'That wouldn't be very nice of me, would it? Another time?'

'I don't think so.' Her eyes flicked to the street once more, seeking the sanctuary of a black taxicab. 'I really do just want to go home.'

'This is ridiculous,' he said.

He took her arm again and marshalled her roughly across the divide to the edge of the furious traffic. He threw his other hand high into the air and yelled for a taxi. One stopped almost immediately. He opened the door for her and she stepped inside, closing the door herself without saying thank you or goodbye.

The taxi pulled away and she looked behind her to see an expression of amused satisfaction on Mac's face before he turned and walked back to the hotel.

Then she saw Chrissie running out, looking this way and that. Standing on the steps, backlit and beautiful, she looked as anxious as Cinderella at midnight. But then the taxi turned into Marylebone High Street and she could see no more.

As she climbed the stairs back to her flat she could hardly wait to crawl into bed and annihilate her sorrow with some television and chocolate, but from the moment she turned her key in the lock she knew something was different.

The light was on. But it was not a stark overhead bulb that confronted her, rather a soft vanilla glow, diffused by the carved wooden screen that created a hallway of sorts in the space, complete with a hook for her coat and a tall, thin table for her keys. She double-checked that she was in the right place, breathed in the smell of fresh paint and stepped inside.

The crappy little bedsit had been transformed.

The single bed had gone and instead an elegant French double was tucked into the alcove where the makeshift kitchen used to be. The kitchen meanwhile was in the opposite alcove and was a clever piece of Swedish design that did a great job of pretending it was a cupboard. The floorboards had been uncovered and left untreated, softened with an enormous sable-coloured rug. The noise from the street flooded in through a crack at the top of the sash window, secured with a new lock that meant fresh air no longer cost security and the gauzy drapes could flutter as they may. Placed in front of the window was a beautiful wing-backed reading chair that made her think at once of her father's and a small table, a delicate art deco lamp casting a puddle of light where a book would go.

In the corner where the disgusting old sink used to be was a sleek bowl of blue glass, partially hidden by three identically beautiful houseplants, taller than she was, silvery grasses in a slim wooden container.

Chrissie. It had to be.

She wandered around her home unable to believe that she lived here. She had to check that all her stuff was still there, and was reassured by the familiar titles of her books on the shelves. Yes, it was still a shoebox. Yes, the creepy guy upstairs would still play house music at four a.m. But it was gorgeous. Sexy. Cool.

How generously her friend had transformed everything, not to Chrissie's personal taste, which tended more towards the ultra-modern than this homely, rustic feel, but perfect for Anna. The chunky raw floorboards, her photographs clustered on the mantle next to a jug of fresh flowers, the old kitchen table refreshed with a lick of white paint, the bed piled up with cushions and throws, ready for anything.

Her first thought was how much her dad would appreciate the old Georgian mouldings that the new paint job showed off to perfection, or the simple beauty of the grain on the wooden floor. He was never likely to see it, and even less likely to remember that he liked such things. So she turned to her second thought: that this was the kind of place she could bring Ben back to without being embarrassed.

Her fingers curled around her mobile phone. Speed dial one.

'Anna?' Chrissie picked up immediately. 'I'm so glad you called. I'm sorry – we both are. Can't you come back? It's no fun without you here, Annie. Come on, we can get drunk and dance the hora. Please? Where are you?'

'I love what you've done with the place,' said Anna.

'You're home already?' wailed Chrissie. 'I was supposed to be there. I wanted to see the look on your face. And now you hate me!'

'Chrissie, how much have you had to drink?'

Her friend sniffed. 'A bit.'

'I don't hate you. I think this is the nicest thing anyone's ever done for me.' She walked across to the window and watched the busy street below. It was the middle of Saturday evening in this most dynamic of cities and there were many people to see. She was drawn to the people walking along in pairs, two by two, watching the tops of heads turned to one another in conversation. Being with Chrissie was the closest thing she'd ever had to being half of something.

The smell of fresh paint and flowers whispered to her, telling her to forget the choking feeling she'd had when she'd caught them kissing. What was one kiss? With her free hand she shifted the photographs around so that the one of her dad she liked the most wasn't hidden behind the others.

'You don't hate me?' said Chrissie.

'No,' she said, noticing for the first time the snapshot of them both that Chrissie had clipped to the edge of the vanity mirror. 'Of course I don't. I love you.'

'Stop. You're going to make me cry. I'll never go near him again, I swear.'

'It's okay,' said Anna. 'You could be very happy together.' She swallowed down the sour taste that came into her mouth and convinced herself that she meant it.

'I'll call you later.'

'I'm going to bed. I'll call tomorrow, okay?'

'I love you too.'

She didn't call the next day, or the day after that. The next few days drifted into a week or two. She wasn't avoiding Chrissie. At least not on purpose. She was just busy, that's all. Sure, maybe she thought about them now and again, wondered if they were a couple now or what, but that was only because they were once her friends. It had nothing to do with jealousy.

The truth was that Chrissie had left a couple of messages Anna had failed to return. She meant to, and she would, but right now she had so much work to do.

She focused on the notes she was reading on the structure of European government, blocking out nagging thoughts of what other women her age were doing on a Friday night like this. Women like Chrissie. Dining, drinking, dating, dancing. Enjoying all the things that you were supposed to do when you were young. Enjoying men. Men like Ben.

Ben hadn't been in touch. Too busy playing with his new girlfriend perhaps? Maybe the pair of them did belong together. Maybe that was why she liked them both so much. And why, once, they had both liked her.

She read the same page of notes for the third time. In just a few months she would take her exams and then graduate from City. She needed to be one of the names people mentioned when they talked about the cream, the pick of her year. She wanted options. And that meant working hard.

And if she did call Chrissie back, then what would she say?

She took a break and checked online for job openings, as had become her habit. There were several leads that looked promising, but as ever she was daunted by the thought of the number of applicants each opening would attract. If only it had been her dream to go into a less competitive field. Law, say, or accountancy. But this was what she wanted, what she had always wanted, and she wasn't about to let go of an aspiration just because it might be hard to achieve.

Her mobile rang and she didn't recognize the number but she answered it anyway, distracted by the thought of what shape her future might take.

'You've been avoiding me, bitch.'

'I've been busy,' said Anna. 'Sorry. I kept meaning to call you back.'

'Yeah, yeah,' said Chrissie, laughing. 'Stuff to do. I've heard it all before. Whatevs.' She launched into a detailed description of the last couple of weeks, which seemed to consist largely of stalking the minor aristocracy in Whisky Mist and various other exclusive nightclubs, the very thought of which made Anna want to count the change in her pockets. She didn't mention Ben.

'What are you doing next weekend?' asked Chrissie, when she had finished giggling at her own wit.

'I . . . um . . . nothing, I suppose.' Anna had never been good at lying on the spot. She thought she might have to get better if she wanted to make it as a journalist. 'Apart from Saturday, obviously; you know I see my dad on Saturday.'

'Don't worry about that,' said Chrissie. 'I spoke to your mum.'

'You did what?'

'She's fine with it, so you can miss a day.'

'Chrissie!'

'What?'

Of course her mum would say she didn't mind Anna skipping a Saturday. Her mum was still proud enough to feel that she should be able to carry the load entirely on her own. 'I just wish you hadn't spoken to my mum, that's all.'

'Honestly, I'm telling you, she was fine,' said Chrissie. 'It's my birthday on Sunday and my dad is throwing me a small but fabulous party. Intimate, you know? I want you to come.'

'Sunday? That's not a problem.'

'It's dinner at his apartment.'

'Sounds . . . great.' And it really did. Over the years she had learnt much about the media mogul, from his press but also from his daughter. Little titbits of information about one of the world's most powerful men that she stowed away as carefully as jewels. The fact that he came from nothing, the frustrations of his early career, his sadness at having only one chid, his expensive divorce, his triumphs and insecurities. Chrissie had been loose-lipped and fascinating. The prospect of meeting him was dazzling.

'In Tokyo.'

'Tokyo, *Japan*?'

'Hence the need to make a weekend out of it, you see? And don't worry about the cost. He'll take care of it.'

Take care of it. Like a weekend in Japan was no more than a bar bill at the end of the night.

She'll hurt you again, whispered the little voice inside that couldn't forget the past.

'So you'll come?' said Chrissie eagerly.

'Of course I will,' said Anna. 'I'd love to.' Meeting Kendall Morton, a free trip to Tokyo, who could say no to an offer like that? 'Who else is coming?'

'It's just me and you, a couple of friends in Tokyo and some people that my dad knows.'

No Ben. What did that mean? That Chrissie had been telling the truth and they had just been messing around at the wedding, nothing had come of it? Or were they a couple but not at the meeting-the-parents stage? Of course, she could just ask. But she didn't.

'I don't know what to say,' said Anna. 'Thank you.'

'Heathrow,' said Chrissie. 'One week from tomorrow. I'll send a car.'

'I can get the tube.'

'I'll send a car.'

Anna had never flown business class before. She tried not to get too excited by the designer travel kit that was placed on her amply proportioned seat, but when the air stewardess offered her a glass of champagne before take-off, which came presented on a silver tray with a single fuchsia orchid, she couldn't suppress a callow little giggle.

'What is it?' said Chrissie.

'I was just thinking that your dad must be pretty generous. The most I ever got for my birthday was a new bike when I was twelve.'

'When I was twelve I got a pony,' said Chrissie.

'You see? A pony! That's every girl's dream.'

'Is it?' said Chrissie. 'It was never mine.'

The truth was that it had never been Anna's either, but only because she was brought up not to have unrealistic expectations. Expectations of any kind were generally frowned upon in her family. They led to disappointment, her dad said. She wondered if her dad had expected to have a brain that functioned into his old age, and if he had lost the capacity to be disappointed somewhere along the way when it turned out that he did not.

'You never told me you had a pony,' said Anna.

'I didn't have him very long.'

'What happened?'

'Shut up and I'll tell you.'

Anna pulled a face, which Chrissie mimicked sarcastically.

'Anyway,' Chrissie continued, sipping her champagne as they taxied along the runway. 'I got this pony, Imperial Idol – that was his name. So grand. We stabled him in Dulwich and I went to visit him every day, because that's what my father expected me to do. I learnt to ride, also expected, and eventually I signed up for my first pony club gymkhana. I knew we'd be up against a whole load of girls who had been riding before they could walk, daughters of my parents' friends mostly, the people who probably gave Dad the idea that I was missing out on something by not having a pony of my own. I knew we wouldn't win, we'd come last, and I begged him not to come and watch. I thought he'd be embarrassed that I was so crap. '

The plane's engines started to roar and Anna braced herself for take-off. It was hard to imagine Chrissie being crap at anything much, least of all doing so in a public competition.

'Did you fall off?' asked Anna.

'I never got the chance,' said Chrissie. 'The horsebox was involved in a terrible crash on the way to the gymkhana, Impy broke both his back legs, a vet came to the scene of the accident and he shot him right there, on the side of the road.'

'Chrissie!' said Anna, horrified. 'That's terrible.'

Chrissie shrugged. 'At least I didn't publicly embarrass my father. I was relieved. God, that's awful, isn't it?'

'Yes,' said Anna, nodding vehemently. 'I'm sure you weren't.'

'I was, I promise you. But I did miss Impy. He had the

softest little patch between his eyes and after every riding lesson he looked at me while I rubbed him down like he knew I'd tried my best. I liked that.'

'And you never had another horse?'

'I begged Dad not to replace him. I said it was too painful, but really I just used it as an excuse. Instead Dad set up a financial holding company in his name that contributed to a bunch of horsey concerns. Imperial Idol. It's still going, as far as I know. Isn't that the stupidest thing you ever heard?' Chrissie's eyes misted, but she turned to the window as the plane climbed and when she turned back her eyes had regained their usual mischievous clarity.

The plane rose into the sky, bursting through the rainclouds into a warm sunset sky and Anna felt sad for a horse she had never known, but more sad for a twelve-year-old girl who couldn't admit to being vulnerable.

'I'm going to sleep, do you mind?' said Chrissie, pulling on an eye mask and obviously not caring about the answer. Anna, who was looking forward to a night of free movies, drinks and food, didn't mind in the least.

She hardly slept and by the time they were pushing through downtown Tokyo in the back of an orange taxicab she really wished that she had. She was about to meet one of the most important men in global media and she looked like death. Her addled brain was being bombarded by a dozen new sensations all at once. There was too much to take in. The noises and smells of downtown drifted in through the open window and she lifted her head to draw them deeper. Nobody on the street looked like she did. The famous Tokyo neon glittered after recent rain, lit up even though it was not yet dark, just waiting for the chance to shine. The traffic heaved into every available space, crawling slowly forward, mopeds and bicycles weaving their way through the crush, those riding the former all wearing helmets, those riding the latter almost all wearing face masks as if they were going into surgery. 'Is the pollution really that bad?' she asked.

'It's not the pollution,' said Chrissie. 'It's the cedar pollen.'

'Hayfever?'

'The Japanese don't like to sneeze.'

She couldn't work out if this was supposed to be a joke and before she had a chance to dwell on it her attention was captured by three girls standing by a metro station, uniformly dressed like surreal cartoon versions of Lolita, complete with heart-shaped sunglasses and schoolgirl kilts. They were surrounded by half a dozen tourists taking their photographs, like a cruise-ship version of the paparazzi. The taxi stopped for a red light and an enormous wave of pedestrians flooded onto the street, seemingly in every direction, so dense that she could no longer hope to see the Lolitas on the other side of the road. After just a few seconds the wave receded, the light changed to green and the traffic moved once more. She looked behind her, watching the crowds amass on the pavements again and waiting for the next chance to cross, but the taxi turned a corner and the spectacle was lost from view. She saw a man, or perhaps it could have been a woman, dressed in orange robes with a conical straw hat, shuffling along the street looking like something from a bygone era, being overtaken on both sides by people who moved three times faster, at a pace appropriate for the modern age in which they belonged. And everywhere the buildings rose too high to see the sky beyond.

'Can you believe my father didn't send a car?' said Chrissie.

'Does he normally?'

'He'll have the doorman pay the driver, but he likes to force me to be independent.'

They stopped in front of a building with the most enormous front door that Anna had ever seen and Chrissie jumped out of the car, leaving the driver to get her bags and take money from the doorman just as she had said he would.

Chrissie said a few words to him in Japanese and Anna was impressed.

'I didn't know you spoke the language.'

'You have to,' she said. 'Otherwise you get ripped off. Come on, we haven't got long before dinner.'

They stepped inside the cool marble lobby and immediately the big city energy was replaced by an austere hush and the hum of air conditioning, the smell of the street supplanted by a light fragrance of lemons and something synthetic she couldn't quite place. The lift was already waiting for them.

'Hang on a minute,' said Anna. 'It's Sunday already?'

Chrissie laughed. 'You really are new at this, aren't you?'

The young Japanese woman who greeted them was dressed in pale blue, and was so delicate and light that she made Anna feel awkward for taking up space in the airy entrance hall of the penthouse apartment.

'This is Fuji,' said Chrissie, 'Dad's PA.'

Fuji bowed, which seemed ludicrous, and then she enquired politely after their flight and general well-being before wishing Chrissie a happy birthday. 'There are gifts for you waiting in your sitting room. Your father will be back shortly before dinner and suggested that you meet for drinks on the balcony before his guests arrive. I apologize, I meant your guests.'

'Don't worry about it, Fuji. I know this party is just a chance for him to show me off. What did you get me this year?'

'Miss?' Fuji's cheeks coloured faintly.

'Come on, it's clothes, right? He got you to buy me an outfit to wear tonight to stop me wearing something he didn't like?'

'It's clothes,' admitted Fuji. 'There are outfits for both of you, except . . . Excuse me, Miss Page, but I think I have made the most dreadful mistake.'

'You didn't know she was fat?' said Chrissie.

'Hey!'

'What? By Japanese standards you're enormous. They don't have tits here.'

Fuji was blushing furiously now. 'I will make some calls,' she said, backing away from them and leaving Anna feeling like she had the largest breasts in Tokyo.

'She'll find you something,' said Chrissie. 'She's incredibly good at fixing things.'

'Do you really think I'm fat? I mean, if you were to describe me is that the word you'd use?'

'Not if it upsets you.'

It didn't, not exactly, but she liked to think of herself as voluptuous or curvy, not *fat*. It was not a nice word.

'Why are you constantly trying to improve me?'

'What?'

'My flat, my clothes, my make-up. I mean, I appreciate it all. But what's next?'

'Don't be so sensitive,' said Chrissie. 'There's no such thing as perfect.'

Chrissie's bedroom was enormous. Four times bigger than Anna's flat, with a spacious sitting room furnished with two grey suede sofas, a coffee table and a widescreen television. A small guest annexe with its own en-suite led off the sitting room. 'No view unfortunately,' said Chrissie. 'Although that does make it somewhat easier to forget where you are.'

There were two cans of Diet Coke on the coffee table, misty with condensation, two glasses and a small bucket of ice. On one of the sofas were two huge white boxes tied with white Prada ribbon. Chrissie popped the top on her Coke and drank it straight from the can. She opened one of the boxes and pulled out a jewel-bright cocktail dress, jade green with a tulip skirt and a pleated neckline. In the other box was a similar dress in purple. 'Not bad,' she said. 'A shame you can't fit into it; the green would have looked sensational on you.'

'I did bring clothes with me, you know,' said Anna.

'Let me guess, the Givenchy? I should burn that thing. I swear to God, if you wear it one more time . . .' She checked her watch. 'Let's take showers and do hair and make-up. Fuji should be back by then. We can't keep Daddy waiting.'

Anna raised an eyebrow. 'Daddy?'

'Dad,' said Chrissie. 'Kendall. Sir. Whatever.'

Sure enough, by the time both girls were washed, brushed and beautified there was a new box nestling on the couch, this one without designer ribbon and decidedly off-white. Anna peeked inside and saw a glint of gold on black between layers of tissue paper. She pulled out a beautiful wrap dress of heavy silk, delicately patterned with gold dandelion clocks on a black background. The material fell through her fingers like liquid and she rushed to the guest annexe put it on, to feel that incredible softness against her skin. It draped over her curves as if it had been made for her, the gold picking out the flecks in her eyes, the black making her red hair glow. The cut of the dress was vaguely suggestive of the traditional Japanese kimono, but not absurdly so. The corners of her mouth lifted as she looked at herself in the mirror. Fat or not, it didn't matter. She liked the way she looked.

Chrissie knocked lightly at the door and came into the room wearing her own dress (she had gone for the purple) and when the two girls stood side by side the contrast between them was marked. 'Great,' said Chrissie, spritzing them both with the same cloud of Chanel. 'Now you look all sophisticated and I look like I'm going out to a nightclub or something.'

'You look gorgeous,' said Anna, sneaking a glance in the mirror in case what Chrissie said was true. But she saw two girls, one quite dazzling and one quite dull. No amount of Japanese silk would ever change that.

'How do you do it?' said Chrissie. 'You're not even from money. I wish I had your style.'

Anna shrugged. Style was one thing – maybe she knew what suited her – but she'd gladly trade it all for half of what Chrissie had. Especially the half that included Ben.

'You'll have to stand next to me all night so at least I look thin,' said Chrissie. 'You ready? Let's go.' She linked her arm through her friend's and together they made their way upstairs.

Was this actually her life? Dressed in silk in a Tokyo penthouse about to meet a man whose influence was unmatched in his field. She had a brief out-of-body experience picturing herself sitting on the sofa at home chatting to her mum over Saturday night television instead of strutting up the stairs with her new best friend, jacked up on excitement and the scent of Chanel.

Chrissie took her hand. 'Don't be nervous,' she said.

'I'm not.'

'Really? Why not? Most people are.'

'He's my best friend's father, that's all.'

'You're so sweet.'

'Could you try to sound a little more condescending?' said Anna.

'Sorry. But this is a huge opportunity for you. My father is a giant in media, a legend. That doesn't make you nervous?'

'It's starting to sound like you're the one who's nervous,' said Anna.

She wanted to find Fuji and thank her for the dress but Chrissie insisted that they didn't have the time. They crossed the main entrance hall and climbed another short flight of stairs before Chrissie, almost running at this point, paused outside beautifully carved cherry-wood doors. 'Take a deep breath,' she said, then she pushed open the doors into the Tokyo night.

Kendall Morton didn't even look up from the view until Chrissie called out to him. He must have heard the clack of the girls' heels on the lacquered tiles but he didn't turn towards them until they were just a few short feet away. Anna was a little disappointed at how ordinary he looked. It wasn't as if she expected him to have a golden aura, or actual dollar signs flashing in his eyes, but she had expected a little something extra. Mr Morton just looked like an average fifty-something bloke, the sort of man who could have been a friend of her dad's back when her dad still had friends.

'This is my friend Anna,' said Chrissie. 'Remember I told you about her?' She gripped her father's arm possessively, gazing up at him with the sort of eager expression that Anna had never seen before.

He held out his hand and she shook it firmly. She prayed silently that some words would come when she opened her mouth. 'Thank you so much for inviting me, Mr Morton. Really, it's very kind of you.'

He shrugged. 'Please call me Kendall. When you say Mr Morton it makes me think I'm still in the office. Chrissie tells me you're her best friend? You're at LSE too, is that right?'

His gaze was direct and penetrating. She had the sense that she was being judged. 'I was there as an undergraduate,' she said. 'I'm doing my master's at City right now, in international journalism.'

'Impressive. Is John Mackintosh still on the teaching staff there?'

'Yes, sir, I have a lecture with him once a month. Do you know him?'

'He has appropriated a desk at the *Herald* though he refuses to go on payroll, which is decent of him as I can't stand him,' said Kendall. 'The man still thinks London is at the centre of world affairs. A hundred years ago, maybe.

The man needs to get a global view and yet he thinks foreign media ownership should be more heavily regulated.'

'With respect, Mr Morton – Kendall – John Mackintosh supports local grassroots journalism, not a London bias. His work as a foreign correspondent is second to none. If I were from Sutton Hoo then he would believe that should be the cornerstone of my world view.'

The corner of his mouth twitched and she felt the hairs on the back of her neck stand in fear. Okay, now she was nervous. 'And the media ownership regulations?' he said. 'I suppose you think Mackintosh is right about that too?'

'Of course not, sir. I think foreign media ownership is a fine idea.'

'And you're not just saying that because you're standing on my terrace, looking at my view, drinking my champagne?'

She wondered if she would be able to wipe her sweating palms on this dress without leaving a stain. 'I think the skyline belongs to everyone, doesn't it?' she said. 'And I'm not drinking anything yet.' She lifted her empty hand and looked at it as if to prove her point.

It was supposed to be a joke.

Kendall paused and Anna held her breath, wishing that she might have been able to hold her tongue in the same way, then he laughed and called out for champagne. 'Quite the little dynamo, your new friend,' he said.

Chrissie was staring at them with an expression of something between horror and admiration. 'That's right,' she echoed. 'A dynamo.'

Anna grinned. She had one shot at getting to know Kendall Morton and this was it. As soon as she saw him, arguably the most influential man in news media today, she had instinctively known that the gap between them was not as vast as she had assumed it would be. Something deep inside her had recognized that fact and taken the opportunity to shine, carrying her corporeal bag of nerves through the entire encounter.

Soon he was telling her all about the *kisha kurabu* system that crippled Japanese investigative journalism and kept the press in the pockets of the establishment. And as he asked her more about her studies and steered the conversation around to her plans after graduation she was delighted that she seemed to be making a brilliant first impression.

Neither of them noticed the deepening crevice in Chrissie's forehead that came from the pressure of keeping the forced smile on her face as her father and her best friend continued to ignore her. Nor did either of them notice that the billionaire had so far failed to wish his daughter a happy birthday.

A short while later the guests arrived. There were twelve in all and only five of them were under fifty: three men who worked for Morton – two Americans and one Japanese man who kept exchanging loaded looks with Chrissie, the sort of looks that nobody would notice except a best friend – and two women (the only women), both with Japanese features but American accents.

Each of the guests bowed when they were introduced, which she reciprocated feeling graceless, and offered her their business cards, which she held in her hand, unsure of what to do with them but sensing it would be rude to put them down. There was an awkward moment while they waited for her business cards, cards that she did not have. Everyone was very quiet and well-behaved. Though the more distinguished guests were clearly very important men she couldn't help but get the feeling that this party might be rather dull. Especially when the conversation was in Japanese, which happened with a regularity she found a little rude.

Eventually the smile on her face became forced and she could feel a dull ache in her jaw from keeping it in place.

She dragged Chrissie aside as soon as she could. 'What's the deal with you and that Rev guy?' she said, nodding towards the handsome man giving the loaded looks.

Chrissie giggled. 'Fuck buddies,' she said. 'Cute, don't you think? Don't tell my dad.'

She was hardly likely to do that, was she? She couldn't even imagine how that conversation would go. So far every conversation she had been able to participate in was to do with work. Thank God she was studying journalism; without that knowledge she would have found it almost impossible to contribute anything at all. Between the shop talk and the Japanese Chrissie must be bored out of her mind. Anna felt like she learnt far more about the world media markets during one round of pre-dinner drinks on that terrace than she had in a whole term of lectures back in London. Her mind whirled with possible futures beyond the shape of her modest dreams. The zenith of her ambition had always been a byline in a national news-paper, a decent living, enough to support her mum and dad during the trying times which surely lay ahead. But what of television, the internet, the global marketplace? What about the world? Impressive though Kendall's guests were, it wasn't such an enormous leap to imagine that one day she might stand in company like this and hold her own.

For this evening's celebration Chrissie's father had commissioned a new room to be built on the west side of his apartment. It had meant sacrificing the terrace leading off the library, but as the apartment had five other terraces and the library was rarely used it was a sacrifice he was willing to make. Anna couldn't help wondering whether, as birthday presents go, an extension on a building Chrissie no longer lived in was about as welcome as a horse she was too scared to ride.

The room was the very epitome of Zen chic. The four elements were starkly represented in the vast expanse of granite flooring, the harmonious wind chimes, the line of delicate tea lights set into a channel along one side of the room and, most impressively, the waterfall that cascaded down one wall as if they were in the lobby of some luxurious hotel and not a dining room at all.

'Do you like it?' asked Chrissie. 'The earth, wind, fire, stone thing? That was my idea. It's traditional in a Japanese banqueting room. And, you know, Feng shui and all that crap.'

'It's a beautiful room, Chrissie, really gorgeous.' Privately she thought that it was overdone, particularly the little fake fish at the bottom of the waterfall, which she strongly suspected would be made out of real gold.

Chrissie waved her hand as if it was nothing special.

Finally Kendall acknowledged his daughter's milestone. 'Happy birthday, princess,' he said. 'May all your dreams come true.' Chrissie smiled happily, then he added the barb: 'Once you figure out what your dreams are!'

His guests laughed politely but Anna noticed the smile plummet out of Chrissie's eyes.

Sake was served in delicate wooden boxes that she found hard to drink from without dribbling. Nervously she glanced down at the chopsticks that were next to her place setting, balanced on a small plinth.

'Do you need a knife and fork?' asked Chrissie loudly across the table.

She smiled. 'I'm fine.'

'You're sure? It's not a problem.'

'Honestly, I'm fine.'

This wasn't the time to tell a party of strangers that once she had been so bored in her lonely little studio flat that she had taught herself to use chopsticks by repeatedly picking up a fifty-pence piece with one of the many cheap disposable sets that came free with every Chinese takeaway. She had never been as grateful for that bored loneliness as she was right now.

The meal that followed was as close an approximation of the formal *Kai-seki* as any westerner could hope to accomplish. She stopped counting courses after the tenth or eleventh and just let the delicate flavours tantalize her taste buds while the exquisite presentation lifted her soul. A single smoked oyster came nestled in a mother-of-pearl shell; a silky pouch of delicate crabmeat was balanced in the bud of a milky white orchid that scented the sweet meat with vanilla; a block of carved onyx displayed fatty tuna sashimi like ruby inlays. Between courses there was more sake, finely sliced ginger, fragrant soups in cups barely bigger than thimbles. There were slivers of quail that tasted of rose petals, a carpaccio of wagyu beef bright with burning wasabi, crisp golden noodles as fine as the hair on her head. As the sake flowed the conversation became louder and more boisterous. One of the older men excused himself from the table and almost fell into the wall on his way out. Chrissie met Anna's eye across the table and they both struggled not to laugh.

The combination of intense conversation, the sake and the rich parade of flavours was making her feel woozy. She pushed her chair back and excused herself, thinking of splashing some water on her face in the bathroom, but by the time she found one Chrissie had caught up with her and squeezed into the bathroom with her.

'Having a good time?'

'That food, Chrissie. My God.'

'I know, the kitchen totally outdid themselves. They must be on bonuses.' She dabbed her fingers under her eyes, cleaning up make-up that was already flawless.

'My father seems to like you. He never usually talks to my friends.'

'I like him too. A man in his position could be intimidating, but he's not. He's quite funny.'

'Funny?'

'You know, witty.'

'I'm so glad you're here,' said Chrissie.

'Me too.'

They grinned at each other in the mirror and Anna felt so mellow that on impulse she asked the question she had been dying to ask for the last few weeks. 'Are you and Ben sleeping with each other now?'

'Why do you ask?'

'No reason.'

'Don't be silly. I told you, we've known each other far too long for any of that sort of thing. He's like a brother or something.'

Anna resisted the urge to question the brotherly love she had seen when she had caught them both flushed and giggling by the bathrooms at the wedding. It wasn't the time to get into another row.

Chrissie flicked her hair out of her eyes and watched with satisfaction as it fell back in its perfect face-framing waves. 'Listen, this is nearly over and then we'll get going, okay?'

'Get going?'

'I want to take you clubbing in Roppongi. Rev'll probably meet us there later and maybe the girls too. But anyway, you'll love it.'

'I'd rather stay here, would that be okay?'

'You want to? Seriously?'

'Can we? Please? I might never get this kind of networking opportunity again.'

'This is my birthday, Anna, not a fucking career fair,' she snapped. Then she caught her breath sharply and smiled. 'But if that's what you really want, then of course we'll stay. Of course.'

Glancing at their reflections in the mirror rather than looking directly at each other it was easy to ignore the sudden presence of something bitter. So that was exactly what they did. They linked arms and rejoined the party, neither of them sure why she felt unsettled, but both of them willing to pay it no heed.

The final course was a bowl of faultlessly prepared rice that was so white it almost seemed to glow. After the procession of complex, exciting flavours it was the perfect ending and a quiet sense of calm fell across the table with nothing but the sound of jade chopsticks against the pewter bowls and the gentle cascade of the waterfall onto those ludicrous gold fish. The windows were thrown open to reveal a pretty winter garden and smoky dark tea was sipped as the conversation ebbed and flowed.

Within half an hour Kendall Morton was challenging Anna to uphold her beliefs in the real world. 'We're all idealists until we face a genuinely blank page,' he said.

'A blank screen is different,' she argued. 'The age of print journalism is over.'

She ignored the frowns from the older businessmen; they clearly thought that her contribution to the conversation should be limited to the occasional supportive comment. Most likely they would prefer all women to keep quiet and look decorative, not unlike the uncharacteristically subdued Chrissie this evening. Anna felt confident that Kendall liked her. The night was drawing to a close and with it her chance to make the best possible impression.

'If print journalism dies then half of my companies die with it,' he said.

'*When* print journalism dies then it will be only the visionaries who can move forward. You saw this coming decades ago, why else would you have diversified into television and the internet so aggressively? And into Asia, for that matter? The Morton Group is forward-thinking, always has been. Surely even an idealist could find a voice there?'

'Or learn to shut the hell up,' he said, smiling and pausing to think a moment before making her the offer of a lifetime. 'You give me a call when you graduate,' he said. 'See if we can't knock that chip off your shoulder with a stint in one of my newsrooms.'

Anna's eyes widened and she opened and closed her mouth a couple of times before she found her voice. 'Thank you, I'll do that. Thank you so much.' She glanced across at Chrissie. Her friend was smiling broadly.

'We could *both* work for you,' said Chrissie brightly. 'Wouldn't that be fun?'

'I don't think so. I'd hazard a guess that Anna isn't in this for the fun, princess. And believe me, if she was she'd be out before her first story made it off the page. Am I right, Anna?'

'There's nothing fun about the news,' she said. 'And anyone who says differently should work in the lifestyle section.'

A few people laughed.

'My daughter *is* a lifestyle section. And a rather expensive one at that.'

And then everyone was laughing.

Everyone except Chrissie.

Ten

Chrissie was in a black mood for the whole flight back to London. She had a headache that not even an upgrade to first could shift. She didn't sleep, trying instead to swallow down the tight little gobstopper of jealousy that was threatening to choke her.

She only had herself to blame. It had seemed like an inspired idea. The superficial stuff she'd been doing for Anna – the apartment, the clothes, the make-up – these weren't making her feel good enough about herself. To feel the kind of moral absolution she craved clearly she would have to do something more meaningful, something with *depth*.

And so she had brought her friend to her father, and to all the benefits that knowing him could bring. A generous and heartfelt offering.

Chrissie didn't like to share.

Technically it was a triumph. Kendall and Anna had bonded and he had practically given her a job, but Chrissie had found herself fading into the background, a place with which she was neither comfortable nor well-acquainted. Was this why she had never had a real friend before? Were those watered-down versions of herself merely accoutrements to ensure that she shone by direct comparison? And wasn't that kind of pathetic?

She had drunk far too much in the end in the hope that she might forget some of what turned out to be an excruciating evening. The contrast between them was not a flattering one. Anna highlighted all her shortcomings. She had brains, wit and a beauty that wasn't about being the skinniest or having the most expensive shoes. Anna had class. More class than the billionaire's daughter. How was that even possible?

The evening had ended shortly after the entire table had laughed long and hard at Anna's silly joke. A joke made at her expense. Did making things better for Anna have to include being the butt of her smart mouth? And was it really so apparent that Chrissie had looks and money where her brain should be? So apparent that to suggest otherwise was comedy?

'I don't know how to thank you,' said Anna, right before she fell asleep in her fully-reclined seat. And that was all. Chrissie waited for some of the weight to lift from her shoulders but it did not. Had she still not done enough? The ever-present guilt was gnawing at her still. How could she possibly be expected to move on and let the debt of shame diminish when her perfect little friend was there as a constant reminder? She watched Anna as she slept, trying to figure out if her raging emotion was love or hate. And if it was Anna or her father who had upset her the most.

If only she had walked away a few seconds earlier that day in the Shaw Library. Life had still been simple then, hadn't it? Being nice to Anna was supposed to make her feel better. Instead it was prying into the cracks of her own life and forcing them wide open.

Back in London it got worse.

'Your father's emailed me,' said Anna as they studied

side by side on the laptops in the main library. 'He says he wants to reiterate his offer.'

Chrissie had a split second of pure joy when she thought that reiterate might mean retract but quickly realized she had been mistaken. She closed down the shopping website she had been idly browsing while pretending to study.

'He emailed you himself? You mean Fuji did?' She peered over Anna's shoulder to look at the email address. But it wasn't Fuji, it was him.

Anna was excited. 'He says I should contact the *Herald*, here in London, and visit them. He's given me a name and everything. One of the UK editors, I think.'

Since when did her father care about anything but money?

'I thought you wanted to cut your teeth on a regional newspaper?' said Chrissie.

'I thought I'd *have to*!' said Anna, laughing. 'The *Herald* doesn't have an open door. You know how many City graduates they've employed over the last three years? One. And he was like some kind of freak genius, an economist type, you know?'

'How do you know all this?'

'I looked it up,' said Anna, as if the answer was obvious.

'When?'

'What do you mean, when?'

'Before we went to Tokyo or after?' For reasons she couldn't explain it seemed important to know if Anna's interest in her father's company had started before or after they met.

'Before. It's a short year. If you want the best graduate opportunities you have to know your stuff.'

Chrissie tried to get her head around the idea of looking for a job a year before you actually needed one. Ambition, she realized, was more than just an attitude.

She tried to see herself as her father must see her. It wasn't pretty.

If she wanted to gain her father's respect then she was going to have to make some changes.

If any of Chrissie's tutors were aware of her renewed enthusiasm for her course then none of them mentioned it. Even when she started getting assignments back with higher marks and more positive comments her new-found dedication was not acknowledged. But they must have noticed, right? She looked at the '71%' scrawled in red across the bottom of her latest essay and wanted to frame it.

On a whim she called her father in Tokyo.

'He's in conference,' said Fuji. 'Is it something I can help with at all?'

'Just tell him –' Chrissie looked down at the essay clutched in her hand – 'tell him I called to say hello.'

'Is everything okay?'

'It's fine,' she said, bizarrely touched. Maybe she was just tired.

She refused invitations from Anna and from Ben, sometimes from both of them together. She spent at least three hours a day reading the background texts on every subject (most of those three hours in the back of a black cab, admittedly) and made actual notes in lectures now instead of doodles, notes that she reviewed every morning in the Shaw Library before her classes. *Before* her classes! She was having to go to bed an hour earlier each night just to stay alert throughout the day. Was it like this for everyone? Or just for her because she wasn't used to it? Or, shamefully, because she really wasn't that clever?

She no longer hid *Elle* behind the covers of something more intellectual. Gradually, as a depth of knowledge started to fill the void where half-baked information had struggled to be retained, she started to respect what she was doing.

'Have you got a crush on one of your tutors or something?' said Anna, when Chrissie was there in the library early on a Saturday morning. 'You are aware that it's the weekend?'

Chrissie merely smiled and turned back to the chapter she was reading on human rights and their relationship with crime and politics, if only because it was more interesting in that moment than a conversation about a crush she didn't have, even on a weekend.

And when she most felt like switching off, like giving up and admitting defeat, she would think of her father and how much she wanted him to talk to her like he talked to Anna. Kendall's respect was something that Chrissie had been craving all her life. Anna had earned his respect in the space of one evening.

Exam season loomed ever closer on the horizon. Revision was the least fun she had ever had. There weren't enough hours in the day to make her clever and so, exhausted, she returned to the master bathroom of the Dulwich house and shook half a bottle of pills into a small white envelope, swapping them later that evening with the same dealer for some naughty salt that she could rub on her gums at that crunch point when her body demanded sleep but her brain still needed to keep on going. And after a while, when she felt she couldn't pilfer any more prescription drugs without fear of discovery, she paid him in cash.

The face that greeted Chrissie in the mirror each morning had lost its looks. Surely it would only be temporary.

Higher education was intense.

Ben insisted that she came to his birthday party at the family estate in Wiltshire over the weekend. It wouldn't be the same without her. 'Anna's up for it,' he said. 'And listen, I said I wouldn't say anything, but she's worried about you.'

She started making excuses before he had finished speaking. It was impossible. Not now, no way. Stuff to do. Have a great birthday and everything, sorry, but no. And she hoped that would be enough. There was less than a month until her first exam. She could ill afford to waste a moment on such frivolous pursuits as partying, never mind a birthday celebration that would surely turn into an entire weekend. Wistfully she remembered how much she liked a good bash. 'I can't,' she said.

'It's not even a real course,' said Ben. 'It's just a diploma, right?'

'Is that what Anna said?'

'Don't snap at me, Chrissie, I've known you too long. God, what's wrong with you? She's right, you know, a break would do you good.'

'You're just saying that because you want me to come to your party.'

'If you walk into your exams wound up as tightly as you are now you'll fuck them up before you even start. You need to chill out. Honestly, we're thinking of you. That's what friends do.'

She forced down the lump in her throat with a deep breath and let a few tears slide silently down her pale cheeks.

'Chrissie? Are you there?'

'I'm here,' she said.

'And you'll come?'

'I'll come.'

The Latimer estate was miles away from anywhere. Had she known quite how many miles and how slowly Anna drove Chrissie might have made other arrangements. Anna was frustratingly cautious, never going anywhere near the speed limit let alone over it. Maybe it was because she'd borrowed the shitty red Volvo from her parents. 'Mum barely uses the car these days,' she told Chrissie. 'And the last time Dad was behind the wheel he stopped at a red light and didn't get going again until someone called the police.'

Chrissie squirmed in her seat, glad of the lift down to Wiltshire, but uncomfortable as ever with talk of Anna's father. They had left at dawn and been driving for over three hours. She was tired and hungry but plans to stop somewhere and get breakfast had been thwarted by a dearth of options; there hadn't even been a single petrol station since they left the M3. They could have veered from their pre-ordained route in search of some sustenance but Anna was sticking resolutely to the directions she had downloaded and the mere suggestion of a detour had been shot down with a dirty look.

'The police were nice enough when they brought him home,' said Anna, checking her rear-view mirror (though they hadn't seen another car for miles) before turning off the narrow country lane into another that was, preposterously, narrower still. 'They said that he thought he was at home, didn't seem to realize he was in the car at all, was quite surprised when they pointed out the line of traffic behind him. Mum put the car keys out of his reach on a shelf in the hallway and hasn't let him drive since. But this still feels like Dad's car to me, you know?' She smoothed her hands affectionately across the steering wheel.

'My father has more cars than I can count. I can't remember the last time he ever drove one of them himself.'

'Then it's a shame he couldn't let you borrow one of them, isn't it?'

Chrissie couldn't detect any sarcasm but she didn't count it out. Anna could be so bloody dry.

The girls were silent for a while until Chrissie pointed gratefully at a small brown sign by the side of the road that read 'The Clockhouse'. 'Look,' she said. 'Isn't that it?'

'Ben's house has its own road sign?' said Anna, signalling and turning down the unpaved road without even looking.

'His father's house,' said Chrissie, shrugging. 'I wonder who'll inherit it now he has the new wifey and everything?'

But as they rounded the final corner and the shadow of the Clockhouse loomed over them, even Chrissie was forced to admit that from this distance the house was impressive. It was a substantial Jacobean house, with various add-ons and outbuildings that gave it the appearance of a small village rather than a private home. As they drew closer they could see that most of the outbuildings were in a state of disrepair. The estate was dominated by a ludicrous clock tower with a gigantic dial and a minute hand so heavy that she could have sworn she heard it turn onto the hour even though it was several dozen feet above them.

'The last time I was here was for Ben's sixteenth birthday,' she said. 'There was a rumour that Ben had sex with Jemima Groves under the buffet table.'

'Jemima?' said Anna. 'My Jemima?'

'What do you mean, yours?'

'I was friends with Jemima Groves.'

'Really? I don't remember that. She turned into a bit of a slut by Year 11.'

'Clearly,' said Anna. 'If she was having sex with Ben under the vol-au-vents.'

'One: I very much doubt there was any truth to that particular rumour, and two: the party was catered exquisitely and I very much doubt there were any vol-au-vents.'

They drove past a gatehouse the size of an average family home, and onto a circular driveway that would once have been very grand but was badly in need of resurfacing, the sparse patches of gravel having packed down into the mud beneath like miniature rockeries for the weeds that grew there. There was a crumbling fountain in the centre that was dry and covered with moss. The clock chimed two (though it was actually eleven) and as Anna pulled the car to a shuddering halt, Ben came shuffling down the front steps, barefoot and wearing a Barbour over what looked suspiciously like a pair of flannel pyjamas.

'Bloody hell,' he said. 'You're early.'

For the first time in weeks Chrissie felt herself relax. Ben had that effect on people.

He got dressed while Anna fixed tea and toast for all of them, making herself at home straight away. Chrissie hovered by the wheezing Aga that was barely warm, afraid that if she sat down in one of those massive armchairs she might never make it out again. She was here to party, not to nap, and luckily she had come prepared with a little something in her back pocket but it was probably too early for that.

Chrissie existed in a state of near exhaustion most of the time these days. Her head actually ached with the effort of learning. If this was what hard work felt like then Anna fully deserved whatever spoils the world was willing to bestow upon her. For as long as she had known her Anna had been diligent about education. She used to think it was boring, now she thought it was bordering on masochistic.

'Can I ask you a question?' she said, watching her friend wander around the kitchen looking for a place to put a soggy tea bag, because of course Anna would never just put it on the side of the sink like normal people.

'What?' she said, flipping open the top of the swing bin she found under the sink.

'You're revising, right? For your exams?'

'Sure. When I can.'

'How many hours, would you say?'

'Hard to be specific, but a couple of hours a day maybe, if I have a free period. I read stuff on the bus on the way to work or to my parents' place. Why?'

'And do you, I don't know, enjoy it?'

Anna laughed. 'Enjoy it? Don't be stupid. Who enjoys revision? That's like saying do you enjoy doing your tax return or buying a television licence.'

Chrissie had never done either of these things but didn't like to say. If they were anything like the brain-numbing tedium of committing facts she didn't care about to memory and unravelling theories that sounded as doubtful as they were dull then she was in no hurry to try. 'But you always seem so keen on the whole learning thing,' she said.

'I am,' said Anna. 'But that doesn't mean I wouldn't rather be reading a book or taking a walk in the park, or having a bubble bath, or drinking pink champagne with my best friend, but none of those things will get me where I want to be. They are fleeting pleasures, and I get to do all of them, just not all the time.'

Interesting. So it was about ambition, then? Maybe her lack of ambition was the problem. Perhaps it wasn't something you could fake. Maybe you really had to want to go somewhere with your life. Right now she felt warm and comfortable where she was and could quite happily stay here beside Ben's Aga for eternity. Especially if it meant she didn't have to make those kinds of decisions. Decisions that would shape the rest of her life tended to scare her. 'Where do you want to be, Anna?' she asked.

Anna sipped her tea and looked thoughtful. 'Is everything okay?'

'Of course it is. Why wouldn't it be?'

'If you need help . . . I know you've been working hard . . .'

How typical that Anna would be the only one who seemed to notice. Chrissie added compassion to the never-ending list of Anna's good traits. 'Me?' she said, injecting her voice with a light-hearted lilt that was a struggle to find. 'Not really. Hey, do you remember the first time we talked at school? You came to find me in the toilets because I was all upset about something, remember?'

Anna laughed. 'You owe me a cigarette.'

'What was I so upset about, I wonder?'

'Ben didn't want to be your tennis partner.'

'That's right. God, how do you remember stuff like that?'

'I couldn't believe that Ben would turn down a girl like you,' said Anna quietly.

'It was just tennis,' said Chrissie. 'Not sex.'

She was expecting Anna to laugh but instead a slightly awkward atmosphere descended and though Chrissie was glad that they were no longer talking about her pathetic attempts at academic excellence she wanted to shift the conversation back to the light-hearted banter she felt more comfortable with.

'So who else is coming to this party, anyway?' she said.

'You'll have to ask Ben. What are you wearing for dinner?'

'Marc Jacobs, probably.'

'As what?'

'What do you mean?' said Chrissie.

'Who are you coming as?'

'Huh?'

Ben appeared, damp from the shower and smelling like amber and old-fashioned shaving soap, his feet still bare but his legs clad in blue denim, teamed with a gnarly old brown jumper that screamed 'country'. 'It's fancy dress,' he said. 'Didn't I say?'

Chrissie said she would gladly miss out on croquet on the south lawn that afternoon and drive into town to hire a costume, but when Ben quite sensibly pointed out that the nearest place likely to offer such a service was Bournemouth, a hundred miles to the south, she allowed herself to be talked out of it. Plus, the most obvious car for her to borrow would have been Anna's – or rather Anna's dad's – and she wasn't sure she could take a three-hour round trip trying to keep a lid on the can of emotional worms that borrowing the car of a man she had wronged could entail.

So here they were, half an hour to go before dinner, and Anna was doing an admirable job of kitting her out in a passable Lara Croft outfit. A pair of khaki shorts and a black vest, hiking boots that Anna had brought, and a plastic water pistol they'd found near the tennis courts tucked into the top of her stockings. Anna left to get her own costume together, upbeat and slightly drunk from an afternoon of Pimm's and croquet, leaving Chrissie to don her Gucci aviator shades and pull her brown hair back in a long plait. The shades hid the dark circles beneath her eyes.

A quick lift and she'd be ready for take-off.

Checking that Anna wasn't coming back she dug deep into the bottom of her make-up bag and unearthed a tiny silver pillbox in the shape of a bullet. She unscrewed the lid and pulled out the minuscule spoon, which had a pinch of welcome cocaine nestling in the bowl. One sharp sniff and she instantly felt better. She'd been so patient.

She stepped out into the courtyard that separated all the guest bedrooms from the main house and enjoyed the tickle of fresh air on her naked thighs. She paused to let the crisp air further enliven her. Finally, before she joined the party she filled her water pistol at the candlelit bar that somebody had set up on the far side of the courtyard, next to an old stone swimming pool that was green with weeds and smelt dank and interesting.

She was here now and she might as well have a good time.

'Hello, sexy,' said Ben as she walked into the main party area, a massive games room with a snooker table, skittles lane and a plasma screen showing Sky Sports.

'Pow-pow,' she said, firing her pistol in his direction.

He ducked and caught some in his mouth. 'Mmm,' he said, licking his lips. 'Tequila?'

'Grappa,' she said.

'Good choice.'

He had aviator shades too, gold-rimmed, plus an Elvis wig and a lei of cheap plastic flowers, the blue jeans he'd been wearing earlier and a white T-shirt.

'Like your wig,' she said.

'Who loves ya, baby?'

'That's Kojak.'

'Oh. Then what's Elvis?'

'It's all in the hips.'

She knew she looked good. She knew that Ben would be watching her arse as she walked away.

She spotted Anna over by the snooker table heckling the players. She was Cleopatra with a black wig and bright red lipstick, an unopened bottle of champagne swinging in her hand. Her eyes were painted like vivid peacock feathers and around her neck was a gold necklace shaped like a snake; other than that she looked like she was wearing nothing but a white sheet. She looked relaxed and happy. How did she manage that without drugs? Maybe that was her second bottle of champagne. The gap between herself and Anna was widening every day. Anna seemed more like an adult now whereas Chrissie still felt exactly as she had when she was fifteen. Had Anna really grown up that much in the intervening years or was Chrissie sort of stunted? She would give anything to have the grace and composure that seemed to come so naturally to her friend. They never should have let their friendship drift. Well, not drift exactly, so much as smash onto the rocks. She walked over to join her, and Robin Hood, a monk and a drag queen. She enjoyed the way the men's eyes ran over her body and Anna seemed briefly forgotten.

'Guys, this is Chrissie, my best friend. Chrissie, um, the guys.'

Within a few minutes of flirting with these three charming friends of Ben's from his City days she was pleased that she had come. The guy dressed as a monk was very good-looking, although maybe the monk thing was giving him a certain forbidden edge. Thanks to the coke and a hearty squirt of grappa Chrissie's spirits were in the ascendant. She laughed and joked, made sassy comments and winked when one of them complimented her legs. Nothing serious, nothing meaningful, just enjoying being young and beautiful at a party in a spectacular location.

Ben's family had excellent taste. This place was stylishly organic, lived-in, each extension and addition telling the story of hundreds of years, odd angles and redundant doorways complementing the nooks and crannies that gave the place its unique character. Every bookcase overflowed, every dusty corner intrigued. Sadly it was shabby and frayed around the edges, the hideous carpets looked as if they had been here since the place was built, and there were ominous damp patches on every ceiling. Still, nothing a few grand couldn't put straight and she wondered why they hadn't bothered.

It could be so beautiful.

The party atmosphere crept under her skin and she remembered who she really was. The studious little recluse she had been for the last couple of months was *so* not a good look for her. After everyone's glasses had been well and truly charged (and she had managed to slip off for a swift pre-dinner toot) they all crossed the vast main hallway, where a music system would later kick in for dancing, and congregated in the formal dining room of the house, yet another impressive room.

The oak dining table was laid for dinner for thirty. Flowers and candlesticks were evenly spaced along the long thin table, and each setting had four glasses and four rows of cutlery too. At a safe distance behind every third seat was a high-hat cradling a bottle of pink champagne in mounds of ice that twinkled like diamonds. A big bay window at the far end of the room looked out over shadowy jade-coloured fields, where the lamb they were about to eat had previously frolicked. Dinner was over an hour late at Ben's urging, and it was getting dark already. Honestly, who wanted to eat anyway?

The place cards went largely ignored. It was a moveable feast, and by the time dessert was served Chrissie had eaten nothing, drunk loads and secured two dates for the following week. One with a lovely looking guy dressed as Death, and the other with the monk. She didn't particularly like either of them but she was sorely in need of an ego boost, and in her experience men stopped being nice to you the minute you turned them down. She could always call and cancel later.

This was what she needed, not 71 per cent of anything, just 100 per cent Chrissie: champagne and sexiness, and so much laughing, laughing, laughing that she had to remember to stop for breath. She had no idea why Anna kept looking at her across the table with a tight little worried expression that did nothing for her and would give her wrinkles if she wasn't too careful.

Anna was dreary when you got right down to it, and Chrissie most definitely was not. There weren't any mirrors in the dining room (sadly) but had she been able to see herself Chrissie wouldn't have been surprised if she actually sparkled like one of the twenty-four sizzling sparklers that studded the tower of golden caramel profiteroles pretending to be a birthday cake.

She was just emerging from the bathroom (again) when Ben snuck up behind her and placed a cheeky birthday-boy hand on her backside. 'Any spare?' he said, then rolled his eyes when she said that she didn't know what he was talking about.

'Don't come coy with me, Chrissie,' he said. 'It might work on all those boys you have in the palm of your hand out there but this is me, remember?'

They ducked back into the bathroom together and she racked up a proper line. 'This is just because it's your birthday,' she said. 'Are you having a good time?'

'It's okay,' he said. 'But I think I might be getting a bit old for this. It feels a bit like everybody's parents will be picking up them up at midnight, you know?'

'Not mine,' she said. 'I'm here all night long.'

'Is that a suggestion?'

'Calm down, you naughty boy.'

He hoovered up his share of the cocaine and pinched his nostrils to get rid of the telltale white residue. 'I didn't know you were into this,' he said.

'I'm not usually, but it's been . . . well, it's been tough lately and I felt like a little pick-me-up.'

'I'm not judging you,' he said. 'How could I when I'm here basically begging you to share?'

'I didn't know you were into it either,' she said carefully.

'I'm bored,' he said.

'Bored? But it's your birthday party!'

'I know.' Ben rubbed his hand across the five o'clock shadow on his chin then grabbed her wrist. 'Come into the garden with me. I'll open a bottle of champagne, one of the decent ones. We'll get pissed and wait for the fireworks.'

'I think I already am pissed,' she said, but laughing she followed him out through the kitchen, where the catering firm were cleaning up everyone's mess, and into the dark garden.

'Are you cold?' he asked.

She wasn't, though she knew she probably should be. The booze or the coke must have been keeping her warm because when she looked up at the night sky and saw the sort of stars you could never see in town, it was their beauty that made her shiver, not the cool night air.

He led her across the manicured lawn to a small gazebo set up by the side of the kitchen garden, shrouded with a budding clematis that had been growing there for years and years. They sat down side by side on a wooden bench inside the gazebo and he popped open the champagne and drank straight from the bottle.

'Do you remember when we used to do this back at St Anthony's?' he said.

'A bottle of cider at the bottom of the playing fields?'

'We used to think you were a total lightweight, you know.'

'Who's we?'

'All of us. The lads. You got pissed just by sniffing the bottle.'

'I was putting it on so that I could get away with being naughty,' she said.

She saw a dark shape move jerkily across the sky towards a small copse filled with pockets of inky darkness. A bat, and then another. The air around them smelt damp and rich with life, the faint scent of thyme from the nearby kitchen garden drifting out and lacing the cold air with warmth.

'Do you ever feel lost?' he said, passing the bottle to her.

'Aw,' she said. 'Is someone feeling a little bit maudlin on his birthday?'

'I'm serious.'

She barely let the champagne touch her lips before passing the bottle back to him. Getting roaring drunk was never the answer, whatever the question. 'Honestly? I'm not sure what that means any more. Doesn't everyone feel lost to some degree? Always?'

Except Anna. Anna probably never felt lost. She had probably known exactly where she was going since her first day at school. How comfortable that must feel.

'Is that what you're doing? Trying to find yourself?'

'I don't know what you're talking about,' she said. She felt the hairs at the back of her neck rise up; if she was a cat she would have arched her back and hissed.

'Come on, Chrissie. The way you've been lately, working and stuff. Every time we ask you to come out you make excuses. You always used to be the first one in the door at a party, that's if it wasn't your party, and I had to twist your arm to get you here, twist it so hard I practically heard it snap. What are you doing?'

'I'm trying to get an education,' she said.

'Why?'

'What do you mean, why? Would you ask anyone else that? Would you ask Anna that?'

'I'm not asking Anna, I'm asking you.'

Chrissie didn't say anything. She was afraid that one day somebody might peel away too many of her layers and everyone would discover that her greatest fear was true. There was nothing there. She tipped her head back to look at the stars, which had the added benefit of keeping any stray tears in check. Was this whole endeavour a waste of time? Suddenly she couldn't see what it was she was trying so hard to achieve. It was too distant, too mysterious, like the stars. 'I'm trying to be somebody different for a while,' she said. 'That's all.'

'Yeah? But the thing is, we liked you the way you were,' he said.

She ripped her gaze away from the sky and smiled at him gratefully. It felt good to have friends.

'I've been fired,' he said.

'Oh.' She sipped some more champagne, mainly because she wasn't sure what to say. She was much better at heart-to-hearts when she was on the receiving end of the sympathy. 'Well, that's unfortunate.'

'Yeah. I haven't told my dad yet.'

'Are you terrified? Will he be very angry?'

His brow furrowed in confusion. 'Angry? No, not with me, at least. Maybe with my boss. But he'll ask me what I'm going to do next and the truth is that I don't have a clue. Some of the guys in there, friends, they're doing a charity trek to Bhutan, helping to restore a monastery or something . . .'

Chrissie pulled a face. 'Hell, no.'

'Exactly!' said Ben. 'Thank you. I could go with them but I can't think of anything I'd enjoy less.'

She was glad of the levity that was back in the conversation. 'Is it one of those treks where there're no hot showers and nobody changes their clothes for four days?'

'You've been on one of those?'

'Please! Me?' she said, laughing. 'What do you think? No, but I've heard the horror stories. It's the classic rich-boy summer, isn't it? Heal the world and all that.'

'I went to Nepal once, with my dad,' he said.

'And at Everest Base Camp you told him that you loved him,' she said in a sing-song voice. 'Benny, every girl at Clareville remembers that story.'

'Really? You know it was total bullshit, right?' He set the champagne bottle down on the ground and took off his jacket, putting it around her shoulders without asking. 'I care about the world, at least I think I do. But I care more about *my* world, this place for example.' He waved his arms towards the house. Shadowy movement could be seen in the dining room and in the room next door. Music could be heard faintly and now and again a burst of laughter or a girlish scream. 'It's falling apart and Dad doesn't give a damn. He's all loved-up with my new step-mum.'

'You like her?'

'She's okay. I'm fairly sure she's pregnant.'

'Yuck. She must be, what, forty-five?'

'Forty-three,' he said. 'And I'm happy for him. If that's what they want, then great. Meanwhile the family home could crumble to the ground and he'd let it. He's not as wealthy as you might think.'

Chrissie snuggled into the warmth of his jacket, enjoying the way it carried a trace of his familiar scent, as if she was wrapped in his arms without the confusion that would bring. 'You should offer to manage the place,' she said. 'You don't have anything better to do.'

'Stuck out here all year round? Wouldn't that be a bit . . . boring?'

She shrugged. 'You're bored anyway.' Without thinking what she was doing she leant over and kissed him on the mouth.

He pulled back.

She smiled and pushed her hair out of her eyes, looking down and licking her lip with the tip of her tongue, a slow smile drifting across her face as she made unmistakable eyes at him from beneath her eyelashes. 'Happy birthday.'

'Wait,' he said.

'Because of Anna?'

He looked confused. 'What? No, because . . .' He trailed off unable to come up with a good reason.

They both moved towards each other and met in the middle, lips and tongues colliding in a hungry, lonely kiss. His hands roamed around under the back of his jacket, catching the nape of her neck and pulling her into him.

She caught his top lip between her teeth and bit gently, pressing her body up against his and tasting champagne. He groaned softly and let his hands drift down to her exposed thighs, tracing the shape of her hips with his open palms, resting them on her waist and then lifting her up as if she weighed nothing to settle her on his lap, straddling him.

She broke off, panting for breath, and slipped her hands up under his white T-shirt, feeling his warm, firm stomach, his hot, broad back. She kept her eyes closed and lost herself in the sensation of his mouth on her throat, his hands tight around her hips. All her thoughts were silenced by the uproar in her nerve endings, the commotion in her knickers. The combination of the coke and champagne, the cool night air, the public place, the platonic friend and the sheer rapture of his relentless kisses induced a lust in her she couldn't hope to control.

Maybe it was a stupid mistake but it didn't feel like it. It felt like just what she needed.

He tugged at the edge of her vest and she lifted her arms above her head so that he could take it off. His kisses fell onto the top of her breasts as his thumbs made lazy circles inside her bra. He lifted himself up against her in hard, thrusting movements and she pushed back against him. They couldn't hear anything any longer except their own balmy frenetic breaths.

Across the garden his birthday party continued.

She flicked open his belt and his button with one hand, delved inside his fly with the other, passing the point of no return. She wriggled out of her shorts and lay back across the bench, pulling him down on top of her as he hastily pushed his own jeans out of the way so that there was nothing between them except cotton and silk.

Then he hesitated.

'It's okay,' she murmured. 'Come on. It'll be fun.'

He was inside her within seconds; it was over within minutes, climaxing in a noisy messy surge that left her grinding against him furiously hoping to ride the tail ends of sensation to an orgasm of her own.

After that they rearranged their clothes and regained their composure. Her plait had come loose and her hair fell in waves across her bare shoulders so she spent a minute or two putting it back as it was. His white T-shirt had picked up a stain and so he wore it back to front and inside out.

'So tell me,' she said, 'was it the Lara Croft outfit or what?'

Ben looked embarrassed. 'It wasn't . . . I mean, this isn't what I had in mind when I brought you out here.'

She raised a doubtful eyebrow.

'Honestly,' he said.

'Shut up now,' she said. 'Or I might get offended.'

She led the way back. Ben was quiet, so subdued that she almost found it uncomfortable. She thought that she recognized his quietness as regret, but she hoped she was wrong.

'I thought you said there'd be fireworks,' she said.

'You mean there weren't?' He winked at her and some of their easiness was restored.

The first person they saw when they walked inside was Anna. Chrissie waited for feelings of guilt and betrayal to surface but they didn't. Perhaps there really was nothing to feel guilty about, after all Anna had had months to make a move on Ben and she'd chosen to remain in a state of platonic continence. Chrissie tried to forget that she would catch Anna looking at him sometimes, when she thought she wasn't being watched, with a sort of yearning expression that would out-class those of the most desperate romantic heroines. And yes, maybe Anna did drop the hand she was holding the moment she saw them, one of the snooker players from earlier if memory served Chrissie correctly, but maybe that was simply to enable her to dash across the room and gather them both up in a flurry of drunken enthusiasm.

'Where have you been?' said Anna, her voice rising above the music with excitement and general good cheer. 'Some of these idiots think it's warm enough to go swimming. You have to talk them out of it, Ben! For one thing it's freezing out there, but for another the swimming pool is clogged with weeds and frogspawn. Quick, come on, put some porn on the plasma or something, cause a diversion.'

They stood in an uneasy little threesome, Ben and Chrissie's secret slicing the air between them, the tension pulling at all points of the triangle. Anna's humour faltered as if she felt the strain.

'Swimming?' said Ben. 'Sounds like a laugh.' And he laughed as if to prove the point but they all knew he was faking it. He went off quickly in the direction of the courtyard, not bothering to look back, stopping to pick up a bottle of Jack Daniel's from the bar. This time there was no mistaking the awkward moment. Whatever. She always suspected Ben was a bit of a wimp.

'You okay?' said Anna. 'Do you think Ben's having a good time?'

Chrissie wanted to laugh but managed not to. 'I'm fairly sure he is, yeah.'

'I am,' said Anna. 'I'm having a wonderful time. I think this is possibly one of the best parties I've ever been to.'

'Oh Anna,' said Chrissie. 'You think every party is a winner. You should get out more.'

'What's wrong with it?'

'Nothing,' said Chrissie. 'But it's Ben's, isn't it? He could invite five people round for DVDs and a pizza and you'd probably say it was the best night ever.'

'You're sure you're okay?'

'I'm great.' She felt better than she had in months. Funny, but it felt like a no-strings shag was the perfect balm for her insecurities.

Except, as everybody knows, there is no such thing as a no-strings shag.

Eleven

Exactly four months after Ben's party Anna walked through central London feeling light-headed. That morning she had sat her last exam, and this afternoon she was speaking to someone at the *Herald* about a summer internship. Making decisions felt good. The Morton Group was vast, the opportunities endless. She couldn't have any of this without Kendall's support; she couldn't have any of it without Chrissie. She was finally taking charge of her destiny, with a little help from her friends, and after so long feeling like she wasn't worth the effort it was about time.

One last summer to tie up any loose ends.

Starting now.

Ben was waiting for her on the steps of the National Gallery, eating an ice cream, seemingly oblivious to the school party that milled around him, a horde of pre-teens, none of them even reaching his shoulder. He saw her and waved, polishing off the ice cream in two more bites and coming down the steps to meet her halfway.

'Congratulations,' he said, and as he kissed her on both cheeks she could smell the sweet vanilla on his breath, still cold. 'How do you feel?'

'Liberated,' she said. Without the pressure of exams, and the wider pressure of what to do after, she was loose and unencumbered, ready to dance in the fountains below them in Trafalgar Square if she so chose.

'It feels like I haven't seen you for months,' said Ben.

'Don't take it personally,' said Anna. 'I've barely seen a soul. These might just be the very last exams I ever take so I wanted to do them right.'

'Chrissie said she hadn't heard from you either.'

'I don't want to talk about Chrissie today,' said Anna.

Ben looked at her strangely but let it pass without comment. 'What do you want to do?' he said.

'I want to have a cupcake and a coffee downstairs in the café, then go and see the Degas. Okay?'

'Sounds perfect. Did I ask you to meet me here today or did you ask me?' he said.

'I asked you. There's something I want to tell you.'

She was fed up of waiting for the perfect romantic moment, fed up of hoping that their eyes would meet across some crowded room and they would suddenly move into that new place with a single kiss. It was never going to happen like that. If it was ever going to happen at all then she had to be brave. She had to look him in the eyes and tell him outright that she was in love with him, no ambiguity, no bullshit. And if he didn't feel the same, and said he never could, then she would be embarrassed, yes, and she would risk losing his friendship forever. Who could ever be friends after such a declaration? But she knew that forever wasn't all it was cracked up to be.

She ordered a lavender cupcake and picked off the little crystallized violets one by one, savouring the moment, not delaying it. In life there are very few days when you dramatically change course and she knew that this could be one of them.

Today everything felt as if it was meant to be. The sun was shining, the sky was impossibly blue, more like the skies you get at the seaside than in the city. She was in one of her favourite places in the world. Ben was in a good mood, she was in an even better one. Their cakes were eaten down to the last crumb and their coffees sipped to the last drop. Conversation was easy, peppered with the usual bursts of laughter or pauses for thought.

It was perfect, he was perfect. God, they could be so perfect together.

'Come on,' she said, balling up her paper napkin and sending it sailing in a graceful arc straight into the waste-basket. 'There's more to this place than cake, you know.' Her fingertips tingled with anticipation.

They went up to the first floor and immediately turned left. In front of them was a painting by Degas. A girl with fierce auburn hair sitting having her curls combed out by a woman who could be her mother, but from the way she was dressed she was more likely a maid. The entire paint-ing was shaded in hues of red and orange and pink, like a blazing fire. Flanked on either side by the artist's pale, insipid dancers, it stood out and was compelling.

It made her feel loved, just as it always did.

'This is the first painting that ever moved me,' she said. 'I was nine years old and I came home from school in tears. A girl in my class, Jane something, had been calling me ginger all day long, throwing the word down at my feet until she made me cry. Dad dragged me into a black cab and we came all the way here.' She closed her eyes, remem-bering, and when she opened them the rapturous girl with burning red hair was still there, enduring in a way that her father's support had been unable to do. 'Matisse owned this painting once,' she said. 'Now it belongs to everyone. How can I look at it and not feel beautiful?'

She reached across with her hand and lightly brushed his fingers with hers like an invitation. Slowly, so slowly it almost made her squeal with anticipation, his hand curled around hers, his little finger breaking with the ranks and doing its own thing on the side of her palm. Thirty seconds they stood like that. A minute. A lifetime.

When she glanced at him he was looking straight at her and she wondered for how long. There was a fluttering in her chest that tickled painfully.

He breathed in and they were so close and quiet that she heard it.

It was going to happen. Her vision swam and the floor undulated beneath her feet. She pleaded with her emotions to behave; she didn't want to miss this moment by swooning like a Victorian heroine when he kissed her. They could spend all afternoon kissing in these quiet hallways and then on the way out they would buy a postcard of the Degas in the gift shop and one day they would tell their grandchildren why it meant so much to them.

He said her name and it had never sounded sweeter. He turned to face her, picking up her loose hand with his so that they were joined, an impenetrable circle of pent-up energy and hope. Hope for the future.

'I have to tell you something,' he said.

'What?'

'Chrissie and I . . .'

What?

'I know you said you didn't want to hear about her but

the thing is . . . we've been seeing quite a lot of each other lately and . . .'

And what?

'One thing led to another . . .'

She swallowed, but it didn't shift the scratchy feeling at the back of her throat. Even then she still could not have imagined what was to come. An affair? Maybe it was inevitable. It wouldn't last. Her mind was slow to take in the possibilities.

'We're getting married,' he said.

She fixed her eyes on the painting. The colours blurred and she felt sick. The sudden ache deep in her chest made her wince. She would never be able to look at the painting in the same way again. From now it wouldn't make her feel better, it wouldn't make her feel beautiful. It would make her feel sad and stupid. So stupid.

'I-I . . .' she stuttered, then held her tongue. Nothing would be right.

'Say something,' he whispered.

Married? 'When?'

'Soon.'

Somehow she made it through the next five minutes while he told her how he and Chrissie had been 'you know' (she didn't) for 'a while' (whatever that meant). That they'd talked about getting married, moving out to Wiltshire, using her money to restore his family home. 'And so we just thought, why not?'

'Do you love her?' said Anna.

'What?'

'Do you love her?'

'I . . .' His eyes were pleading. He was still holding her hands.

'Your turn to say something . . .' she whispered.

It was as if he was asking her permission, her blessing. Either that or he wanted her to talk him out of it. The silence stretched between them and she wanted it to snap cleanly. She could have told him then, perhaps, she could have said, 'But *I* love you,' and it might have made a difference. But her friends were going to be married. And Anna loved them. There was only one way to respond to news like that and hope to keep hold of both of them. She reached across to kiss his cheek and then she dropped his hands. 'I couldn't be happier,' she said.

It wasn't a lie. She couldn't be happier. She doubted very much if she could ever be happy again.

Chrissie couldn't wait to get her involved with the wedding plans. When Ben said 'soon' he hadn't been messing around. 'The grounds of the house are far more attractive than the inside,' said Chrissie. 'And if we wait until next summer we might change our minds.'

She was trying on dresses and her disembodied voice floated over the thick velvet curtain. 'Isn't it exciting? I wanted to tell you myself,' she said. 'But Ben thought it would be better coming from him.' Anna took advantage of the fact that she could not be seen and pulled a face. Only mid-grimace did she remember the discreet sales assistant waiting patiently with a rack of 'maybe' wedding dresses for the bride-to-be to try on. She checked. Yep, she'd been seen. But the twinkle in the stranger's eye made her think that she was amused rather than appalled.

'What about telling me together?' she said. 'Didn't you think of that?'

'I thought that would be rubbing your face in it a bit.'

'Rubbing my face in what, exactly?'

'You know,' said Chrissie. 'Our love.'

This time Anna stifled a little snort with the back of her hand and saw the sales assistant smirk conspiratorially. 'I couldn't be happier,' said Anna.

'Really?'

'Really.'

'This dress is vile,' said Chrissie. 'I told you we should have gone to Temperley.'

They went for a glass of champagne instead. It was Chrissie's idea. Anna had hoped that the longer Ben's bombshell had to settle on her the better she would feel about it, but it wasn't working out that way.

'So tell me how it happened,' she said, asking the question that had been spinning in her bewildered mind all along but had been subdued by her romantic disappointment. She could no longer contain her curiosity. Masochistic though it may prove to be, she wanted to understand.

'What?' said Chrissie, perusing the tea menu. 'Do you want to get a cake and I'll have a sliver?'

'You and Ben,' said Anna, ordering a slice of ginger cake because she might need the sustenance.

She didn't. It was not a long story.

'We shagged at his party,' said Chrissie, 'and the sex was great, really great. He doesn't know what to do with himself and neither do I and so we just decided, why not do each other?' She laughed and flicked back her hair.

'That's . . . um, lovely,' murmured Anna. 'But marriage, it's such a big step. Couldn't you just have, you know, gone out with each other?'

'What? With me living in Dulwich and him pounding the streets in the City looking for another job? I don't think so. There's a grace period after you get married. People leave you alone to get on with the important business of making babies, which – believe me – is *not* going to happen.'

'And by people, you mean . . .?'

'Daddy, who else? Plus Ben was getting all sorts of pressure from his father about selling up in Wiltshire, which would've been such a shame; it's a gorgeous piece of property and a bloody awful time to sell. We can hang around down there for a couple of years. It'll be fun. I needed direction, right? Daddy was livid, but he's coming round.'

Anna knocked back the rest of her champagne and fleetingly wished that they had ordered an entire bottle. 'Do you love him?' she said.

'Ben?' said Chrissie inexplicably. 'I adore him. Always have.'

As an awkward schoolgirl, as a student, and now as a soon-to-be brand-new employee at the *Herald*, the flagship European publication of the Morton Group, Anna's sense of duty stopped misery from consuming her. Only a fool would sabotage a dazzling career from the very start because of a little inconvenient heartbreak and Anna had been a fool for long enough. So every time her thoughts drifted to Ben and Chrissie together and the huge mistake she was sure that they were making she would force herself to think instead of deadlines and column inches and sources, her name as a byline, her view of world events.

What was a romantic mistake in the context of the rest of her life?

By neatly side-stepping her emotional responses she was able to muddle through and at times even convince herself that she was absolutely fine.

The first thing she saw was the newspaper's logo, six foot high and proud, behind an empty reception desk. It was oddly quiet and there was nobody in sight. Her very first day. It felt as if she had made it. The only problem was that she wasn't entirely sure what to do next.

She lingered a while, shifting her weight from foot to foot. After a minute or so, she leant across the desk to see if there was a bell or something, like in a hotel, but there was just an idle laptop computer, an open can of Diet Coke and a copy of *Grazia* left open at the horoscopes.

The phone started to ring and she ignored it until she could ignore it no longer, then she slipped behind the desk and answered it. It was someone asking for features, and there was a list of department extensions in front of her so it was easy enough to put them through.

She sat down.

The next caller asked for someone by name, which was more difficult, actually impossible, so she took a message instead but that made her so nervous that she vowed not to answer the next call and just let it ring out.

Except she could no more leave a phone to ring out than she could let a cut bleed unchecked; she tried but it was impossible. So regardless of whether or not it was the right thing to do she popped on the headset, closed the magazine and tried to put the calls through to the appropriate departments. She was just starting to rather enjoy herself when a sudden voice took her by surprise.

'Who are you?'

She jumped up so sharply that she forgot she was connected to the headset and it pulled taut, tipping up the can of Diet Coke, which spilt over the magazine. She fussed around trying to contain the mess and so it took her a long moment to recognize the man who had spoken.

It was John Mackintosh. Scratching his uncombed hair with a ballpoint pen and grasping his ever-present packet of Lucky Strike cigarettes in his other hand. How unfortunate that the first person she should see was the one person who thought she was an idiot. And more unfortunate still that she was acting like one. She hoped that it wasn't a sign.

'Hello,' she said.

He didn't reply. He looked tired. His head was cocked to one side and he regarded her curiously, as if he was trying to place her. She smoothed down the front of her smart little wrap dress and hoped the splattering of Coke didn't show too badly. Should she introduce herself or just assume that he remembered who she was? And if he didn't remember should she remind him that she was the quiet one from the back or the sobbing girl he had put in a black cab several months before?

'Sorry,' she said. 'There was nobody here. I wasn't really thinking, and picking up the phone is an instinct, isn't it?' She was waffling, edging from behind the desk, ignoring the bemused expression on his face that hadn't shifted since he first set eyes on her. 'I took a message for Sandy Coronado,' she said. 'I didn't recognize her name. It's here.' She held out the yellow Post-it note with the caller's

information on it. 'Should I leave it here or give it to ,
or . . .' She trailed off but realized that he was not about to
fill in her blanks. Instead of remaining calm she opened
her mouth and started apologizing all over again.

He sighed deeply and looked as if he sincerely regretted engaging with her at all. 'Don't make me ask you
twice.'

'What was the question?'

'Who are you?'

'Shit, I mean, yes, sorry. I mean . . . Anna Page. It's my
first day.' She smiled and hoped that might explain everything. Maybe he hadn't rated her work at City but this was
a brand-new start. 'Did you need anything?'

He smiled at last, vaguely and without really looking at
her. 'A reliable source at the CPS? Or failing that a warm
bath and a glass of Zinfandel.'

'At nine in the morning?'

'You're saying sources can't be reliable before lunch –
Anna, was it?'

'Anna Page,' she said.

'I'm Mac.' Candidly his eyes travelled the length of her
body and it almost felt as if he was touching her. She
shivered and tried not to mind.

'I know,' she said. 'You're John Mackintosh. We've met.'

'You're at City?'

She nodded. 'I was. International Journalism. I had you
once a month.' An awkward pause. 'For your lecture, I
mean. I had you for your lecture.'

'Thanks for clearing that up,' said Mac. He took a cigarette from the packet and tapped it on the edge of the
desk. 'What did you say your name was again?'

'Anna Page.' She watched as he briefly trawled his

recollection for the name and obviously came up with nothing. 'Then we met again briefly,' she said, 'at the Latimer/Cross wedding at the Landmark.'

'I was pretty drunk at that wedding,' he said.

'Oh,' she said. 'Well, we did.' Could she sound any more like a featherbrain?

'For your information, little Anna, Sandy Coronado is a he, not a she.'

She blushed and pushed her mistake aside. 'I'm supposed to find Lionel Sloane.'

'Lionel? Really? What makes you so special?'

She felt patronized. She didn't like the way he was looking at her either, as if she was nothing more than fresh meat; but to an ageing playboy like Mackintosh she supposed that was probably exactly what she was. 'Kendall Morton is a family friend,' she said coolly, and watched as Mac's eyes widened momentarily.

'I didn't know he had family,' he said. 'Or friends.'

Anna noted that his shoes were the most polished thing about him. His blue eyes sparkled mischievously, like those of a young boy. 'Lionel will get you to confirm all his lunch appointments and then give you some filing to do,' said Mac. 'You should you tell him you're in with the boss if you want something better.'

'Thanks for the tip.'

'Take the weight off those long legs of yours,' he said. 'The girl who is supposed to be here at all times will be back shortly, I presume. She'll help you.' He started to walk away then paused, turned back and said, 'Unless you fancy a cigarette?'

She'd heard once that the existing journalistic establishment could be split keenly down the middle between old school and new, and it was nigh-on impossible to have a foot in both camps. Mac was most definitely old school, he had inky fingers and a dirty mouth, and Anna was unmistakably new. She believed in global media and the internet and citizen journalism. All things that she knew Mac would abhor. But they could learn from each other. Or at least, she could learn from him and see how they went from there. She sensed an opportunity to use his weakness for women to her advantage. For the next few years, if called upon to explain her bad habit, she would say that it was all Mac's fault she started smoking again.

He seemed to like her. But then Mac liked everyone as long they were wearing a skirt.

Mac was right about Lionel: he treated her like a PA. And so after a week of keeping his lunch diary and printing out his emails she drifted towards the news desk, and when Mac suggested that she perched in the background wherever he was working on any given day she readily accepted.

'Except Thursdays and Fridays,' he said. 'When I work from home. Unless you want to trek to the country to watch me type.'

'That's all you do on Thursday and Friday? You type up stories?'

'I smoke, occasionally I eat. It's spectacularly unimpressive.'

He was the sort of man that it was hard to picture in any kind of domestic scene. If he had said that he lived out of a suitcase in a bedroom at the Groucho Club it would have been easy to believe him. Obviously he was being nice to her because of her connection to Kendall Morton; either that or he wanted to sleep with her. Perhaps she should have cared more about his motives, but she wanted to learn and that meant getting away from Lionel as soon as she could.

'You can help me with background on this Bolivia thing,' he said, after she'd been in the office a while, elevating Anna above the research assistants who had endured three years of library grunt work to be given just such an opportunity.

'It's not what you know . . .' sneered a junior someone as she passed by them on her way to the archive.

'What was that?' she asked sweetly, daring them to say it to her face.

'Wouldn't it be nice if we were all as chummy with the boss?'

'Not for me,' she said, unconcerned. 'If everyone was chummy with the boss then I'd lose my advantage.'

She threw herself into the task Mac had given her and when she presented him with a two-hundred word side-bar and a sheaf of accompanying notes for his okay a few hours later, he raised an unruly eyebrow, impressed, and told her to take it straight to editorial for final checks and typesetting. 'Good job,' he said as Anna walked away, and that same junior research assistant swapped envious and amazed glances with another, praise from Mac clearly being as rare as reticence at a press convention.

'How do you know Kendall anyway?' said Mac one day when his name came up in connection with the Humanitarian of the Year award.

'His daughter, Chrissie. She's my friend. I've known her for years.'

'He has a daughter. Did I know that?'

'I have no idea,' said Anna.

'It feels like I should know that.'

'Maybe you don't know as much as you think,' she said.

Mac grinned and let her get away with it. Their office banter had not gone unnoticed by the rest of their department, who probably thought they were sleeping together, but what did it matter? Most of them had made their dislike of her perfectly clear the moment she stepped over them to progress. She had no intention of getting romantically involved with Mac; her fingers had been badly burnt by Ben and so for now she wanted nothing more than friendship.

'And her name is Chrissie? What does she do?'

'She's a student. I mean, she was. She's getting married in a couple of weeks.'

'And?'

'And what?'

'And then she'll just be someone's wife?'

'I suppose.'

'Not quite Elisabeth Murdoch, then?'

'No,' said Anna, 'and don't be mean, she's my best friend.'

Much to Chrissie's disgust she had been unable to interest OK, *Hello!* or *Tatler* in the upcoming ceremony without a cast-iron guarantee of her father's presence – something she was embarrassed to say was not a given. When they met for a quick bite near the office she asked Anna to make sure that someone from her father's newspaper would be covering the occasion. 'He owes me,' she said. 'He had all kinds of press opportunities when I was growing up but he said he was –' she made air quotes with her fingers – 'protecting my privacy.' She finished picking the

Parmesan out of her rocket salad and pushed the plate away.

'Maybe that's the truth,' suggested Anna.

'Ha! Then he could have asked me. Like I care about privacy. Couldn't be bothered, more like. What little girl doesn't want to be in glossy magazines next to her daddy? I don't have a single decent photograph of the pair of us together.'

Anna's mantelpiece had a framed snapshot of herself and her father that made her smile when she looked at it every morning. It was taken on a beach in France when she was about thirteen, before Clareville, before Alzheimer's. They had been swimming in the sea before breakfast and were both still soaking wet. He was holding a tiny flat fish they had caught with a stick and a piece of string, his arm wrapped around her and his chest puffed out proudly as if it was a forty-pound barracuda. Anna was laughing so hard she'd had to run into the sea and do a wee immediately afterwards.

'I'll check with regions and make sure they're sending someone,' she said. 'You'll get some good shots of the pair of you at the wedding.'

'Maybe,' Chrissie said. 'Though I think he might be pissed off that we're doing it in Wiltshire instead of Tokyo. Like *that* was ever an option.'

The white and gold folder which went everywhere with Chrissie these days made an appearance and Anna braced herself for further instruction. At least the minutiae of the wedding provided a distraction from the bigger picture, the one of Ben and Chrissie getting together and moving to Wiltshire as soon as they returned from honeymoon. She could visit, sure, but it wouldn't be the same.

For one thing she would know beyond all hope that things with Ben would never be the way she wanted them to be, and for another they would inevitably drift away from her in the way that married friends and people who moved to the country did.

There would be no more impromptu cocktails followed by greasy-spoon breakfasts, no more giggles and the feeling of being comrades-in-arms. There would be no more short swings through new exhibitions followed by long drinks at old drinking holes. When bored she wouldn't be able to call one to talk about the other. When lonely she wouldn't be able to call them both and talk about herself. In short, things would go back to the way they were before they all made friends again, back to the time when she had convinced herself that she was perfectly happy, something she doubted she would be able to convince herself of ever again. She missed them already. Him, especially.

Thank God for the Morton Group. There was an opening on the foreign affairs desk in Singapore that Kendall was pushing her for once her summer internship was complete.

She forced herself to focus on the bride-to-be, who had opened her folder and was talking colour schemes.

'I sent Daddy my swatches by FedEx, so he could coordinate. I thought he would have been in touch by now. Will you call Fuji and find out what time he's flying in? What else?'

Anna made a note to do so at the bottom of her list of tasks – *confirm delivery of flowers and cake, pick up bridesmaid's dress, purchase real rose petals (cream), provide caterers with map and floor plan of Wiltshire house, arrange hen night* – the last was proving particularly tricky. 'About a hen night . . .' she said.

Chrissie looked up from her own list, which Anna noticed was considerably shorter.

'What would you think about bypassing it in favour of something a bit more sophisticated?'

'Carry on,' said Chrissie, unconvinced.

'A big group of girls on the town? Isn't it all a little, well, trashy?'

'I think that's the point.'

Despite Chrissie's sceptical frown Anna pressed on. It was a problem. A trawl through Chrissie's Facebook had unearthed a few old names but nobody she would presume to call a close friend. A similar trawl through the wedding-guest list revealed more men than women, most of them closer to Chrissie's father's age than her own, friends of the family, not of the bride. How did she explain to a bride that she had been unable to summon enough friends to make it an occasion? This was the most popular girl in school after all.

'What if it was just us two?' she said. 'I could take you for a day of pampering, a massage, get your nails done, maybe in Wiltshire somewhere? Babington House? Then afterwards we can go for dinner.'

'Can I get drunk?' said Chrissie hopefully. 'Come on, it's traditional.'

'As your bridesmaid I think I'm supposed to look after your welfare.'

'You're also supposed to boff the best man but I don't see that happening, do you?'

'I don't know,' said Anna. 'Ben's dad has a certain older-man appeal.'

'Yuck,' said Chrissie. 'Though I think it's bizarre that his dad is his best man. Is it sweet, or is it pathetic?'

'It's sweet,' said Anna.

Chrissie looked as if she might beg to differ, but before she could say anything further her attention was caught by something outside the window and her eyes lit up. 'There he is!' she said, her hand raised in a small wave.

Anna spun around to look. 'What? Who?'

'Ben. I asked him to meet me here because we're going to the vintners this afternoon to choose champagne. I suppose you could come with us if you like.'

Anna saw Ben, and saw him freeze, his hand in mid-air, when he noticed her, and then saw him quickly recover. She knew without looking in a mirror that she had gone pale. So far during this whirlwind engagement she had done a discreet but effective job of avoiding the bride-groom completely. In less than a minute Ben was upon them and Anna tried not to wince when she saw them kiss on the lips for the very first time, tried not to draw any attention to the fact that everything had changed.

'Hey, Anna,' said Ben.

'Hey.'

'You two chat,' said Chrissie. 'I'm just going to nip to the bathroom and make myself look beautiful.'

The others both paused a fraction too long, Anna because she was pretending to look at the dessert menu, and Ben because he was looking at Anna. He snapped to attention first. 'You look beautiful already, gorgeous.'

'Don't call me gorgeous,' said Chrissie. 'I told you, I don't like it.'

And then they were alone. 'So . . .' he said. He was bent over the table in a defeated posture, shy almost.

'So . . .'

'Haven't seen you for a while.'

'I've been busy,' she said, wishing that she had known he was coming so that she could have given some thought to the way she looked but simultaneously despising herself for caring at all.

She looked down at his hand on the table, clean straight fingernails, the tips of them white against a summer tan. She hid her own chewed afterthoughts in her lap. To her dismay they were trembling slightly. 'Not long now,' she said.

'Until what?'

'Until the wedding.'

'The wedding,' he said. 'Yeah, I suppose.' He ran his hand through his hair and she was reminded of the very first time she saw him, standing on the stage at Clareville House, making three hundred teenage girls weak at the knees with that same simple movement. He still wore his hair the exact same way and she was seized by the urge to give him a buzz cut and see if a man emerged from beneath the floppy schoolboy fringe.

'She's my friend, Ben,' she said. 'You could at least *try* to sound excited.'

He nodded slowly. 'I just . . . I've been thinking about you a lot and . . . seeing you here . . .'

She held her breath and waited for him to speak. Could anything happen with Ben after all? Could they run away together? Chrissie would never forgive her, but . . .

Then he straightened up, pressed his lips together and smiled without showing his teeth. It could almost have been a grimace. 'You're right,' he said firmly. 'I'm sorry. Of course I'm excited. Chrissie's fantastic.'

'Fantastic,' she echoed faintly and felt her romantic, treacherous daydreams drift away to nowhere once more.

That afternoon she was on fire, throwing herself into her job with a ferocious single-mindedness in an effort to forget his face, to forget that she ever thought herself in love with him. It was busy, very busy, almost busy enough to carry her away from her feelings.

She was marshalling calls into the *Herald* on an unfolding situation in northern Spain involving a man in an illegally parked car who was either dead or asleep, wearing a belt either of explosives or of questionable taste, either a suicide bomber or an innocent man in a chunky belt taking a nap in his car. They had two correspondents on the scene and a list of sources growing by the minute. The area had been evacuated and armed police were on the scene, but it was hard to separate speculation from fact, and the foreign desk were holding three column inches on the fourth page in case he blew an enormous hole in the Bilbao Guggenheim.

Although it could be nothing.

Anna's job was to log and précis every call before it went to Mac, who was tying together the various strands of the story (or non-story) and had just an hour or so left before making the decision on what to report or not to report. It was confusing and tense. And so when her mother called Anna was quite short with her at first, until she realized something had happened. Something bad.

Her guts twisted when she heard the clipped tones that meant her mother was trying to stay calm, trying to hide something.

'I'm so sorry to do this to you,' said her mum. 'You know what? Forget it. I shouldn't have called.'

'I'm on my way,' she said.

'Are you kidding me?' said Mac. 'Get back here. You don't run out on me when I need you, I don't care who your best friend's father is.'

It was the first time he had ever ordered her to do anything, the first time he had come close to raising his voice. Across the office curious colleagues peered over to see if there was going to be a confrontation. There wasn't.

'Family emergency,' said Anna and she grabbed her coat and her bag as she simultaneously updated her spreadsheet and fired off a quick email to one of the researchers, attaching the work and begging him to take over her desk. 'I'm asking Sam to cover for me,' she said. 'You won't even miss me.'

'Which one is Sam?'

She left without answering. Mac would work it out. This time tomorrow her early exit would be forgotten. People moved on quickly in the newspaper business; it was one of the things that she liked best about it.

Her mum answered the door within moments, as if she had been standing behind it, waiting for the knock since she had called her daughter for help. The left side of her face was red and livid, the start of an indigo bruise blossoming with sickening speed. Yet on the untouched right side of her face it was clear to see how pale she was.

'God, Mum, what happened?'

'I don't know,' she murmured. 'One minute I was just talking, and the next . . .'

Anna pushed inside and closed the door, helping her

mum, who was unsteady on her feet, her eyes cast with the dazed expression usually found in the eyes of her other parent.

'Where is he?'

'Upstairs.'

Anna's eyes flicked nervously upstairs and her mum noticed. 'Don't worry,' she said. 'I gave him a pill. He was perfectly docile about it all afterwards.'

'Tell me,' said Anna.

'I was folding laundry,' she said. 'He was standing on the landing, you know, like he does, and I was chattering away. Then out of nowhere he was running at me, my face went into the side of the airing-cupboard door.'

Anna swallowed down her fear and her grief. 'Ice,' she said, trying to be practical, wanting to be able to do something real, to delay the conversation they must have now. He had never been violent before, but she had read enough to know that it happened. And often. Alzheimer's sufferers, through frustration or chemical imbalances in their brains, or perhaps a combination of them both, nobody knew for sure, would turn on the very people who cared about them most. You always hurt the ones you love.

'I put a bag of peas on it,' said her mum, 'while I was waiting for you. Don't worry.'

'Don't worry? Mum, what the hell do you mean? Don't worry?'

'He didn't mean it.'

'I know.' But that didn't make it any easier to stomach. She was angry with her dad. The truth was she had been angry for a long time, but irrationally, childishly angry. This latest incident might be just the thing to tip her feelings out of their carefully contained box.

'It's not as bad as it looks.'

'Don't lie to me. Please.' She was fed up of her mother defending him. When he was well they had argued like any other married couple. Sometimes he was wrong. Just because he didn't know what he was doing didn't make it right.

'We can try altering his medication. And the doctor said that most likely it's a phase.'

'Meaning what, exactly?'

'Meaning that it will pass.'

'When did you speak to the doctor?'

Silence.

'Mum?'

'The last time.' Her head ducked down and her hair dropped across her face so that Anna could no longer see her eyes. She suspected that if she could there would be shame there as well as tears.

Fury steamed deep inside her like a hot spring. Looking down at the floor to avoid a scene was one thing if you were a child telling fibs or a teenager caught with cigarettes but the only person who should feel ashamed here was her dad.

She took a deep breath and counted to three. Then five. Then ten, but she stopped counting when she felt confident that she would not show her mum how cross she was with her for not asking for help before now. 'Okay,' she said, 'okay, here's what we're going to do. They gave you all the material, didn't they? Before?'

'The material?'

'You know what I mean,' she snapped. 'About respite nurses, and care homes. When he was diagnosed. I saw it. I know you think that I didn't but I did. It's in a big brown envelope, like the ones you keep bills and stuff in. Fetch it for me, please. We're going to go through it together.'

Her mother pushed the hair back from her face and stared directly at her daughter for the briefest of moments before her eyes, then her mouth, then her forehead crumpled and dissolved into a single, choking sob. She tipped back her head in an effort to staunch the tears but they fell across her upturned cheeks and onto her neck, silently and heartbreakingly. 'I'm j-just not ready,' she stuttered.

'Ready for what?' Anna's composure was stretched as thin as tissue paper over the tumult of emotions threatening to engulf her. One of them had to be strong. It had been her mother for so long, now it was her turn.

'To say goodbye.'

A few hours later Anna burrowed down deeper beneath the duvet in her old bedroom and let the tears flow freely. It had been a long and emotionally exhausting few hours, and they hadn't even made any decisions, not really. But at least her mother had finally admitted that she had come to the end of what she could do herself; it was time for some real help. Anna sat beside her as she made phone calls to book an appointment with the doctor and with a private care firm.

Anna felt too young for this. She had nowhere to go with the resentment she felt as she tried to make considered judgements about this care home or that one. Did she care that they had film nights twice a week? That the menu rotated on a fortnightly basis and contained a selection of seasonal organic veg? That he could pay extra for a view of the garden, less for a view of the street? Wasn't it months since he had appreciated a view, let alone a movie?

'You don't know that,' said her mother. 'Just because he can't tell you, doesn't mean he doesn't feel anything.'

But that just made her feel worse. She would rather he felt nothing, rather he was just a shell, than cling to the idea that some remnant of the man who used to be her father remained. Her whole family, everything she held most dear, was unravelling in the most awful way that she could imagine. When she thought of how happy they had once been she felt like crying, but when she thought of how things were now she felt worse. She was excessively anxious that she hadn't told her father she loved him, not often, and hadn't told him she loved him as much as she did. And now he would never know. They hadn't ever been a family for gushing declarations, theirs had been a love that showed itself in actions and shared experiences, but suddenly all she could do was wish that she had said, 'I love you,' at least once a day.

He awoke briefly, ate quietly and went to bed meekly. They gave him another pill just to be sure that they would all be well rested for the big decisions that needed to be made the following day and then both stood over him until he was almost asleep.

Just before she closed his bedroom door she whispered it. 'Love you, Dad.'

His sighed and turned over and for a moment she thought that perhaps he did hear her. Maybe in those mysterious moments between wakefulness and sleep he was himself again.

She took the small brown bottle of sleeping pills from her mother's hand and tipped them back and forth, listening to the innocuous little rattle as the pills moved around inside the plastic. They were used rarely, only in emergencies such as this. Anna suspected that they scared her mother with their potency. These magic pills that the doctor would only prescribe a dozen at a time for reasons that chilled her heart. Did he think her mum would hurt herself, or hurt her husband? Some tacit instinct made her keep them in her room that night.

She fancied that she could feel the shape of the tiny terrible bottle beneath her tear-stained pillow all night long.

Twelve

The next day was her wedding day. Chrissie kept reminding herself of this fact in the vague hope that she might
stop feeling slightly sick when she thought about it. It was
just nerves, right? It didn't mean she was making a mistake
or anything. Marrying Ben was the perfect focus for the
next few years. He wasn't Mr Right necessarily, just Mr
Right Here and Now. Oops, there was that sicky feeling
again. She took another swig of the excellent white bur-
gundy and tried to relax.

A few miles down the road Ben was getting married the
next day too. She wondered how he was feeling and hoped
it was a little less nauseous.

Earlier that day they had almost ruined the eve of their
wedding with a spat about everything and nothing. It
started harmlessly, sexily, with an argument about whether
or not they were allowed to sleep with each other on the
day before they became man and wife.

'I don't see why not,' Chrissie had said gamely, checking
the time to make sure she had the necessary spare moment
before the next stage of her elaborate bridal beautifica-
tion. A masseuse was due at two, followed by a manicure.

'Tradition.'

Chrissie had assumed he was joking and started to
laugh accordingly but stopped as soon as she saw the
thunder clouds gathering on Ben's face. 'Oh what now?'
she said.

'It's just a joke to you, isn't it?' he said. 'Our marriage is a joke.'

'Of course not. Listen, Ben, don't start. You're probably just nervous, that's all.'

He stared at her, saying nothing. She began to feel uncomfortable and started to go but he stopped her by putting both his hands on her shoulders and piercing her with his gaze. Chrissie had always hated it when people did that. What did they expect to see in there? Her secrets? No chance.

'Do you think we're making a big mistake?' he said.

'Well, you obviously do,' she said, 'or we wouldn't be having this conversation. If you don't have the balls for it, just say so.'

'It's a bit late for that,' he said.

Thank you, God. She would have killed him if he had called her bluff and called it off. She might even have been tempted to literally kill him. Dealing with the fall-out from a dead body might be preferable to explaining to their guests, and her father, that they had decided not to rush into this after all.

She swiftly went into damage-control mode, pressing herself up against Ben in the manner that had proved extremely successful over the last few months. 'Babe,' she said, 'don't worry. Everything's going to be okay.' She toyed with the top button on his Levi's and ran her other hand up his back, under his shirt, scraping lightly with her unmanicured fingernails. 'I want to marry you tomorrow. It's what I want more than anything in the world.'

'Really?'

'Really.'

'You're not just trying to get your father's attention?' he said lightly.

She flinched, but he couldn't see because her face was pressed into his shoulder, and he couldn't feel because the bulk of his sensation had headed south in the way that it tended to do when Chrissie wanted something.

'I love you,' she said. Because really she knew that was all he wanted to hear. 'I want you,' she added, because that was the truth.

Being engaged to Ben had shown her all sorts of different sides to him. He wasn't anywhere near as confident as he had always appeared to be. He wasn't as strong. This malleability certainly had it benefits – she could generally get him to do whatever it was that she wanted, their impending marriage being a case in point – but at the same time it made her lose a little bit of respect for him. Had he always been this way? Or was she perhaps even more manipulative than she knew herself to be?

The power she held over him was both intoxicating and repellent. The more he bent to her will the less she wanted to marry him.

But he was right about one thing. It was far too late to change her mind.

It was a warm evening and she sat quietly with Anna in the garden of an old stately home turned hotel, the scent of late summer roses hanging in the still and sultry air. It was just starting to get dark. Soon they would have to think about moving inside. Her father was also staying at the same place and was due there later that night. Chrissie was jumpy waiting for him to arrive, constantly checking her nails (buffed to subtle perfection that very afternoon) and drinking more wine than might be advised for a dewy bride.

'I'm young,' she insisted, when Anna gently pointed out the cosmetic effect of a nasty hangover, 'my body can take it.'

'Whatever you say,' said Anna. Almost snappish.

Straight away Chrissie knew that there was something terribly wrong. She was a really intuitive person. Besides, Anna looked awful, worse than usual. And she'd arrived late at the hotel, leaving Chrissie, the bride-to-be on the eve of her wedding, alone for almost a whole hour. So it must be something pretty major. Honestly, who knew that being a bride could be so fraught with snags?

'What's happened?' she said. 'Is it the flowers?'

Anna picked up the white and gold folder and started going through the final checklist with a red pen.

'The flowers are fine, Chrissie.'

'The cars? What?' And then a belated thought. 'Is it Ben?' For some reason she just assumed that the flowers or the cars would be more susceptible to last-minute glitches than her fiancé. Any more laid back and he'd fall over.

'It's nothing,' said Anna, forcing a smile onto her face that wasn't fooling anyone. And Chrissie was not just any-one.

'Look, clearly something has happened. Is it my father? Is he still coming? He's not coming, is he? I'd rather know now than later. I'm sure you've got it all under control, but it's my wedding and I think I have a right to know.'

Anna slammed the folder closed and smashed it down on the table between them. 'For God's sake, Chrissie, give it a rest. It's not always about you.'

'*Excuse* me?' Chrissie would have laughed if she were a little drunker. 'Are you serious? Tonight it is, tonight it's most definitely all about me. I'm getting married tomorrow.' Saying it aloud didn't make it any less stressful. Jesus, what was Anna's problem?

'You're right. So let's drop it, okay?' Anna picked up the folder again and started up where she left off, red pen in hand, slowly and methodically ticking off the inconceivably long list of individual tasks that had added up to a spectacular, but subtle, summer wedding.

Anna was so good at all of this stuff. She was organized. Chrissie wasn't the list-making type; if there wasn't room for it in her head then there wasn't room for it in her life. Simple.

'I think that's everything,' said Anna, and she crossed off the last item on her list with a flourish.

Chrissie peered over her shoulder. 'Really?'

'Yep.'

'Fabulous,' said Chrissie. 'Just as long as it doesn't rain.'

'It's supposed to be lucky, you know,' said Anna, 'if it rains on your wedding day.'

'I don't care,' said Chrissie. 'Please, please don't let it rain.'

'I'm afraid that's the one thing I cannot do,' said Anna, closing the gold and white folder with a resolute snap and pushing it aside.

'I really am incredibly grateful, you know,' said Chrissie, awash with a sudden wave of affection for her oldest friend.

'Grateful for what?'

'For you, for all your help. I couldn't have done it without you.'

'Course you could,' she said. 'You'd have paid someone.'

'Wait until you see your present,' said Chrissie. She had

splurged and bought Anna a pendant from Tiffany, and not a cheap one either, a dragonfly of diamonds and emeralds. So dazzling she was sorely tempted to keep it herself, except that the emeralds would pick out the green of her friend's eyes perfectly.

'You didn't have to get me a present, don't be silly.'

'Of course I do. It's traditional to give the bridesmaid something. Besides, we wanted to because you've been . . .'

She stared in horror as Anna's face crumpled and those green eyes filled with sudden tears.

'Oh God, what?' said Chrissie. 'What is it?'

'I'm sorry, it's . . . I'm not good when people are nice to me.'

'Just tell me.'

'I don't want to spoil your evening.'

'You're already spoiling it.'

'It's my dad,' she whispered.

Chrissie froze. Every time she managed to successfully smother her guilt and convince herself that her friendship with Anna was honest and strong she would suddenly be brought back to reality with a bump and the threat of discovery would loom alongside the remorse. 'Is he . . . okay?'

'Oh Chrissie, it's just awful.'

It was the first time she had seen Anna cry for years. An instinct that she hadn't known she would possess made her open up her arms and lead her sobbing friend's face to a soft shoulder, with very little care for the ivory cashmere that covered it.

'I didn't want to say anything . . . You're right, this really should be all about you. But he's . . . it's all got too much, and my mum and everything.'

Soothing noises came out without thought. All these

years she had been feeling guilty, then trying to do the right thing by her friend and maybe what she needed most of all was a good cry, with a real friend. Is that what real friends did? Even the constant shame was alleviated a fraction by this simple act.

'Is there anything I can do?' she said, and she really meant it. In that moment, feeling like some kind of mother goddess, she would have moved the earth if it meant her friend would feel better. She would even – she paused for a moment's thought – yes, she would even have postponed the wedding. God, she was a *saint*!

Thankfully that wasn't going to be necessary. Besides, the moment passed.

'It's all right,' said Anna. 'The last couple of days have been tough, that's all, and I don't want to get upset in front of Mum. Really, you're the only one who knows about it, about him, I mean. Maybe I need to talk about it more often, stop letting it all build up, you know, in my chest, in my heart, until I explode. Like this.' She pulled herself out of Chrissie's embrace. 'I'm really sorry.'

'Don't be ridiculous. If you ever want to talk, I'm here.' She could only hope that she never would. It was a pretty good bet; Anna was the secretive type. Come to think of it, they both were.

She wasn't sure what to say, but Anna didn't seem to mind. She was staring into the middle distance and taking deep breaths. After a few minutes to compose herself, hopefully they could move on to other things.

Her gaze drifted back to the door. Her father was late. What if he didn't make it? She'd have to walk down the aisle alone. The part where they walked down the aisle together, arms linked, father and daughter, was a huge part of her wedding dream. She didn't know if she could do it without him, didn't know if it was worth doing without him. Surely he must have dreamt of it too? What father didn't think of her wedding day when he had a daughter?

Poor Anna, though, it sounded like her dad would be too far gone if and when she ever got around to finding someone to marry.

Damn. Why was she thinking of him?

'There was something I wanted to ask you,' said Chrissie. 'I've wanted to ask you for a very long time.'

'What?'

'It'll sound silly.'

'Much of what you say sounds silly to me,' said Anna, a sparkle coming back into her eyes. 'Ask away.'

'That night in Hampstead . . .'

'What night?'

'I think you know,' said Chrissie, narrowing her eyes and making it impossible for Anna to play dumb. 'I'm marrying Ben tomorrow and I think I have a right to know if my best friend and my husband were lovers once.'

'Lovers? Have you asked him?' said Anna.

'I'm asking you.' She just wanted the truth. It wouldn't change her relationship with either of them, but she hated not knowing, she had hated it for years, and somehow it was easier to ask Anna than to ask him. Chrissie and Ben didn't have that kind of relationship, the kind where they talked about their exes or their past; in fact, they really didn't talk about much of anything at all. Plans for the Wiltshire house mainly, the wedding. Generally they just had sex or drank wine or watched television. Sometimes all three at once.

'Did you have sex with him?' she asked bluntly.

Anna took an agonizingly slow sip of her wine, or perhaps it just felt that way.

'That night in Hampstead?'

'You remember?' she prompted. 'You were wearing my Vivienne Westwood corset and you were drunk. I sent Ben in to look for you and you were both gone for ages and when you came back you'd missed a button, one of those hook and eye things, remember?'

'I remember,' said Anna.

'And?'

'And nothing, Chrissie,' she said, laughing at last as the colour flooded back into Chrissie's face, Chrissie, who was trying so hard to act nonchalant she was practically rigid with fear.

'Nothing happened,' said Anna, 'not like that.'

Chrissie allowed the rush of relief to flood her like endorphins, unclenching a tiny fist of dread, dread that she wasn't the most desirable girl in the room, that Anna had been there first, that she was marrying her best friend's leftovers. 'Nothing happened?' She wanted to make this absolutely clear.

'You really want to know?' said Anna. 'I threw up. Dark and Stormies, wasn't it? I can barely look at a bottle of rum now without shuddering. Ben found me with my head down the toilet bowl. He was really sweet and, well, some of the – you know – sick had got on your corset and so I tried to wash it off as best I could and I had to undo it a bit and sort of swivel it round . . .'

'You got puke on my Vivienne Westwood?' said Chrissie. 'Sorry.'

'God, that's disgusting. I *wore* that! Loads!'

'I know.'

'You're gross.'

'A bit, yeah.'

The friends smiled at one another and Chrissie forgot to be anxious about her father walking her down the aisle, about her wedding, about how Ben didn't truly excite her, about how she didn't love him, not really, and only thought about this friendship and how – oddly – it was the one thing in her life of which she could be proud.

If this friendship of which she was so proud was hiding a dirty secret then how could it be true? And if it was the one constant in her life, the one thing she could count on, then it had to be true, didn't it?

She would have to tell her.

She would have to tell her tonight.

If she lost Anna as a result then perhaps that was no more or less than exactly what she deserved.

Another drink and then, quickly, she would rip the dark truth from her guts and maybe the doubts and fears which plagued her life would be ripped out with it and she could marry tomorrow with a pure heart. And perhaps even fall in love with her husband for real.

Wouldn't that be nice?

A deep breath. Her hand shook slightly as she poured them both another glass of wine.

'I did love him, though,' said Anna, so quietly that Chrissie was sure she must have misheard.

'I'm sorry?'

'Ben. I was in love with him. I think a little part of me always will be, even though he's marrying my best friend. That's bad, right?' She wasn't so much avoiding Chrissie's eyes as wrapped in her own thoughts, toying with the rim of her wine glass, a sad smile playing across her beatific face, and Chrissie knew that if Ben saw Anna like that, and heard her talk like that, then her claim on him would be lost.

'You're in love with my husband, is that what you're telling me?'

Anna giggled. 'I'm so stupid. Carrying a teenage crush around with me all this time. But you knew, didn't you? You must have known. God, I was so obvious.' She giggled again.

'I suspected.'

Anna's eyes glinted with resentment. 'And yet you slept with him anyway.'

'Hey, I asked you if you still liked him,' said Chrissie defensively. 'I asked you a bunch of times. And you had ample opportunity to hook up, so in the end I said to myself that I'd have to trust you. That you must have been telling the truth when you said that any feelings you might have had for him were in the past. We were friends, why would you lie?'

'I suppose sometimes even best friends lie,' she said.

Chrissie bristled. It was the night before their *wedding*. If Anna had a problem with it she really should have spoken out before now. Little drama queen. God, some people. She refused to feel guilty for this. For other things, yes, of course, but not for this. She jutted out her chin, ready for battle, and was momentarily wrong-footed when Anna reached out to take her hand.

'It's fine, Chrissie,' she said. 'You look like you want to slap me. Yes, I was sad when you got engaged, I honestly thought my heart was breaking, but if I really cared that much, wouldn't I have said something? It was the fantasy

I was having trouble letting go of, just the daydream, because I never had Ben, not at all. A few teenage kisses a thousand years ago, that's all I ever had and I built a dream around them.'

Chrissie crossed the fingers of her spare hand. 'You're sure? Because I would never . . .'

'You and Ben are getting married tomorrow. It's time for me to be happy.'

'You forgive me?'

'There's nothing to forgive. You two make a far better couple than we ever would.' She shook her head, as if shaking away long-held concerns. Another wry laugh emerged from her mouth. 'I'm going to have a good time at your wedding tomorrow, you know that? I'm going to get drunk and dance with as many handsome strangers as I can. I've wasted . . . well, let's just say I've wasted far too long. Maybe I just need to get laid.'

'I believe there're a couple of cousins?' said Chrissie.

Anna's smile broke into a grin. 'You're my best friend,' she said.

It was like saying, 'I love you.' It *was* saying, 'I love you.'

Anna took a deep breath. 'I know I can be distant, I'm secretive and I work too hard, and I worry too much, but I don't know what I'd do without you. I never talk about my dad, not to anyone, only you. So of course I forgive you. There's nothing you could do that I couldn't forgive. Nothing.'

It was a night for secrets. It was the perfect time.

Tell her.

'About your dad . . .'

'Oh let's not talk about him, daft old bugger. He's on a bunch of new tablets so he just sleeps. We'll find him a nice home, with a cute nurse, and maybe that's what we should have done years ago. But the guilt, we were afraid of the guilt, that's all. Guilt can cripple you, you know that? I hope you never know guilt like that, it's not fun.'

Chrissie already knew. Guilt was the great black dog of her life; guilt was everywhere, tainting every decision, every failure, every moment. Everything that she did not have. Without that guilt what kind of person might she have been, what kind of person could she still be? She was a good person. She had to be.

'Please, Anna, listen to me . . .'

Chrissie's tears surprised both of them. They swept down her cheeks with great force as if they had been dammed for years, waiting to burst through in a silent torrent. She felt a painful heaving in her chest and a great gush of emotion as the past rushed forward to meet the present. After being buried for so long her secret bloomed inside her, reaching for the light.

'What? Chrissie, what is it? What's wrong?'

They were both still. Looking at each other with hushed connectivity. Sensing that things would never be the same again.

But at that precise moment Kendall Morton swept into the rose garden shouting his daughter's name with abundant joy.

The girls stared in horror, first at him and then at each other. Then Chrissie felt the secret scurry back under the rock of her resolve and faced her father with a fake smile so practised and so perfected that out of everyone in the world only Anna was able to spot its insincerity.

Kendall grinned back and threw open his arms. Fuji was hurrying along behind him snapping Japanese down her mobile phone. He swept his daughter up into an embrace so unexpectedly fierce that she was able to pretend that was why she was crying, because she loved him so much, and she turned the tears into squeals of delight when he presented her with keys to the darling little terrace on Dovehouse Street. Because that's what brides do the night before their wedding, isn't it? They're supposed to cry.

Because they are so happy.

Thirteen

As soon as she woke up the next day Anna knew it was going to be hot. Not a pleasant English summer's day hot, every bride's delight, but what the weathermen would refer to as a heatwave and the tabloids would refer to as a scorcher. It was just past six and already she could feel the suffocating heat to come, hanging in the deceptive cool breeze that came in through the open window of her hotel room, lurking in the shaft of light that fell onto her pale body. At some point in the night she had thrown off her covers. That's how hot it was going to be.

The big day had arrived at last.

There was no denying it. She was sad.

She retrieved the white sheet from the floor, wrapped it around her and walked over to the window, looking out onto the countryside, a shimmering green baize of calm. She thought of the house a few short miles away where already the caterers would be unloading the ingredients for the canapés, and the sit-down lunch, then the buffet later. The marquee and the rented furniture would have arrived by now and there would be a team of people transforming a huge swathe of the grounds into an enchanted forest. Shortly the entertainers would arrive so that guests would pick their way through the flags and fairy lights to stumble upon a juggler in the gazebo, or a contortionist by the duck pond or a musician leaning against the trunk of a willow tree. At Chrissie's behest

Anna had even found a local ballet school willing to send little winged cherubs to frolic for a couple of hours trailing brightly coloured ribbons behind them.

She made a mental note to make sure that the cherubs were wearing sunscreen. It wouldn't do to send the local children home with sunstroke and third-degree burns.

Chrissie coped well in the heat. Her tawny complexion never burnt, only glowed. Anna, on the other hand, with her red hair and milk-white skin tended to look parboiled whenever there was a break in the clouds. Mournfully she realized she would have to coat herself in factor fifty, never mind the greasy pallor it would bring to her complexion. Better to look oily than fried.

All this preparation and still the wedding was referred to as 'small' by everyone from the caterer to the happy couple themselves. This wasn't small. Small was barefoot on a beach, a wedding chapel in Vegas. Small was Gretna Green, or the local town hall on a Tuesday afternoon. Small was not one hundred and twenty guests at a price per head that made Anna tighten her grip on her wallet. It may have been Chrissie's dream wedding but it certainly wasn't hers. What was, then? She closed her eyes and tried to picture her dream wedding but it was clearly pure fantasy because the only people standing beside her were her mum and dad and they both looked hale and happy. That was never going to happen. So perhaps just the man she loved and some stranger to do the official bit. The picture refused to form in her mind's eye. Perhaps that meant she was never going to be married at all.

Guests would start arriving at noon. As bridesmaid she should be there well before that. In fact she could be useful there now, overseeing the final details, being the voice of the bride, who would be far too busy being prettied to bother that the fruit in the Pimm's was cut too small or the cured ham on the plates of tapas was fridge cold when it should be served at room temperature. Team Chrissie, as they referred to the hair and make-up team (it had started as a joke but the name had stuck solidly), were due at the hotel in little more than an hour.

A room-service tray was outside the door to Chrissie's room. There was a glass of orange juice and a pot of coffee. Anna peeked under a silver dome and pinched a piece of melon from the fruit salad before knocking.

There was no reply.

'Chrissie? Rise and shine, it's me.'

She heard movement inside and then the door opened and Chrissie was there, wearing a white robe and dark glasses.

'You're getting married today!' said Anna, bending to pick up the tray and entering the bedroom.

It was dark in there and she threw back the curtains, eager for Chrissie to see what a gorgeous day it was outside.

Chrissie recoiled from the light. 'Don't,' she said, holding up her hand. 'Not yet.'

'Are you okay?' She pulled the curtain partway closed so that light fell more gently into the room but opened the window to let in some air. It was stuffy in here, oppressive. An atmosphere of gloom hung in the shadows and made her uneasy.

Slowly Chrissie removed her sunglasses and Anna could see that her eyes were red and puffy. Either she'd been punched in the face or she'd been crying all night.

'I have to tell you something,' said Chrissie. 'I haven't been able to sleep. If I don't tell you now then I might never sleep again as long as I live.' She looked up at Anna as if she was about to beg. 'Did you mean it when you said that you could forgive me anything?'

Anna nodded, but she was scared. Chrissie should be dancing around her room, the windows open wide, a glass of chilled champagne in her hand. Outside the birds sang and butterflies danced on any breeze they could find. The scent of summer roses clung to the warm air and made her think of summer holidays and childhood. Nothing bad could happen on a day like today. So why did she get the feeling that the sky was about to fall?

'It's okay,' she said, meaning it. 'You can tell me.' Maybe it was nothing. A change of heart about the dress, a crisis of confidence in her ability to carry off the elaborate up-do. Or maybe Chrissie was about to tell her that she'd cheated on Ben. Maybe she was about to leave him at the altar. She couldn't help the glimmer of hope and excitement that came with the thought. Even at this eleventh hour Anna was praying for a miracle.

Chrissie took a very deep breath and rocked her head back and forth on her shoulders, a little like a boxer preparing for a fight. 'I want you to know that I am very, very sorry. I couldn't be more ashamed,' she said, her voice so solemn that it was absurdly comic. 'Hardly a day goes by when I don't hate myself for what I did. And what you said last night, about being friends, it goes ten-fold for me. You're the best friend I ever had, which is what makes this so hard.'

'Tell me.' Okay, maybe it was something else.

'I told a lie,' she said. 'I told a huge lie about your dad, back at school. I said that . . . that he and I had been having an affair.'

'What?' Who and who? What was Chrissie talking about now? 'Say that again?'

'That we'd been sleeping together. When he was a teacher and I was a pupil.'

'You and my dad?'

'I lied,' said Chrissie. 'I wanted to get back at you. They fired him.'

The words hovered in the air, almost as if they could be swiped down with a dismissive wave. She could still hear them but they didn't make sense. Chrissie was joking. It was some sort of crazy joke that she wouldn't get until the punchline. Typical Chrissie, making up a drama just to see the look on her face. It wasn't a very *funny* joke though, and Chrissie had stopped talking and was waiting anxiously for her to say something, so perhaps she had finished, perhaps there wasn't a punchline, which would mean . . . which would mean . . . that this wasn't a joke. The words hanging in the air would not fall down. They were there to stay.

A memory: her dad walking unexpectedly into the back garden when she was still a teenager and catching her smoking, her heart lurching painfully into her throat preparing to be lambasted, but then he didn't say anything, just hello, like she had always smoked. Later he told her that he just assumed it was something he had forgotten and he was trying to cover himself. A few months later he forgot her name.

She forced herself to listen to the explanations and excuses pouring from her friend's mouth, even though it was impossible to process what she was hearing.

'I was a silly, spoilt little teenager,' said Chrissie. 'By the time I found a shred of decency it was too late to make things right. I can't tell you how many times I thought about walking into Clareville, even after I left, to confess. But . . .' She trailed off, her face as pale as the ivory wedding dress hanging in the corner of the room. 'It was a terrible thing to do,' she said. 'I know that. Despicable. There's no justification, there's nothing I can say.'

Another memory: her mum standing in the doorway, her painfully bruised face a gift from the man she would always love no matter what.

'And when you told me he was sick, well, I just fell apart. I wanted to tell you. But I was afraid. I felt like it was all my fault. It was a stupid, stupid thing to do.'

Next week they were sending him away. He would leave the house he had worked his entire life to pay for, it would be put up for sale, he would leave the family he had built there and the memories he could no longer recall. He would leave behind the man he once was. He would go into a shared home with nurses for family and residents for friends and her mum would struggle with that decision for the rest of her life.

Because of Chrissie?

She couldn't think. Instead she fumbled in her pocket for her mobile phone. 'Here,' she said, holding it out to Chrissie. 'Call my mother and tell her what you just told me. Then after that you call Clareville and you tell them.'

'I . . .' Chrissie looked down at the phone and back up at Anna. 'Is that all you want to say?'

It wasn't nearly all she wanted to say. Not nearly. She wanted to tell Chrissie the story of her father's life so that she might know exactly what she had ruined. She wanted to pound her pretty face into the floor of this bridal suite.

She wanted to ask for details. When exactly? What precise words did she use to destroy the career of a man who had done absolutely nothing to harm her? Take me through it, she wanted to say, moment by moment, because then I might understand how you could do such a thing.

And underneath it all a certain knowledge.

Because of me. Her stupid teenage argument with Chrissie was at the root of this. Knowing that made her want to hurl herself off a cliff into oblivion, but there was no cliff, there would be no oblivion. She had to live with it.

His career had never recovered after Clareville. It had been a strange and unusual time. When things got worse it was easy to pinpoint that moment, the end of the career, as the beginning of the end of it all.

'Go on,' she said, 'call them.'

Chrissie shrank away from the phone as if it was something nasty that she didn't want to touch. 'Now?'

Anna nodded.

'I think Clareville will have broken up for the summer holidays.'

'My mum doesn't take summer holidays. She hasn't taken one for seven years now.'

Chrissie's brow furrowed and her tone of unconditional contrition glinted with a little self-defence. 'What happened to him, after all this, it was a tragedy, but that wasn't anything to do with me. I looked it up, when you told me. He would have . . . gone down that road anyway, there's no direct connection.'

'Don't you dare presume to lecture me about Alzheimer's,' spat Anna. 'Don't you dare.'

'I wasn't.'

'I know more than you about most things, I should

think, but about this? Trust me, Chrissie, I'm an expert. So if you want to talk about the link between stress and Alzheimer's, go ahead, let's talk about it. Let's talk about frontotemporal dementia and neurogenesis, let's debate the erosion of glucocorticoids and the effect on long-term mental health. You want to do that?'

'No,' whispered Chrissie.

'What was that? I didn't quite hear you. Maybe I have an excessive amyloid build-up in my brain.'

'I said no.'

'There's a link, Chrissie.' She concentrated hard on keeping calm; she could feel her own heartbeat, the pulse of her blood, and she wondered if it was loud enough for Chrissie to hear. 'They might not have proved it in the lab but there's a link. You only have to live through it to see that. And I've lived through it, we all have, my whole family. I'm surprised we're not all loop-the-fucking-loop by now. If you've managed to persuade yourself otherwise that's just too bad, because you're wrong.'

'I didn't mean any harm.'

'But you *did*,' said Anna. Her throat contracted painfully and it hurt to breathe, and she fought back furious tears. 'You knew *exactly* what you were doing: you wanted to get rid of him so that you could get rid of me. It wasn't a prank; you knew it would have consequences, serious consequences. God, how could they believe a girl like you?' She answered her own question. 'It was your father, wasn't it? He threatened them with something.'

'Not him,' whispered Chrissie. 'One of his lawyers.'

'Because you thought something had happened with me and Ben?' She wanted to understand how this could have happened. Still, in a clumsy, desperate way, she hoped it was not true. 'And we fell out? That's why? Chrissie, you can't . . . it wasn't . . .'

Chrissie sat down on the edge of the bed, dropping her head so that she was staring at the floor. Tears that rested in her eyes dropped silently to the floor, blooming dark damp patches on the oatmeal carpet. 'I was angry,' she said. 'Humiliated. I knew it was wrong, but I wanted you out of my sight and it was the only way I could think of. I've tried so hard to make it right.'

'What? How?'

'It doesn't matter. Obviously nothing is enough.'

'Wait a minute, what do you mean? Make it right how, exactly? By being my friend?' She dropped her voice to an incredulous hush. 'Chrissie? Is that why we're friends? Because you owe me?' She felt unsteady on her feet as the oldest friendship in her life was swept out from beneath her. 'You selfish, hopeless little cow,' she said. 'You always get what you want, don't you? Always. You wanted me to be your friend and I was, you wanted Ben and now you have him too. But why would you do that to my dad? He never did you any harm. He never did anyone any harm. He was a good teacher, Chrissie, he was a good father and a good person. You ruined him. Out of spite. How could you?' Anna knew she was crying, and that her words were strangled, maybe even incomprehensible. The rasping pain in her throat grew worse as sob after wretched sob tore through her. Everything was all Chrissie's fault, so why did she feel so guilty? If only she hadn't made friends with her, allowed her into their lives. If only she hadn't fallen out with Chrissie that night, or had made it right somehow. All the things she had said to her dad, all the awful things. And none of it was his fault.

'Anna?'

Chrissie was looking up with those big brown Bambi eyes that had never failed to get her out of all kinds of trouble. 'It's my wedding day,' she said mournfully. And damn, if there wasn't hope in those eyes. Hope that she would be forgiven, hope that confession brought with it automatic mercy, that her bravery would be met with kindness. And hope that mere circumstance – a wedding, guests gathering, small children trailing ribbons on a beautiful summer's day – would absolve her.

'Do you believe in karma?' asked Anna. 'What goes around comes around?'

Chrissie didn't say anything, she had said enough.

'I don't know how,' she continued, 'but you'll pay for what you did to him. You'll pay. I promise you.'

She walked towards the door.

'Wait,' said Chrissie. 'Where are you going? Anna, please . . .'

They say you can choose your friends, but you can't choose your family. So when something happens and the bonds of friendship shatter into a hundred lethal pieces you have nobody to blame but yourself. The very first time she met Chrissie Morton she knew she was a bitch and yet she didn't listen to her instincts. It sickened her to think of the things she had overlooked. Why? What was so special about Chrissie?

You choose your friends. Just like you choose your enemies.

Fourteen

Anna left her bridesmaid dress hanging on the back of the bathroom door and threw her overnight things in a bag, wiping her tears away angrily before slamming the door behind her with such force that she made herself jump. She had to drive to the Wiltshire house to collect her laptop and the rest of her clothes. Then she could put enough distance between herself and her poisonous best friend to ensure that she never had to feel this way again. Halfway down the twisting country lane she needed to stop because she thought she was going to be sick, but nothing came up so she parked for a while as the morning sun grew stronger and the day started to get really hot. She felt very tired. If she closed her eyes she could imagine that she was back in her hotel room an hour or so previously and that everything was still okay. Then she panicked because she thought that Chrissie might be trying to come after her and she abruptly started the car again and carried on.

She reached the house and managed to retrieve her belongings without bumping into anyone and was about to make a clean exit when she remembered that she had stashed her boots in the cupboard under the kitchen stairs.

Leave them.

It was still early, the caterers would only just be unpacking, so she could slip in and out before anybody noticed her and started asking where they should stack the canapé trays.

She raced to the kitchen and opened the cupboard, snatching up her favourite brown leather boots and allowing herself a moment's relief. It was short-lived.

'Good morning!' There was no escaping Ben. He grabbed Anna's waist and spun her around to face him, sounding as happy as any bridegroom ever had. 'What a great day to get married.' He tried to spin her again, like a dance, but she stiffly resisted and he realized that she was upset.

'Anna? What is it? What's wrong, gorgeous?'

'Don't call me gorgeous,' she snapped. 'You shouldn't say things that you don't mean. Why does everybody around here have to lie?'

Chrissie would break his heart. She didn't know how and she didn't know when but she had no doubt that it would happen. 'You deserve each other,' she said, but she didn't mean it.

'You need to calm down,' he said.

'Who are you to tell me what I need to do?'

'I'm your friend.' He grabbed her wrist and stopped her from leaving. A sob caught in her throat and her face contorted with the effort of keeping it down there.

'It's nothing,' she said. 'I have to go. Please let me go.'

'Is it Chrissie?' he said. 'What's she done now?'

'You don't know Chrissie like I do,' said Anna impulsively. 'If you marry her today you'll be tying yourself to her forever and she'll find a way to ruin your life. That's what she does. She ruins lives. Don't marry her.'

Even as she spoke out Anna realized that she was trying to wreck Chrissie's chances of happiness. It made her feel ugly. If she tore Chrissie's day apart, if she spoilt her future, wouldn't that make her no better than Chrissie?

'But I love her,' said Ben. 'I mean, yeah, I do. I think I do. And besides . . .' he gestured at the mounting chaos around them, the caterers bustling around in their smart white uniforms, the bar staff polishing glasses in their contrasting black. Through the door they could see people carrying silver chairs across the lawn past the kitchen garden. 'You girls,' he said. 'So emotional. Why pick today of all days to have one of your little catfights? Is Chrissie okay?'

'She's fine,' said Anna. 'Chrissie is always fine. Haven't you noticed?'

'Do you know where the people from the flower place are supposed to set up base camp?'

'It's your house, Ben,' she said. 'It's your wedding. It's your life. What's it got to do with me?' And with that she left.

It was a miracle she didn't have an accident. Her eyes were on the road but behind them her mind was churning. When she thought of how horrendously she had treated her father in the wake of his decision to leave Clareville she felt ill. It hadn't been his decision at all. If only he'd told her. Come to think of it, why hadn't he told her? She was so agitated that when she pulled up a couple of hours later outside her mum and dad's house she blinked in defeated surprise as she hadn't consciously decided to pay them a visit.

She used her key without really thinking and found her mum out in the garden wearing a big sunhat and deadheading the roses. There was no sign of her father; he was probably asleep.

'What a lovely surprise,' said her mum, putting down

262

her secateurs. For a moment she was blinded by the sun but as she walked closer her smile faded. Anna was a mess. All those tears had left her face puffy and weakened. She saw her mum's gaze flick subconsciously up to the bedroom where her father would be sleeping. 'What's happened?'

'Chrissie Morton told me,' she started, 'she told me what really happened at Clareville.' Her mum sighed and took off her hat so that she could wipe the hair from her damp forehead. Anna always thought she looked more like her dad, but there in the garden with the sunlight catching the sudden sadness in her mum's face and picking out the auburn glints in her hair she thought she caught a glimpse of how she would look in twenty years' time. 'You knew,' she said, 'didn't you?'

Her mum nodded.

'Why didn't you tell me? God, why on earth didn't you tell me?'

'Your father didn't want you to know.'

'Why not? You let me stamp my feet and make all that fuss. I was horrible. I hated him,' said Anna. 'And I'm so scared that's all he will remember, that I hated him.'

'Oh Anna.' Her mum reached out and caught her in a hug. Anna leant her weary head on her mum's shoulder and inhaled grass and roses. 'You never really hated him. Don't you think he knows that? He'll remember bedtime stories and camping holidays and looking at the stars. He'll remember you.'

'Why didn't you tell me?' she repeated.

'Because your father thought that you might believe Chrissie.'

Anna pulled away sharply. 'What?'

'She was your best friend, we were your parents. You were absolutely besotted with her. She could do no wrong, whereas we . . . well, we could barely do anything right.'

'I would never . . .' said Anna, but her voice trailed off because she could remember thinking that Chrissie was the only one who understood her. How could she unequivocally state that she would have put that aside and stood with her parents against her? 'I'm sorry,' she said. 'I really am so sorry.'

'He knows that.'

She couldn't go back to work at the *Herald*. Of course she couldn't. She would sooner build her career from nothing than build on the cracked foundations of a ruined friendship. She sent a brief email to Lionel Sloane, thought briefly of sending one to Mac but decided against it, and she never went back. She kissed the prospect of a reference goodbye and started to hunt around for an alternative job.

She never heard from Chrissie, not a single word.

The months that followed were frustrating and lonely. All the decent graduate opportunities had been snatched up while she was busy focusing all her energy on the Morton Group. Anna was forced to go back to her old job teaching French to teenagers while simultaneously trying to get the odd freelance piece published here and there with varying degrees of success. Finally, and against her better judgement, she took an assistant's position at a radio news agency that entailed very little in the way of journalism and a lot in the way of running around after her new boss and making him feel important.

She thought about Chrissie every day and pondered the paradox of hating someone and missing them at the same time. For a while she had fantasies of getting even some-how, of how and when she would get her own back, of how she would wipe the smile from Chrissie's perfect face once and for all. But after a while she stopped because it just didn't make her feel as good as she thought it would.

Once more Anna's dreams had come to nothing, so once more she stopped dreaming altogether.

Fifteen

More than two years later Anna missed her dreams. She missed many things.

Sometimes her self-doubt would consume her and she would cry for a few minutes before making herself a cup of tea or pouring a glass of wine and counting her blessings. She was still working as an assistant for the radio news agency and the job turned out to be every bit as frustrating as she had feared. But it was a job, a good one.

Perhaps her dreams had always been too big. Perhaps that was the problem. Perhaps that had always been the problem. No wonder she was always disappointed.

Once she would have thought covering a party political conference for a national news agency sounded impossibly glamorous. She would have pictured herself trailing after party leaders, chasing down policy stories, and breaking big news as fast as the world turned beneath her feet. She would not have imagined this: waking up in her hotel room on the first day at conference shortly before dawn, terrified that her career was already irredeemably average.

What was she doing with her life?

She was not trailing after party leaders and chasing down stories, but instead trailing after a boss who seemed intent on getting pissed and shagging as many junior policy shoppers as he could fit into his diary. She filed thirty-second updates and one-page briefings on his behalf, anything else would be surplus to the requirements, and she felt like a middle-man, passing press releases from one place to the next largely unchanged.

No wonder she couldn't sleep.

The bed whined as she dragged herself from it and walked over to pull back the daisy-strewn curtains in the sweet little bed and breakfast she had found within her budget. Her boss was staying down the road and she was thankful about that. She peered hopefully out at the 'sea glimpses', of which the landlady had seemed so proud. It promised to be a beautiful autumn day, no wind and a sky already streaked to the east with the colour of a ripe Victoria plum.

With every new day Anna tried to stay positive.

This English seaside town in which she found herself had been dragged from its out-of-season slumber and was humming round the clock with the chatter of a hundred parties, meetings and focus groups, any of which she could probably charm her way into with her press pass and her way with words.

So last night why had she ordered a takeaway pizza and holed up in her room with a good book?

The beach at dawn was deserted, the sea washed gold by the slowly gathering light. She stripped off her clothes, down to the bathing suit beneath the layers, and breathed in the salty tang. It looked cold. But her father had taught her that autumn was the best time for sea-swimming, that the sea would retain the heat of the summer in a way that the air and the ground could not. He liked to swim out until he could no longer touch the bottom. She would swim with him and learnt how to overcome her dread of what might lurk in the dark spaces beneath her paddling feet.

'You should never fear the unknown,' he said. 'There's a fifty-fifty chance it might be wonderful.'

This was something she thought about when she saw him now. Lost somewhere mysterious within his own head. Who could say that it was not wonderful there? She didn't know. Nobody did. Not for sure.

The first few steps into the water took her breath away, but as the waves cascaded over her hips and then shoulders she thought that she could feel the warmth of the summer after all.

As soon as she could she kicked out hard and swam until her breath came in steady pants and her legs started to ache. Then she turned back, treading water for a while. She thought about her job. It was a decent enough company: safe, established, reliable. It was a line on a résumé for most, but a life's work for many. The trick, someone there told her, was to move on before you became a part of the furniture, otherwise you'd get stuck. And two years was starting to feel like about half a year too long. It was not her dream. She had to find a better job. It was that simple. Do not fear the unknown.

Anna was about to wade into shore when she saw a man kicking curiously at the small pile of clothes she had left on the beach. He looked out at the water and she instinctively ducked her head beneath the surface as if she was doing something wrong. When she resurfaced he was walking away.

Quickly she clambered out through the surf, dried herself as best she could, and dressed, squeezing her damp feet back into her shoes, sand and all. The cold air made her shiver. She wanted a warm shower and a full English. Already she felt far better than she had when she woke up.

She was about to head back up the cliff when she heard someone shouting. The man she had seen earlier, this time accompanied by a policewoman, was heading towards her and looked worried.

The man who had been kicking her clothes was John Mackintosh. Mac.

Had they almost been friends once, had they gone some way towards being friends, or was that another unrealistic expectation that would have led to disappointment? Why would a brilliant man like Mac want to be friends with her?

Of all the journalists gathered here he might be the one she would least want to see. At least in her current state. She kept her gaze averted and hoped that he wouldn't be able to place her. Bedraggled and clammy was not her best look. Mac, she noticed, hadn't aged a day and looked his usual cocky, casual self.

The policewoman was slightly irritated. 'It seems you were wrong,' she said to Mac.

Mac lit a cigarette before responding. 'That hardly ever happens,' he said.

The policewoman tutted but was halfway to being charmed.

'Good morning,' said Anna, confused.

'Sorry, miss, but the gentleman here found a pile of discarded clothes on the beach and expressed concern.'

'These clothes?' said Anna, tugging at the lapel of her jacket.

'They look better on you than they did on the ground,' he said. Then he lifted his left eyebrow in recognition. 'I know you.'

'Hi, Mac.'

'Karen?'

Who was Karen? 'I'm Anna,' she said.

He shrugged. 'I was taking a wild guess.'

The policewoman drifted away, back up to the top of the cliff to marshal the protesters that would already be starting to gather in their pre-designated area some distance from the conference centre.

'Sorry,' yelled Mac, as she left. 'Overactive imagination.'

'You thought someone had walked into the water and killed themselves?' said Anna.

'Either that or been eaten by a shark.'

She wondered if her lips were turning blue.

'I remember you now,' he said. 'The *Herald*, right? A couple of years ago. You were there for about five minutes?'

'Three months,' said Anna.

'And then you did a moonlight flit.'

'Personal reasons,' she said.

'Yeah? What were they?'

'Personal.'

Neither of them said anything for a while after that and by unspoken consent they walked off the beach together and headed left on the promenade, up the cliff and back towards town.

'I had no choice,' she said eventually.

'Sorry?'

'Leaving the *Herald*. I had to. I think I was handling background on a couple of stories for you. I'm sorry. I hated to leave like that, but, well . . .'

'You had no choice?'

'Exactly. It's a long story.'

He accepted this with a lazy shrug that might have been

nothing more than a minor shoulder adjustment against the heavy strap of his bag.

'Want to tell me later over a drink? Or are you going to the Margaret Howell party?'

'No. I mean, I'm not going to the party, so yes.'

'Yes what?'

She smiled. 'Yes, please?'

They met in front of the conference centre and he said he knew a good place. A few blocks from the seafront there was a cellar bar that didn't look open but was. Mac ushered her down the stairs in front of him and though she wasn't usually keen on walking first into somewhere totally unknown she wasn't about to admit that to him. Pretending to be more confident than she was she heaved open the heavy wooden door.

She didn't see anybody she knew, nor anybody she could instantly peg as a politico or a journalist, and there was a distinct lack of the usual chattering agendas. Heads turned when they walked in but not many, most of the scattered patrons were too busy watching the young singer perched in a blue spotlight in the corner of the room with her guitar on her naked knee. The music was low enough to be unobtrusive but loud enough to give the place an atmosphere.

He asked her if she wanted a beer and she asked for a vodka and Diet Coke. He refused to order it on the grounds that it was a sissy drink so she had a beer after all.

'I'm fairly sure we'll be on our own,' he said. 'It's too much like London-on-Sea at those bars down by the conference hall. You've been to the Exeter?'

She nodded, which was half true, in that she had

delivered a package to her boss who was staying there, but she guessed that he meant the hotel bar, which would be crawling with hacks round about now and exactly where she was probably supposed to be, networking and trying to get a better job. But this was something, a one-to-one with John Mackintosh, and who knew where it would lead?

'I hate the Exeter,' he said. 'It's the same every year. Hack central. Foreigners in the isolation ward out back, natives glued to the bar, divided by media. Radio, print, TV and so on.'

'What about the internet?' she asked.

'Over by the DJ listening to the Europop with the wannabes and the women,' he said.

She laughed and sipped her beer. 'So I imagine that's where you'd be?' she said innocently, with a beat for good measure. 'With the women,' she added.

'Yeah,' he said. 'I love the tunes, can't you tell?'

There was a polite smattering of applause as the winsome blonde playing guitar finished her song, then a pause before she started another.

'She's good,' commented Anna.

'She's my girlfriend,' said Mac.

The blonde guitar player looked about seventeen years old. Anna gulped her beer, embarrassed and not sure what to say. She opened her mouth but then thought better of it. Then opened it again and said, 'She's very pretty.'

'Anna, I'm kidding,' he said, disappointed. 'Did you always take everything so literally?'

'I just didn't think it was particularly funny,' she fired back. 'Or particularly unlikely.'

'You don't like me very much, do you?'

'You're growing on me,' she said. 'So, tell me what you're doing here.'

'Same as you,' he said, 'covering the conference.'

'You're not a political reporter, you're international,' she said. 'You report to the foreign desk, that's your comfort zone.'

'Hey,' said Mac, 'I object to that. It wasn't all that comfortable in Liberia last week.'

'You know what I mean,' she said. 'You don't want to tell me. Why not? What's the bigger story? There must be one.'

He remained infuriatingly tight-lipped, smiling at her with a sarcastic half-smile she had seen him use on students and editors, but logically she knew she must be right.

'I could help you,' she said. 'Research, background, context. I know how you like things done.'

'Thanks,' he said. 'But I think I can handle it.'

'I hate my job,' she said suddenly. 'I'm asking you to consider me.'

'I don't need anyone,' he said.

'Many people like to think that,' she said, 'but it's rarely true.'

Halfway through her second beer she realized she was flirting and tried to stop. For one thing he was about fifteen years older than her, and for another it would be a terrible idea to have a one-night stand with a man she thought she would walk over hot coals to work with. It didn't matter how attractive he was starting to look, sitting there tugging on his eyebrow, his gaze blatantly dipping to the swell of her breasts from time to time.

Wait, did he just ask her a question?

'You're a swimmer?' he repeated.

She shuddered. 'No. But my dad has this crazy tradition; he has to swim in every ocean that he lays eyes on.'

'Otherwise what?'

'I'm not sure. But it's been that way ever since I was a kid, you know? I like it. It connects you to something, to all the other seas, to something else, the elements, the universe. I like it. You probably think it sounds pretty stupid.'

'I doubt anything you do is stupid,' he said.

Somehow he managed to make that sound like it wasn't a good thing.

'Tell me your story,' he said. 'You went back to work, albeit with some Mickey Mouse radio news agency, so whatever personal issues you had were not with working as a broad concept, they were Morton Group specific.' He made the word 'issues' sound like a dreadful affliction. 'I'd guess specifically Chrissie. I know you didn't go to her wedding.'

'What? How?'

'I saw the pictures.'

'And you missed me? A few hours ago you thought my name was Karen.'

He shook his head and rolled his eyes. 'Anna Page. It's been a long time, you and I,' he said, blatantly enjoying her state of bewilderment. 'You used to write these long passionate essays that were ninety-nine per cent fact and one per cent bullshit. Then we saw each other at that wedding, didn't we? Something had happened. I'm guessing it was either to do with Chrissie or a man, maybe both. Both?'

'But that means . . .'

He smiled gently, allowing her time. 'I know who you are, Anna. I've known you for a while now. You probably don't realize that you make a lasting impression. But why would I want you to know that?' He shrugged. 'Old journalist's trick.'

'What's that? Tell lies?' she said.

'Let them do all the talking.'

The guitarist played a final flourish and then fell silent. The spotlights dimmed and there was applause as light as the rain outside. The bartender started wiping down.

'Tell me about Chrissie,' said Mac.

And so she did. Because she'd had a couple of beers to melt all those cold edges, and because she was in a strange town with a man she felt undeniably drawn to, whose opinion she had trusted long before they even met. She told him about her dad getting a job teaching at Clareville, about her friendship with Chrissie. She even told him about Ben.

'I had a crush once,' he said. 'Clare Pearson. I used to let her borrow my bike whenever she wanted. Then she got engaged to a guitar player called Martin something. Never known pain like that.'

'A crush,' said Anna.

'It's a noun and a verb,' he said.

Then she told him why her father had been forced to walk away from the only career he'd ever had.

'And they took her at her word?' he said. 'Just like that?'

Anna shrugged. 'It's a prestigious school. The scandal wouldn't have been worth it. Believe me, I don't like it either. But that's the way it is. Who in their right mind would try to pick a fight with a Morton?'

'So you never thought of doing anything to make her pay?'

'Like exposing her?'

'Like suing her.'

'I looked into it,' said Anna. 'It wouldn't be worth it. She'd probably stick to her story; if I was her lawyer that's what I'd tell her to do. In slander cases the onus is on the prosecutor to disprove. And my dad . . . well, he's not exactly in a position to defend himself.'

He tapped the edge of his beer bottle softly. 'He passed away?'

She shook her head and told him the rest.

'It's a cruel disease,' she said, painfully aware of the inadequacy of her words to explain the heartache. By the time she had finished Mac was on his third beer while hers sat untouched on the table between them.

'You could go to the newspapers,' he said. 'Then the onus would be on Chrissie to refute you.'

'I know, but it seems cheap. Not enough. Plus, what about my dad? Putting him under a spotlight. He wouldn't want that. He needs dignity, whatever he can scrape together. It would be . . . I don't know, crude.'

'Here.' He handed her a paper napkin to blow her nose. She hadn't realized she was so obviously close to tears. 'How's your dad now?' he asked.

'The same, more or less. He's comfortable. It's a really nice place. I visit him a couple of times a week. Maybe he knows it's me. Sometimes I think he does and other times . . .' A vision of his happy, empty face swam unbidden into her mind's eye, swiftly replaced by another of the way he used to be when she was young. It was always the same when she thought of him, as if her mind protected her from the present reality by reminding her of the past. 'I think he likes it when I read to him,' she said.

'What do you read?'

'Non-fiction mainly,' she said. 'I can't see how we would keep track of a narrative from day to day. The newspapers. Some travel books. Political stuff.'

'You ever read him one of mine?'

'All of them.' She had sat by her father's side hour after hour reading Mac's incredible books, his journals of the civil war in Sri Lanka, some more about the South American drugs trade, and his study of the human-rights violations in Liberia. And it had helped; it had been a relief to absorb them both, for however brief a spell, in the misery of others, in tales of human tragedy. It made her feel humble. And blessed. What were the chances of being able to explain that to the author without sounding trite? 'I'm a big fan,' she said candidly, because what reporter wouldn't like to be told they were reaching people?

He brushed off her compliment. 'We should go,' he said and she noticed that apart from a young man in the corner who appeared to have fallen asleep they were the last people left in the bar.

'You feel like dropping in at the conference, make sure we haven't missed anything important?'

'You haven't,' he said.

'Still, I'd like to be sure before I go to bed.'

'Then I'll walk you back, but after that you're on your own.'

Outside it was still raining. The short walk back was necessarily brisk and the conversation was left behind in the bar. The lights from the police cars sliced through the veils of falling rain, their wheels making swishes in the puddles as they passed.

'Will I see you again?' she said before she walked beneath the brutal lighting of the conference centre.

'It would seem you and I are destined to cross paths from time to time,' he said.

It was a funny kind of answer, but then it had been that kind of night.

There was somebody knocking at the door of her room. She awoke disoriented, feeling as if she had not long been asleep. It was still dark and she scrambled for her mobile phone. Six in the morning. The knocking continued as she scrabbled around for some clothes to pull on and wondered if the T-shirt she found would cover her bum or whether she should find some knickers too.

'Hold on,' she yelled.

'I brought coffee.'

Mac.

She stopped dead in the middle of the room and enjoyed the sensation of all the fine hairs along her bare arms standing on end one after the other. Had she dreamt about him? His voice made her shiver. Knickers, definitely, and a quick sweep around her face with a wet wipe. 'What time do you call this?' she called back.

'Six a.m. or thereabouts. I checked the sea but you weren't there. Not swimming today?'

She opened the door and glowered at him. He was dressed in jeans and a dark grey shirt; he looked refreshed and she felt frumpy. 'The swim was a one-off, not a habit. I'm not some kind of maniac.'

'I have a job for you,' he said.

'I already have a job.'

'And we both know how you feel about that,' he countered. 'I want to take you up on your generous offer to help me out. Although, really, considering I'm giving you the opportunity to work with me on something like this, it's me that's helping you. I'm just saying some thanks would be appropriate. We'll think of how you can thank me later.'

'How did you find me?'

He raised both eyebrows at once, implying that the answer to the question was both obvious and confidential. He was one of the finest journalists of his generation. He had found deposed despots and disgraced politicians. Finding one woman in a small seaside town would have been a breeze.

'Come on, let's get something to eat.'

'I can't go out dressed like this!' She pulled back.

'I think you look great.'

She smiled. 'Two minutes, okay?'

'I'll give you ninety seconds.'

He took a slim black folder and passed it to her. Inside was a single sheet of A4 paper with a short list of company names.

'I'm looking for background on these companies. Memorize them, ask around. If you see a flicker of recognition, dig deep. Plus, you can Google them into oblivion. Anything you can get linking them to British politics, I'll take. Or any names, actual names, of people involved.'

'Why?' she said.

'Because I can either pay a researcher I don't trust or I can ask you to do it for free.'

'I don't mean why ask me to do it. I mean are you not going to tell me what I'm looking for?'

'Nope, can't.'

She thrust the slim folder back at him. 'Then maybe you should do your own grunt work.'

'Do you always act like this when you get what you ask for? I don't usually let anyone in on a story, let alone one this big.'

'You're not letting me in.'

'Not yet,' he said. 'I'm asking you because nobody here has a clue who you are. If I start asking questions then someone else asks some more and so on. You're subtle. I like that about you.'

She glanced back at the names and when she did her breath caught in her throat and she struggled to keep her composure.

There, somewhere near the bottom, was a name she recognized. A company set up thirteen years ago by Kendall Morton.

Imperial Idol.

'Sure,' she said. 'I'll do it. What's the pay like?'

The press enclosure was buzzing, readying itself for the party leader's speech in a few hours' time.

She found Mac drinking cold coffee by the gallery, looking down at an empty stage.

'What's up?' she said. 'Wondering if the empty stage could be used as a metaphor for something or other?'

He grimaced. 'You're a better writer than that.'

If that was true then why was she stuck working at IRN?

She knew she could be in possession of some privileged information. As soon as Mac left her room that morning she had put the name Imperial Idol into every search engine and every news archive and had yet to find anything linking the company to Kendall Morton. And if the worldwide web didn't know then surely it was likely that Mac wouldn't know either. After all, who would care about a twelve-year-old girl's dead pony? The provenance of the list was still unclear but it was a dreadful list to be on. All of the companies were cloaked in murky silence and the only time a search popped up any results was when one or another had been charged with criminal activity or blacklisted by the United Nations. Imperial Idol was keeping some pretty dishonourable company.

'I've decided I'm not speaking to you again until you tell me more about your precious list.'

'You don't think that's a little immature?'

She stuck out her tongue at him and he laughed.

'Haven't you figured it out yet?' he said.

'It's something to do with UN trade embargos,' she said. 'To Africa.'

'There's a trade embargo against Africa?' he said. 'The whole continent?' He feigned shock and she rolled her eyes.

'Fine,' she said. 'Don't tell me. But I know something.'

'What?'

'It's not a "what",' she said. 'I saw a name I know. It's a "who".'

'So who?'

'Facts are power. I think you taught me that in one of your lectures. So I suggest we trade.'

'I wish you wouldn't quote me back to me, it's very disconcerting.' He eyed her with something approaching respect. 'Okay,' he said. 'But not here.'

They bought cones of salty hot chips from Harry Ramsden's and walked along the old promenade towards the pier at Boscombe, where a dozen or so hopeful surfers braved the cold to ride the stormy swells.

They found a wooden bench and he swept it clean of drifted sand before he would let her sit down.

She threw a chip onto the sand just to watch the seagulls swoop down and screech, fighting among themselves over one lousy chip. She saw Mac grinning and was embarrassed. He was here working on an important story and she was here doing little more than taunting seagulls with fried food. They lived in different worlds.

'I like spending time with you, Anna,' he said.

She wasn't sure what she was supposed to say. It was like the opening of a joke and she waited for a punchline, but when it didn't come and she hadn't replied she started to wonder if he had said anything at all. Perhaps she had imagined it. After all, he was usually so sharp and sarcastic, why would he say something so sweet?

He wasn't watching her any more. The seagulls had dispersed and he was watching the waves rolling in.

'Tell me,' she said.

'You first.'

'No way.' It was the first time since she met him that she had the upper hand and she loved the feeling. She couldn't stop smiling. Neither of them could. He was enjoying the power shift too. And the buzz that comes with a story, an angle, a lead.

'Otherwise I'll just assume you're bluffing,' he said, 'and we can both go back to the day jobs.'

She shivered. And not just because it was cold. This was a moment in her life, she recognized that, this was one of those moments that should be cherished. She forced herself to catalogue the feel of the air on her skin, the smell of brine, the sound of the waves, and the amused look on Mac's face as he tried to figure out whether or not he could trust her. 'Tell me,' she said again.

'No. Give me a name.'

'Imperial Idol,' she said.

'And?'

'And what?' she deadpanned. 'I gave you a name.'

The smile dropped out of his face. 'This is serious stuff, Anna. You want to know? You're sure? I'm talking about civil war, Liberia, Sierra Leone. These people on my list make money by raping a country's natural resources – the timber, the diamonds – then buy arms, and sell them back to the warlords. They turn trees and stones into guns and bullets. And we know it happens, and we try to stop it, but these companies are getting very, very good at hiding, and the UN security council has to go ten rounds of resolution and ratification, and, frankly, I don't have that kind of time and I don't think the kid staring down the barrel of a gun has that kind of time either.'

When she last saw Kendall Morton he had been smiling, a happy father on the eve of his daughter's wedding. 'My God. You're sure?' she said.

'It's Morton, isn't it?' he said.

'What makes you say that?'

'He's the only powerful person you know. Those little emails he used to send you? There was a rumour doing the rounds at the *Herald* that you were his London piece.'

'Piece?'

'Of skirt.'

She grimaced.

'Mainly just in the sports department,' he added.

'Please, he's my best friend's dad.'

'Like that matters.'

There was no mistaking the pull between them now. She placed her hands in her lap to try to calm herself down but that didn't work so she sat on them instead.

'Actually, I kind of liked him,' she said. 'Not in that way, but he was decent to me, you know? I think he found it so hard to be good to Chrissie, to show her that he loved her, she was always fighting him about something or other, and it was easier just to help out her friends. He seemed . . . nice.' There was no point in trying to hide the truth; she wanted to tell him. 'Imperial Idol is the name of a company he set up about thirteen years ago.'

'Any particular reason?'

'To honour a dead horse.'

If Mac found this unusual he didn't say. 'If you think he's such a nice guy then why did you tell me?'

'It will destroy Chrissie,' she said.

'Then I think it really should be your story, don't you?' He stood up, and held out his hand. 'Come on,' he said. 'I'll help you.'

They stayed up talking until very late. Drinking excellent Californian Zinfandel that he kept in his suitcase and smoking too many cigarettes. At one point she caught sight of herself in his bathroom mirror. Her make-up had long since worn away and her hair was suffering from the cold and the damp, her pale skin was showing blatant signs of tiredness, but she liked what she saw, the bloom of excitement on her cheeks, and she couldn't wait to get back to the story, to Mac, to the wine, not knowing which one was more intoxicating.

Back in his room she sat down on the bed, leaning

against the headboard, her bare feet stretched out in front of her, cherry-red toenails a splash of colour against the crisp white hotel sheets. He was sitting in a chair by the window, the black and grey static of rain and sky behind him. He got up to refresh her glass.

'Chrissie used to tell me stories,' she told him, tipping her glass towards him, 'about her family, about him. I think I know a lot about him that might be useful. Background. I know you like a bit of background.'

'You know, nobody has ever written Morton's biography, not a good one,' said Mac.

'They should,' said Anna. 'He's got history. He made his first million by the time he was seventeen, did you know that? Advertising, marketing – he saw that the future of sales was selling empty space, selling nothing. Selling ideas, concepts, thin air. And it's made him rich.'

'It's a good idea,' said Mac. 'You should do it.'

'Do what?'

'Write a biography.'

'Me? No.'

'You said yourself that you've heard all the stories. You know the background. If not you, then who?'

'A writer,' she said.

'You're a writer.'

'I mean a proper writer. Someone like you.'

'I think,' said Mac, taking the glass from her hand and setting it down on the bedside table, 'that you're far more proper than I am.'

He leant over and kissed her on the mouth. Pizza, coffee, cigarettes and wine. And her cherry-red toes wiggled in appreciation, nerve endings jangling while she kissed him back. The flat of his hand slid down the side of her body, into the curve of her waist, and rested there as he pulled away. 'I think you're a little drunk,' he said.

'So?'

'I don't make a habit of going to bed with drunken women young enough to be my daughter,' he said.

'That's not what I heard.'

He kissed her again, entirely without urgency. His hand stayed where it was and it felt perfectly placed. She relaxed into the kiss, hardly even curious as to where this would lead them. It felt like a natural extension to their conversation, and so after they broke apart again she picked up on his suggestion without a pause.

'I think if I told Chrissie that I had decided to forgive her, she'd believe me.'

'Really?' said Mac, passing her her wine glass and taking a sip from his. 'Her ego's that big?'

Anna nodded. 'We could be friends again.'

'You'd be on the inside.'

'You think I could persuade him to talk to me?'

'I think you should try. Conference ends tomorrow and I have to go to New York, but you could go to Wiltshire and see some old friends.'

Her mind was racing with ideas. There was far too much to all of this, to her relationship with the Morton family, for one little article to do it justice. If she did a book, she could bring him down from his lofty heights, and he would drag Chrissie with him.

A father for a father.

'If she found out what I was trying to do she would do everything she could to ruin me,' said Anna.

'That's the way it goes.'

'You don't think I would be doing this for the wrong reason?' she said.

'What would that be?'

'Personal revenge.'

'Revenge is a classic,' said Mac. 'I think it's the best reason there is.'

She jumped up from the bed.

'Where are you going?'

'I want to get started,' she said. 'Get these ideas down on paper while they're still fresh, just some rough notes.' Then she paused. 'Oh.' A few moments ago they had been kissing, and she had been enjoying it. Was she being rude? 'You don't mind, do you?'

He shook his head. 'Go on. I'll see you later. We'll talk some more.'

She kissed him once more and then she left.

The thought of contacting Chrissie again made her excited. They wouldn't really be friends. How could they after everything that had happened? But still, she wondered how she was, what she was up to, if she was still outrageously selfish and shamelessly funny. Not because she cared, but because she had a job to do. That's why she was excited. That's all.

A moment later she fired up her laptop.

Dear Chrissie . . .

Sixteen

Chrissie never thought that she would miss Tokyo as much as she did. The revelation came somewhere in the early hours of the morning, dancing with a stranger in Ageha nightclub. She had been dancing solidly for an hour, perhaps more; her clothes were clinging to her body with a thin layer of sweat. Her make-up was a mere memory. Her throat was crying out for a cold drink of water but she ignored it. She felt as if she was hearing the music with her entire being, not just her ears. Then, for a moment, she could hear nothing, only her own breath, her own heartbeat, the sound of young and vital blood pumping through her veins. She stopped. Nobody stared at her, static in the midst of a gyrating crowd, because this was Japan, where nobody ever stared at anything. You could shoot your own puppy in the middle of the street and people would still bow when they excused themselves to walk around the mess.

The man whose name she did not know continued to dance, smiling at her, wondering what drugs she was on (if he'd asked she would have told him: none), and Chrissie tipped her head towards the rainbow of lights above, but it didn't stop the tears from sliding down her face.

She was happier than she had been in years.

In a rush of sound the music was within her once more and she threw out her arms and started to laugh.

Ben who?

Their wedding day had been something of a disaster. She looked atrocious, for a start; a few thousand pounds' worth of dress and shoes and jewels could not disguise how tired and anxious she was, although Ben – superficially charming as ever – said she had never looked more beautiful. This was to be the first of many lies that passed between them in the months to come. Kendall walked her down the aisle, the cellist played sweetly, the weather was glorious, everybody said and did exactly what they were supposed to do. The house looked the best it ever had, before or since. The ribbon-trailing urchins were an unbelievably cute touch. But Anna wasn't there. And Ben missed her the most.

'What do you mean, gone?' he'd asked.

'We had a fight.'

'What about?' he'd pressed.

She had said the first thing that came to mind. 'About you.'

After a few short months in Wiltshire Chrissie knew two things for sure. She didn't like the country and she didn't like her husband much either. He was handsome and attentive and kind and he bored her to tears. Literally.

Soon she was dashing up to Dovehouse Street for weekends, inventing girlfriends to go shopping with, developing a sudden and fictitious closeness with her mother so that she could escape to the gritty, grimy city and breathe. She simply wasn't cut out to be a wife. Being a wife meant being with the same person all the time. It meant being half of something, but something that didn't make her feel whole. When she was with him she didn't feel settled and safe, she felt itchy and panicked.

'I'll come up with you,' said Ben, when she arranged another visit to London, this time to visit the new baby of an old friend, both of whom were pure fabrication, conjured to allow her three days of space from her increasingly claustrophobic life. So she created a cancellation – 'a touch of jaundice, she said, but I don't think it's serious' – and booked a flight to Japan.

Lying had always come easily to Chrissie. She used to think it was a talent that would take her far in life; now she wondered if it wasn't one of the reasons she felt like she was getting nowhere. Yet she seemed unable to stop.

'Do you want to come to Tokyo?' she asked, knowing that he wouldn't. He didn't like the culture, or the weather, or his father-in-law. She suspected that Kendall terrified him, as if he could see straight past Ben's lack of ambition to the work-shy pretty boy she had discovered him to be.

Once she was in Japan it was easy to extend her week-long stay to a month.

Here, in the enormous joyful crowd at Ageha, she wished that she could stay forever.

On a whim she bought a table in the VIP room and invited the six people nearest to her to join her. The stiffness of her rusty Japanese caused one of the girls to giggle and Chrissie decided that girl would become her new best friend.

The girl asked her what she was doing in Tokyo and Chrissie just laughed and laughed, as if it was the funniest question in the world.

Because she had never known what she was doing. It hardly mattered where she happened to be.

Once they were installed in the Loft with its stellar views and mellow sound system, Chrissie ordered two bottles of champagne for the table and a round of shots. She tipped the alcohol down her throat before the glass had even touched down on the table. Outside the city skyline winked at her and reminded her of just how much distance there was between her and her husband. Happy days. Perhaps she could consider a permanent move.

A little while and most of the second bottle later they were joined by a group of very funny teenage girls who were bemoaning the state of the Roppongi Hills development. Once, they said, a pretty young thing was practically guaranteed to meet a man with money, a jolly *gaijan*. Now all the brokers and hedge-fund managers had scuttled back to London or New York or Sydney and the Hills Tribe were having to pawn their Hermès Birkin bags and various other gifts to maintain the lifestyle to which they had become accustomed. They weren't hookers, they said, just girlfriends. Unless the money was exceptional.

One of the girls started telling a story about a particular *gaijan* – and as soon as she started the others tittered in recognition – who only wanted to sleep with virgins. What made the story funny was that after a few months the exact same girl could revisit him and pass herself off as someone new. 'Fucking *gaijan*,' she said, 'they think we all look the same anyway.'

'But rich though?' said Chrissie's new best friend.

The girl telling the story tapped her ears, where a pair of Bulgari diamonds glittered, diamonds that Chrissie had assumed must be fakes. 'Rich enough,' she said.

'Did you see the new dining room he's had put into his apartment?' said one girl, laughing. 'He thinks it's authentic Japanese but it looks like the inside of Onyasai restaurant on Kyodo.'

'That waterfall!' said another.

'The fish!' said two in unison.

'He has these fake goldfish made out of real gold,' explained the first girl.

But Chrissie felt sick. She knew they were talking about her father. The giggles of the teenage girls crawled over her skin. She stood up too quickly and had to grab on to the table when she felt woozy. Her new best friend cackled with laughter and Chrissie snapped at her to shut up.

She walked back into the main club, thinking that maybe if she danced again she might reconnect with that state of grace she had felt earlier, but the boom-boom-boom of the techno music was making her head ache and the bouncing crowd full of carefree high spirits was no longer somewhere she could imagine feeling comfortable.

She wanted to go home. But none of the places that might fit that description felt right. Out of nowhere came the urge to be held in Ben's undemanding arms.

How much had she had to drink anyway? She walked up to the first decent-looking man she saw and attempted to start a conversation, but her tongue felt too big for her mouth and she stumbled over the language until he suggested that they switched to English because he couldn't understand what she was saying. But then she fumbled in her mother tongue and she watched as what little interest he had in talking to her melted away with the ice in his drink, a drink that he finished too quickly so that he had an excuse to leave her. He offered to fetch one for her but she knew he wouldn't be back. A guy doesn't go to the bar if he's interested. He either waits for a waitress or goes thirsty.

The next guy that she approached didn't even try to

come up with a decent excuse; he just looked at her with undisguised repulsion and walked away.

They couldn't have been more than seventeen, those girls. One of them had been wearing a Hello Kitty backpack from the children's department.

She staggered back out onto the VIP terrace and checked her phone for a signal.

What time would it be in England? She wasn't sure. The relevant information had dropped out of her head. She had no idea what Ben might be doing no matter what time it was. It occurred to her that maybe if she paid him more attention, if she strove to be a better wife, they could have a better marriage. She resolved to try.

The phone in their house, the stupid old-fashioned thing that she never used and hated the sight of, rang out. She tried his mobile. Nothing.

Then she called Rev, her old lover, because that's what she always used to do when she was feeling lost and lonely in Tokyo.

Seventeen

The Wiltshire house looked exactly as it had when Anna last saw it three years ago. What had happened to all those ambitious plans for renovation? Ben's family home (now Ben and Chrissie's, of course, imagine that) was dying on its feet. The old dry fountain in the driveway was thick with moss and dead leaves covered the mosaic at the bottom. The mortar between the honey-coloured stones had crumbled so badly that in some places the walls looked as if they would give way with a decent shove. The trees that framed the frontage were unkempt and stark naked. She could see neither curtains nor any lights, which gave the impression that the house was deserted but for the same battered Land Rover parked on the gravel. She pulled the Volvo up next to it thinking that she hadn't changed her car so why should they?

What had she expected?

She turned off her engine and watched the rain stream down her car windows, avoiding taking the few short steps to the front door. She needed to convince Chrissie that they could be friends again, close enough to regain Chrissie's trust and to renew her acquaintance with Kendall. The truth was that it was the thought of restored friendship and not the thought of revenge that eventually propelled her out of the car and into the rain, up the steps until she was banging on the front door with one hand and pushing wet hair from her face with the other.

Three years was a long time. They used to speak to each other every day. Was Chrissie as apprehensive as she was?

She heard footsteps coming from within the house and braced herself to see her old friend, not knowing whether she would want to embrace her or slap her, but curious to find out how she would feel. She heard the sound of sheep coming from somewhere beyond the house and wondered how Chrissie coped so far from civilization.

The door opened. Warm air flooded out, bringing with it the smell of something that couldn't possibly be home-baked bread, could it? Ben stood there in front of her, smiling, hustling her in from the rain with a single touch, welcoming her to his home with a few jovial words that passed her by. She felt herself spiralling helplessly into the vortex of his presence once more. Ben.

Ben.

Not still after all this time surely?

She had been so focused on Chrissie, and on Kendall, on the job she was here to do, that she had barely thought of Ben at all. And yet now here he was in front of her talking about things in the oven (that delicious smell) and acting as if it had been weeks, not years, since she had so abruptly severed their friendship.

'Shame about the weather,' he said. 'How was the traffic?'

She lurched through a few sentences about the rain and the drive and how she was quite well thank you, and wished that she could think of something more meaning-ful to say, something witty, even something flirty would do, but instead she was confused by the surge of hyper-awareness that meant she was self-conscious and slowly winding up so tightly that soon she wouldn't be able to speak at all.

'You look great,' he said. 'I mean, you know, you look well.'

'You too.' Where was she? Where was Chrissie? Her fingers curled around the packet of cigarettes in her bag and her eyes flicked around for traces of her old friend.

'How've you been?' he said.

He looked different. The same of course, but different. His hair was a little longer and still looked as though it would be impossibly soft to the touch; he was clean-shaven and as rosy-cheeked as a farm boy. He could no longer be described as lean, but had some way to go before fat. It was easier than ever to see the resemblance to his father and the man he would one day become. The thought of that man growing old beside Chrissie was still something she struggled with.

'Where's your wife?' said Anna, trying out the word for the first time and feeling a sharp pain quickening somewhere in the region of her heart.

He looked embarrassed. 'I'm sure she'll be back any second,' he said.

He made her a very good cup of coffee and allowed her to chain-smoke without stepping out of the house into the rain, even though the search for something to use as an ashtray made it obvious that nobody who lived here had the habit. She kicked off her shoes and made herself comfortable, surprised at how easy it was to do so. He wouldn't sit down, though, and his skittishness started to irritate her.

'Is something wrong?'

'Wrong? No.'

'It's just that's the fourth time you've checked the oven in about fifteen minutes. I was wondering how you'll avoid eye contact when whatever's doing in there is done.'

'I'm sorry,' he said. 'I suppose I'm nervous.'

'Why?'

'Why do you think?'

'I honestly have no idea.'

He twisted up the tea towel between his hands, one way and then the other then back again until she thought she might scream. But then he slapped it down on the kitchen counter with a crack. 'Christ, Anna, it's been three years and I still wonder what might have happened if I'd run after you. When she told me.'

'When she told you what?'

'When she told me how you felt about me.'

'Excuse me?'

'Chrissie told me. The day of the wedding. She told me why you disappeared.'

The rain slowed to a gentle patter and she walked over to the battered old French windows leading to the quaint little kitchen garden and pushed them open so that she could light yet another cigarette without completely smoking out the room. 'What did she say?' Already she could tell that it had not been the truth.

Ben untwisted the tea towel, folding it into four, then unfolding it, until she wanted to snatch it from his hand.

'What did she say?' she repeated.

'She said that you were . . . you know . . . in love with me,' he said. 'That it would be too painful for you.'

His eyes met hers and she held his gaze knowing that he was far more embarrassed than she was.

'But you know what?' he said.

'What?'

'While she was telling me, I kept thinking how would I feel if it was *your* wedding day, if I was having to watch you devote your life to another man and pretend to be happy about it, pretend to be happy for you.' He walked across to join her at the open doorway, his eyes still fixed on hers, and she was reminded how dark and sad they could be. 'Because I'd be pretending, Anna.' He took the cigarette out of her hand and flicked it into the garden where it fell into a puddle with a small hiss, soaked up rainwater and fell apart. 'I think maybe I should stop pretending, don't you?'

He leant over and kissed her gently on the mouth. His lips were warm and dry and a dart of heat and shock whizzed through her. She kissed him back, her arms hanging limply by her sides, lifting herself on her toes so that her lips met his more comfortably, and they stayed like that, joined, until she lost her balance.

'It really is good to see you,' he whispered, touching his finger to her bottom lip.

'Don't,' she murmured. 'Ben, come on, don't.'

The rain stopped and almost immediately a hopeful bird trilled into the dripping dampness outside. They stared at each other. She could still feel the warmth of his lips on hers, like an echo, and when she drew in a deep steadying breath there was the new and unfamiliar smell of him, not altogether pleasant and nothing like the sexy mixed-up scent of Mac.

And then they both caught the bitter scent of burning flour and in a flurry of tea towels and smoking ovens the moment was saved from being more awkward than it already was. The tea towel was too thin for the job and so Ben burnt his hand in the rush to save his precious baking. He dropped the red-hot tin with a yell of pain and it clattered onto the flagstone flooring, coming dangerously close to one of Anna's bare feet.

She squealed and hopped away, watching him from a distance as he chased the tin around the floor with a solitary floral oven glove too cumbersome to allow him to get a proper grip.

A few minutes later they were both staring mournfully at a loaf of bashed-up, overcooked bread.

'It's black,' said Ben.

'Brown-black,' said Anna. 'Like mascara.'

'It's ruined.'

'Do you still have ducks?'

'The first time I ever make bread and it's a complete disaster. I won't be trying that again. And it took bloody ages as well.'

She laughed.

'What's so funny?'

'I thought you'd turned into some sort of domesticated house-husband.'

'Are you disappointed?'

'Relieved, I think.'

'I told you,' he said. 'I was nervous. About seeing you again.'

If she was to succeed in getting close enough to injure Chrissie then she would need every ally she could get. And she would have to avoid complications. As far as she could tell Ben had the potential to be both an ally and a complication. Where was the harm in letting him continue to think whatever he liked?

They both turned at the sound of the front door slamming. Chrissie was home.

'I'm sorry, I'm sorry, I'm sorry!' she called, the sound of her voice drawing closer with every reiteration of remorse. 'I'm so late. The traffic!' She piled into the kitchen, throwing her coat across a chair and her bag on the table, then she lifted her nose into the air and sniffed. 'Has somebody been smoking?'

'I burnt something,' said Ben, shooting a glance at Anna.

'Me,' said Anna. 'I've been smoking.'

A look passed between Chrissie and Ben.

'It doesn't matter,' said Chrissie, waving away whatever protest she might have liked to make. She pushed open the other French window before she moved to embrace her old friend. 'It's good to see you,' she said. 'How are you? We missed you, didn't we, Benny?'

'We did,' he said.

There was a gentle pause until Chrissie and Anna turned at the exact same moment to look pointedly at Ben, who folded under the pressure. 'I'll leave you ladies to chat,' he said.

'Wine? I bought a cake,' said Chrissie. 'Shall I open a bottle of champagne?'

'What are we celebrating?'

'Us. You and me. Back together again.'

'You make us sound like a couple,' said Anna. 'What makes you think I'm here to get back together?'

'Aren't you?'

Anna felt like lighting another cigarette but she didn't. 'A glass of wine, then,' she said. 'But not champagne, not today.'

The wine poured, the two women sat at either end of a faded Liberty sofa.

'You told Ben I was in love with him,' said Anna.

'I had to tell him something, didn't I? Isn't the best lie always one that's closest to the truth?'

'And you'd know everything there is to know about lying, I suppose.'

'Christ! Did you come here just to make me feel like shit? Because if you did you're wasting your time. I don't need outside help to feel like shit these days.'

'Trouble in paradise?'

'Do you care?'

'Not really.'

'So why are you here?'

After more late-night discussions with Mac, Anna had concluded that for all her egocentricity Chrissie might be suspicious if she suddenly turned up pretending that all was forgiven. It was unrealistic. Far better to approach this with a set of demands. It should be hard, but not too hard. More like walking over gravel than over broken glass.

Chrissie swirled her wine and then knocked it back. 'I don't know if there's anything I can do, anything you need, but . . .'

'Are you offering me money?' said Anna, aghast.

'Money, or help of some kind, I don't know.'

'I don't want your money.'

'Then what do you want?' pleaded Chrissie. 'I really am sorry, I think you know that, and I will say so a thousand times but it's not going to change anything.'

'Honestly?' said Anna. 'I want to be friends again.'

'What?' said Chrissie.

'I know it's probably wrong, but I do. I've missed you. All the things that have happened these last few years, tiny

things, things that wouldn't be funny or interesting to anyone else, I've wanted to tell you. I've picked up the phone
to call you but I've got this cold river of hate for you deep
down inside me, in my blood, like poison, and I can't get
it out of me. I thought if I came here, if you made amends
somehow ... I don't know. It was stupid.' The words
came easily, of course they came easily: they were the
truth.

'I've missed you too, Anna, so much.' Chrissie's eyes
grew moist. 'So what now?' she said. 'Is there a way past
this?'

'Maybe,' said Anna. 'There's a couple of things I want
you to do.'

'Just a couple?' she quipped.

'Are we doing this or not?'

'Yes, sorry, yes, what do you want?'

'I think it would be appropriate for you to make some
kind of donation to an Alzheimer's charity. I don't know
quite how it works when you have money, if indeed you
have any of your own, but perhaps you could speak to
your father. There are some wonderful places doing very
good work and money like yours, well, it could really make
a difference.'

'Oh,' said Chrissie and she smiled unexpectedly. 'But I
already did that.'

'You have?'

'I had to. As soon as you told me, of course I had to,'
she said. She named a well-respected research charity and
a figure far beyond generous. 'Of course, if there's somewhere else you'd prefer . . .'

Anna stared at her, speechless.

'What? I can show you the paperwork if you don't

believe me. I love charity. Plus, my financial adviser tells me it's extremely tax efficient.'

'I'm, well, surprised, I suppose, that's all.'

'That I have a heart? It's just money, Anna. You'd do exactly the same. What's the other thing?'

Oh yes, the other thing. This one was a deal breaker. 'I want you to meet my father,' she said. 'All that guilt you talked about? The remorse? I want you to explain all of it to him. If he can forgive you, maybe I can too.'

'But isn't he . . . you know, past caring?'

'He's sick, not dead. Don't you think he deserves his apology? Is he no longer a man?'

'But it won't make any difference.'

'It will,' said Anna. 'I think it will make a difference to you. To us. It should be difficult for you, and it's right that it's difficult.'

A small crease on Chrissie's forehead that hadn't been there three years ago deepened and she looked fearful. 'And if I say no?'

'I'll tell everyone what you did,' said Anna. 'Starting with your husband and your father, and probably a few of those magazines you used to love so much too.'

'You hate those magazines.'

'They pay a lot for these kinds of real-life stories. I've been looking into it,' she lied.

'Can I think about it?'

'I suppose.' Anna pushed her wine aside. 'I'll give you half an hour. I'm going to take a walk. You'll come and find me when you've made up your mind.'

She could not be sure that Chrissie would agree. If she called her bluff then Anna wasn't sure how to proceed. But she was counting on the fact that Chrissie was still addicted to drama and the chance to be centre stage would be as irresistible as ever. Plus, she genuinely seemed to have missed her. The old spark in her eye was notably absent, awakening some long-dormant sense of concern in Anna, who instinctively wanted to know what was wrong.

'If you're looking for Ben he'll be in the old dairy,' said Chrissie. 'It's his favourite place on the estate. The crappy little building right past the orchard. You can't miss it, it's a bloody eyesore.'

Anna had a sudden urge to tell Chrissie that Ben had kissed her in this very kitchen ten minutes previously, just to see the look on her face. But she resisted. 'Half an hour,' she said. 'And Chrissie?'

Chrissie looked up from pouring her second glass of wine.

'I really did miss you. It's just hard for me, that's all.'

'I'm glad you came,' said Chrissie.

Anna avoided the orchard and the old dairy, preferring instead to wander along the east side of the house, along overgrown pathways beside which you could still very faintly see the old shadows of formal planting – box hedges and rose bushes now tangled and gnarly. She made a complete loop until she found a small gazebo overlooking the kitchen garden and sat on the wooden bench there, smelling damp earth and thyme. She pulled her mobile out of her pocket and called Mac.

'I don't care who this is but it better be life or death,' he growled.

'Not really,' she said sweetly. 'I just had a little time to kill.'

She heard the flick and flare of a lighter and his rushing inward breath.

She pictured him settling down in his bed with a cigarette, the phone cupped against the warmth of his face and yet again she was surprised to find how much she liked that image. She missed him, never mind that he was too old, too coarse, too *intelligent*.

'What's the matter?' she said. 'Did I interrupt something?'

'You want me to tell you I'm alone?'

'Well, are you?'

'Sadly, yes.'

'I'm at Chrissie's,' she said.

'How is it?'

'Okay, I think. I did my bit and now she's thinking about it, but I'm pretty sure she'll say yes, she's just being theatrical.'

'You think she might guess you have an ulterior motive?'

'I don't think so, no. She seems lonely actually. It would be easy to get stuck into the wine, have a laugh, and forget all about the past. Just for one night.'

'That's a bad idea,' he said. 'Seriously. It's not about the past any more, it's about the future. Your future, the future of Kendall Morton. It's about nine-year-old boys with guns in their hands.'

'Thanks, I needed that.'

'Is *he* there?'

She grinned. Mac was funny when he acted jealous. 'He is,' she confirmed.

'You saw him? You spoke to him? And?'

'And what?'

'You still in love with him?'

'That's a bit personal, don't you think?'

'A bit, I suppose,' he conceded.

'I don't know,' she said honestly. 'He . . . kissed me.'

'Anna,' said Mac, 'you're breaking my heart. You realize now I'll have to go out tonight and find a pretty young thing to help me get over you?'

'So soon? I thought you'd hole up there with some chocolate ice cream and listen to sad songs about love. Watch old movies. Cry.'

'I'll wait until you come and visit, then we can do that together,' said Mac. 'I'm guessing that's your idea of a good time.'

It had started to spit with rain again but the clematis rambling over the gazebo kept her mostly dry. 'She's changed,' said Anna. 'Chrissie, she's not the same as she was.'

'People don't change,' said Mac. 'Not really.'

'I used to think so,' she said. 'But now I'm not so sure.'

Eighteen

Chrissie took the bottle of wine upstairs to help her think. From the window of the lavender bedroom she could see Anna talking on the phone out in the garden. To her mother probably. Perhaps they concocted this humiliating little plan together. Let's get Chrissie out of her comfort zone and condemn her. Wasn't that the purpose of this undertaking? It wasn't about atonement, it was about disgrace. Besides which, wasn't it cruel? From what Chrissie knew about Alzheimer's he wouldn't even know she was there, let alone care that she came to apologize. It was just plain spiteful.

Of all the things she had taught Anna it would seem that how to be a bitch was the one she might come to regret.

Anna was laughing at something. She couldn't hear her but judging from the way she threw back her head so that her gorgeous hair caught the traces of hopeful sunlight peeking through a rip in the clouds, it was hilarious. Some joke at her expense no doubt.

Chrissie closed her eyes and focused on the pleasant buzz that came with downing two glasses of Pinot in quick succession. Why was it that every time she saw Anna she looked happier with her lot than Chrissie did? Wasn't she supposed to have ruined her life?

She hated this bedroom. Named for some long-forgotten aunt and painted the sickening colour of Parma violets in case you didn't catch on the first time. There was an ominous dark stain on the ceiling, which she'd first caught a glimpse of when they were doing it in here on the cast-iron bed. It had sounded fun, to christen every room during the first month of marriage, but when you start noticing damp in the midst of passion it was a sign that all was not well. This room had been among the first to be tackled in her renovation proposal, but since it had become clear that Ben expected her not only to pay for the work but to actually pitch in and do it herself, and to his helplessly rustic taste, progress had stalled at the drawing-board stage.

Often she wondered if life might have been a whole lot more enjoyable if she'd just gone out to work like her father had wanted her to. Look at Anna.

How stupid she had been to look forward to seeing her. A couple of hours ago she could have almost torn her nails out with frustration, stuck behind a tractor on the single-lane road that she was forced to tackle every time she wanted to taste civilization. She had been out to buy cake and champagne. What an idiot.

She had managed to convince herself that they could be friends again. Instead she had been forced to think yet again about making things right. One mistake, that's all it was. One mindless mistake. And yet here it was, years later, spoiling her buzz.

Chrissie couldn't stop thinking how much she had missed Anna too, how many times she had wanted to share the snakes and ladders (mostly snakes) of her newly married life. She'd wanted to tell Anna about the chocolate Labrador that Ben bought her last Christmas and how she'd had to fake allergies to persuade him to get rid of it shortly after New Year's, by rubbing lemon in her eyes to make them red. About the arguments they'd had over renovating the house, so many that they'd got no further than an unplumbed en-suite off the planned master bedroom. How they still had sex but only because they didn't know what else to do with each other. She'd wanted to tell Anna, and only Anna, the first time she was tempted to sleep with someone other than her husband so that she could talk her out of it, and the first time that she went through with it so that Anna could talk her down from her lofty despair with that wonderful, quiet way she had of listening without judging. She wanted to tell Anna all of this. And if she could suck the poison out of their friendship with her own mouth then she would, gladly, because, as always seemed to be the case when Anna found her, she needed a friend.

It sounded like Anna needed her too, and the frustration at both basically wanting the same thing was immense.

Was pride a good enough reason to hold back?

Chrissie considered her options and Anna's threats. She pressed her eyes shut and tried to imagine what her father's reaction would be. She knew that it might not be the morals of her actions that upset him the most but the associated publicity, the disrepute that she would bring on his house. Clearly the man had spent far too much time in Asia.

As for Ben. Whatever. She could tell him. Perhaps it might be just the impetus they needed to get divorced.

And then she thought of speaking to that man, Anna's father. It would be a short, sharp encounter, and she'd get over it. Plus, if she took a Valium beforehand that would take the edge off.

But what if it was all for nothing? What if it was insurmountable, the challenge, the obstacle, the past itself? And Anna might decide that her friendship wasn't worth it. Of course it wasn't. Anna wasn't exiled out in the sticks as she was. Anna was in London and when she wasn't in London she was probably off on some far-flung foreign adventure, reporting back to the world, pursuing her career dreams. She had made something of her life. What would she want with a friend like Chrissie? A housewife, basically, who dreamt of nothing more than an easy resolution to the problem of her life being an endless charade. She spent the first twenty years of her life trying to be the perfect daughter for a man who couldn't seem to care less, and now she seemed destined to spend the next twenty trying to be the perfect wife for a husband who felt the same.

The only things she ever seemed to make in her life were mistakes.

Outside, Anna had finished her phone call. Chrissie went downstairs, pushed her feet into a pair of Wellington boots and met her as she rounded the hedge between the east lawn and the kitchen garden.

'Fine,' she said.

'You'll do it?'

'It seems fair.'

'Okay,' said Anna. 'So I'll expect you on Friday. I'll send you the address.'

Chrissie nodded. 'Friday,' she said. 'Let me walk you back to your car.'

As they headed for the driveway around the side of the house Ben came running across the lawn. 'You're not leaving?' he said. 'I thought you'd be staying over. I wanted to show you the dairy. I'm turning it into a micro-brewery.

Real ale. All organic. The market for that kind of thing is massive. Massive.'

Without meaning to, Anna caught Chrissie's eye and the pair of them did a synchronized eye-roll, too subtle and sly to be caught by anyone but them.

A flicker of suppressed laughter floated across Anna's face and Chrissie tried to coax it from her. 'Massive,' she echoed.

Ben hesitated, sensing some joke that he was a part of but not party to.

'I have to get back,' said Anna.

'We'll see you soon though?'

'Maybe,' she said.

They reached her car and there was an awkward moment as they all stood there waiting for something, but they weren't sure what. A hug, a handshake? How do you say goodbye to an old friend who hates your guts?

In the end Anna took the initiative and bestowed perfunctory kisses first on Ben's cheek and then on Chrissie's.

Together they watched her pull out of the driveway and when Ben reached over and took her hand it was surprising, but not unwelcome.

'What did the two of you talk about?' asked Chrissie.

'Nothing much,' he said. 'She was only here a few minutes before you got back. What about you two? Did you have a fight or something?'

'Why do you say that?'

'She didn't stay very long.'

'It was a flying visit,' said Chrissie. 'I'm going up to see her in London on Friday. I'll probably stay for the weekend.'

She took a deep breath and as she exhaled she let go of all the tension she had been holding onto these last three years without realizing why. She had been waiting for this. She had been waiting for Anna's return shot. A contrite confession to a man she would never see again? She was getting off lightly.

Standing outside a converted Victorian mansion block somewhere in the boondocks of south-east London the following Friday Chrissie was no longer so sure. The Valium hadn't worked out the way she wanted it to; all it had done was make her brain fuzzy and more prone to confusion than ever.

What was she doing here?

She reached out to stop Anna from walking ahead. She needed a moment to compose herself. The truth was she needed a week. 'What do you want me to say?' she asked.

'That's entirely up to you,' said Anna, and she continued walking up the long front path to the main entrance of the nursing home where her father lived.

Hardly. If it was entirely up to her then she would say nothing at all, apart from maybe to compliment the stained-glass panels in the front windows. She wondered if anyone inside knew they were reminiscent of the windows at the Ivy. Or if they'd care. She sensed she might not have a chance to mention it.

Inside it was horrendous. Oh, the building itself wasn't too awful, the grounds were really quite lovely and the furnishings were modern and comfortable, but was she supposed to just ignore the smell that got down into the back of her throat and almost made her gag? It was a combination of hospitals and canteens, both of which she avoided as a matter of principle.

She wished that she could just wait in the car; maybe

she could send Anna's dad an email or something? But she couldn't see Anna going for that. They were here to try to right a wrong. That was important, weighty, and she sensed it was not the kind of thing that could be done by text message. So here they were.

Calling this place a 'home' was so far wide of the mark that she wondered why they bothered. Homes generally didn't have grab bars in every bathroom and endless yards of dull linoleum flooring connecting all the communal areas. Homes didn't have communal areas, they just had rooms. The dining room in a home didn't seat fifty at fifteen tables or have dull knives and thick water glasses that reminded her of being at school. A home generally didn't have bright and breezy staff constantly checking the clock to see how soon they could leave this place and head back to their houses where they could probably make whatever they liked for dinner and watch whatever they chose on television, sitting on a squishy sofa with plenty of room, and then go to bed, sharing a double with somebody they loved, an alarm clock by the bedside rather than an emergency buzzer. That was a home. This place was not. It was the saddest place that Chrissie had ever seen.

Anna walked beside her with the grim determination of someone who knows exactly where they are going because they have been there many times before. They may not want to, but they go anyway.

The irrepressibly vivacious nurse on the front desk greeted Anna by name and she felt her old friend make the effort to respond in kind, but she also felt her shudder when the nurse buzzed them through a door that looked innocuous enough but closed behind them with an unsettling finality.

'He has a private room,' said Anna. 'It's one of the best ones, I think. He has a view of the garden. Not that he was ever much of a one for gardens but it was that or the road, so there's not really any comparison. Unless you like roads, I suppose, or cars maybe . . .' Her nervous prattle trailed into nothingness.

Chrissie reached out to touch her arm, hesitated, but went through with it, an awkward pat that was supposed to convey support but probably just felt patronizing and was hellishly inappropriate. 'From what I remember of your father,' she said, trying to make it better, 'he would encourage us to make our own entertainment. Use our brains.' She cringed. 'I mean, our imaginations.'

'I'm not sure how much he has left of either,' said Anna.

They came to a stop outside a dark wooden door much like all the others along this corridor except that it was open. Wordlessly they peered inside and saw him, sitting in a wing-backed chair by the window looking out at the bare branches of a cluster of sycamore trees as they rattled in the wind; a book on his lap was open but ignored.

Anna pushed ahead into the room, kissing her father and perching on the bed near where he sat, leaving a hard-backed chair for Chrissie. 'Hey, Dad, how are you?'

Chrissie crept into the room reluctantly, her feet feeling heavy, her mind pulling back with painful resistance from the first proper look at his face in more than a decade.

He was recognizable, but so old. Like the same man she remembered except aged up in stage make-up for the penultimate scene of a film, the one right before his funeral. His hair was completely white, his face was the dull grey colour of old potatoes, but what startled her most were his eyes. They were tiny islands of black lost in oceans of palest green, open and trusting as they turned to her with no note of recognition, not of the girl she had been nor even of her as a stranger in his room. It was as if she had always been there.

'This is Chrissie, Dad,' said Anna. 'A friend of mine.'

'Hello, Chrissie,' he said jovially, then turned back to his daughter, a question in his eyes.

'I'm Anna, Dad. Don't you know that by now?' She kept her tone light and teasing, reaching out to the bedside table to tidy away a few bits and pieces and perhaps to distract herself from the ugliness of the benign insult, a man denying his own daughter. 'Anything interesting outside that window, then?'

He stared at her with a curious half-smile. 'No, is there supposed to be? I keep looking but nothing ever happens.'

Anna picked up a book from his pillow. Andrew Marr. 'Have you been reading?' she asked.

'A little bit,' he said. 'At night. I'm having trouble sleeping. They have me on these pills, you see, to keep me awake. And I need to piss. All the time I need to piss and they won't let me just walk to the bathroom, oh no, I have to push this button, see?'

He held up a button, a black plastic one from a coat or a jacket, attached to nothing, just a button. 'I press it and I press it but nobody comes.'

'So what do you do?' asked Anna.

'I go to the bathroom,' he said, looking at her like she was crazy. 'Were you not listening to me? I *need* to go.'

He turned to Chrissie and she paled. This was weird shit, snaking Alice-in-Wonderland conversations, except this wasn't a story and it certainly wasn't Wonderland.

Please don't ask me anything.

'And who's this?'

'I told you, Dad, this is Chrissie. Actually, you two used to know each other. You were a teacher once, and Chrissie was one of your pupils.'

'Really?' he said, with polite interest, as if Anna had just told him that Chrissie was from Surrey and liked Italian wine.

'She has something she wants to tell you. I'll go and get us some tea. Would you like some tea?'

Chrissie's nostrils flared with alarm. *Don't leave me.*

Anna bent over her and said, gently but firmly, 'You can do it, you'll be fine.' And then she left.

Chrissie could feel small beads of sweat popping out onto her forehead and wondered if she was coming down with something. You could pick up all kinds of things in these places. That would also explain why she felt nauseous and her throat had gone all dry and scratchy.

Really, she didn't have to say anything, did she? When Anna got back she'd just say that she told him and that he commented on the shape of a cloud outside. She could make up any old thing and he wouldn't be able to refute it, would he? They could just sit here in this creepy silence and she could return his vacant smiles until his daughter came back. Job done. Would that be so hard?

He was gazing out of the window once more and seemed remarkably uninterested in her presence. She watched him. Here he was, the man that she had wronged, the source of all the guilt she had been carrying on her shoulders, the same guilt that she blamed for her tendency towards unhappiness. The truth was that she didn't know what would happen if she let that guilt go. She had been carrying it around for so long that it was a part of who she was, it was to blame for all the bad things that had happened to her. If she made this right, if karma was restored, who could she blame then for the mess that she was making of her life? Not that she blamed him, of course not, well, not really. But he didn't exactly make it hard for her, did he? He allowed himself to get into a compromising position and then when she made her allegations he didn't even fight back, not one little bit. She had been shocked at how easy it was.

And why didn't he tell her back then? Tell Anna? She supposed that she should be thankful they'd chosen not to. Yet wouldn't life have been a whole lot easier if they had? Anna would have cut her out of her life long before her wedding day and she wouldn't be sitting here now with a sense of dread, waiting for the judgement that she had managed to escape for so long.

She would have lost a friend earlier, that's all. Same result.

She was jolted from her thoughts. He had stopped looking out of the window and was staring at her. Was something sparking back there in what was left of his mind? Just as Chrissie had lived through many years during which her regret had been allowed to dig deeply and burn, he'd had the same years when hate and resentment could have grown and festered. Maybe something survived.

'Chrissie,' he said, his eyes still wide and his smile still vacant.

'That's right,' she said.

'Little missy.'

'What?'

'Do you work here?'

She shook her head, convinced that she must have imagined the lucid darkness that flitted across his time-worn face. For years she had imagined seeing him again. That time had come.

The silence stretched out between them as thin and taut as the strings on a violin. She could barely breathe in the full force of her shame. No longer just a name, a face, the father of her oldest friend, this man sitting in front of her was living, feeling flesh and the pain she had caused him was palpable.

'You won't remember,' she said, 'but years ago I did something very bad to you. I was very young. I know that's not an excuse but it's the only defence I have. It was wrong of me. Very wrong. I have lost sleep. I have lost any hope of integrity. But worst of all I have lost the only true friend I ever had.'

That was good, sort of, but it sounded hollow as it rang out into the aching empty space. How could she quantify loss to this poor man? The brief sense of excitement she had felt a few days before, seeing her old friend sitting in her kitchen, had flickered out as soon as the purpose of her visit became clear and the illusion that they could be friends once more was shattered. But that wasn't loss. Loss was what this family had faced day after day. And though she might not be responsible for his absence she was indisputably responsible for the ugly flaws running through the final years of his marvellously ordinary life.

'And so I wanted to tell you that I'm sorry, so very sorry,' she concluded, and lifted her head, wondering why she had ever thought this would be easy.

'You're sorry?'

'I am.'

'And now I forgive you?'

'Yes. I mean, if you want to, then yes, I suppose you do.'

'Okay then.'

He smiled at her with something resembling a real smile, then, as she started to cry, he shuffled to his feet, walking over and patting her on the arm, making soothing noises and eventually resting his head awkwardly on her heaving shoulder.

'I-I don't know why I'm crying,' she stammered. 'It's just been such a long time.'

'Forgive and forget,' he said. 'Forgive and forget.'

When Anna came back carrying two cups of tea and smelling of cigarettes Chrissie's eyes were discernibly pink around the edges and she was reading to him from Andrew Marr. He was gazing out of the window and if you hadn't known that he was sick you might have said that he looked blissfully content.

'Everyone okay?' said Anna.

Chrissie's chair made a horrible squeaking noise as she pushed it back and stood up, placing the book on the bedside table. 'I need a minute,' she said, clawing at the neckline of her dress which had been choking her since they first walked into this place. She had forced herself to wait until Anna was back, and now she was back and Chrissie hoped that she would never have to step inside this room ever again. 'I'll see you outside in a little while?'

'You don't want any tea?'

Chrissie shook her head. She just wanted out, out, out. 'Goodbye, Mr Page,' she said.

'Goodbye, dear.'

She waited until she stepped outside the door to break into a run, driven by her shame, blinded by her tears.

It was almost an hour before Anna came to find her. She was getting cold sitting on the bench just outside the main front door. Anna said she'd been looking for ages but it honestly hadn't occurred to Chrissie to go back inside.

She'd had almost an hour to think about what had just happened. It didn't make any difference that he was in no fit state to hear her or to properly respond, if anything that made it harder. Looking at him, seeing him destroyed like that, only reinforced how savagely she had treated him.

Anna sat on the bench beside her and lit a cigarette.

'Those things will kill you,' said Chrissie.

Anna shrugged. 'You spoke to him?'

She nodded. 'It got pretty intense in there.'

'Poor thing,' said Anna sharply. 'I imagine you'll get over it.'

That was it. She'd had enough. She'd done what she had been asked to do. 'Is it always going to be like this?' she said. 'I miss you, Anna, and I get the feeling that you miss me too. I want to be your friend, but I can't cope with sly little comments the whole time. Honestly, I'll crack up. What I did was shitty, you're right, it was criminal. But I need you to forgive me now, I need you to forgive and forget.'

Anna's head jerked up and Chrissie could see that she was struggling to hold back tears, they both were. 'That's what he always used to say, my dad, forgive and forget.'

Chrissie felt Anna's hand reach across the space between them and briefly grasp hers. It was a small gesture, so quick that she might have imagined it, but it felt like the first step on the road back.

'I want to, I really want to. I just don't know if I can,' said Anna.

'Can you try?'

Anna stared at her thoughtfully, as if trying to do so right now. Chrissie felt judged and exposed, as if she should rattle off some altruistic achievements in order to help her case.

Finally, after a silence so long it was in danger of becoming strained, Anna blinked twice and then she nodded. 'Okay.'

About time too. Chrissie was sad and repentant and everything but she didn't want to drag out this painful part of reconciliation any longer than necessary. When could they get to the fun part of being pals again?

'There's just one more thing,' said Anna.

'What?' *What now?*

'I want to interview Kendall.'

'Daddy? Why?'

'For a book I'm writing.'

'Okay, that should be easy enough.' There was nothing her father liked more than talking about himself. And what's more he had always seemed irritatingly fond of Anna.

He would be glad that they were friends again.

Nineteen

Anna took all the annual leave she had left at work and started writing her book the following week. She wasn't sure of the exact shape it would take, but she headed off to the British Library to read every article on Kendall Morton and every archive she could find. Not the famous British Library at St Pancras, where she had pretentiously spent many undergraduate hours, but the rather less glamorous branch in a north London outpost called Colindale, which held copies of every newspaper since the beginning of time and so much microfiche that she always came home with a headache that didn't leave her until after she'd had a shower and stared into the middle distance for a while.

He became her whole life. It reminded her of when she was obsessed with Ben and she would look up things about him on the internet or write down little things that he said or expressed an interest in. She wanted to become an expert in everything he thought. That's how it was with Kendall: a fascination that felt a lot like love.

Gradually she was able to piece together a comprehensive picture of his early life and his rise to prominence. A chapter on his childhood, a chapter on his first million, another on his family life, another on his move to Japan. The words that she was writing began to feel like more than an article, more than an essay, they started to feel like a part of something bigger.

'Are you sure?' she said to Mac on the phone one night. 'Are you sure that Morton is involved in the arms trade?'

'Imperial Idol is,' he said. 'Very involved. Proving the link between Morton and Imperial is up to you.'

'Any suggestions?'

'You're a clever girl, you'll figure it out. But if you want to publish you'll need more than just Chrissie saying so. You need hard evidence, paperwork, computer records, otherwise there's not a publisher on earth who'll touch your book. It needs to be bombproof.'

'Okay.'

'Use your feminine charms if you have to,' he said.

'You're giving me permission to sleep with him?' she said. She was kidding. For one thing she would never sleep with a source to get a story. For another, *eugh*.

'It's sweet that you think you need my permission.'

'I don't,' she said.

She told him about her two-hour round trip to Colindale, the amazing Chinese restaurant where she sat every day, read a newspaper and had lunch.

'Which newspaper?' he asked.

'The *Herald*,' she said. 'Don't worry, I'm not cheating on you with another broadsheet.'

Her research had just taken Anna to the point where Kendall married and started a family. From the dates of the marriage certificate and the birth certificate it was obvious that the bride had been almost four months pregnant. An accident, then, and perhaps not a happy one. Unwanted, maybe? And everyone wants to be wanted, don't they? If Chrissie had always known this then that might be one reason why she could be such a bitch. The other was that she was just extremely good at it.

She was reminded of something that Chrissie said once as a schoolgirl when Anna had asked her if she had any brothers and sisters. 'My parents decided not to have any children after they had me,' she said. 'I was enough for them.' At the time Anna thought it sounded like a typically egotistical thing for Chrissie to say, half in jest. But now she wondered if the young married Mortons had decided that one child was more than enough. A mistake they didn't intend to make again.

As a girl Anna had navigated adolescence with a permanent sense of frustration. At university she had worried that she took things too seriously, that she should be out drinking and clubbing and screwing, that by concentrating too hard she was missing out on the bigger picture. Then at City she had been torn between her education and the obligation she felt towards her parents. And lately, in her crappy little job for a mediocre news agency, she had doubted – no, not doubted – she had known that she was making steady progress down the wrong path. Nobody ever changed the world without voicing a single opinion. But this, this felt like something she was meant to do.

After stumbling through the first and second cocktail nights with Chrissie, by the third time they met up there was no mistaking that their friendship was back on familiar turf. Or at least that Chrissie was convinced it was. Anna was not so sure. The lines were blurring dangerously between faking it for the good of her book and actually being pleased that they were friends again. But it didn't matter either way. The end result was what was important, not the methods she employed to get there. So what if she enjoyed a few cocktails on the road to the truth? That didn't make her a liar.

'I miss London,' said Chrissie, sucking down her first Singapore Sling in record time and immediately ordering another. She casually slipped off her wedding ring and deposited it in her Prada clutch.

'What are you doing?' said Anna.

'Trust me, the chances of meeting any interesting men are *zero* when you wear a wedding ring. They don't even strike up conversation, let alone buy the drinks. I used to think some men were generally nice. Turns out they all just want to get you into bed, even the nice guys.'

'Why do you want to meet men?'

'You know,' said Chrissie. 'For fun. Why? Don't tell me you've finally met someone?'

Finally? The use of the word needled her. Still, she didn't feel like telling Chrissie she considered herself to be very much single. So instead she said, 'Maybe.'

'Tell me.'

'He's older. Forty something.'

Chrissie waved away any concerns. 'That's nothing. Rich, then? Must be, otherwise how would he be sleeping with a gorgeous twenty-something like yourself?'

How rich was Mac exactly? Probably very. 'He does all right for himself, I think,' she said. There was no need to tell Chrissie that so far their relationship consisted of a few kisses and a lot of flirting.

'Don't think,' said Chrissie, 'know for sure. I thought that Ben's family were bound to have squills stashed away but some prick of a great-great-uncle pissed it all up the wall a couple of generations ago and now we're all hopeless.'

'But Ben's dad . . .' said Anna.

'Ben's dad has a career. Ben, on the other hand, thinks we're going to home-brew ourselves out of a gigantic crater of debt if only he can think of the perfect label design for his beer, which, by the way, tastes of dog.'

'Don't put that on the label,' said Anna.

'No,' said Chrissie. 'Best not.'

She wasn't quite the same old Chrissie. Something had quashed that irrepressible spirit she once had, the childlike enthusiasm for every day. Now when she talked about herself there was a bitterness about her life, like somebody had squirted lemon over her particular bowl of cherries.

The thing with the wedding ring was silly. Had it really taken Chrissie all this time to realize that generally men were most comfortable in the company of other men unless there was the possibility of sex? She wondered if Chrissie had had an affair, or perhaps more than one.

'On the phone you said you had something to tell me,' said Anna, hoping that she didn't sound too eager. 'Is it about Kendall?' She could feel herself creeping safely into Chrissie's confidence; it wouldn't do to make her suspicious.

'My father remembers you,' she said. 'He'd be happy to speak to you for your book. He asked me what it was about, but I didn't know.'

'The influence of foreign ownership on worldwide media,' she said. A lie of course, but a topic she knew was close to his heart.

'Yeah,' said Chrissie. 'I told him it was something boring.'

Anna pulled a face because she didn't know if their friendship was quite secure enough to flick her the V-sign.

'So anyway,' Chrissie continued, 'how would you like to come to his sixtieth birthday? Very exclusive, very luxurious. Frankly, you'd be doing me a favour. I'd be bored stupid if it was just me and Ben trapped on a boat with nobody to talk to but each other.'

'A boat?'

'Aye, aye, captain. He asked me to invite you. So you'll come? We fly out to Tokyo next Wednesday. I'll have Fuji get in touch and arrange everything, yes?'

She was due back at work next week. She knew they wouldn't allow her any more time off. Unless she faked an illness of some kind, perhaps a minor operation?

'Yes?' prompted Chrissie.

'Yes,' said Anna firmly. 'And thank you.'

While writing to tell her employers that she would not be returning to work, not ever, she paused for thought. Can you start a letter of resignation with the phrase 'I regret to inform you' if you're almost certain that leaving will turn out to be the best thing you ever did and that you'll never regret it, not for a moment, not for as long as you live.

The following Wednesday she collected a ticket for a direct flight from the British Airways desk at Heathrow terminal five and was slightly disgusted with herself for being disappointed that it was an economy-class ticket. Business-class privileges were obviously not extended to Chrissie's friends when they were flying solo.

Chrissie had gone on ahead to spend a couple of days with her father. 'He called it "quality time",' she'd said, making air quotes. 'Do you think that's what I'm down as in his schedule?'

'Better than Daughter – brackets – Chrissie – close brackets,' she'd replied.

Chrissie always said that he loved money more than he loved her. Considering what Anna and Mac had uncovered about his ethics, or treacherous lack thereof, she was now convinced that this was true. Anna may have lost her father but at least he had never given her cause to doubt where she came in his priorities.

As soon as she had checked in she changed into a baggy jersey tracksuit, the kind that some people might wear to go to the gym but she only ever wore for travel or marathon television sessions. She rolled up her street clothes tightly and stashed them into her hand luggage.

She dithered over books or magazines in the departure lounge and in the end chose neither. She could work on the flight, or if not then watch movies and sleep. She had to be careful what she spent her money on now. A few more short weeks and she would start nibbling into her precious savings account. The book could take many more months to finish and then who knew how long to find a publisher? For the first time in her life she was being financially irresponsible and it wasn't as terrifying as she'd thought it would be. If asked, not that anyone ever did, she felt she could legitimately refer to herself as a freelance journalist.

She accepted all the cabin crew's offers of free drinks and snacks immediately after take-off then, pen and paper in hand, she got to work. She needed to finalize two sets of questions basically asking the same things. One set if he permitted her to write a book all about him, and one more subtle set in case he did not. She also needed to find a way to ask his permission without being too direct. After all, if he didn't like the idea she still intended to write the book and she didn't want him to throw her overboard before she had a chance to quiz him at all.

A few minutes later there was movement in the seat to her left. She didn't pay it much attention as she was absorbed in crafting the first of what she was sure would be many lists. She chewed the end of her pen as she considered probing him on his politics. Perhaps if she asked if he'd ever consider running for public office . . .?

Then she had a new neighbour. With a familiar voice and a familiar smell and a familiar hand that reached over and took the pen from her mouth.

'Don't chew on that,' he said. 'If you want something to put in your mouth so badly give me fifteen minutes then meet me in the bathroom.'

'Mac!' If they hadn't been strapped in she would have thrown her arms around him. As it was she settled for grasping his hand while bouncing up and down as much as her limited freedom would allow.

'You're pleased to see me,' he said, grinning.

'Despite that dreadful line, yes,' she said.

'You're not a mile-high-club fan?'

'Never had a chance to find out.'

'I make it ten hours and forty-five minutes remaining.'

'Sorry, I should have said never been tempted to try.'

'Ten hours and forty-four.'

He looked good in a cool, crisp blue shirt that she knew would be getting all crumpled and dirty sometime soon. He never stayed smart for long. She became aware of her own baggy tracksuit and inwardly cringed. She had missed him these last few weeks, but of course she would never tell him that, he was cocky enough without her compliments. She turned over her notepad so he couldn't see what she had been working on. Her scratchings and scribbles were incoherent and felt decidedly amateurish.

'You're going to Tokyo?'

'Not really,' he said. 'I've got to get back to New York, but I wanted to see you.'

'You did?'

'Here.' He passed her a plain brown A4 envelope. 'I thought you might like a little dossier on Imperial Idol. There's a guy I know, ex-Wall Street, good at getting into other people's computers. Anyway, he put this together.'

Her eyebrows shot up.

'Don't worry. I didn't mention the link to our friend. You're still the only one that ever came up with a name. It's useful information about the company. If nothing else it'll come in handy when you start to feel emotionally involved.'

'What do you mean?'

'Come on, it's your best friend's dad – you're basically a good person and you might need a reminder of the bigger picture.'

She stashed the envelope in her hand luggage. 'You could have just emailed it to me.'

'But then I wouldn't get to see how good you look in leisure wear.'

'Enough of the sarcasm, Mackintosh, what is it that you want from me? An exclusive, a co-author credit? What?'

The cabin crew were passing round wine before dinner. He got them a tiny bottle of red each and then stealthily procured two more as the trolley passed them by. The stewardess spotted him but turned a blind eye with an indulgent smile.

'That's not very nice, Anna. I don't want anything from you. At least not professionally. I do okay in that area by myself.'

'And you're flying straight back to New York?'

'A three-hour layover,' he confirmed.

'So basically you booked a seat on this flight to Tokyo just to spend time with me?'

He nodded. 'Ten hours and thirty-one minutes,' he said.

For the next hour she listened with engrossed amusement as he told her about the trouble he'd had getting his latest story together, with total focus when he gave her some tips on getting closer to Kendall without revealing her hand, and with barely concealed admiration when he told her how he'd made the decision never to work for the Morton Group again. 'How could I,' he said, 'now we know what we know?'

She liked his use of the word 'we' and wished that she could say it out loud just to roll it around her tongue and feel how good it felt.

That raffish charm he had, his way of making brash jokes and looking so pleased when she laughed at them – she realized it wasn't always confidence, sometimes it was sweetly concealed insecurity, doubt that a girl like her could enjoy spending time with an old cynic like him. He wasn't being flip or insincere with his compliments or with his talk of something more for them both. She had to face the very real possibility that he liked her.

'Whatever,' she said. 'I'm still not having sex with you in the bathroom.'

'That's okay,' he said. 'Maybe we can just, I don't know, hold hands?'

And so as the flight soared high above northern Russia, that's exactly what they did.

When they landed at Tokyo he had to move fast to make his connecting flight back to New York but he made time for a kiss that made her go weak with desire and wish she hadn't been such a tease about the mile-high club.

'Don't forget,' he said. 'Use those feminine charms.'

'You think?'

'Well, it worked on me.'

So far three people had told her that Kendall Morton's yacht, *Crystal Dawn*, was small for a reason. It was an open sports yacht, and as such was the biggest model in the world. Not small at all, then. Whatever. It seemed huge to her anyway.

'One hundred and sixty-five feet,' said the maid who led her to her cabin, echoing the captain, and the nice young man who had met her at the airport and accompanied her all the way out to Tokyo Bay, where the boat was moored for the night. Cabin? Was that the right word for such a luxurious room, complete with plasma screen and en-suite? She could have been in a boutique hotel ashore, surrounded as she was by enough rich caramels and bronze accents to make her feel instantly more sophisticated. 'Mr Morton is enjoying pre-dinner drinks outside,' said the maid, with a smile that hadn't wavered since she first met Anna from the zippy little tender that had brought her out to this floating palace.

Like his Tokyo apartment, this boat exuded Kendall Morton's love of subtle yet unabashed luxury and she was already thinking about how she would describe this toy of his in her book.

'Is Chrissie, uh, Miss Morton with him?'

The maid bowed slightly and backed away. 'Ms Morton and her husband are expected back shortly.'

Expected back? From where? She pinned her hair up to disguise its need for a good wash and blow-dry and put on the least creased thing out of her suitcase, glad that the red and black wrap dress was vaguely sexy. She wasn't here to spend time with Chrissie; she hated Chrissie. Kendall was the prize and right now he was enjoying pre-dinner drinks. So she had damn well better be thirsty.

I just hope he remembers me.

She shivered when she stepped outside, the cool air reviving her travel-weary bones. The vast deck was as luxuriously furnished as the quarters below, a semi-circle of soft seating wrapped around a white oak coffee table, and behind that was a fully stocked bar. A tuxedo-clad waiter appeared at her side with a single glass of champagne on a tray dressed with a spray of white orchids and she took the glass, glad of the opportunity to delay joining the small group of people gathered by the railings looking at the twinkling Tokyo skyline across the water, which was gradually lighting up like Christmas illuminations. Nobody noticed her, and why should they with such an impressive view to distract them? It was her nerves and not her sea legs that were in danger of defeating her. The scent of the sea and sway of the water were both barely noticeable, but the enormous birds flying en masse to roost as the sky fell dark reminded her that they were all afloat.

Seriously? Was she expected to *dupe* a business lion like Morton?

The conversation was hushed and sparse and she walked over to the group as slowly as she possibly could, trying to clutch onto the thin shred of confidence that she knew must be in there somewhere. She pushed aside the strands of hair that the gentle breeze had lifted onto her face and she opened her mouth to speak. Just 'good evening' would surely be enough.

Then the stillness of the evening was pierced by a shout of anger. It carried across the water from the small motor boat close by, which had chosen that unfortunate moment to kill its engine and coast into the side of the *Crystal Dawn*, presumably so as not to disturb the peace on board.

'You can go back to England tonight if you like!' It was Chrissie's voice and it was shrill and annoyed. 'Go on, why don't you? Piss off.'

One of the women on board giggled uncomfortably. Kendall's face darkened. Anna walked up to the group and took his arm. 'Kendall?'

He placed her immediately and he knew that they both recognized that voice across the water. She was here to save him.

'Anna Page!' His enthusiasm was surely more about distracting his guests from the continuing argument aft than a genuine delight to see her. 'Everyone, this is Anna. She's an old family friend and a rather excellent writer.'

'How nice of you to remember,' she said, and kept hold of his arm as he introduced her to the group. She was more animated and slightly louder than she might usually be – acting drunk almost – and in the flurry of introductions the overheard quarrel seemed forgotten and Chrissie and Ben were able to board at the stern unobserved, except by Anna, who caught a glimpse of Chrissie slapping away Ben's hand as he tried to help her step aboard.

'My daughter tells me you are writing a book?' said Kendall.

She nodded. 'I'd love to talk to you about it at some point,' she said, fixing him with a shy and hopeful smile.

'We have a few days,' he replied. 'Tell me, have you visited the Ryukyu Islands before?'

'I've only ever been to Tokyo,' she said.

'They are sensational,' he said. 'Best seen from the sea, of course; step a few hundred yards past the palms and the post-war concrete rebuild rather spoils the illusion of paradise.'

The small crowd laughed politely and she joined in, then listened closely as they filled out their names with a few details. She recognized two of the men as Morton executives, already subject to a footnote or two, the nearest thing that Kendall Morton had to friends. Mac had been right: she was in a unique position to a write a book, *the* book, on Kendall Morton. Which other writer could stand here so innocently overlooked yet altogether accepted by such a powerful crowd?

There was a squeal followed by the rapid tap-tap of heels on the solid walnut deck. Chrissie careered across and smothered her in an embrace, squeezing both her arms tightly. 'What do you think? Isn't she gorgeous?' She was talking about the boat. And Anna knew just what was coming. 'You know, she seems small but for an open sports yacht she's actually the biggest in the world,' said Chrissie.

'So I hear.'

'And don't you think it's sweet that Daddy named her for me?'

'What?'

'Crystal Dawn.'

'Your name is *Crystal*?' Anna clamped her lips together to stop herself from laughing but it came out of her nose instead. 'You're kidding me.'

Chrissie gave her a withering look, the sort that Anna had seen her perfecting since the day they met. 'If you'd made it to my wedding,' she said snidely, 'you'd know that already.'

'Okay, *Crystal*,' said Anna, unable to contain her mirth, knowing that it was getting on Chrissie's nerves. 'Where's Ben?'

'On his way,' she said, waving at her father and his friends. She grabbed hold of Anna's arm and pulled her close, hissing into her ear. 'I have to talk to you. It's important. Don't go anywhere.' Then she sailed across and greeted the rest of the guests, regaling them with tales of her dreadful day ashore.

Where, pray, was she expected to go, exactly? She was on this boat for the next eight days and at dawn tomorrow they would begin racing south towards the tropical Ryukyu Islands and she wouldn't get her land legs back until they got there.

She saw Ben approaching and stayed where she was, slightly separate from the rest of them, knowing that he would come across to her first and say hello, imagining that he might feel as out of his depth here as she did and that they would be useful to each other over the days ahead.

He looked pale and very tired. 'I feel like getting hideously drunk,' he said. 'Are you with me?'

'Hello.'

'Yes, hello, hello, kiss, kiss. Drinking or not?'

'Not,' she said.

'Please yourself.' He summoned one of the barmen and asked him for a large vodka rocks, which appeared in his hand before she'd even finished telling him that her flight was fine and that she was tired but fine and that yes she was impressed by the boat, small though it was.

Ben kept shooting looks towards his wife. They'd been shopping all day apparently. 'Shopping,' he said, as if it was a disease. 'She didn't even want to stop for sushi or sake, both of which are her favourite things. I think she was punishing me actually.'

'What for?'

'Being me?'

Anna cringed. 'Ouch. I was hoping this trip would be, you know, fun.'

'That's why you need a drink,' he said, beckoning to the barman to keep them coming and holding up two fingers. She didn't stop him even though she didn't intend to drink a sip. The champagne was enough. She wanted to be clear-headed in order to spot opportunities and to write up her notes every night. Besides, if Ben wanted to host some sort of self-pity party by hitting the hard liquor then he was on his own. That wasn't her idea of a good time.

She felt him tense as Chrissie headed straight for them. He turned away and she avoided looking at him. 'Come down to my cabin, Anna,' she said. 'I have to show you this dress I bought.'

'Our cabin,' corrected Ben.

'Mine,' said Chrissie. 'You're my plus one, darling. I would have thought you'd be used to that by now. Don't get too drunk, there's a good boy.' She gave him a silly little wave and dragged Anna away with her.

They went down some stairs and made more turns than seemed possible in such cramped quarters (feeling more cramped with every passing moment) until they ended up in a cabin even more luxurious than her own, with a separate dressing room and his and hers en-suites. A maid was in there emptying out the pile of shopping bags on the king-sized bed and carefully hanging up the clothes she found. Chrissie tipped her a folded thousand-yen note to leave them alone. The maid walked out backwards, bowing at the waist. Chrissie wasn't looking.

She perched at the dressing table and gazed at her reflection in the mirror, pulling back the skin at her cheekbones to smooth out imperceptible wrinkles. She picked up a hairbrush and started brushing her golden brown hair, watching herself critically, turning her face from side to side and pausing between strokes occasionally to touch her hand to some imagined flaw.

Anna waited. 'You wanted to show me something?'

'No,' said Chrissie. 'Let's just sit for a while, okay? I'm so glad you came.'

'I'm grateful to be invited,' said Anna. 'If I can get some time with your father then it could change everything. My book, I mean. I've been considering . . . how do you think he'd feel if I altered the focus slightly, the spotlight? The impact of foreign ownership is such a broad subject, don't you think?'

'Ben and I are getting a divorce.'

They had been married just over three years, little more than a heartbeat compared to her parents, the marriage she knew best. 'Are you upset?' she said.

'Do I look upset?'

Chrissie looked exactly the way she always looked: beautiful and cold. Her brown eyes were defiant.

'No,' said Anna. 'I'd say you're coping. What about Ben?'

'He doesn't know.'

So it wasn't a done deal, and Chrissie's propensity for drama and exaggeration could mean this was nothing more than a spat. 'Maybe you guys could work it out?'

Chrissie snorted. 'I don't think so.'

'It was a very quick marriage, you didn't even live together first. Maybe you need to give it a chance. Any . . . conflicts could really still be written off as teething problems.'

'I'm pregnant,' said Chrissie flatly.

'Really? I mean, are you sure?'

'I took the test three times. I'm almost three months gone. I'm starting to show, for God's sake.'

Anna walked across the room to embrace her friend in a hug that didn't really work out. Chrissie was rigid and unresponsive. For a few seconds Anna forgot that she was supposed to hate her – she wanted her so much to be happy. Forgive and forget, wasn't that what her dad had said? Perhaps she should. Revenge was for the merciless.

'Isn't this a good reason for you and Ben to try again? The perfect reason.'

Chrissie pushed her away. 'Don't you get it?'

Ben would be so happy; she just knew that he would. He would redeploy his effort ten-fold to make the marriage work. He would move back to London if that's what Chrissie wanted. It was the logical next step for any young couple. And then suddenly she realized why Chrissie was getting a divorce. Suddenly, she got it. This was Chrissie, so nothing about this situation would be logical.

'Is it his?' she said. 'The baby? Is it Ben's?'

Chrissie shook her head.

'Oh.'

'Yeah. And I've got about six months before that becomes glaringly obvious to everyone.'

'What do you mean?'

'You remember Rev?'

'The Japanese guy?'

'Korean.'

'Oh.'

'I'm fucked, aren't I?' said Chrissie.

'Well,' said Anna, 'it would seem you certainly were at least once.'

When she woke up the next day the engine whispered beneath her feet and Anna wished that she had jumped ship while she still had the chance. Now the voyage was underway she was stuck. Chrissie showed absolutely no remorse. The only time Anna saw her show anything approaching regret last night was when she had to pass on the champagne that sloshed around the yacht like rain wash, citing a detox. Other than that the forthcoming implosion of her marriage was merely one more thing she wished that she could delegate.

'What should I tell him about first?' she asked. 'The divorce or the pregnancy?'

'Have you thought about talking to your father?'

'Him? Why on earth would I talk to him?'

'You know,' said Anna. 'For advice.'

'Oh, Anna, I learnt a few things about my father's idea of a relationship that make that an even worse idea than it already is.'

'Things like what?' said Anna casually, her mind twitching into action.

'Do you know what he does for fun?'

'No, what?'

'Teenagers.'

Then there was Ben, constantly badgering Anna to have a good time, like that would solve everything. 'Let's get the jet-skis out,' he suggested. 'Come on, it'll be a laugh.'

'You go,' she said. 'I'll watch.'

'What's wrong with you? You used to be fun.'

I used to be a lot of things, she thought, but I'm learning.

She wanted to be left in peace, ostensibly to relax but really to ingratiate herself with Kendall, but their host seemed to spend most of his time playing cards in the spacious grand salon and forty-eight hours into the trip she found herself without having had so much as a single meaningful conversation.

The food and drink – western, sinful, ample – kept coming at regular intervals and the deep blue East China Sea sparkled beneath them like quicksilver as they made indecent haste towards the tropics.

'I saw some dolphins,' said Ben, and reluctantly she lifted herself from the shaded lounger where she had been pretending to sleep, but when they got to the viewing platform the dolphins had gone. She doubted they were ever really there in the first place.

'She hates me, doesn't she?' he said.

'I'm sure she doesn't.'

Standing in front of the midday sun she had to shield her eyes to see him and even then she couldn't see him properly. Instead she saw a vision of the boy he once was, hopeful and strong, with every opportunity ahead. She had taken that from him, Chrissie; she had taken from him the chance to be anything he wanted to be, by offering him false promises all wrapped up in her perfect packaging. And she had taken from Anna the only two men she had ever loved. She would never see either of them again. Her father was trapped inside a body that was failing him, and Ben was trapped inside a failing marriage.

'Perhaps you should think about leaving her,' she said tentatively.

'But I love her,' he said. 'I don't want to, of course I don't, I'm no masochist, but I do.'

She knew exactly how he felt.

Yet sometimes, when she had no idea she was being watched, Chrissie would look at Ben with utter tenderness, the same way she looked at her father, and Anna would be overwhelmed with the desire to protect her from both of them. Their love for Chrissie came with conditions and compromise. At times like that she would try to catch Chrissie's eye and make her laugh somehow, or whisper some little joke in her ear as light as sea spray, and momentarily they would be girls again, best friends as they had always been.

Remember what she did.

Chrissie and Ben were trying so hard to avoid each other that it surely wouldn't be long until one of them asked her to ask the other to pass the salt at dinner.

'Is this why you wanted me to come?' she asked Chrissie on the third night, when they danced with each other so that Chrissie didn't have to dance with her husband.

'But you're having a good time?' said Chrissie.

Later on, after a nightcap in Anna's room (green tea for Chrissie, stiff gin for Anna), she had to force Chrissie to go back to her own suite.

'But I can't sleep,' said Chrissie. 'I lie there next to him and I think about waking him up and telling him what a dreadful person I am.'

'You're not a dreadful person,' said Anna automatically. But that wasn't what she thought. Chrissie ruined everyone she came into contact with; it was just that sometimes in the middle of a joke or a moment of shared understanding it was easier to overlook her flaws than judge her for them.

Anna decided to force Kendall to get to know her better. She dressed up for dinner that evening and sat down next to the head of the table, disrupting the seating plan which had been in place since the first night. 'You don't mind, do you?' she said sweetly to the wife of one of his colleagues with whom she had swapped.

'What about me?' hissed Chrissie, who she had left stranded at the other end of the dining table with only her husband and a middle-aged businessman for dinner conversation.

'What about you?' said Anna, knowing that Chrissie would fume through dinner but forgive her over dessert.

She spent the meal discussing all the subjects that she knew Kendall liked best, letting him talk and talk and wishing that she had thought to secrete her Dictaphone under her skirt.

'You have to give me a chance to get some of this down for my book,' she said, 'and this steak is delicious.'

Kendall drank deeply from his red wine glass and poured some more, waving the waiter away so that he could do it himself. 'Tell me more about this book of yours,' he said.

'I've been thinking of narrowing the focus,' she said.

'Onto what?'

How much had he had to drink? How much was he enjoying her company? How much impact had her gentle flirting had? Would she scare him away if she moved too fast? She had only a few days left. 'Onto you,' she said, and made a face, like she expected him to be angry. 'I think what you have to say is too important to share space.'

At the far end of the table both Chrissie and Ben were watching her with something between curiosity and alarm. She tuned them out and focused all her considerable attention on the host.

'Have you ever considered running for public office?' she said.

He regarded her thoughtfully and she tried hard to project professionalism and sound judgement.

He took a cigar from the box on the table and sliced off the end in a move that she suspected might be designed to intimidate. 'You think you're the first person that ever wanted to write a book about me?' he said.

'Of course not,' she replied. His daughter trusted her, his son-in-law did too. All she wanted was for him to do the same.

'I have work to do tomorrow,' he said. 'You'll go onto the island with the others and when you get back we'll talk, yes?'

The desserts arrived, thick with cream and alcohol, and he barely took his eyes from her as he devoured it in a few mouthfuls. The way he watched her made her wonder if, despite her best efforts to appear professional, her feminine charms were working some magic after all.

*

Ben was the only man on board who wasn't invited into the salon to play cards. It was an obvious and humiliating slight but he really wasn't doing himself any favours by hanging out at the bar and steadily working his way through a bottle of vodka every night. After the card game had started he was predictably easy to find.

'You and Kendall looked very cosy tonight,' he said.

'He's interesting,' she said.

'I'm not,' said Ben. 'I'm boring. Ask Chrissie.' He waved his arm extravagantly towards the foredeck where Chrissie and some others had started watching a brand-new film on the giant plasma. He was already drunk.

'I don't think you're boring.'

He lunged towards her and she didn't have time to pull away. His face was looming down and she probably grimaced. His wet lips fell on hers and he wobbled on his bar stool so that he had to cling onto her to stay upright.

She stared at him in horror.

'Don't look at me like that,' he said.

'Like what?'

'Pity. You pity me.'

She glanced around to make sure that his clumsy pass had not been observed. It was over and he was already embarrassed. 'A bit.'

He rubbed his mouth with the back of his hand. She resisted the urge to do the same. 'I thought that was what you wanted,' he said. 'I thought you loved me.'

'I thought so too,' she said. 'But not any more.'

'Oh,' he said. Then: 'Sorry.'

'Don't worry about it.'

He was so lost that a part of her wanted to take his hand just to show him the way to a future that could hold so much hope for him. A future where he would have to forget that he was once the most popular boy in school, the one who could have everything, and figure out what it was he wanted most. From where she was standing it looked as if Ben hadn't changed at all. But she didn't love him. Perhaps she never had.

Later, under the stars, Chrissie took her aside. 'I'm telling Ben tomorrow,' she said.

'What?'

'All of it.'

'Chrissie, are you sure?'

'I thought you'd be happy,' she said viciously. 'Ben will leave me, and then he'll be free and then you can have him. Isn't that the way it should be?'

'I don't want him,' said Anna.

Finally, she felt free. And the first person that she thought of was Mac.

When they reached the island of Iriomote it was evident that four days out of the office were three days too many for Kendall, but it was his party and he'd work if he wanted to. His guests were piled into tenders and taken ashore while he remained on board with Fuji. Nobody really had any say in the matter.

Anna slathered on her factor-fifty sun lotion, pulled on a wide-brimmed hat and a pair of sunglasses, then found herself on a boat with Chrissie and Ben. It appeared that relations might have thawed a little. At least they weren't arguing. Anna could hardly look him in the eye and yet he didn't seem at all embarrassed by the memory of last night's blundering kiss.

'It's stunning,' he said, as they neared the picture-perfect tropical island.

'Once upon a time you said that about me,' said Chrissie.

'Have you got a bikini on under there?' he said, tugging at the straps of her maxi-dress. She batted his hands away and Anna could guess why. How on earth had Chrissie managed to keep her pregnancy a secret from her husband for this long?

Her mind was still turning over everything Kendall had said last night. She had stayed up late writing down what she could remember, making notes on her notes to double-check dates and facts and old quotes from other sources. She tingled with anticipation when she thought about him now. She could hardly wait to see him again.

Their small boat pulled into a shallow bay, scraping across the butter-coloured sand, and they stepped out into water that was so clear Anna could see the tiny silver-white fish nipping at her ankles. She was immediately offered a pristine towel to dry her feet, but she preferred to sink them into the soft warm sand and enjoy the connection with solid ground after four days at sea.

They were led to a charming restaurant a short distance away between the palm trees, where the plan was to have brunch on the beach and then take a jungle river cruise inland to a series of waterfalls. Across the water they could see the gleaming lines of the *Crystal Dawn*, towering above a handful of neighbouring yachts moored out at sea. They sat down at a long table and admired the bounteous feast placed in front of them one dish at a time. Fresh fruit, silken tofu, honeyed yoghurt, salads of watermint and bean sprouts, tiny pink shrimp in shredded green mango and small glasses of ice-cold sake or lime water. The restaurant was luxurious and yet rustic, crumbs which fell onto the rough-hewn mango-wood tables were swept away within moments by attentive waiting staff, but only as far as the sand beneath their feet.

'Are we still in Japan?' said Anna, as she speared a piece of papaya. This paradise seemed too far removed from the frantic modern pace of Tokyo. Butterflies danced in circles across the water and the dappled sun fell on them through the trees. Behind them a haze of steam lifted up from the jungle in the growing heat of the day and she thought she saw fish jumping in the water, prompting birds to dive in and make splashes every now and again.

'I love it here,' said Chrissie. 'When I was little my father taught me to swim in this bay. It was so shallow that it probably didn't even come past my waist, but I still thought I might drown until I got the hang of it. He kept going even though I got upset. By the end of the week I was snorkelling.'

Anna's mind spontaneously conjured an image of father and daughter together twenty years ago but she had to push it back. Father was a warmonger and daughter was a sworn enemy. That was the only way this could work.

Ben was at the other end of the table chatting with the others.

'It's like a meeting of the geek squad down there,' said Chrissie, referring to the enthusiasm everyone was showing for the various cameras and bits of kit they had all brought with them. Anna giggled like a schoolgirl.

Ben looked up and saw them watching. He smiled and lifted his glass to them.

'You two seem a little happier,' said Anna.

'I've been nice to him,' said Chrissie. 'Guilt, I suppose.'

'Maybe there's a chance that he'll forgive you.'

'What makes you think I want him to forgive me?'

Their party lingered for a long time over the tiny cups of bitter coffee that came at the end of their tropical brunch until eventually someone suggested it was time to move on. They organized themselves into three groups to travel in golf carts to the start of their jungle cruise.

At the last possible moment Chrissie announced a change of plan.

'Anna and I are going to hang out here,' she said. 'You guys go ahead.'

Chrissie's grip on her wrist was as tight as a handcuff. Ben made a token protest but he had been one of the most enthusiastic about the adventure since the start of the day and so it was clear that he wasn't about to give up on the opportunity.

'Don't worry about us,' said Chrissie. 'Honestly. Anna feels a bit sick, that's all.' She looked across for support and Anna obligingly pulled a stricken face.

'The thought of another boat . . .' she said.

'As long as you're sure,' said Ben, looking over his shoulder and seeing the first golf cart already pulling away.

'We're sure,' said Chrissie, linking her arm through Anna's and waving them off. They both watched until the carts turned a corner and were gone, then they walked back towards the restaurant.

To Anna's alarm it looked as if it was packing up for the day. 'Was all that just for us?' she said, as four waiters carried away the very table they had been sitting at.

'Probably,' said Chrissie.

Without the restaurant the beach was completely deserted. The small boats that had brought them into shore had long gone and she was alone with Chrissie. A dart of apprehension made her shudder but she brushed away her concerns.

They found a spot of cool sand beneath a low-slung palm and Chrissie made absolutely sure they were alone before peeling off her dress. Her stomach curved gently outward with such determined progress that Anna gave a small gasp of surprise.

'Is it horrid?' said Chrissie, holding both palms protectively over her little bump.

'Of course not,' said Anna. 'But it's real.'

'I told you.'

'And you're sure it's not Ben's baby?'

'Ben and I don't have that much sex,' she said frankly. 'That month we didn't have any. I was away.'

'In Tokyo?'

Chrissie nodded and had the good grace to blush. 'I never mean to cause trouble, you know,' she said. 'Things just sort of happen, and it feels like I have no control.'

'Do you love him?'

'Who? Rev? I don't think so. Besides, he wouldn't want me.'

'Why not?'

'I think he's engaged.'

Anna drew patterns in the sand with her fingertip and tried to think of something comforting to say but came up with nothing. Wasn't this kind of mess exactly what Chrissie deserved?

'My father will be furious,' said Chrissie. 'You've never seen him angry; it's not fun. I probably shouldn't even be having it. I know there was an easy way out, but I want this baby. I don't love Ben, or Rev, but I love this little thing, I love it already.'

'Everything will work out for you,' said Anna. 'It always does.'

Chrissie made a noise that sounded halfway between a snort and a sob. Then she started to laugh until her eyes were watering and she was struggling to breathe. 'Is that what you think?' she said, between gasps. 'That things work out for me? Are you mad?'

After a while she stopped laughing and there was that awkward silence that follows a bout of hysterics, punctuated only by the occasional gulp as Chrissie brought herself back under control.

'Tell me about your new man,' she said eventually, folding up her dress and putting it under her head as she lay back on the sand with her eyes closed. 'You never tell me anything any more.'

So Anna told her a little bit about Mac and then, because it made her feel good to be talking about him, she told Chrissie a little more, until she was telling her everything. How much she liked him, although she was scared of his reputation with women, how inspiring he was, how helpful, but how much fun he was at the same time. How passionate.

'And I keep thinking: this is why women always fall in love with him,' she said. 'Because he's exactly like this with all of them.'

'Maybe not.'

'But maybe so, right? I get the feeling all I'm going to get out of it is a broken heart.'

'Not if you keep it casual.'

'I'm trying,' said Anna. 'Honestly.'

'Where is he?'

'New York,' said Anna, thinking how even the sound of the city turned her on.

Chrissie's nose was turning a delicate shade of pink and so Anna unearthed her sun lotion from her bag and passed it over.

'Ugh,' said Chrissie, smearing some of it on her face. 'This stuff is like porridge. No wonder you never get a decent tan.'

'Or skin cancer,' said Anna, 'or wrinkles, or old before my time.'

'Blah blah blah,' said Chrissie.

'I missed you, you know,' said Anna, and she meant it. She could forget her agenda for a couple of hours and pretend they were friends again, just like they used to be, laughing together and talking about boys. The sun softened her desire for vengeance, if only for the afternoon, and she tried to remember how it felt to be fifteen, when you had no notion of consequence.

'After everything is settled,' said Chrissie, 'I think I'll move into Dovehouse Street. It's small, but maybe not by your standards,' she added. 'I was thinking, there's a spare room, two actually, and maybe you'd want to move in for a while? I could probably do with some help, you know, with the baby and everything, so I wouldn't expect you to pay rent. It might be fun, don't you think?'

'Maybe,' murmured Anna.

'Just think about it, okay?'

'Okay.'

'Come on, let's get in the water.'

They splashed through the shallows until they could swim and then by mutual consent they made their way over to a rocky outcrop on the west side of the bay and rested there for a while, perched on the smoothest bit of rock they could find, letting the gentle waves wash over their legs, Chrissie's brown ones and her milky pale ones. Their toenails were the exact same shade of red.

'I'm glad we're friends again,' said Chrissie. She leant over and kissed Anna on the cheek then slipped back into the water with barely a splash, like a mermaid. 'Last one back to the beach is a freak,' she said.

When they were all back on board Chrissie and Ben were conspicuously absent from that evening's dinner yet nobody mentioned it. It didn't seem appropriate with her father at the table. After dessert Anna returned to her quarters, showered quickly and then continued to work on her book until there was a knock at the door. She quickly shoved the folders under her pillows. 'Hello?'

The door opened and Fuji stood there politely asking if she'd had a good day and then launching into an itinerary of times and flights so complicated that it took her a while to realize that Fuji had gone to all this effort for her, and her alone.

'Wait,' she said. 'Start again.'

'We can get you to Okinawa in a few hours and there's a commercial flight that will take you to London with an overnight stay in Tokyo. Alternatively, you could fly via Osaka and Paris but you won't get back until the following day.'

'I'm sorry,' said Anna. 'Who told you I was leaving?'

'Chrissie. She asked me to make arrangements to get you back to London as soon as possible,' said Fuji, in her soft precise English. 'Is that not the case?'

If Chrissie wanted her gone then shortly she would be gone. What else was she supposed to do? Cling to the railings refusing to disembark?

'Let me speak to Chrissie,' said Anna. 'I'll confirm things with you first thing tomorrow, would that be okay?'

'I'm afraid that won't be possible.'

'Why?'

'Chrissie and Ben are staying on Iriomote tonight. They left some time ago.' Fuji smiled, but it went nowhere near her eyes and so she ended up looking slightly sinister. 'It will be very romantic for them. You have less than an hour. Shall I find someone to help you pack?'

She packed all by herself, struggling to keep tears of frustration at bay. She used the satellite phone to place a short call to Mac, dragging him out of an important meeting. He listened sympathetically and then he said, 'Ben must have told her that he kissed you.'

'You think?'

'In my experience women tend not to look too fondly on their husbands canoodling with their friends.'

'Canoodling?"

'It's a word.'

'You don't think she might have found out what I'm really trying to do here.'

'No,' said Mac. 'I think she's mad at you for making out with her husband.'

'He kissed me, you know. Not the other way around.'

'But it's your own fault for being so irresistible.'

She would have laughed but it didn't feel funny.

She ventured out onto the deck. Two of the men were drinking at the bar, but there was no sign of Kendall. She made enough small talk with them to ascertain that Kendall had retired for the night and she told them that she was doing the same.

As far as she could tell, Fuji was the only person who knew that she was leaving.

She gathered all her personal possessions, including her tape recorder and her notes, and crammed them into her small backpack. She left her suitcase with one of the stewards, who was readying the tender to take her to shore. They would leave in around ten minutes. Fuji was to personally escort her to the departure gate. 'Chrissie insisted on it,' she said.

All that work, for nothing. She needed to find the irrefutable link between Imperial Idol and Kendall. That would be a start. If she could prove that single fact then people would listen to her opinion.

Anna ventured downstairs to the owner's suite. The only part of the boat she hadn't seen. It was a floor below the rest of the accommodation and she knew from Chrissie's description that it had twin en-suites, twin dressing rooms, a study and a private terrace. If he was there then she would simply say that she had come to say goodbye, to thank him. He would like that.

She knocked but there was no reply.

She pushed the door, expecting it to be locked, but it opened under her touch and she was standing in the hallway to his palatial master bedroom listening to the sound of a shower running from behind a door to her left.

The glass doors that led outside to the terrace were like mirrors and she could see herself reflected against the backdrop of the sea at night and beyond that the sparse scattered lights of Iriomote, where Chrissie and Ben would be.

Would she tell him about the baby tonight? Would she tell him all of it? Or would she avoid the truth as long as she could, carrying another guilty secret with her every-where she went? Once upon a time she had wanted to be Chrissie and have everything that she had. Now she thought that Chrissie might just be the loneliest girl in the world. If you pushed people away the moment that they didn't give you exactly what you wanted then eventually you would be left with nothing at all.

There were three other doors leading off the master bedroom. The owner's study was behind the second one that she tried. She left it open so she could hear the shower and she fired up the enormous computer on his desk, determined to think clearly, trying to make the most of the opportunity. Her heart hammered in her chest and the adrenalin made her razor sharp and quick-fingered. She searched for Imperial Idol: nothing. She cleared the search history. She started to look through the desk drawers, frustrated by those she found locked. Then she went back to the computer and searched for locked files.

There were several. All password-protected.

The shower fell silent.

She rapidly turned off the computer and as she did so she spotted a small laptop on one of the shelving units. Without much forethought she threw it into her bag and left the study, stepping clear across the owner's suite in four huge strides and out through the door. She thought she heard him emerge from the bathroom just as she closed the door behind her.

Her breath came in huge anxious gulps. Back up top she apologized profusely to Fuji for keeping her waiting, clambered down the ladder to the small tender and waited while the steward cast them off, all the time expecting a damp and towel-clad Kendall to emerge on deck yelling at them to stop her. The laptop in her bag felt like snakes: alive, dangerous and terrifying.

The engine hummed gently as they edged away from *Crystal Dawn* at an achingly slow pace. As soon as they were a decent distance away the steward opened up the full throttle and with a lurch they began to bounce across the choppy water.

She wouldn't allow Chrissie to ruin things for her all over again. Forgive and forget, that's what her dad had said, but he wasn't in his right mind. He hadn't been for a long time. His advice was nothing more than an echo of something he had once heard long ago, a neural tic fired by a random memory.

She didn't want to forgive. She didn't want to forget.

At Okinawa airport Anna allowed Fuji to check her onto a flight to London with a change in Tokyo. Then she went to the bathroom, doubled back, and checked herself onto a plane to New York City.

By the time anybody realized that Anna had stolen the laptop nobody would have any idea where to find her.

Twenty

Every morning Anna needed to step out onto the fire escape and take in her view in order to convince herself that it wasn't a dream. She was living in Manhattan while she concentrated on writing her first book. If she stood on one of her kitchen chairs she could even glimpse the east side of the Chrysler building. She left a chair out there for a while, but somebody complained and the superintendent for the Murray Hill apartment building left a brusque note in the mailbox warning her that she was contravening fire regulations, so she had promptly taken the chair inside again.

But every morning, not long after dawn, she looked at the New York skyline until she heard the chugging bubble of her stove-top espresso pot. Then she would fix herself a cup of coffee, a bowl of frosted All-American cereal and sit down at the kitchen table to write. She forced herself to stay there even as the words dried up, staring at the screen if she had to, until she heard movement from the bedroom a couple of hours later and knew that Mac was awake.

Then she would smile, without fail.

She hadn't known where to find him, hadn't known her way around Manhattan at all, but she called him from the airport and he came to collect her, and when she passed it to him it was the first time the laptop had left her side.

'It's Morton's,' she said.

'You stole it?'

She nodded. She had slept barely two hours out of the last twenty-four. Fear and fatigue had carved deep lines into her face.

'I thought maybe your friend,' she said, 'the one who's good at getting into other people's computers . . .? I don't know, perhaps it will turn out to be the most stupid thing I ever did. Will I get into much trouble? Will I go to jail? I left the country with it and everything. I wasn't thinking, it wasn't something I planned to do, it was just there and I just . . . I saw this flight. I don't know why I'm here. I'm sorry.'

'Relax, Anna,' said Mac. 'It's not like you killed anyone.'

She started to cry. 'Should I have come?' she asked.

'Where else would you go?' He pushed away her tears with his thumbs, one for each cheek, patiently stopping each fresh tear as it fell until they stopped altogether. Then he held the sides of her face and made sure that she was listening to him properly. 'I've been waiting for you,' he said. 'I've been waiting a really long time.'

Their kiss tasted of tears and by the time it ended she knew that she was exactly where she was supposed to be.

He looked around at the chaos of JFK. 'I hate the airport,' he said. 'Come on, let's go.'

She couldn't remember him inviting her to move in but he didn't seem to mind. She stayed there that first night, and she never left.

It was a typical bachelor pad, sparse and functional, an old-fashioned typewriter taking pride of place in what was probably supposed to be a dining nook but was an office crammed with reference books and notepaper and postcards and Post-its, the only space in the apartment that was full of life.

'You write on this?' she said, running her hands over the cold keys of the Olivetti.

'I write with a pen,' he said. 'I type with that. I don't trust computers.'

'You're showing your age,' she said.

'And you're asking for trouble.'

They had their morning ritual. Together they'd slowly stroll to a diner on 17th Street and she'd eat eggs Florentine and drink coffee, except on Sundays when she had pancakes and bacon, drenched with syrup. Often she'd talk to him about her work, asking his advice on a point of fact or a discrepancy thrown out by her tireless research, but equally often they'd make plans for the evening to come, a restaurant to try or a film to see, or a night at home with take-out and television and lots and lots of sex.

He asked her once if she was in love with him. She had laughed but he had pushed her until she said that she was getting there. 'Why?' she'd asked. 'Do you love me?'

'What do you think?'

'I think you want me to say it first.'

'Say what?'

'Don't try to trick me with your clever little wordplay, Mackintosh. I'm onto you.'

He'd grabbed her and pulled her onto his lap. 'All this and brains too,' he'd said, kissing her. Then one thing had led to another and they were in bed. Again.

One Sunday after breakfast they were walking through Union Square having just browsed at the Farmer's Market and bought precisely nothing, as they always did. Next stop would be Barnes and Noble, where Anna would spend the money she had fully intended to spend on artisan bread on a new bestseller that would make Mac sneer at her taste – 'or lack thereof' – at which point she would smack him round the arm with it and he would grudgingly allow her to add the book to the growing stacks of her things in his study when they got home.

Halfway across the square she slipped her hand into his and closed her eyes.

Years ago, walking hand in hand with Ben in the woods, she had felt a sense of freedom. Instead of the birds and the hushed sound of the wind in the trees she could hear the laughter of children, the constant drone of New York traffic, the chatter of passers-by, the thrust of a city that was always on the move and that she was lucky to be a part of. She allowed Mac to lead her through it all, trusting him, and in that moment she realized that this was more than just a crush, a fling, a love affair on the way to something more permanent. She realized that this could be all of those things, and maybe more.

He stopped. And her eyes flew open.

'What the hell are you doing?' he said.

'I'm letting you take the lead.'

'Well, don't,' he said. 'I'm not looking for a follower. I have enough of those already.'

She smiled. 'What are you looking for, exactly?'

'Someone exactly like you.'

The book came together, word by word, chapter by chapter, and she knew that it was a damning indictment. The laptop revealed its secrets after a few hours with Mac's friend and there was enough there to tie Kendall to

Imperial Idol so tightly that no amount of lawyers would be able to untangle him. He would be ruined.

For weeks she waited for the knock on the door. She had left Fuji waiting for her at Okinawa airport and it wouldn't have taken a clever woman like Fuji long to raise the alarm. How long before the laptop was missed? Would the police be called? Or would Kendall keep them out of it, knowing that one stolen computer was nothing compared to the monstrous crimes he had committed?

She waited. But the knock on the door never came and after a few months she started to trust that it never would. Only when she acknowledged this with a trace of disappointment did she realize she had hoped the knock on the door might be Chrissie.

She conquered her nerves and made a flying visit to Tokyo, asking around at the nightclubs until she found some teenage girls willing to talk to her about their nights with the rich *gaijan* with the gaudy apartment.

'Sex sells,' said Mac.

But the more she wrote the less satisfied she felt.

One morning she saw a photograph of Chrissie in the society pages of the *New York Post*. Chrissie looked amazing cowering from the rain under a charcoal umbrella, perfect make-up, perfect outfit, perfect pregnancy bump. And she could make out a dignified Asian man standing beside her. Rev. So what had happened to Ben? The article said that she lived in New York now, and the knowledge that her friend was somewhere close in this same city was at once appealing and horrifying. She studied the picture for several minutes trying to work out if Chrissie looked happy but it was too difficult because she was smiling.

Soon the book would be published and her revenge

would be complete. A complete triumph. A triumph that left her feeling hollow and cheap.

'It's a good thing you're doing,' Mac reminded her. 'People should know the truth about him.'

'I know,' she said.

She wasn't a girl of fifteen. She knew that there would be consequences. She was ready to face them.

'I think I need to speak to Chrissie,' she said.

'Why?'

'Because she's my friend.'

She finished her book at the end of summer, just as the New York evenings began to feel colder and start earlier, but the golden light still blazed down the long straight streets at sunset. She waited in a diner with the one and only copy of her completed manuscript on the table in front of her. Months of work. Headlines waiting to happen.

She ordered another cup of coffee and waited for Chrissie.

She had been competing with Chrissie in one way or another since the very first day they met. Once it had felt that all she ever did was lose. Today she would win with the knockout punch, a punch from which Chrissie would never recover.

The door opened and a breeze tickled the top sheet of paper, and she turned around to see a beautiful brunette enter the store, her warm brown eyes firmly fixed on the bundle that was harnessed around her mid-section, a small baby swaddled in a cosy-looking sling. The baby let out a small mewing cry and Anna thought that the sound was pretty amazing, the sound of her best friend's baby, until she remembered that they weren't friends any more and they hadn't been for a very long time, not really.

Chrissie offered the baby her little finger and the mewing sound stopped, then she looked around and she saw Anna and they both grinned without thinking about what they were doing.

'Congratulations!' said Anna. 'She's gorgeous. What's her name?'

'Dawn,' said Chrissie.

'As in Crystal Dawn?'

Chrissie laughed but Anna thought perhaps it really wasn't worth laughing about. The baby girl had golden skin and eyes like melted chocolate; she looked up at Anna with total disinterest before turning her face to the side and going to sleep.

Chrissie sat down carefully so as not to wake her.

'How are you?' said Anna. 'I saw a photo a few months back. You're with Rev?'

'Not any more. It's just the two of us now, isn't it, babes?' She stroked her sleeping daughter's head. 'I heard that Ben's engaged already. Maybe it's for real this time.'

A fleeting pinch of nostalgia and then . . . nothing.

'How about you?' said Chrissie.

'I'm good, really good actually.'

'You look great. Either you're having the best sex of your life or you're in love.'

Anna smiled but she didn't say anything.

'*Both?*' Chrissie's voice roused the baby briefly and the soothing that ensued gave Anna the perfect excuse not to answer. She didn't want to tell Chrissie anything more about Mac. She didn't want to let her anywhere near it.

'How's your dad?' said Chrissie.

Anna started to shred a napkin between her fingers. She hadn't expected to feel like this, to feel protective of Chrissie and her baby, to feel that inescapable pull to be friends with her again. Chrissie's concern about her father might be ironically inappropriate but she found that she welcomed it. 'The same, more or less,' she said. 'Mum is better though. She has a job now, a life. Friends. I always thought she needed me close by but it turns out she needed me to be wherever I was happy.'

'That's good,' said Chrissie. 'I'm glad you're happy.'

After everything that Chrissie had done to her Anna could barely forgive herself for being nervous. She focused on hating her. She should do it right now. She should show Chrissie what she had and bring her world tumbling down around her. The father that she worshipped, the name that meant she never had to try as hard as other people, the charmed life: gone.

'Here,' she said, pushing the manuscript across the table.

'What's this?'

'It's a book I wrote. It's about Kendall.'

'What about him?'

'Everything about him. It took me six months. There're bits about you too.'

'Which bits?'

'The very worst bits of you, Chrissie.'

Chrissie turned to a random page and her brow furrowed in confusion. 'Why are you giving it to me?'

'I think you should know who Kendall really is,' she said. 'Perhaps then you'd stop caring so much what he thinks of you.'

'I doubt he thinks of me at all,' said Chrissie. 'As you

can imagine he wasn't pleased about, you know –' she gestured towards her baby – 'everything. He hasn't even seen her yet.'

Anna wanted so much to hate her, but she could not.

'Read the book, Chrissie. Maybe he's not someone you should love as much as you do. You have to stop trying to impress him.'

Chrissie shrugged. 'He's my father. Have you stopped trying to impress yours?'

The baby shifted and started to cry again. Chrissie took the manuscript and put in her bag.

Anna's heart had lurched as she passed it over. That book could make her rich and famous. It would change her life forever. Was that what she wanted? To change? What would her father do?

As soon as she thought about it that way the moral high ground was clear to see.

'I'm not going to publish it,' said Anna. 'That's the only copy. It's yours. Read it, burn it, I don't care. I don't want it.' She waited to feel disappointment, but all she felt was relief, and somewhere soon to come she sensed happiness.

'Why?' said Chrissie. 'If you worked so hard?'

'I'd be doing it to get back at you, Chrissie, only I doubt it would make me feel better. I don't want my life to be wrapped up with yours any longer. It's over. You and me. It's over.'

The baby started to cry properly.

'I only ever wanted to be friends,' said Anna. 'Why did you find that impossible?'

Chrissie shushed her baby, rocking her with increasing intensity. She offered her little finger for the baby to suck on but she didn't want it. Around them people pretended not to stare. 'You only ever wanted to be friends with me when you thought I could help you,' said Chrissie. 'You wanted to be popular, you wanted to belong, then you wanted Ben, then you wanted a career. Now you come after my dad. Don't pretend to be perfect, Anna, because you're not.'

Anna turned her head away. Chrissie had always known how to hurt her.

'We should go,' said Chrissie. 'I'll read this. I expect my lawyers will be in touch.'

Mac was furious. 'You're a writer,' he said. 'You have a responsibility to tell the truth.'

'I have a responsibility to be true to myself,' she said. 'I couldn't live with it, ruining somebody like that. I'm too close. It wouldn't be just his life; it would be Chrissie's too, her baby's. What about all the people that work for him? And for what? Because a thousand years ago Chrissie made a huge mistake? She was just a teenager. It's not enough. Personal revenge is never enough.'

'It's more than that. This is bigger.'

'Not to me. Nothing is bigger than that.'

'You're mad,' said Mac. 'You're an idiot.'

'Maybe.'

He stormed out of the apartment, slamming the door behind him so hard that the keys in his typewriter rattled.

She waited for him to return, but night came and still he hadn't. It didn't feel right sleeping in his bed without him. She felt unwelcome. So she watched old movies on cable television and eventually fell asleep on the couch.

In the morning she didn't know what to do. She had no book to write and nobody to share the start of her day with. The skyline seemed less magical without him around and the eggs she ordered for breakfast were tasteless and dry. The day passed and still he didn't return.

What if he never came back? She knew he had a home in England but she had never thought to ask how long he was staying here for, how long she had him with her until he was off again to some far-flung corner of the world reporting the truth in a way that she had been unable to bring herself to do. She was haunted by the realization that every single time she let Chrissie into her life it was ruined in some way.

She spent more nights on the couch. She wandered the streets of Manhattan and didn't know where to turn. She stopped smoking. It was easy. It was good to feel in control of something. She called her mother and pretended that everything was fine.

She curled over Mac's desk and tried to write, to work, but nothing came easy; she didn't know what it was that she wanted to say. In the end the only thing she was able to finish was a series of letters to her father telling him the story of the last few months, the last few years, really, and trying to explain how grateful she was to him. How much she loved him. No matter what.

Then, on the morning of the sixth day, he came back.

'Here,' he said, tossing a copy of a British broadsheet down on the table in front of her. 'What's the term? Hot off the press.'

It was the cover story. The Kendall Morton story. Her story. With Mac's byline on it.

She picked up the newspaper, turning to the two-page spread, unable to speak, hardly able to think. 'What have you done?' she whispered.

'You'll thank me later,' he said. 'So why don't you just thank me now?'

'For what? How could you?'

'I'm a journalist, Anna. How could I not? You knew that, you must have known. As soon as you came to me with that red-hot computer and those big green eyes of yours – help me, Mac – you really think I wouldn't have made a copy of everything for myself?'

'But . . .'

'If you're worried about Chrissie, don't be. She's already signed an exclusive with one of the tabs plus a picture deal with one of the glossies. They say she'll be famous. From everything you've told me, I'm guessing she'll be perfect for the gutter press.'

'And Kendall?'

'Prison, I expect, unless his lawyers can keep it away from The Hague. I turned everything over to the police. Which is exactly what you should have done. But you got scared. And it's okay that you got scared.' He reached out for her.

'Get away from me,' she said.

'Anna . . .'

'I said get away.'

Anna ran out of the apartment taking the newspaper with her and kept running until she found a payphone and then she was dialling the house back in London where she grew up and praying that her mother would answer. But it rang and rang and she hung up in despair realizing that it wasn't even her mother that she really wanted to speak to but her father.

*

She found somewhere to sit and read the article. It was brutal and brilliant. It was everything she would have hoped it could be and far better than she ever could have written herself. It had his name on it. But it had hers too. 'Additional Reporting – Anna Page.' After she had finished she read it for a second time and then sat there wondering what on earth she was supposed to do with the rest of her life.

'Well?'

She looked up and Mac was staring at her, smoking a cigarette and shuffling from foot to foot, uncharacteristically nervous.

She couldn't find the words to express how moved she was by what he had written. 'You've changed the world,' she said.

'I love you,' he said.

'We've stopped smoking.'

'We have? Okay.' He threw his cigarette aside. 'Is there anything else you want to tell me?'

'That you were right.'

'What about?'

She looked down at the newspaper in her hands and no longer felt angry or betrayed. In fact, she felt proud, proud of Mac for doing what she hadn't had the nerve to do. 'Well, it's later, and I do want to thank you. He deserves everything that happens to him.'

'I think you'll find I'm right about a lot of things,' he said. 'So that's something that you're going to have to get used to.'

He pulled her to her feet. 'Maybe the life is not for you,' he said. 'You shouldn't be chasing after bad guys and lying to the source, shaking his hand while taping your conversation. You're not ruthless enough, you're not cut-throat. You care about people, Anna Page.'

'You say that like it's a bad thing.'

'It was supposed to be a compliment.'

'So what now?' she said. The biggest opportunity of her career and she had handed it away. So perhaps she wasn't going to shape the world at all. She had no idea what she could do with her life if she wasn't going to make it as a reporter.

'Breakfast,' he said. 'Then a walk, but a short one because I'm shattered, so a little siesta, then maybe later we could try that new place by the park or we could just get take-out . . .'

'Breakfast sounds good,' she said.

Later that day they walked back to the apartment, the harmony between them restored. Anna had started to think that maybe she would just hang out in New York with Mac for a while and then if he needed to travel on assignment perhaps she could go with him, ride his slipstream into adventures.

'You don't want to waste your life running after an old guy like me,' he said, when she put it to him.

'It wouldn't be a waste,' she said. 'And maybe you'd be running after me before too long.'

'I've been running after you for months,' he said.

'And now you have me,' she said.

Then suddenly, a few steps from the apartment, Mac stopped dead in the middle of the sidewalk. Anna looked at him, confused, and then followed his gaze to the entrance of the building, where Chrissie was sitting on their stoop, waiting. In her hand was a folded-up copy of the fateful newspaper with her father's name across the banner headline. She looked up. Her Bambi brown eyes were as inscrutable as they had been when she was a girl of fifteen.

'I'll be okay,' said Anna, and Mac squeezed her hand before slipping past Chrissie, up the stairs and through the door.

'That's the guy?' said Chrissie.

Anna nodded. 'That's the guy.' Perhaps she should be afraid but she wasn't. For the first time she faced Chrissie and knew that for all their mistakes, all their lies, all the wealth and good fortune, the tragedies large and small, old and new, for the first time they were more or less even, more or less equals. Forever and ever.

'Where's your little girl?' said Anna.

'I have a nanny.' Chrissie rolled her eyes. 'I'm not, you know, a peasant.'

Anna sat down next to her, on the cold stone steps, as if they were two schoolgirls waiting for the bus.

'So you read it?'

Chrissie looked down at the newspaper and then back at Anna. She paused and tipped her face to the sky and Anna thought that she was holding back tears. She swallowed the lump that had surfaced in her own throat and fought the urge to reach out and comfort her friend.

'You know what's funny?' said Chrissie, laughing in a strangled way that betrayed how it really wasn't funny at all. 'I always hated how much my father liked you. He thought you were everything that a young woman could be, everything I should be. I used to think that when he looked at you all he saw was everything I am not. He's completely beside himself, he's furious, destroyed. And he sure as hell doesn't like you very much any more.'

372

'No,' said Anna. 'I don't suppose he does.'

'You've ruined him.'

'He deserves it.'

To her surprise, Chrissie nodded slowly. 'I know,' she said. 'He does. And so do I. That's what I came to tell you. It's okay. And I forgive you.'

They both sat there for a while and Anna wondered if Chrissie was waiting for her to say the same thing but she knew that if she did then it would be a lie, and there had been enough of those passing between them already. Enough for any lifetime.

'We can't be friends, Chrissie,' said Anna. 'It's just impossible.'

'Really?' said Chrissie. 'Is that what you think?'

'Why? What do you think?'

Chrissie walked over to the kerb and looked down the one-way street. She saw a yellow taxicab with its light on and whistled for it loudly with two fingers. It pulled over and came to a stop a few inches from her high-heeled toe.

'There are all kinds of friends,' said Chrissie. 'And I think we're friends whether you want to be or not. So I'll see you, Anna, okay? Take care.'

She stepped into the taxi and slammed the door. It sped off down the street and Anna was left alone. 'Take care,' she echoed, and waved, just barely. And even though Chrissie was probably too far away to be seen Anna thought that perhaps she could make out Chrissie turning in the back seat of the cab, flicking her perfect hair, and waving back.

Acknowledgements

I am happy when I am with books, whether they are my own or other people's, and I am so grateful that I get to write every day. With thanks to Judith Murdoch, Lydia Newhouse, Mari Evans, Alice Shepherd and everyone at Michael Joseph and Penguin who make my books real. Also thanks to Lynne Bowers, Sally Harris, Lizzie Cullen and Hannah Davis, because this is a book about best friends.

ALISON BOND

HOW TO BE FAMOUS

Stars, secrets and celebrity obsession

Your invitation to the most glittering premiere of the year introducing ...

Lynsey Dixon
An employee at a top London talent agency that specializes in looking
after neurotic actresses, like Melanie Chaplin. After keeping her cool in
a crisis, Lynsey is offered a transfer to LA to help Melanie make the
most of her big break in a new TV show. And Lynsey knows an
opportunity for sunny days and serious star-spotting when she sees one ...

Melanie Chaplin
Star of a new hit TV series and the object of desire for LA's hottest
players. She has everything – except Davy Black: the gorgeous
director who is married in real life, but not in Melanie's dreams.
And celebrity has a dangerous habit of occasionally making you
forget which is which ...

Serena Simon
Serena didn't exactly choose Hollywood; when you're as beautiful as
she is, it's the only place to go. Serena has a plan – and it's working;
stardom is just a photoshoot away. But she also has a little secret.
And in LA, secrets rarely stay that way for long ...

Three very different girls whose dreams all depend on one another –
and who are all about to realize the true price of fame ...

'How dare Alison Bond write a debut novel this good? We defy you
not to be glued to its pages from beginning to end' *Heat*

ALISON BOND

THE TRUTH ABOUT RUBY VALENTINE

Imagine being a nobody

When Hollywood legend Ruby Valentine shocks the world with her mysterious suicide, Kelly's father reveals something even more shocking – it seems she's Ruby's daughter.

Who suddenly becomes a somebody

So Kelly sets off for Tinseltown to find some answers, diving headfirst into Hollywood society with her new family of jet-setters and fashionistas. But she soon discovers that Ruby's real life was laced with more drama, tragedy, and intrigue than any screenwriter could imagine.

Because of something you can't tell anybody?

When Ruby's fortune turns out to be non-existent, and Kelly learns of the intense relationship her mother had with her slick, powerful agent, she begins to get suspicious about what's really going on. And the more she digs, the closer she gets to uncovering the most unbelievable secret of them all.

ALISON BOND

A RELUCTANT CINDERELLA

Samantha Sharp turned seventeen, left her old life behind and moved to London, determined to make her fortune. Ten years later and she's a super-agent to the stars, with her name in the papers, millions in the bank, and one success after another. Love has taken a back seat because her past has put her off relationships for good.

Everyone's got a history but Samantha's is particularly murky. What's more, she hasn't got to the top of her game without collecting a few enemies along the way. So when she meets a man who might be a little bit dangerous, someone she's finally close to loving, is there anyone to tell her what a terrible mistake she's making?

Will Samantha find her happy ever after? And if her carefully hidden past comes into the light, will her fairytale coach turn back into a pumpkin?

Samantha Sharp needs to find a way to cling onto her sparkle . . .

He just wanted a decent book to read ...

Not too much to ask, is it? It was in 1935 when Allen Lane, Managing Director of Bodley Head Publishers, stood on a platform at Exeter railway station looking for something good to read on his journey back to London. His choice was limited to popular magazines and poor-quality paperbacks – the same choice faced every day by the vast majority of readers, few of whom could afford hardbacks. Lane's disappointment and subsequent anger at the range of books generally available led him to found a company – and change the world.

'We believed in the existence in this country of a vast reading public for intelligent books at a low price, and staked everything on it'
Sir Allen Lane, 1902–1970, founder of Penguin Books

The quality paperback had arrived – and not just in bookshops. Lane was adamant that his Penguins should appear in chain stores and tobacconists, and should cost no more than a packet of cigarettes.

Reading habits (and cigarette prices) have changed since 1935, but Penguin still believes in publishing the best books for everybody to enjoy. We still believe that good design costs no more than bad design, and we still believe that quality books published passionately and responsibly make the world a better place.

So wherever you see the little bird – whether it's on a piece of prize-winning literary fiction or a celebrity autobiography, political tour de force or historical masterpiece, a serial-killer thriller, reference book, world classic or a piece of pure escapism – you can bet that it represents the very best that the genre has to offer.

Whatever you like to read – trust Penguin.